The

WRIGHT

BOSS

ALSO BY K.A. LINDE

AVOIDING SERIES

Avoiding Commitment
Avoiding Responsibility
Avoiding Intimacy
Avoiding Decisions
Avoiding Temptation

RECORD SERIES

Off the Record
On the Record
For the Record
Struck from the Record

ALL THAT GLITTERS SERIES

Diamonds
Gold
Emeralds
Platinum
Silver

TAKE ME SERIES

Take Me for Granted
Take Me with You

STAND-ALONE

Following Me
The Wright Brother

ASCENSION SERIES

The Affiliate
The Bound

The WRIGHT BOSS

K.A. LINDE

Visit my website at www.kalinde.com

Join my newsletter for exclusive content and free books!
www.kalinde.com/subscribe

Photographer: Wander Aguiar Photography,
www.wanderaguiar.com
Cover Designer: Sarah Hansen, Okay Creations.,
www.okaycreations.com
Editor and Interior Designer: Jovana Shirley,
Unforeseen Editing, www.unforeseenediting.com

This book is a work of fiction. Names, characters, places, and
incidents either are products of the author's imagination or
are used fictitiously. Any resemblance to actual persons, living
or dead, events, or locales is entirely coincidental.

ISBN-13: 978-1948427029

To Katie Miller,
for pink champagne, epic desserts,
and many more adventures to come.

One

Landon

Fuck, my wife was ruining my life.

In fact, Miranda had been ruining my life since the day we met. I hadn't known it at the time. I wouldn't find out until much later. But, now, the fact was undeniable. Miranda was a cancerous cell eating away at my body. If I didn't get away, she would destroy me.

My phone buzzed and I glanced down to find Miranda's name on the screen.

For the hundredth fucking time.

"Fuck," I groaned, ending the call.

She had been calling me nonstop since I walked out the door without her. But I had just landed in Lubbock on the last plane of the day, and frankly, I didn't want to talk to her. Not after what she'd done. Not after what she had been doing to me for years.

Of course, I didn't blame her for freaking out when I was on my way to my ten-year high school reunion without her.

I cringed at the thought. I'd wanted to come back for the reunion at the top of my game. I'd spent six years working as a professional golfer out of Tampa with a few PGA Tour victories under my belt, but I'd wanted to come home having won the Masters with my sexy wife on my arm, living the dream. I'd wanted to make my name as someone *other* than a Wright.

As proud as I was of my family and Wright Construction, the largest construction company in the nation, I wanted my own life. Now, I was returning at twenty-eight years old without my wife and with my golf dreams in ashes.

I shrugged off those depressing thoughts and exited the plane. The Lubbock Airport was compact, to say the least. I'd only brought a carry-on, so I bypassed baggage claim and exited the sliding glass doors out to my hot and dusty home. After Florida summers, where you drink the air, Lubbock felt more like breathing sandpaper.

A shiny red Alfa Romeo zoomed up to the spot in front of me, and my brother Austin rolled down the window. He honked the horn and flipped me the bird. He was two years older than me but frequently acted as if he were the younger brother.

"Hey, get in!" Austin yelled. He popped the button for the trunk.

"Nice to see you, too," I said sarcastically.

"Where's your other half?" Austin asked.

"Couldn't make it."

Sure, Miranda couldn't make it. That was the lie I was going with for a woman who didn't work, spent my money like it actually grew on trees, and was practically attached to my hip.

"Cool," Austin said with a shrug.

I knew he was the only one of my four siblings who would buy that explanation.

I slid my suitcase into the trunk and slammed it shut.

"This car is so fucking tiny," I said after I sank into the passenger seat. "The trunk barely has enough room for my suitcase."

Austin zoomed away from the airport. "Keep complaining, and I'll make you stay with Jensen."

I sat back and stared out the window. "Yeah, I'd rather not have to hear him banging my ex-girlfriend."

"I'm sure he could put your ass on the other side of the house. Then, you'd only have to imagine him with Emery."

"Thanks. You're *really* helping."

"That's what I'm here for," Austin said with a grin.

Even though my oldest brother, Jensen, had started dating my ex-girlfriend Emery eight months ago, it was a little weird for me. Not because I had feelings for her. But I couldn't erase the two years we'd dated in high school. The whole thing had added to my irritation with Miranda. How could Jensen be so happy when I was stuck in a miserable, loveless marriage?

God, everything came back to Miranda. My phone even buzzed, as if she had known I was thinking about her.

I checked the message.

> *Babe, answer your phone. We need to talk about this. I cannot believe you left without me. What am I supposed to do?*

Fuck that noise. I turned my phone off.

"God, can we get fucked up before this thing tonight?" I asked in desperation. Alcohol would numb the pain for a night.

"Now, *that* I can help with," Austin said with a grin.

I probably shouldn't be contributing to my brother's alcoholism, but fuck, I needed a drink. Austin had been drinking heavily ever since our dad died ten years ago from an overdose. Golf had always helped me manage my vices and the characteristic Wright addictive personality. Without it, I didn't know if I'd have ended up just like my old man.

Twenty minutes later, we showed up at Austin's house in Tech Terrace. He'd had it gutted and redesigned after he closed on it. So, even though the construction was built in the sixties, the house was brand-new. It had the advantage of being located within walking distance of the best bars, which I thought was the reason he'd bought it. But this also meant I could walk my drunk ass to and from the reunion down the street.

Austin parked in the garage, and we entered the house. After depositing my suitcase in his guest bedroom on the first floor, I came back out to find Austin already at the wet bar. It was fully stocked with as much alcohol as the nearest liquor store. It even had some top-shelf whiskey that wasn't available in stores but had to be purchased straight from the distributor. He took drinking very seriously. It was maybe the only thing he took that seriously.

Austin poured me a glass of whiskey, and I sank into the sofa. He crashed back into a chair and turned on the big screen to *SportsCenter*. It was at that exact moment when golf stats were on for the British Open, a tournament I should have been at.

I downed my entire glass in one gulp. "I'll take another."

Austin gave me a strange look, as if he knew something was wrong, but he didn't say anything. He just changed the channel. "Help yourself."

That was the best thing about Austin. He didn't pry.

We sat around for a couple of hours, watching some baseball game neither of us cared about while drinking ourselves stupid. When it was almost time for me to go to Flips for the reunion, Austin finally turned to look directly at me.

"Bro, you should probably come up with a story to tell Jensen," Austin said.

"About what?" I played dumb.

"Whatever the fuck you're dealing with. You know he's going to ask, and you're a shit liar."

"I'm not dealing with anything."

"Like I said," Austin said, refilling my glass one last time, "shit liar."

I laughed and raised my glass to him. "Maybe I'll tell him the truth."

"Nah, you won't. That's not the Wright way."

Now, that was a true statement. We were a family of five, ranging from thirty-three to twenty-one, and we hid the truth from each other like we had been made for it. We'd learned that from our long-ago dead parents. Our mother had never told us about her cancer, and our father had lied about the alcohol, even on his dying breath. Maybe it *was* the Wright way.

Either way, I didn't argue with Austin on that point. I'd deal with Jensen when I had to.

With my head sufficiently foggy, I changed into a pair of khakis and a light-blue button-up. Then, I waved good-bye to Austin and walked the few scant blocks to Flips. The last time I'd been there, I'd found out that Jensen and Emery were dating. It had been a weird fucking night, and I was really hoping not to have another one like that any time soon. I wanted to get tanked, talk to some of my old friends, and forget about the shit I'd left behind.

I signed in at the front and then angled straight for the bar on the left side of the room. I almost made it when Jensen stepped right in front of me.

Great. Just the person I didn't want to talk to about my problems.

"Hey," Jensen said.

"Hey, bro."

"Where's Miranda?"

"Don't know. Where's Emery?"

Jensen pointed behind him, and I saw Emery leaning over the bar in an all-black ensemble, gesturing to the bartender.

"What do you mean, you don't know where your wife is? I'd rather not have her run into Emery. She still acts like a..." Jensen looked at me, and his eyes said that the word he was looking for was *psychopath*, but he didn't want to say it in front of me. "Well, she doesn't like Emery."

"Nothing to worry about then because I didn't bring her," I said. Then, I tried to push past him to get my drink.

Jensen grabbed my arm. "How the hell did you get away with that?"

"Give it a rest, Jensen."

He sighed and dropped my arm. "What happened?"

"Look, we had a fight, and I left without her. The end."

"Must have been a pretty big argument for her not to come with you," Jensen prodded.

Jensen, like the rest of my family, hated Miranda with a fiery vengeance. He might think he was able to keep his distaste for her under wraps—unlike my sister Morgan—but he didn't fool me. Only my youngest sister, Sutton, was any good at pretending that she liked Miranda. Not that I blamed them at this point.

"I'm leaving her, man. Is that what you wanted to know?" I spat at Jensen.

He stared back at me, stunned. Maybe he never thought I'd actually do it. Miranda had pushed and pushed and pushed, and I'd never broken. There were reasons for all of that. Reasons I'd handled the Wright way with no one else knowing about them. But she'd crossed the line, and I'd had enough.

"Landon, you know that I just want you to be happy."

"Yeah, well, I need a drink, not a lecture. Leave it be."

I stumbled over to the bar and ordered that drink, making sure to angle away from Emery. We were on all-right terms now, but since this was all about high school, I didn't want to dredge up those awkward memories. Maybe I'd find some of my old football buddies.

Or the blonde at the pool table in the back of the bar.

My eyes found Heidi Martin, Emery's best friend, as she stood up to her considerable height. She was surely making a fool out of her opponent since I'd personally seen her hustle more than her fair share of unsuspecting victims.

We'd known each other for years. She'd been a cheerleader when I was the starting quarterback in high school. We'd hung out more times than I could count while I was dating Emery. But, when I'd come back over for Sutton's wedding, it was like seeing a whole new Heidi. She oozed confidence and power, she made everyone smile, and she did it all effortlessly. Heidi Martin had completely come into her own.

We'd started talking after the wedding. Nothing serious. Or at least that was what I had told myself. Our conversations became intimate...and then New Year's had happened. We'd almost kissed, and fuck, I'd wanted to. But it hadn't been fair to Miranda. And so, after that, I'd cut off all contact with her.

Time to fix that mistake.

I strode down the bar and straight to the pool tables. Heidi curved a ball and knocked it into the pocket. Her blue eyes lifted from the table and landed right on me. Her smile grew but warily. She hadn't forgotten how abruptly I had ended things.

"Heidi," I said, taking her in like a breath of fresh air.

"Hey, Landon." Her eyes looked over my shoulder, as if she were trying to figure out if I was alone. "Where's your wife?"

"She's not here."

"Oh," she said. Though she didn't seem upset by that notion. "Sorry she couldn't make it."

"Are you?" I asked curiously.

She laughed and shook her head. "Are you drunk?"

"I might be a bit inebriated, yes."

"Ah. *Inebriated*, are we?" she asked with an eye roll. "Guess you can't be too drunk then."

"Never know. I'm still an intelligent drunk."

7

"Sure you are." She pushed her blonde hair out of her face and smiled, as she seemed to be warming up to my presence. The next person missed his shot, and she proceeded to run the table. "Another round?"

The guy shook his head. "No way in hell. Find someone else to embarrass, Martin."

She shrugged and leaned on the pool stick as she turned her attention to me. "So, what's new with you?"

"A lot actually," I told her. "Can we go somewhere to talk?"

"Somewhere, not being here?"

"Somewhere…more private." Then, I dropped my voice. "I just…don't like the way we left things."

"Oh, Landon," she said with her characteristic laugh, as if nothing bothered her. Even though I knew it did. "Don't even worry about it."

"Heidi," I said softly, stepping closer to her. Her body tensed as I drew near, and she took a shallow breath. "Please."

"All right," she said, stumbling backward a step. Her eyes were wide and desirous, but she quickly hid her emotions. She put on a big smile. "Sure, I'd love to catch up."

She placed the pool stick back in its slot and then nodded her head to the side. I followed her to a booth in the back of the room. A handful of people from our senior class plus their dates were already at the reunion. I knew right away that talking in a booth in the back of the room was tantamount to announcing that something nefarious was going on. I didn't want anyone to overhear us. I didn't want anyone to see us.

I might not care that ten years had passed. I was a different man. I was a professional golfer. I had my own life. I didn't live in town. But no one could escape high school gossip.

"Let's go outside," I suggested.

"Landon, I don't think that's a good idea."

"Fuck good ideas." I took her hand in mine and gently tugged her to the emergency exit. It had been disabled for as long as I could remember, and we breezed through it and out into the hot summer night.

"All right, we're outside. What's up?" Heidi asked. She leaned back on the brick wall and popped a foot up against it. "The last time we spoke, you said that we shouldn't talk anymore. You said what was going on between us wasn't fair to your wife."

"That was true," I agreed.

But my body and addled brain couldn't care less about what I'd said all those months ago. January felt like a lifetime ago. The reasons I'd had for reacting that way no longer applied.

"This probably isn't fair to her either, Landon."

I stepped into her personal space, and her breathing hitched. My hands went on either side of her face, boxing her in. She swallowed but fiercely met my gaze. I'd thought she'd push me away. I'd thought she'd stop me.

"Do you still feel the way you felt back then?"

"Landon," she whispered. Her words came out breathy and soft. "Don't do this."

"Do you?"

"I haven't spoken to you in months. At the time, Emery suspected what was going on, and I'm her best friend. There's girl code to consider. I can't do this. I can't answer you."

"She's dating my brother. I don't think that applies anymore, Heidi. Just answer me this; do you or do you not still care for me?"

She paused, frozen in place, with her ice-blue eyes boring into mine. She was trying to find where this was a trick or a joke. But she wouldn't find it with me.

"Yes," she whispered.

Without another thought, I pushed my hands up into her wild blonde hair and brought my lips down onto hers. I tasted her like a luxurious delicacy and then devoured her as if I could never have enough.

K.A. LINDE

Fuck everything else in my life.
This was the moment when I made Heidi Martin mine.

Two

Heidi

Landon Wright was kissing me.

It was amazing. The best thing that had ever happened to me. He was fulfilling every fantasy I'd had in the back of my head over the last eight months. *How many times had I imagined him doing this exact thing?*

Last winter, when he'd driven me home from this exact bar, all I'd wanted to do was lean over and kiss him senseless. I'd wanted him to take me up to my apartment and fuck me. I'd wanted so much. And New Year's, we had been so close to giving in and ending up in this moment together.

Yet, even as drunk as I had been on both occasion, I'd known he was married. I'd known how wrong it was to even want that from him. And I'd walked away.

Now, he was finally kissing me and answering all my silent pleas, and I had to stop him.

Fuck.

I shoved Landon backward with as much force as I could. Then, I moved away from the wall and wiped my mouth.

Fuck!

"Whoa!" I yelled at him. I took another step back from him. Putting distance between us was the only way I wasn't going to give in again. "Whoa! Married!"

Landon leaned into the space I had vacated and sighed heavily. "Yeah."

"Are you completely insane?"

He turned to face me, pressing his back against the bricks. His eyes were bright and full of lust. I could understand that look. I was sure it mirrored mine. But he also looked... remorseful. Like the last thing he had wanted to do was hurt me. Again.

"Uh, yeah," Landon said, "a bit insane at the moment."

"Well, Jesus Christ, what were you thinking?"

Because I needed an explanation. What the hell had changed that he would go from cutting me off entirely to making out with my face? If we hadn't gone through with it on New Year's when we had both been in the thick of it all, I couldn't fathom how he could do it now.

"That I really wanted to kiss you, and I'd wanted to do it for too damn long."

I held my hand up and tried to breathe shallowly. "You can't say things like that to me."

God, he's drunk. Of course, I'd known that before I came out here with him, but I hadn't expected our conversation to veer so far left. And, now, I would never be able to get the feel of his lips or the brush of his tongue or the taste of whiskey mixed with something purely Landon out of my head.

I couldn't think about that or I wouldn't be able to think about anything else. Ever.

"I can," he said, meeting my gaze. "But you act like I shouldn't."

His dark brown eyes nearly made me lose it. He was too much. Tall, dark, and handsome was too cliché for Landon with his deep tan from endless days on the golf course and soulful expression. He was a man who had known loss and understood depression but had risen above. There was more to him than the gorgeous Wright looks. But it didn't excuse his actions.

I didn't want to be some mistake he'd made when his wife wasn't in town.

"No, you shouldn't," I said. "I won't do that again. I will not be that kind of girl. It's disrespectful to me, and it's disrespectful to Miranda. And…it's just bad," I rambled on because, if I stopped, I knew I'd be done for. My fingers were itching to grab him and crush his mouth to mine again. I'd wanted this for months. Even though there were a million and a half reasons that it was a supremely idiotic idea, I still wanted him.

And that had made dating nearly impossible. Somehow, Landon had become the standard that I held all other guys to. Not that I'd had much luck outside of Tinder hook-ups, and I refused to date my coworkers. That was the number one rule. One I had always completely adhered to. No matter how cute the new guy ended up being.

"Yeah, bad idea," he agreed slowly. "I'm not trying to make you that kind of girl, Heidi."

"Good, because that would never happen."

"I'm just lost, and I want you to find me."

I knew he was drunk, but damn it, that was cheesy. And, fuck me, I hated that I still thought it was sweet of him to say it to me. Even if he wasn't allowed to.

"Stop that! No sweet talk."

"I wasn't—"

"How about no, Landon?"

Then, with all the strength I could muster, I strode back toward the emergency exit. I could do this. I was a strong, fierce, independent woman who worked in a male-dominated field and shattered glass ceilings. I could walk away from one boy. Even if he was a Wright.

Then, he touched me. His hand gently landed on my elbow. He wasn't demanding my attention, just drawing me away from the door.

"Heidi."

"What?" I asked in frustration. How was I supposed to leave him behind when he was being so irresistible?

"I'm sorry," he said.

"Stop," I said. "Please."

"I'm leaving her."

My heart stopped beating. My lungs stopped working. My brain stopped functioning. What he was saying was *impossible*. I honestly couldn't even believe that those words had come out of his mouth. There was no way in *hell* that he was leaving Miranda.

"Come again?" I whispered.

"I left Miranda at home to come here because I'm leaving her."

My mouth fell open. He had said those words. He'd repeated them. He was *actually* leaving Miranda.

This isn't a drill, team. This is the real deal!

My brain tried to catch up with the rest of my body, but instead, I stood there, like an idiot. There had to be a catch. There had to be some big joke that was being played on me. Because Landon leaving his wife was way too good to be true.

"Wow," I said. Then, I blinked rapidly a few times and tried to recover. "I mean…how awful. That has to be so hard, Landon."

He laughed humorlessly at me. "Heidi, you're cute."

I arched an eyebrow at him in question. "I tell you I'm sorry about your wife, and you tell me I'm cute?"

"You can't hide how much you hate Miranda any more than my family can."

"Hey," I said, holding up my hands. "I don't hate Miranda. I don't even know her."

"Well, if you knew her, you'd hate her, too."

"Maybe so," I conceded. "But that doesn't make things any easier for you. Clearly, you must have loved her."

"It's just…yeah," he said. "I don't know. It all happened today."

"No wonder you're drunk and acting like a fool. Maybe we should have addressed you leaving Miranda first and made out second."

He grinned devilishly. "So, we're going to make out again?"

"No," I said, smacking his arm. God, I could hardly keep my mind out of the gutter. I was never going to succeed in keeping his out of there, too. "We shouldn't have kissed in the first place."

He might have left Miranda today, but who knew what tomorrow would bring? I doubted he had even filed paperwork for a divorce. I had so many unanswered questions that, even though I wanted to kiss Landon…to give in to this thing between us, I couldn't do it. I knew it was wrong.

Not just because of Miranda, but also because of all the women I'd seen my dad with.

My mom had died in a carjacking when I was in middle school. She'd been brutally murdered, and I'd been a zombie through much of middle school. Without Emery, I never would have made it.

But my dad had coped with women. He'd go from girlfriend to girlfriend—regulars who came to Hanks, the bar he owned. I knew the signs for when he settled for married women—when a woman flipped the diamond over or took it off, leaving a pale stripe on her ring finger, or when I'd find a wedding ring on the sink at night. I'd decided at a young age that I'd do anything to be a different person than my dad. I wasn't about to let Landon Wright fuck that up.

15

"Yeah, I probably shouldn't have kissed you," Landon said. He scratched the back of his neck and winced. "But I'd been thinking about it since New Year's."

"Landon, you can't come here and talk to me like this. If you want to talk about Miranda, I'm here." I held my hands up in supplication. I wouldn't deny him a friend or a shoulder to cry on, but that was it. "We can talk after the reunion, but now, maybe try to forget about it."

"About Miranda or you?"

"Both."

"Not going to happen." He stepped toward me and cupped my cheek. "There's no way I could forget about you, Heidi."

"You've done fine so far. Do what you've been doing, Landon, and you'll have no trouble," I said with a bit more heat than I'd intended. Then, I turned and walked back into Flips.

Three

Heidi

Leaving Landon standing outside felt horrible. I knew he was in a rough place, and he needed someone to talk to. I was happy to be that person. Even if the last thing I wanted to hear about was Miranda. I couldn't do that while we stood out back where we had just kissed. I trusted myself with most things, but Landon Wright was not one of them.

I glanced over my shoulder to make sure that Landon hadn't followed me. The last thing I wanted was for people to see us coming in from outside together. When we'd walked out there, only a handful of people had been in attendance, but already, the bar was filling up. I recognized nearly everyone and was stopped constantly as people wanted to say hi to me.

In high school, I'd been a cheerleader, class vice president, and student council vice president. I'd been very involved. So, planning this evening with Meredith and Dave—the class president and treasurer—had been a blast, but it'd also put a lot of pressure on me. I was the only one who still lived here. That meant I was the one who'd had to do most of the groundwork. The benefit of that was, we got to have the event at Flips.

"Tequila?" the bartender, Peter, asked when he saw me approaching.

I nodded my head and held up two fingers. *Yeah, make it a double, buddy.*

Peter knew what kind of alcohol I was into based on my mood. That was how often I was in here. It was a little scary honestly.

"Care to toast with your bestie and roomie?" Emery asked, sidling up beside me.

"The shots are not celebratory unless I am licking them off your stomach," I informed her.

"Let's do it, baby!" Emery said. She leaned back on her chair and hoisted her black tank up to reveal her flat stomach. "Peter, I need the salt!"

"Oh God, are you two doing this again?" he asked. He tilted his head and judged us, as per usual.

"Hand it over!" Emery crooned.

"It's really not a reunion if we aren't drunk and ridiculous," I said.

"Let's be real," Emery said. "It's not a reunion if we're not drunk on wine coolers and running from the cops because Landon has pot and is afraid he'll get arrested."

Emery hoisted herself up onto the bar and lay down. She balanced the shot on her stomach and started shaking salt next to her belly button.

"Honey," Jensen said, appearing at her side, "what in the hell are you doing?"

"Body shots. Don't tell me you've never done one."

Jensen's face pinched. "*Who* is doing a body shot off of you?"

"Heidi, of course," Emery said with a grin.

"Yeah, Wright, get out of the way." I nudged Jensen, and he gave me a pained expression. I knew how much it hurt him not to get to take that shot, but I wasn't giving it up. "This is my girlfriend, and we might or might not have done this once or twice in high school."

"There were a lot of things you two did in high school that don't need to be repeated," he said.

"Party pooper," Emery called at him.

"Don't listen to him, Em. He's jealous because I get to take the shot. We all know he's done worse."

Jensen shrugged and didn't deny it.

Emery winked at her boyfriend and then placed the lime in her mouth. She made a come-and-get-it gesture. I laughed at my best friend and felt unbelievably grateful for having her. Even if she didn't know something was wrong, she allowed me to completely forget about what had happened.

I bent down, licked the salt from Emery's stomach, and then downed the shot. After I swallowed the tequila back, I took the lime straight from Emery's mouth. She hollered with excitement as I sucked on the lime. My grin was magnetic as I raised my arms like I'd won a gold medal.

"What did I miss?" Landon asked as I turned around to face the rest of the crowd.

I dropped my arms and shrugged. "Body shots."

"Ah, like old times then."

"You don't have any weed on you, do you? Emery reminded us that you used to be a pothead."

Landon raised his eyebrows at me and then shifted his attention to Emery. "I was *not* a pothead."

Emery hopped off the bar. "Nah, you were too scared of getting caught to be a full-blown pothead."

"Actually, I think he was too afraid of our dad," Jensen chimed in.

Landon shrugged. "Well, he could be a scary motherfucker."

"Landon! Brah, I didn't know if you'd come," a guy said from behind him.

My eyes moved from Landon's gorgeous face to the guy behind him. Brandon McCain. My lucky number twelve in high school. I'd been obsessed with him all four years, and I had even adopted his football number as my favorite. Emery liked to make fun of me about it. I couldn't even remember all the times I'd mooned over him, but nothing had ever come of it. He'd had a serious girlfriend all four years of high school and never looked my way. But, as far as I knew, he was single now and lived in Los Angeles as a wannabe actor and model.

"Brandon," Landon said. They firmly shook hands. "Good to see you, man. I didn't know you were going to be here either."

"Fuck, man. I wouldn't have missed it. High school was the shit," Brandon said. "Though who am I kidding? You killed it in high school, and look at you now! Fucking PGA Tour!"

Landon winced slightly. I narrowed my eyes at that movement.

Why would he flinch about being on the PGA Tour? That was his dream. That was his life. He loved golf with everything in him. It seemed odd that he would be uncomfortable with discussing it. I'd never seen him upset about golf.

"Thanks, man," Landon said.

Brandon's eyes shifted from Landon to me, and his smile grew. "Heidi Martin. Fuck me," he said, pulling me in for a hug. "You look even hotter than you did in high school, and you were fucking gorgeous ten years ago."

When Brandon said that, I searched Landon's face, and he went from wincing to pissed in a second. If I wasn't mistaken, he was remembering that crush I'd always had.

"Thanks, Brandon," I said, stepping out of his embrace. "You look great, too."

"We should definitely catch up later." Brandon pointed his finger at me and winked. "Definitely. But, first, I'm going to steal Landon here," he said, throwing an arm around Landon's shoulder, "and get the rest of the football team together."

Landon shot me a grieved look but disappeared with Brandon. I could already see that a huge group of football players was convened in the back. Landon was their star. Of course they had come to collect him.

I'd really wanted that interaction with Brandon to make me feel better about the whole Landon situation, but it didn't. Brandon McCain was still really good-looking. Los Angeles ate people alive if they didn't stay in shape. It was clear that he had been putting in a lot of time at the gym, but I didn't feel the same spark as I once had.

Goddamn it, Landon. Even guys I *could* hook up with were tainted by him.

All I'd wanted for four years was this one sexy guy. Now that we were here and I definitely had not misinterpreted his catch-up-later line, I was meh about the whole thing.

"Whoa!" Emery said. "Brandon McCain is so fucking into you. Hello, dream come true!"

"Yeah," I muttered. "Dream come true."

Emery wrapped her arm through mine. "Okay, roomie, we're supposed to be having a good time. You know I hate reunions and basically all things high school. But I'm here for you because I love your face. Tell me what's wrong, so I can fix it."

"Nothing's wrong."

"News flash, Martin! Brandon fucking McCain just hit on you, and you're sad. You would have blown that guy behind the bleachers after a game if he'd let you. What part of him thinking you're super hot is a bad thing?"

I cleared my mind of everything I'd been dealing with since Landon had stepped back into my life. Landon Wright was not right for me. There was no future for us. I didn't know if he would go back to his wife tomorrow. I didn't know if he'd ever file divorce papers. I didn't know if that kiss was a bullshit rebound move. Stressing over it would only ruin my high school reunion. And I had put too much effort into this reunion for that to fucking happen.

I was the life of the party. I was smart, beautiful, and confident. I could rock this reunion with or without Landon Wright.

"You're so right," I said, bolstered by my own pep talk. "There is not a damn thing wrong with that."

"You sure? You seemed a little out of it. Maybe you and Landon…"

"Please, do not finish that thought. Landon and I do not belong in the same sentence. You've bugged me about it in the past, Em, but he's married. You know what my dad was like. You know I could never do that. And I could never do that to you."

"But it doesn't bother me."

I held my hands up. "Irrelevant. It bothers me! Now, let's talk about Brandon McCain and how he just hit on me."

Emery gave me a look that said she didn't believe my bullshit, but she wasn't a pusher. She wouldn't bother me until I gave up the info.

"Okay, are you going to hook up with him? Because he went from being like gruff hottie in high school to being an LA pretty boy," Emery observed. "I don't know if you could fuck a pretty boy."

"Oh, I could. I assure you."

"Plus, he used *brah* in a sentence without irony."

I snort-laughed and signaled for another drink from Peter. "So, he's not the sharpest tool in the shed. As long as he has a big, long tool I can use, then we're good to go."

"Oh my God!" Emery said, busting out in laughter. "I pray that he does, for your sake, Heidi."

We hung out at the bar as more and more people showed up. It was even more than I'd anticipated. A lot of the local crowd hadn't RSVP'd, so I'd thought it was mostly going to be out-of-towners. A lot of people had complained about the location and lack of food and it not being kid-friendly…and on and on. So many complaints. But it looked like a ton of people had shown up anyway. Probably because of the open bar I'd finagled.

By the time it seemed like most people had finally arrived, the bar was packed. Meredith had planned to make some kind of speech, but with the crowd, that would be impossible. I wasn't worried about it, but she was.

Eventually, she gave up and turned on the slide show she had prepared with all the pictures that everyone had turned in for the reunion. The whole thing was a walk down memory lane.

I had only turned in a couple of pictures of me and Emery together, but it was almost obnoxious, how many images there were of me. It was never clearer to me that I had been totally obsessed with popularity. I cared nothing about it now, but I had deeply stressed over it at the time.

I was sure I had my dad to blame for a lot of that. We never had much, but he'd indulged me with everything I'd wanted at the time. I'd taken every cent. Man, how that had all backfired.

The football team was hooting and hollering over all the images of them. Landon was in nearly as many as I was. Then, one stopped on him in a high school golf polo, holding his club. My eyes shifted over to where he had been sitting all night with an IV of whiskey practically hooked into his arm. When he saw the picture, he openly cringed at it.

Then, his gaze found me. I quickly looked away.

I shouldn't be looking at him. I shouldn't be worried about him. I shouldn't be wondering why golf was a trigger for him.

But I couldn't seem to focus on anything else.

I'd tried to forget him.

I'd tried to stay away from him.

I'd tried not to look at him.

All I did was fail.

Our eyes met across the distance, and my heart tugged in his direction. He nodded his head back toward the exit. It was a question and a promise. I knew that, if I went out there, he'd kiss me again. And I would give in to him. Because I wanted to.

"Ugh, who sent in these pictures?" Emery asked from next to me.

I guiltily looked away from Landon and stared at the picture. It was Emery and Landon together after a football game. She was in his letter jacket, and they were laughing. The next one was of them seated side by side for their Best Couple shot for the yearbook. The one after that had Emery sitting in his lap by a bonfire. I was sitting next to them, grinning like a fool.

There were three or four others, all in a row. A barrage of Emery and Landon. One big fat reminder that the guy I was dreaming about had dated my best friend.

This wasn't like Jensen, who hadn't known Emery when she dated Landon. I'd been there with them through everything. I knew the good, the bad, and the ugly. Emery and I had spent hours lamenting over our love lives.

There was no way in hell that I should be interested in Landon. I wouldn't allow it. I promised myself that I wouldn't look in his direction again. No way, no how.

And, when Brandon McCain moseyed back over to talk to me, I let him hit on me and told myself I wasn't going to feel guilty about it.

Four

Heidi

"Well, I'd call this a success," Emery said a few hours later with a yawn.

"A rousing success," I agreed.

"Way better than the five-year reunion."

"Yeah. This time, they let me have it at a bar. People are way better when they're drunk."

"True. Also, people have actually changed...sort of... since then. Everyone had just graduated college at the five-year."

"Or they were on their second kid," I reminded her.

Emery laughed. "Or that."

"I'm glad you came. You're going back with Jensen now, right?"

Emery gave me a sheepish look. "Don't act like you know me."

"Of course I know you. We've been best friends since kindergarten, and now, we live together!"

I pulled my bestie in for a hug, and we swayed back and forth in a tipsy sort of slow dance.

"You're the best," Emery said.

"You're the bestest."

"Sorry to break up the romantic moment," Jensen said with an amused grin, "but I don't think we can go home until we get Landon safely back to Austin's."

Emery groaned. "But I'm so tired! I want to go home."

"As do I, but if you haven't noticed, he's totally fucked up."

I nodded my head. I had definitely noticed even though I was trying not to. Though people had slowly been leaving the place, most of the football players were still being rowdy in the back. Landon, who had never been the type, had even started to join in with their antics. It made me cringe. He must really be going through something to allow himself to be this far gone.

Emery yawned long and dramatically, as if to say, *Please, dear God, let us go now.*

I laughed at her.

"I'll make sure he gets into a cab. I have to be here until bar close to settle up with Peter anyway. I won't let Landon do anything stupid," I told Jensen.

"Are you sure?" he asked. He got that look in his eye, like he was the older brother and had to guarantee the safety of all of his siblings. It was adorable.

"Yep. No worries. We have cabs coming at closing to get people. I'll make the football players carry him into one. No big," I told him.

Emery arched an eyebrow, and we had a silent conversation.

You're going to help Landon into a cab, huh?

Yeah. So?

And there's nothing going on?

No!

Sure.

There's not.
I don't believe you.
Fuck off, Robinson.
Whatever, Martin.

I laughed and pushed her toward Jensen. "Don't worry about a thing. Go have a lot of monkey sex."

Emery groaned. "I hate you."

"Love you, too, hooker."

"Thanks for doing this, Heidi," Jensen said as he motioned for Emery to precede him out of Flips. "I really appreciate it. If anything goes wrong or if you need me, don't hesitate to call."

God, Jensen is such a nice guy.

"I won't, but don't worry; it'll be fine."

"Famous last words," he muttered before following Emery outside.

I wanted to laugh off Jensen's comment, but with the Wrights, something always went wrong.

Without Emery, the reunion deflated for me. I hadn't kept in contact with anyone else from our senior class, other than Landon. We were all friends on Facebook and Instagram, but I wasn't involved in their lives. I could go hang out with the cheerleading crowd, but I didn't fit in with them now that they had their own mommy circle. I knew everyone, but suddenly, I felt very alone.

I slunk back over to the bar where Peter was cleaning a pile of glasses, generally looking exhausted.

"Long night?"

He shrugged one shoulder. "Pretty busy in case you missed it."

"Noticed that."

Peter dragged a hand back through his shoulder-length hair and sighed. "You've got company."

I whirled around at that comment, expecting to find Landon. Then, I quickly hated myself for that expectation.

Instead, I found Brandon had returned with his pointed grin and flirtatious dude-bro personality.

"Hey, Brandon," I said with a smile.

"Heidi," he said, leaning me into the bar. "You want to get out of here?"

Just like that. No preamble or anything.

"I actually have to close down the bar for the reunion."

"I can wait," he said with a magnetic grin that I was sure worked on girls in LA.

"No, it's okay. It'll be boring, and I should just go home after that."

Brandon's grin slipped, and I could tell that his drunken mind was irritated. He hadn't expected me to turn him down.

He twirled a lock of my hair around his fingers. "Come on, baby. I know you were into me in high school."

I gently extracted myself from him. "That was more than ten years ago, Brandon."

"Couldn't have changed that much."

"Funny you say that," I said with growing aggravation. "I would say that I've changed a lot, but you wouldn't know that, as you've spent the entire time talking to me about your awesome life in LA and all the roles you could have gotten but missed. I'm not interested. You missed your chance to get someone as amazing as me."

I turned and strode away from him, feeling unbelievably empowered. Even though I could hear the words *bitch* and *led me on* being muttered under his breath. It might have been nice to flirt with him, but that didn't guarantee that I had to go home with him. And it most certainly didn't mean that he could push me around because of something I'd felt as a teenager.

Meredith announced from the front of the room that it was time for the bar to close and that everyone should head out now. A few people mentioned an after-party to the reunion, and groups started arranging to go to someone's house to keep hanging out. I had no intention of doing that at all. I'd promised I'd get Landon home, and that was it.

When I found Landon, he was drinking straight out of a pitcher of beer someone had purchased for a game of beer pong on the patio attached to the side of the building. My eyes were round with concern at his level of inebriation. His eyes were glassy, and he was sloshing beer everywhere.

"Landon, I told Jensen I'd get you into a cab at bar close. It's two. Time to go back to Austin's and sleep this off."

"Heidi, Heidi, Heidi," he crowed, his words slurred. He slung an arm around my waist, ignoring the looks from the remaining football players in his crowd. "Don't listen to Jensen. He doesn't know shit."

I easily slipped out of his grip. "Time to go, Landon."

He placed the pitcher down on the table and stood up to look at me. But his balance was total shit. He stumbled forward into me, and I had to lean him up against the booth for him to stand straight.

"God, you're fucked up."

"Heidi," he said again.

"What?"

"You heading out with McCain?"

I gritted my teeth. "What if I am?"

"Have at it, Martin," Landon said, swinging his arm. "He only fucks anything that walks. Go for it, if you're into that."

"Even if I *were* into that," I said in irritation, "it would be none of your goddamn business."

"None of my business?" he said with a sharp laugh. "Right."

His buddies patted him on the back and nudged his shoulder as they passed.

"See you at the after-party, Landon!" one guy called.

Landon yelled and held his hands up, "Yeah, man!"

The other guys cheered him on and then disappeared out of the now-empty room.

There was no way I was going to let him go to some party; that was for damn sure. He was too drunk to go anywhere.

"Landon, you're drunk. Can you let me get you home, so I can fulfill my promise to Jensen?"

"Fuck Jensen!" Landon announced.

"I think Em has that covered," I growled in frustration.

"Awesome. Another thing we have in common. Shitty wives, a penchant for whiskey, and my ex."

"Would you cut it out?"

"I'd normally say blondes, too," Landon said. He ran his hand through my long blonde locks and grinned at me.

I slapped his hand away from me and tried to remain calm. "Time to go. Let's go. Right now."

"Fine," he grumbled as I shoved him toward the door.

We made it halfway across the room, veering awkwardly in his drunken stupor, before Peter came over to help me walk him outside. Only one more cab was waiting, and I breathed a sigh of relief. I could get him home. Then, this crazy night would be over.

Peter and I finally maneuvered Landon into the back of the cab.

"Thanks, Peter. I appreciate it."

"Be careful, Heidi," he said with a knowing look. "Wrights aren't always right." Then, he winked at me.

I felt my face flame at his words. From anyone else, I probably would have blown it off, but Peter didn't say much. He watched and observed. If he had noticed something, then it was because it was blatantly obvious with just a look.

"Thanks for the advice, but you don't have to worry about me."

"I know," he said with a nod. "You're a fighter, just like your old man."

I winced slightly at the comment. Perhaps that was supposed to be a compliment, but about my father...I could hardly take it as one.

"Thanks," I muttered, trying for a smile. "You're the best."

I hopped into the cab behind Landon and coaxed Austin's address out of him for the driver. I nearly kicked him when I found out it was only three blocks away. Not that I could have walked him down those three blocks, but I felt ridiculous, having a cab take him a walkable distance.

Getting him out of the cab was about as difficult as getting him into it, and I got the cab driver's number, so I could call him when I needed a ride home. I didn't think getting him inside was going to be any easier.

Eventually, we made it into Austin's home and to the first-floor bedroom. I thanked the Lord that he wasn't on the second floor. I wasn't sure what I would have done about getting him up the stairs. I probably would have had to leave him on the couch.

I pushed him down onto the bed, and he tumbled backward.

"God, I'm drunk," he muttered.

"Welcome to my world."

"I never expected that you'd be the one taking the initiative," he slurred. "You like it on top?"

"Don't mess with me right now, Landon."

"Hey, you pushed me back onto the bed."

"Because you're wasted, and I wanted to get you somewhere safe. Now, I'm going to go home, so I can get some sleep."

He sloppily reached out for my hand. "Stay with me."

I slipped my hand out of his with a shake of my head. "Not happening."

Then, I went about finding water, Tylenol, and a small trash can to put beside the bed. He might get sick, and I didn't want him to throw up all over Austin's room.

"Guess we're skipping that talk," I muttered when I walked back in with my supplies to find Landon passed out.

I placed the water and Tylenol on the nightstand and proceeded to take off Landon's shoes. He could sleep in the rest of his clothes for all I cared. I patted down his pockets to remove his wallet and cell phone. I dropped the wallet next to the provisions and plugged in his phone to the charger curled around the lamp.

The screen lit up, and for one nosy second, my eyes dropped down onto the screen.

I cringed when I saw the entire screen was full of messages from Miranda.

I pulled my eyes away. Here I was, taking care of someone else's husband when his wife had been messaging him nonstop. No matter what he had been going on between us— the feelings we'd been harboring for too damn long—I knew we were in the wrong.

We were so in the wrong.

My eyes landed on the lit screen one more time, and I guiltily read a few of the messages. I knew I shouldn't, but if I saw what she was saying to him, then maybe it would give me the push to put this whole thing behind me for good.

> *Landon, I love you so much. Please, answer your phone.*

> *I'll always love you. I know we have a future together. We can't be separated. Think about all we've been through.*

> *We can make this work, Landon. I'm so sorry. I wasn't in my right mind. I can't imagine my life without you. Please, please, my love, please let's work this out.*

I jerked away from his phone, as if I'd put my hand into a bed of red-hot coals.

Holy fuck!
Miranda is a wreck!

She was a total wreck. And she had no idea that *I* had contributed to this in some way. She had no idea that her husband had come here and promptly kissed another woman. And that was all I was—the other woman.

He might be separated, but they weren't over.

I stared down at him sleeping peacefully on the bed and wanted nothing more than to curl up beside him. But I wouldn't.

Landon Wright didn't belong to me.

He belonged to Miranda.

I wouldn't be stupid enough to forget it again.

Five

Landon

"Fuuuck," I groaned.

My stomach heaved, and I rolled over to find a conveniently placed trash can for me to empty my stomach into. *Thank fuck!*

After I was finally able to sit up, I squinted into the brightly lit room and tried to remember where the fuck I was. It looked like Austin's place, but how had I gotten here? After kissing Heidi and seeing her talk to Brandon McCain, the rest of the night got kind of fuzzy.

I fumbled for the bottle of water on the nightstand and downed three-quarters of it before realizing there was Tylenol next to it. Someone must have read my mind. There was no way I'd gotten this all together last night. Not if I couldn't even remember it.

Fuck, I mean, my shoes were off, my wallet was out of my pocket, and my phone was even charging on the nightstand. I couldn't have come home alone; that much was for sure.

Austin wouldn't have gone to the trouble. I wasn't sure he even got hangovers anymore.

Slowly, I eased into a standing position and took the Tylenol for my splitting headache. I stripped out of the clothes I'd worn last night and found a pair of basketball shorts and a T-shirt. Then, I palmed my cell phone and headed out into the living room.

"Morning, sunshine," Austin called from the living room. He had *SportsCenter* on in the background and was drinking a Bloody Mary.

"How can you even look at alcohol?"

"We have a special relationship."

I laughed and then held my head in pain. *A special relationship to say the least.*

"What time is it anyway?"

"One in the afternoon," Austin announced.

"Fuck," I groaned.

I slouched into a chair and pulled up the messages on my phone. I'd ignored Miranda all day yesterday, but fuck, she had filled up my text messages, and I had seventeen voice mails. *Christ!*

No way was I in the mood to listen to any of those. From a brief scroll through the texts, I could already see that it was her same shit. I'd deal with that conversation when I got home. I didn't want to talk to her about the shit she'd tried to pull or the argument we'd gotten into.

I rolled my eyes. I wasn't an idiot. She had tried to hide shit from me and then acted like a cornered animal when I'd confronted her. Despite our long and damaged history, she hadn't thought I'd call it quits. No matter that I'd wanted to divorce her a year ago. I'd drawn up papers and everything, but she had gotten pregnant and I'd said I'd give us one more chance. Then chance after chance after chance after marriage counseling chance I'd given her until her latest bout of bullshit. I'd given her so many chances she never thought I'd walk. Now that I'd finally had enough, I knew what she was really freaking out about—losing her paycheck.

"So, you banging Heidi now?" Austin asked.

I jerked up so hard that I winced and cradled my head. "I'm *what*?" I shouted.

Austin's eyes narrowed. "She was here last night. Saw her come out of your room when I got back around two thirty."

"She was *here*?"

"Bro, were you that fucked up that you don't remember fucking her? Because that would explain why she looked so upset," Austin said.

"You think I slept with her?" I asked, getting paler by the second.

"I mean, I don't know for sure, but why else would a hot chick be leaving your room at two thirty in the morning? Plus, with the shit going down with Miranda, I thought you'd wanted some fun at this reunion."

"What stuff with Miranda?"

"Dunno, man. Can't be good if you're here without her."

"Wait, wait, wait," I said, my brain finally catching up. "Heidi was upset?"

Austin shrugged. "You really don't remember shit, do you?"

"Fuck. I'm screwed, aren't I?"

"As far as I see it." Austin pushed his Bloody Mary toward me. "I think you need this more than I do."

"Thanks, but I have to figure out what the fuck happened last night." I tried to shake out the cobwebs in my mind, but everything was just missing. I hadn't blacked out like this since college. *Jesus, I had been an idiot.*

I hauled ass back into the room I was staying in and dialed Heidi's number. It rang and rang and rang before her voice mail finally picked up.

"Hi, this is Heidi. You know I hate voice mails. If it's important, text me."

Beep.

I hung up before leaving a message she'd never listen to.

"Fuck, Heidi," I grumbled as I dialed her number again.

It didn't even go through all the rings before pushing to voice mail.

A minute later, Heidi sent me a text.

Let's just end this the way we did last night.

I stared at that text message with a growing sense of panic in my chest. *What the hell happened last night? Where did we leave things?*

I didn't want to call and be like, *Hey, did we fuck last night?* I was sure I would have remembered that if we had. I couldn't imagine having sex with Heidi being anything less than unforgettable.

I responded to her message.

Not good enough for me. Answer your phone.

I dialed her number again, and this time, at almost the last moment, Heidi answered. It was as if she hadn't been sure she was actually going to do it.

"Hey," she said softly.

"Hey. Thanks for answering."

"I'm not sure why I did."

"Because leaving me at two thirty in the morning, drunk off my ass, is not how you wanted to end things."

"Yeah. How are you feeling this morning?"

"Hungover and with a severe lack of memory of several hours of last night," I admitted.

"I see," she said.

"Care to fill me in on the details?"

"Nothing happened, if that's what you're asking," she said with bite in her voice. "I told you I wouldn't do anything with you while you were still with Miranda. Anyway, do you think I'd take advantage of someone as drunk as you were last night?"

"No, I didn't think you would. I just didn't know if I'd made a total fool of myself in front of you."

"If insinuating that I was going to fuck Brandon McCain because he'd flattered me with his obnoxious attention, getting so wasted that you were drinking beer straight from a pitcher, and blacking out as soon as I got you into bed make you a total fool, then yes."

I winced. *Great.*

That was all pretty shitty, but at least I hadn't had sex with her and somehow forgotten. That would have been way worse.

"Yeah. Sorry about all of that."

"It's fine, Landon. It's fine. I should just go. I don't think we should be talking anymore."

"Heidi, please. You said that we were going to talk."

"Yeah, and then you got wasted!"

"I know. Have brunch with me."

"You cannot ask me out!" she cried.

"It's just brunch, Heidi. You said we'd talk after the reunion. Can I call in that favor?"

"No."

"Heidi," I groaned. "Please."

She sighed heavily into the phone and left me waiting and wondering. "Fine. Brunch. Half hour enough time?"

"Yes, that's plenty of time. Thank you. Café J?"

"All right. I'll see you there, Landon."

I hung up the phone with a sigh. I could make this right. I hadn't done anything unforgivable. Heidi would come around. I might be in the process of leaving Miranda, but I didn't want to lose ever having a chance with Heidi.

The next twenty minutes, I showered off the alcohol still oozing from my pores, shaved, and changed into navy chinos and a polo. I still had plenty of time to get to Café J, which was one of my favorite restaurants in town. I grabbed my phone, and it started ringing.

Jensen.

I rolled my eyes. At least it wasn't Miranda.

"Hey, bro," I said when I answered the phone. I busied myself around the room, stuffing my wallet into my pocket and throwing on my large-faced watch.

"Landon, I hate to call you so early in the afternoon, considering your condition last night," Jensen said.

He was all business. It was the tone of his voice that finally stilled me.

"Yeah. Last night was rough. What's up?"

"Miranda just showed up at my door, demanding to see you."

"She did what?" I cried.

"I guess she took the early flight out of Tampa this morning and just got into town. She came straight here, thinking that you would be here."

"Did you tell her I was at Austin's?"

Jensen sighed. "Of course I did. She's your wife."

"Fuck, Jensen."

"Handle your shit, Landon, or let me help. Otherwise, you're going to keep ending up right back at this same place."

I cursed Jensen under my breath. He was right, which was why I hated him more for saying it. "Thanks for the heads-up."

My mind was reeling as I hung up. I should have known that Miranda would follow me. What had I expected from her? She had done crazier things in the last couple of years than hop on a plane to see me in Lubbock. And, with the way I had left things, I should have anticipated this. But I'd been so pissed that I wasn't thinking straight, which was becoming more apparent as the day went on.

I rushed out to the living room. Austin was lounging back with his Bloody Mary, texting.

"Miranda is on her way," I told him. I could hear the panic in my voice.

Austin turned his head to look at me and grimaced. "That's bad, right?"

"Probably. I have to make a phone call. Will you answer the door if she shows up?"

"Well, I was going to see if you wanted to get lunch with me and Patrick, but that sounds out of the question."

"Yeah, I don't think I'll be able to hang with you guys now." Not that I'd planned to for lunch anyway. "Can you answer? I have to make a call before she gets here."

"I'll run interference," Austin agreed, waving me away.

I dialed Heidi's number as I dashed back into my room.

I was going to be late. Definitely late. *Fuck, I might have to cancel.*

No, that wasn't an option. I had to talk to her. I had to apologize for last night and explain what was going on. If she knew the truth, then she would understand where I was coming from.

After a few rings, the line cut to her voice mail. I hung up and blew out a harsh breath as I dialed her number again.

"Pick up, pick up, pick up," I breathed over and over as the phone rang.

She must be in the car or something because it went to voice mail again. I swore loudly and was about to dial her number again when I heard the doorbell.

"Fuck," I cried.

I pocketed my phone and exited the room. Austin had already set down his Bloody Mary and swaggered over to the front door. He shot me a curious look over his shoulder before opening the door.

"Miranda," Austin said, as if he were surprised. "I wasn't expecting to see you."

"Where's Landon?" she cut in, skipping all pleasantries.

"He's a bit hungover, but he's here."

41

Miranda elbowed past him to get inside.

He blew out a breath. "Come on in."

Miranda's eyes found me across the room, and I saw the determination in her gaze. She was a woman on a mission. She had clearly thought of nothing else but getting to me since I left. But she still managed to look perfect. Her long bleach-blonde bob was straight and pristine. Her makeup was flawless with cherry-red lipstick. Even her outfit—a white knee-length skirt paired with a hot-pink silk blouse—was pressed and perfect. If I hadn't known her, I never would have guessed that this was a woman who had been falling apart.

"Landon!" she said, rushing over to me. She threw her arms around my neck and pressed her body against mine. "I've been so worried."

I patted her back. My eyes found Austin's across the room. His expression was pinched. He still thought that I'd slept with Heidi last night. He must be thinking horrible things about me. Either that or he truly despised Miranda as much as everyone else and had hoped this wouldn't happen.

"Hey, what are you doing here?" I asked. I held her at arm's length.

"What am I doing here?" she asked in disbelief. "After you walked out of the house without me, what did you expect me to do?"

"Stay home in Tampa."

Her eyes widened. "I could never do that, Landon. You had to know I could never watch you walk away and be okay with it. I was devastated. I had to follow you. I had to make this right."

Austin cleared his throat. "Sorry to interrupt. I'm going to…head out and get some lunch with Patrick. Let me know if you need anything."

"Thanks, Austin," I said with a sigh. I waved at him as he practically bolted out of the house to avoid the conversation that I so desperately wished to back out of.

As soon as Austin shut the door, Miranda reached for my hands. "I'm so, so sorry, Landon. I am. Truly. You have to know how sorry I am about all of this."

I pulled my hands back from her. "I don't actually. You seemed like you meant what you said."

"You know I didn't. I was frustrated and worried about you when you heard me on the phone with Janice. It's not every day that we have to face the news from your doctor that you might never be able to play golf again."

The breath left my lungs in a whoosh, and I took a step back. Even hearing those words out of her mouth made my stomach clench and my body seize. I'd tried not to think those exact words. I'd tried to block out the doctor telling me that I'd reinjured my back in the same spot as before. I'd tried to forget him telling me that, if I didn't stop, if I didn't take time off to heal, I would never golf again. And, even then, there were no guarantees.

"No, I'd hoped to never have to hear that," I said. "But I also didn't expect for you to tell Janice that you didn't want to have kids after we'd spent the last year doing everything possible to make that happen, then blow up on me when I asked you about it."

Tears welled in her eyes, and within seconds, she was sniveling into her hands. Her shoulders were shaking. Her body was racked with sobs. The composed woman that I knew disappeared.

"I'm sorry," she blubbered. "I'm so sorry. It was a joke between girls. I swear."

"Well, it wasn't a funny joke considering we lost a child and I've catered to your every whim the last *year* in an attempt to make it right. Then you tell her that you don't want a kid to end up like a Wright so you're not having one. Excuse me if I don't think that's funny."

"It was stress," she went on. "I know I shouldn't have said it. I didn't mean it. Everything I said was me being worried about your career and came out all wrong. It wasn't anything else. I want you to get better. I want you to do what you love again. You know that you're my first priority. Always. And I flew all this way to make it right."

Her eyes came up to meet mine. They were bloodshot, and tears streamed down her face.

"Landon, let me make this right," she gasped out.

My phone buzzed in my pocket, and I knew exactly who that was. I knew where I was supposed to be and what I was supposed to be doing. But here was my wife, my callous and hardened wife, laying it all out for me. I was so tired of all the shit that we had been through. I didn't know if I believed her when she had she had been joking or that my career was her first priority, but I'd have to be a different man, a worse man, to not hear her out.

"One more chance, Miranda," I told her. "Just one and if I ever feel this way again. I'm gone. Do you understand?"

She nodded fiercely. "You never will. I promise."

Heidi

Going to Café J to have brunch with Landon was an idiotic idea. I knew that down to my bones, yet I couldn't say no to him. I'd tried, but when he had pleaded with me, I had been a goner.

There was never going to be a real relationship between us. I wouldn't come between him and Miranda. I wouldn't be that kind of girl.

But, still, I hoped.

I hoped for the day when he would tell me that he wasn't just separated, but that he'd finalized a divorce with Miranda.

It was a bad, cruel thing to hope for.

Asking for a marriage to be ruined was bad Karma, and I needed all the good vibes I could get in my life. I'd had enough hard times, and I knew better.

Still…it made my chest ache to think about that one kiss. And, even though he'd been drunk the night before, my blood had heated when he asked me if I liked to be on top. It had taken all the willpower in my body not to give in and forget about being a responsible adult for once.

Yet here I was, driving out to see him.

As if I honestly believed we could go back to being friends after that kiss.

He'd cut off all contact with me because our conversations had gone from him finally having someone he could talk to in his life to deep, emotional conversations. To talking late into the night. To wanting to wake up and call him. To wanting to talk to him every day just to tell him about my day. To wanting to fly out there and see his smile to match the laugh I could draw out of him.

And then New Year's. When our conversations had gone from everything but admitted feelings to almost crossing a line we would never have been able to come back from.

He'd ended it for a reason.

We probably should have been smarter and stuck to that.

Too late now.

He'd had his tongue down my throat, and I certainly wasn't about to forget it. Even though the sane side of my brain told me I should want to forget.

I pulled into the Café J and killed the engine. It was busy, and the parking lot was full. I hurried inside, and after looking around and seeing Landon wasn't there, I put my name down for a table for two.

"Should be about fifteen minutes," the hostess said.

"Thanks."

I took a seat on the bench to wait for Landon and pulled out my phone. I had two missed calls from him but no voice mail or text messages. *Odd.*

I dialed Landon's number and waited. He wasn't like me. He didn't avoid phone calls like the plague. He almost always answered immediately. But, this time, his voice mail actually picked up.

"Hey. This is Landon Wright, and you've reached my voice mail. I'm not here right now, but if you leave a message, I'll get back to you."

Beep.

I ended the call. If I hated voice mails, I wasn't about to leave one for him. Still, it was strange.

"Martin," the hostess called.

"That's me!" I waved my hand and stood.

I let the woman escort me to our table in the back of the room and ordered a glass of water for each of us. I assured the waiter that Landon was on his way and would be here any minute.

After about ten minutes of radio silence, I craned my neck back up to the front to see if maybe he was waiting and didn't realize that I'd gotten a table already. But he wasn't up there, and my phone hadn't rung.

Landon was late.

Seriously, this was annoying. *Why insist on seeing me if he was going to show up late?* He was probably just working off that hangover or something, but it was crappy not to at least text.

I tried calling one more time, but he didn't answer. *Huh.* I chewed on my lip. This wasn't like Landon. Maybe something had happened. *What if he'd been in a car accident or something? What if something had happened to him or Austin, and he couldn't get to his phone?* A slew of other worst-possible scenarios ran through my head.

With fear driving me, I sent Landon a text.

> *Hey, is everything okay? I'm worried about you. Call me back.*

I bit my nail down to the quick as I waited for what felt like an endless amount of time. I shooed away the waiter more than once as he came by to check on me. Ten minutes turned into twenty, and twenty was quickly approaching thirty. I hadn't eaten anything, and I had gone from worried to pissed.

47

Landon Wright had made me come here, only to abandon me.

He'd stood me up.

My heart beat rapidly in my chest, and I could hear whooshing in my ears, as if I were going through a tunnel. A flush of embarrassment coated my cheeks, and anger suffused my system.

I didn't know what was going on in his life. I didn't know what was really happening with Miranda. But this wasn't acceptable.

I clenched my hands into fists and stood from the table.

Landon had made an idiot out of me.

I knew I'd been right the first time. I'd left Austin's house last night, visibly upset about what I'd come to realize. Landon and Miranda had shit to work out, and I'd happened to be the closest person for him to channel his anger into. That was all it had been.

When he'd called this morning, I'd thought that maybe I'd read the situation wrong. Maybe I shouldn't have left last night. Maybe we could see where things could go between us. Maybe he did want me.

Now, I had to keep my hands from shaking. I was so angry with him. He'd proven me right, and I didn't like it at all.

I stormed out of the restaurant and back to my car. My breathing was coming out in furious hyperventilating-induced sputters. In all my life and all the horrible dates I'd been on, I'd never once been stood up and made to feel this stupid.

I turned over the ignition as my phone started vibrating next to me. I almost ignored it. If it were Landon, he was too little, too late. I was an afterthought. I wasn't important enough to even be told that he couldn't make it. I didn't want to talk to someone who could treat me that way.

But my hand reached out, and I looked at the screen anyway.

A sigh escaped me when I saw that it was Emery, not Landon. Somehow, I had still gotten my hopes up that it was him. But I had to put that all away now. I couldn't let Emery know why I was so upset. Landon was off-limits. He was not a conversation I wanted to have with my best friend.

I answered the call, "Hello?"

"Hey! I just got home. Where are you?" Emery asked.

"I went to get some food but lost my appetite and didn't eat anything."

"That's lame. You should probably eat something. Want me to make you something at home?"

"No, that's okay." I really was not hungry any longer. My anger had burned away my need for food. "What's up?"

"I have so much to dish to you. I wanted to tell you as soon as I got home. Are you going to be out long?"

"I'm on my way home actually," I said as I turned over the ignition and pulled out of my parking spot. "Be there in, like, ten minutes."

"Okay. Well, I can't wait that long," Emery said. "Miranda showed up at Jensen's house this morning."

I gasped as everything seemed to crystallize, "Miranda? Like…Landon's wife?" My voice was brittle, as if I were a cracked eggshell, ready to shatter.

"Yeah. Like the crazy bitch lady who screams at me every time she sees me even though she knows that Jensen and I are together and I have no interest in Landon. She's a total monster. Jensen detests her, to put it mildly."

"What was she doing there?" I managed to get out as I drove blindly across town. I couldn't recall any of the drive. Stoplights and traffic signals and lane changes had all happened, but I was on autopilot.

"She was looking for Landon, but as you know, this trip, he's staying with Austin, not Jensen."

"Right." Because I'd gotten his drunk ass home last night. "But…what did she want?"

49

"Not sure. What I gathered from her clipped conversation with Jensen was that they'd had an argument, Landon had threatened to leave her, and she was here to make things right. Whatever the hell that means."

"Yeah," I whispered.

Miranda was here to make things right. And, now, Landon wasn't returning my calls or answering any of my messages.

My throat felt dry and cracked. My hands were stiff on the steering wheel. My heart constricted painfully.

Of course.

Of course this was what it was.

It was as if those messages I had read last night on Landon's phone and the conclusion I had drawn from them came true. Landon wasn't leaving Miranda. Landon was never going to leave Miranda. Even Emery had said that Landon had only threatened it. He wasn't really going to follow through.

I didn't know what this whole brunch thing had been to him. *Had he been trying to break my heart once and for all? Had he decided it would be easier for me to know how worthless I truly was to him if he led me on and then blew me off?*

I was feeling about two inches tall at the moment, and blood was roaring in my ears.

"Heidi? Hey, are you still there?" Emery asked.

I hadn't even realized that she was still talking to me on the phone. "Yeah, sorry. I'm driving."

"That's cool. You went quiet on me there."

"I don't think I'm feeling that great," I admitted.

"Oh no," Emery said. "We'll have to do some Netflix and chill."

I laughed softly. "You do know that means we're going to have sex, right?"

"And?"

"Count me in," I said the words, but they held none of my normal lighthearted enthusiasm. I couldn't muster up the humor for the conversation.

"Heidi," Emery said again.

"Yeah?"

"Is this about Landon?"

"Is what about Landon?" I asked, panicked that she had correctly interpreted my silence.

"You know…about him and Miranda."

"No. I don't know."

Emery sighed. "I know you like him, Heidi. You don't hide things from me as well as you think you do."

"I don't like him," I insisted.

Right now, I definitely hated him.

"Okay," Emery said disbelievingly. "Well, I don't know what's happening with Miranda, but if Jensen has anything to say about it, they'll be divorced sooner rather than later."

"I won't hold my breath."

"Well, come home, and we can eat ice cream and binge-watch *Buffy*, okay?"

"Sounds good. See you soon." I ended the call and drove straight home.

When I pulled into the parking lot of the apartment I shared with Emery, a text popped up from Landon.

> *So sorry about brunch! Something came up, and I couldn't get away. Can we talk later? I'll explain everything.*

I shook my head in exasperation. He hadn't even mentioned Miranda in the text. *Something had come up. Yeah, right.* What he'd meant was, his wife had shown up, and if I'd stayed the night, she would have busted us. Even worse, if he had been at brunch with me, she could have shown up there while we were together. *What the hell would he have done then?*

Landon wasn't being honest with me, and worse, it didn't seem like he was being honest with himself. He wasn't leaving Miranda. Talking to me was only going to cause him trouble.

I had no interest in a battered love triangle.

I had no interest in fighting for someone who was unattainable.

I had no interest in losing my heart to someone who could only break it.

I tapped out a message to Landon, letting my anger guide me. I knew I was doing the right thing. Reconsidering had been the wrong move. Waiting around for him when he was late had been a desperate one. Agreeing to talk to him again after all of that would be utterly stupid.

> *I know Miranda is here. This is over. Don't ever talk to me again.*

Seven

Landon

Heidi's text was explicitly clear.

Don't ever talk to me again.

Fuck.
Fuck.
Fuck.

I had fucked up. I could feel her anger in that one message. She was beyond pissed. I didn't know how she had found out about Miranda, but that was not good. Worse was, I hadn't told her myself that Miranda was here. Now, she probably thought that I was hiding it from her. Who even knew what was going on in her head? It couldn't be good. And, by the sound of it, our friendship wasn't even salvageable.

With Miranda here in Lubbock, I had no chance to make things right with Heidi. Even to apologize and let Heidi be. It might be for the better to keep her out of my baggage at the moment, but I still felt bad. Standing her up after how I'd acted last night had been unnecessarily cruel. I would never have done that if I'd had a way to get away.

Instead, I'd stayed at Austin's and listened to Miranda talk for hours. Maybe she *was* serious about making things right. I wasn't sure. I'd need some more time to process. Between my injury, golf, and Miranda, I needed more than a day to figure out what to do with my life.

After a painful afternoon, I decided that it would be better for the two of us to go home. With the reunion over and Heidi refusing to speak to me, there was really nothing for me in Lubbock. I had another doctor's appointment on Monday. I had serious pain in my lower back, and I knew it was fucked up. I was really not looking forward to him talking to me about it some more.

But that wasn't an option with my career on the line.

I shook my head to clear away the cobwebs. Everything felt as if I were walking on a tightrope without a net. One wrong move, and I'd lose it all.

Miranda must have noticed my somber mood because she dried her tears and became completely compliant. I might be pissed at her for the argument we'd gotten into before I had left. After overhearing her conversation with Janice and confronting her about it, she'd tried waterworks. When she realized that wouldn't work, she'd screamed that it was true.

Fine, she didn't want kids. Was I happy?

Happy?

How could I possibly be happy?

I'd stayed with her for the kids. For the possibility to fix our marriage with children.

Now, she was saying that she hadn't meant all of that. She'd sounded pretty fucking serious when she'd said it. Both to me and Janice. And I didn't know if I could believe her even though I kept doling out second chances to her like candy. We'd see how this one went, because I fucking meant it. I'd stick to my word. This was the last one she got. I couldn't keep living my life like this.

⸻

Sunday morning, I dialed Jensen's number as I was packing up my meager belongings. I knew he would answer. My eldest brother was a bit of an insomniac vampire.

"Hey," Jensen said groggily into the phone.

I startled at him sounding tired. That was new. "Hey, did I wake you up?"

"No, no. Go back to sleep," Jensen whispered. I assumed he was talking to Emery. Then, he was back to me. "Sorry about that. I'm up. What's going on?"

"I wanted to let you know that Miranda and I are taking an early flight out this morning."

Jensen blew out a harsh breath. "You're leaving already?"

"Yeah. I think I need to get back to my life and figure out what's going on."

"With Miranda?"

"Yes," I said slowly. "And golf."

"Your injury isn't healing," Jensen guessed. "I noticed you were careful with it at the reunion."

I winced. I hadn't even realized I'd been doing that. I'd had some pain ever since I injured my back four years ago, and I'd had to pull out of the middle of my last tournament. Then a couple weeks ago I'd completely thrown it out. It was no surprise that I was hurting the way I was.

"Yeah. We'll see what happens."

"And you're going to miss church," he accused.

This was the hardest part about telling Jensen that I was leaving early. Church was a Lubbock necessity and a Wright tradition. Our mother had gone to church every Sunday, and we continued to do so in her memory every single Sunday.

Leaving ahead of church was nothing short of blasphemy, and I was doing it. Again.

"Yeah, sorry. You know I want to be there, but—"

"Yeah, yeah. Just figure out your life. Call me if you need me…or a lawyer."

I sighed. "Thanks, man. I'll keep that in mind."

After I hung up, I said my good-byes to Austin and then Miranda and I headed to the airport. Our flight had a layover in Dallas, and Miranda insisted we upgrade to first class for the long leg of the flight. I didn't want to argue, so I just did it. She ordered a mimosa as soon as we were in the air again. I didn't need a drink; I needed a new body.

The landing was hell on my back, and in that moment, I was glad for the first-class seat. If the pain could flame up that quickly, I had a feeling that surgery was going to come sooner rather than later. A problem for another day.

After we picked up Miranda's bag from baggage claim, we walked out to my Mercedes SUV parked in the deck and drove into Clearwater. We lived in a gated country club on the water with a full golf course that, up until this recent injury, I had played at nearly every day. Big enough to house a college spring break, our house was a sprawling two-story overlooking the Gulf of Mexico with a pool and hot tub out back.

Miranda had been silent and fidgeting the entire drive from the airport. She hopped out of the car as soon as I pulled into the garage. She seemed nervous, and I didn't know why. But the vibe from her was coming off strong.

I didn't really want to deal right now. I wanted to get our luggage inside and pass out for a few hours. I had not gotten enough sleep this weekend.

With a groan, I pulled Miranda's enormous suitcase out of the trunk. Why she'd had to bring a full-sized suitcase for a last-minute weekend trip, I would never understand. My back certainly didn't approve. Then, I lugged it along with my own bag inside.

And I stopped dead in my tracks. "What the fuck?"

The house was a wreck.

I'd left it in pristine condition, and I came home to find it…vandalized. The furniture had been moved, and pillows were scattered across the room. Pictures had been ripped off the walls. All the frames of me and Miranda had been overturned, or the glass had shattered onto the hardwood floor. Some decorative display with green glass pebbles had been strewn across the room.

Miranda whirled around with her brows scrunched together and her mouth open. "I can explain."

"You can…explain?" I asked in confusion. "We've been robbed."

It was the only explanation that seemed to fit. Someone must have broken in and trashed the place, looking for money or valuables.

"We haven't," she said softly.

"How the hell do you know that?"

I dropped the luggage and slammed the garage door behind me. My fury reignited, like pouring gasoline on a flame. I'd been gone for three days, and this had fucking happened!

"Because I did it," she whispered.

"You did what?"

"I was upset, and I got carried away," she said so evenly that it was as if she were delivering news about where we were going for lunch. It was nothing of importance. Just something that had happened. Something she hadn't even blinked at when she left the house like this to come get me from Lubbock.

"You trashed our house," I said slowly through gritted teeth.

"I said I was upset." She lifted one petite shoulder, as if to say, *Oops.*

My gaze shifted around the room once more. *This* was what had happened when she was upset. She had turned into a Tasmanian devil and leveled the living room. *What in the hell was wrong with someone who could do something like that?*

Finally, my eyes landed back on her.

She seemed perfectly content. We'd talked. I was home. Her world was in the right.

But I was seeing a different person.

I was seeing the person my family had been warning me about for years. The one I had known existed and been willing to walk away from a year ago. The woman that I'd given everything…and then she spat in my face.

I'd been played.

As I stared around at the destruction, it was so fucking obvious. Miranda hadn't been sad or upset after I'd left. She'd been *pissed*. Then she'd used that anger to come up with a plan to get me back. No matter how much she had to lie and act. And it had fucking worked.

But the evidence of her scheming was before me.

"Don't worry," Miranda continued. "I'll have someone come to clean it up. It'll be fine."

"Fine," I whispered.

"Yep." She grinned at me. She thought this was all better now. Her plan had worked. She got another chance, and now she could go back to how things were. "I'm going to go up and change. I scheduled a massage and facial for later today. After this horrible weekend, I need to detox."

Then, she traipsed upstairs, as if the entire world was at her feet once more.

But, really, it was crumbling all around me.

"Fuck this," I muttered.

Without another word, I turned and walked out the front door. My feet carried me down the street and onto the golf course. I found the nearest green and stood there, watching as a couple tried and failed to get their ball into the hole.

This was what it all came back to.

This was where I was home.

This was my whole life.

Now, I couldn't even use a putter, let alone swing a club. I might be in a midlife crisis or something, but everything I'd known and everything I'd associated with as a person felt over.

I might get back to golfing. I might not.

I might save my marriage. I might not.

I might have a family one day. I might not.

All I knew was, I wouldn't continue with how things were.

My family hated Miranda. Everyone hated Miranda. The only reason that we had stayed together this long was because of the pregnancy, and after that display, how could I possibly want kids with her. How could I want to bring a child into a world where his or her mother acted this way?

I was done catering to Miranda. I was done dealing with this shit. I had nothing left in me. No more chances.

Why should I keep putting myself through this?

I didn't even love her.

With a sigh, I felt a weight fall off of my shoulders. I finally knew that I was doing exactly the right thing.

I pulled my phone out and dialed the last number I'd called.

"Landon?" Jensen answered on the first ring. "You back in Tampa?"

"You said that you'd help me," I said to him.

My eyes were locked on the green before me. Jensen was a fixer. We could do this together.

"Miranda?"

"I think I need a lawyer."

Jensen slowly breathed out. "I was afraid it would come to this."

"Yeah. I'm done. I'm so done."

"I'll get on it right away. Florida is a no-fault state. You know she'll be getting half of your golf money, right?"

"Fuck my money," I growled.

"Just letting you know. Half of everything after the prenup."

"It doesn't matter. Something has to change. She's not the woman I married. She's not the woman I want to be married to."

"What are you going to do in the meantime?" he asked. "You can't live in that house with her."

"I don't know. I have a doctor's appointment tomorrow. I'll know more about what is happening with golf then. After that...I'll figure it out."

"Focus on getting better. Let me handle the rest."

I nodded, and we ended the call.

I took a deep breath as the divorce that had been a long time coming was finally put into motion. It was as if I could finally take a breath, and I knew then that I was doing the right thing.

But I sure was not looking forward to breaking that news to Miranda.

Eight

Heidi
One Month Later

"I don't know about a third date, Julia," I said, leaning my hip against the side of her desk. "Nick was almost too nice, too normal."

Julia rolled her eyes. "You *need* nice and normal, girl. All you have been dealing with are assholes, douche bags, and jerkfaces."

I shrugged at my closest work friend. "So, I have a type."

"You do not have a type. *I* had that type, remember?" She held out her arm to reveal the tattoos peeking out of her blouse and then ran one hand down the array of studs in her ear. "Bad girls attract bad boys. You are like the prom queen."

"I was *not* prom queen."

"Your hair is bleach blonde to your waist, and you're wearing more bright colors than I have in my whole wardrobe. Plus, high heels," she added in triumph. "I attract the bad boys. You go looking for them."

"So what? I'm only twenty-eight. Live a little."

Julia laughed brusquely. "Oh, I've lived way too much for the both of us. I'm content with *not* living like I used to and finding a nice and normal dude."

"Like Trevor?" I asked.

"Yes, like Trevor."

Julia and Trevor had started dating at the beginning of the summer. He worked in accounting, which made him completely off-limits to me because of my no-dating-coworkers rule. But he had a cute friend, Nick, who did not work for Wright Construction and whom I had now gone on two double dates with. He was exactly as I had described—nice, normal, and baggage-free.

That might be why Julia liked Trevor, but sometimes, I found it all a little dull. I was notoriously picky, and though I thought he was an all right guy, I didn't get any vibes off of him that he was *the one*.

But at least I was dating.

Seeing Landon again at the reunion last month had been a wake-up call. I'd been wading through life, waiting for a guy as awesome as Landon and coming up short every time. Turned out, Landon wasn't as great as I'd thought. He was essentially the same guy who had dumped my friend on graduation day ten years earlier. I clearly hadn't been giving any other guys the time of day.

Now, I was.

"Just give Nick another chance," Julia encouraged. She flipped her shoulder-length auburn hair to one side, revealing the shaved undercut she had gotten earlier that week. She was obviously the coolest person I knew.

"All right. I'll go for date three," I told her with a shrug. "What else am I going to do this weekend besides plan Emery's surprise birthday party? Do you think you can make it?"

"Next Monday?" Julia asked.

"Yep."

"And she still has no clue?"

"Emery hates, hates, *hates* birthdays. She does not suspect that I have anything planned."

"I might have to be late. Is that cool?"

"You'll miss the surprise part." I pouted.

"Okay, okay. I'll reschedule my hair appointment. The girl is so hard to get in to see."

"You just got your hair done!"

"Upkeep, bitch," Julia said with a laugh. "I don't look this fabulous for nothing."

"Yes, you do. You always look fabulous."

Julia rolled her eyes and waved her hand, as if to say, *Whatever.* "So, is, uh…Austin going to be there?"

I grinned wide and crossed my arms, giving her *the look.* "Are you ever going to tell me what happened with you and Austin Wright after the office Christmas party?"

"Not a chance," Julia said, standing abruptly. She was in an all-black getup—pencil skirt, button-up blouse, and ballet flats. "Austin Wright completely proves my point of the bad boys finding me. I like to file him under The Past I Will Never Look at Again."

"At least he hasn't been in your office as much lately," I conceded.

Julia was head of HR for the entire company. She was excellent at her job. But Austin got more HR reports against him than anyone in existence. Apparently, being drunk daily on the job got him into a lot of trouble. If he were *anyone* else other than a Wright, then he would be gone. Right now, he got paid to drink at his desk and dick around. He had a problem, but no matter how many complaints he got, his family wouldn't throw him into rehab.

"He comes and goes, depending on the week." Julia shrugged. "I don't want to talk about Austin. Let's talk about Nick. Do you think you guys are going to have sex?"

I shrugged. "I think we have a while to go. We've kissed, but it wasn't really anything."

Of course, it was impossible to have a life-altering kiss like I'd had with Landon at the back of Flips that night. Shouldn't have allowed it to happen, but damn, he was a good kisser.

Fuck, I'm doing it again.

How many times did I have to remind myself that I couldn't think about kissing someone else's husband?

It was bad enough that Emery had been pushy about Landon after the reunion. I'd finally had to shut her down completely and tell her that, like her, I had sworn off the Wright brothers. She, of all people, should understand that I didn't want to hear about Landon or talk about Landon. Whatever had happened with us was over. The idea that people actually went from friends to lovers was ludicrous. Friends to lovers didn't exist any more than Landon and I did.

"Ugh! I just want you to fall in love, like me!" Julia confessed.

"It'll happen. Maybe. Someday. Never."

"You're ridiculous."

"Hey, Heidi," Jim said, popping his head into Julia's office. "Morgan came by and asked for the entire engineering and project team to convene in the conference room. Some announcement."

"What announcement?" Julia asked.

"I don't know what it's about, but I need to steal Heidi."

"Okay, I'll be right there," I said. I turned back to Julia with a shrug. "I guess I'll go see what that's all about."

"Keep me in the loop."

"Will do."

I hopped off her desk and strode out of her office. My office was on the other side of the floor with the rest of engineering. The engineering and project team worked closely together here at Wright Construction headquarters. I was lucky to be on the same floor as Julia even though our jobs were night and day.

I was the only woman working in engineering, and I was damn proud of it. Even if I did have a tiny cubicle, unlike Julia's swank office. I'd been climbing the ladder to this job my whole life. I'd graduated at the top of my class in civil engineering at Texas Tech and started working as an intern at Wright right out of college. I'd worked my way up and up and up. My job was my life. I made great money, and I loved what I did. I felt so fortunate to be where I was.

"Hey, Heidi," Matt said, coming up beside me. He had a pink-and-blue plaid shirt under his navy blazer with a bow tie. With him, every day was more eclectic than the next.

"Hey, do you know what this announcement is about?" I asked as we walked to my cubicle. I rummaged through my purse and grabbed my phone. If this meeting was boring, I was going to need something to occupy my mind while I pretended to take notes.

"No idea. You?"

"Nope," I said, glancing down my nose at him.

I was already five foot seven without my heels on, and I made it a point to wear my heels into work. I liked to be as tall or taller than a lot of the guys on the team, so they couldn't look down their noses at me.

"Jim thinks someone is getting fired," he told me, trailing behind me, as I moved toward the conference room.

From the outside of it, I could tell that it was already crowded. Matt must have waited for me. He would follow me around a lot, like a lost puppy.

"Why would they bring everyone together to fire someone? Isn't that kind of personal?"

"Yeah, true. Maybe it's a new project or something."

"After we took over Tarman Corporation last year, I do not want to think about adding on another new project. I feel like we've *finally* caught up from how shitty they were."

Matt laughed and held the door open for me. "Yeah, definitely."

We stepped into the brightly lit conference room. It was full to the brim with men in cheap suits who just wanted to go on a coffee run. There were a few guys, like Matt, who were around my age, but most of them had been with the company long before Jensen took over. Those guys really did not think too fondly of women in engineering, even when I schooled their asses.

Or maybe because I did.

I wasn't sure. Nor did I particularly care.

As much as I detested the blatant sexism that ran rampant around the office, I *was* getting paid as much or more than my colleagues. Unless someone was sexually harassing me, I wasn't about to complain to the higher-ups that my colleagues were douche bags.

But that was neither here nor there. I was waiting to find out what the big announcement was, and I'd completely zoned out on Matt.

"What?" I asked, glancing back over to him with wide blue eyes. "Sorry, I missed what you said."

"Uh…I was seeing if you were free on Friday night."

Even though he was kind of short and wore strange clothing, he was a cute guy. He just…wasn't my type. Not that I would date him because of my number one rule—*do not mix business and pleasure.*

"Oh," I muttered. "That's sweet, Matt, but I'm kind of seeing someone."

Sort of true. If I considered date number three with Nick to be seeing someone. And it counted right now.

"Right. Totally. Of course," he said the tips of his ears going pink.

I gave him a smile that said, *I'm sorry,* and then faced the front of the room again. That was when Morgan Wright stepped into the conference room. It went from a loud buzzing to almost complete silence in a matter of seconds.

Morgan had that effect on people. She was two years younger than me, and we had cheered together in high school. But she had been bred for her position as a senior vice president of the company since birth. Some people said she ran the business even better than Jensen. It was clear to me that she enjoyed it more.

She commanded attention and respect, and these men, who gave it out so rarely, dished it to her in spades. It didn't matter what she was wearing or how she looked or how pretty she was—those things that men would never consider about other men but usually judged women on. What mattered with Morgan was that she was smart, loyal, fierce, motivated, and hardworking.

If she didn't know how to help you with your job, she would *learn* how to help you. She would go out to the construction sites. She would get her hands dirty if she had to. Morgan Wright was unstoppable.

"Thank you for convening here on such short notice this early in the morning. I'll make it brief, so you can go back to your coffee breaks," she said with a mischievous smile.

The men laughed at what wasn't exactly a joke. I loved how sarcastic Morgan could be without ever breaking character.

"I wanted to let you know that we have reorganized the company a bit, and we're adding a new level of management to this department that has been needed for some time."

A rumble of confusion followed that statement.

We needed better management? That was an odd thing to say.

Engineering and project teams along with a few smaller departments all reported directly to their supervisors, and the supervisors met with a team manager for the department. Then, the team managers reported up from there. The way things had worked had never been a problem before.

"Don't worry. It doesn't change anything with what you already do. We have recently hired on a new employee who will be filling the void in this area. Is that clear?"

The answer was essentially no.

"We can work out the kinks as we go, but I think this will be a good solution for everyone involved. Let me introduce you to your new boss," Morgan said.

With a giant grin, she pressed the door open, and in walked none other than Landon fucking Wright.

Nine

Heidi

All eyes turned to Landon, and a short smattering of applause followed his entrance, but I was frozen like a block of ice in the Arctic.

What the hell was Landon Wright doing at Wright Construction, on my floor, in my department? Why was he even in Lubbock?

And, oh my God, he was in a suit. A sharp-cut, clearly custom-fit black suit with a crisp white shirt underneath and a patterned blue tie. His hair was cut shorter than normal, and his dark eyes were aimlessly wandering the room, as if he were lost. A lost, lost puppy trying to find his way in this strange world of corporate America.

Then, his eyes, those puppy-dog eyes, landed on me. He found me standing in the back of the conference room, shell-shocked. Surprise was written on his face, but mine only revealed horror.

Had he really not known that we would be working together when he showed up?

I didn't know the answer to any of these questions. I didn't know why he was here or what had happened, but none of it mattered.

Landon Wright was my *boss*.

He was my boss.

Fuck, he was my motherfucking boss.

I couldn't process that information. I couldn't process what Morgan was saying, and I certainly couldn't understand why he was here, standing a few feet in front of me.

Why would Landon be my boss?

Sure, he had a business degree from Stanford that he'd gotten while on a golf scholarship. He knew his shit. He was perfectly competent. And he was a Wright. But it still didn't make sense.

It didn't help the knot that had formed in my stomach and weaseled its way up to my throat. My mouth was dry, and I felt sick. As if it weren't bad enough that I had kissed him while he was married even if he had been legitimately separated, I didn't know if I could handle seeing him day in and day out.

I slowly inched toward the door. I couldn't be here a second longer.

Work was my safe place. My happy place.

He couldn't take this away from me.

We were still staring at each other, even as he spoke to the department about how excited he was to be here. Though he said it with no enthusiasm. He wasn't convincing me at least. I knew a lot of the guys looked up to him for his PGA wins, so maybe they didn't hear how he really sounded. Or they didn't know him like I did.

I had known him.

Past tense.

Previously.

In another life.

Big difference.

Without a second thought, I broke eye contact, yanked the conference room door open, and disappeared down the hallway. Our side of the building was a graveyard, and I jogged in my high heels down to the restroom.

I burst through the door of the vacant room and pressed my hands onto the counter. I leaned forward and tried to catch my breath. I felt as if I were hyperventilating. Unable to get enough oxygen to feed my brain. My utterly confused and bewildered brain.

"He can't be my boss," I whispered to myself. "He can't be."

I wanted to call Emery and demand answers. *How could she not have known that Landon was coming back to town? How could she not have told me that he would be working here?*

Of course, I couldn't call Emery. And the reason I hadn't known was because I would completely shut her down anytime she tried to talk about Landon with me. I'd said time and time again that there was nothing between me and Landon. Emery had had him first, and I would never break girl code like that. Yet here I was, having a mental breakdown because he was here.

As it was, Emery was too suspicious about me and Landon. Calling her and demanding answers would only prove her point. And nothing was going on.

Not anymore.

Still…I had so many questions to ask him. They all flew through my brain at lightning speed.

Why was he in Lubbock? Why was he working for Wright Construction? Why wasn't he golfing? Had he known he'd be my boss? Had he asked to be my boss? Was he here with Miranda? Had their relationship recovered? Did she know that we'd kissed? Did he think about that kiss like I did?

Fuck!

No!

71

I looked up at myself in the restroom mirror, took a deep breath, and straightened to my full height. I needed to get myself together. This was not the end of the world. Landon wasn't my direct supervisor. He wasn't even my supervisor's supervisor. I didn't have to see him. I wouldn't have to come in contact with him. This didn't even have to be a thing I stressed about.

Besides all of that, this made our entire situation easier. I would never jeopardize my career, the most important thing in my life, for anything.

Rule number 1: Don't date your coworker.

Rule number 2: Definitely don't date your boss.

Rule number 3: Forget the taste of your boss's lips.

Okay, the taste of his lips was a new one, but I needed to follow it anyway because, sometimes, that taste of whiskey would creep right up on me.

The truth was, I had worked too damn hard for this job. Nothing and no one was going to distract me. Not even Landon Wright.

I left the restroom with my head held high. I could do this.

The meeting had been adjourned when I got back to my desk.

Matt gave me a sympathetic look. "Are you okay?" he asked.

I nodded my head. "Totally fine. Just had an emergency. You know, girl stuff."

His face paled, and he looked away.

Easiest way to get a guy to stop talking to you was to bring up your period.

"So, did I miss anything?" I asked.

"Nah, you were there for most of it. All the Wrights are under one roof now."

"Well, not Sutton. She just had her baby."

"Right. True," Matt agreed. "What did she name it? James?"

"She named *him* Jason."

"I still can't believe that he took her last name instead of the other way around. I can't imagine ever doing that."

"Ah, yes. How ever did women survive all these generations, dealing with changing their name?" I said with an eye roll. "It makes sense that he'd change his name, considering who Sutton is. Then, they can have the baby be a Wright."

"It's emasculating."

My eyes nearly popped out of the sockets. "And how do you think women feel, having to change their name to fit a man?"

He looked at me like a fish out of water. He had clearly never thought about it before.

"Forget it," I muttered. I was still irritated about Landon. "A lot of women really love the idea of changing their name. Maybe Maverick suggested it. Maybe it wasn't emasculating to him at all. At the very least, I'm sure that he wanted his son to be Jason Wright instead of Jason Johnson."

Jim saved Matt from having to come up with an answer to that. "Hey, Heidi. The new Wright boss wants to see you in his office."

"Right now?" I asked, clenching the edge of my desk.

"Uh…yeah, I think so."

"Oh, okay. Where is his office?"

Jim pointed down the hall and in a corner. I could see the office from where I was seated at my desk. If he stepped up to the door, then I would be able to see him. I'd have a clear line of sight on Landon every single day. He wasn't pushed off into some solitary corner or even on the other side of the floor by the project team.

No. Of course, they had picked the only vacated office left in the area.

And, now, I could see him *whenever* I wanted.

Great.

"Thanks," I muttered, unable to conceal my sarcastic undertone.

Without another second's hesitation, I marched down the hallway to determine my fate. And, even though I was solid and dignified in my approach, I felt as if I were trudging through waist-deep water. My brain was telling my body not to go through this. Not to endure what was to come. But I knew I could handle this.

I knocked twice on the open door, and Landon's head whipped up. He looked...out of place. I'd seen him in a suit before, of course. He wore it well. But he looked the most comfortable, happiest in golf clothes. I'd watched him on TV. Golf was a mind game, and everything else disappeared when he played. Some players tensed up and let the game get to them but not Landon. All the pressure and all his worries eased away until there was only him and the game that he loved to play.

He looked the opposite of that now.

"Heidi," he said. "Please come in. Shut the door."

I arched an eyebrow, but did as I had been told. Being alone in Landon's office with the door closed was a pretty terrible idea, but it didn't stop me from doing it anyway. Or stop me from being pissed at how calm he seemed. Or stop me from wanting to throw him onto that desk.

"You asked to see me," I said, keeping my voice neutral.

"Yes. I've decided to meet with everyone on my team to get to know my new employees."

I pursed my lips. A million questions threatened to fly out of my mouth, but I wouldn't give him the satisfaction of knowing my curiosity. "And you decided to start with me?"

Landon stood and came around to the front of his desk. He buttoned the top button of his suit coat, as if he were dressing for a theater production. "Yes," he said simply. "I decided to start with you."

"Let's not do this, Landon. I'm pretty sure we already know that you know me better than most of your employees. And that's all I am—an employee."

Landon stared at me across the scant feet of space between us. Both of us were mired in this moment and the impenetrable distance. It might as well have been an ocean because I couldn't cross it. What had happened a month ago hung in the air like a thick fog obscuring our view.

"Don't you want to know why I'm here?" he asked finally.

I held my hand up. "It doesn't matter."

He shot me an incredulous look. "Heidi—"

"It really doesn't. This is my career. I've worked hard to get to where I am. I wasn't born into this."

Landon's face was a mask. I was sure that I had hit a nerve with him, but he didn't show it. I wasn't used to that from him. He usually wore his emotions on his sleeve. But I guessed he couldn't do that here.

"Not that you don't deserve your position or anything," I added. "But I think we should keep our relationship professional. Having conversations with the door closed…is probably not a good idea. There's no reason to muddy the waters. You know…what's done is done."

"Right. Good. Yeah. Professional." His voice was clipped.

"Good. I'm glad," I said with no enthusiasm.

This wasn't how I'd expected our next encounter to happen. I'd oscillated between yelling at him for standing me up and crushing my lips to his. I hadn't anticipated indifference. Or for him to agree.

"I believe that is all then, Miss Martin," Landon said formally. His jaw twitched.

I inhaled sharply at his comment as my fingers curled into fists at my sides.

Miss Martin? Fine. Fucking professional then. Whatever. It didn't even matter.

"I'll just get back to work then…*boss*."

I turned on my black platform high heels and ripped the door back open. I exited his office like a thunderstorm.

God, I felt like an idiot. I knew I had done this to myself. I could have gone into that room sympathetic and full of questions. I could have told him that, yes, in fact, I *did* want to know what he was doing here. I wanted to know a lot of things. But I couldn't allow myself that modicum of curiosity. If I gave an inch, I'd give him a mile and more. And I couldn't.

I wish it hadn't felt so good to see him. God, that suit. That face. And it wasn't purely physical. Seeing him had felt… right. Like a piece of the puzzle had been missing, and he fit in perfectly.

"Fuck," I grumbled when I sank into the seat at my desk.

This was never going to work.

Landon

"This is never going to work," I groaned.

I crashed into my office chair and rested my head back. I was totally fucked. This was a disaster. Of all the things to happen when I started working for Wright Construction, I had to end up as Heidi's boss. *Could the universe be any crueler?*

The way she had looked at me just about put me over the edge. So cold and emotionless. Like seeing me was a minor irritant. But I knew she was upset. After how things had ended with us, how could I blame her?

Now, we were in unfamiliar territory. And any chance I'd thought I had at reconciling with her went out the window when she blew me off. But I wouldn't let her go that easily. Not after the hell I'd endured to get here.

If being her boss were the issue, then I'd do what I could to change that.

I darted out of my chair and ignored the questioning look from the manager who worked directly below me. I knew he wasn't pleased that he was now answering to me. He, like Heidi had insinuated, believed I had gotten this job because I was a Wright. And the fact that it was true only made me hate the position more.

My feet carried me to the elevator, which brought me up to the second highest floor in Wright Construction. The top floor was a fancy restaurant that the company used for business meetings, catering, and big events. But I wasn't looking for the restaurant. I needed to talk to Morgan.

She was on the phone when I sidestepped her secretary, a tall and trim white dude, and entered her office. Her eyebrows rose when she glanced up at me. She held up a neatly manicured finger in my direction.

It was strange to take orders from my twenty-six-year-old sister. I'd bossed her around enough when we were younger, so to see her like this, it always amazed me. She had been made for it, of course. Even more than Jensen, who had always been more interested in the architectural side than the business side.

When she finally hung up her phone, I was leaning against a chair in front of her desk, trying not to be impatient.

"What's up?" Morgan asked.

"I appreciate everything you did to get me this job."

Morgan furrowed her brow. "Are you quitting?"

"Um...no?"

"Who are you? Ben from *Parks and Rec*?"

I laughed and shook my head. "Last I checked, I wasn't an accountant who kept refusing to work for you."

Morgan grinned. "Well, what's the issue?"

"I want to switch positions."

"You...what?"

I walked around the side of the chair and sat down in front of my sister.

She knew why I was here and what all had happened in the last month. After all, she was the head of Operation Miranda, the silly name my family had given for trying to break us up. She despised her more than anyone.

"I think I need to be in a new job," I repeated.

"Landon," she said, steepling her fingers and looking at me over the top of her hands, "do you know what we went through to get you this job on such short notice? We had to shuffle and reorganize the company. I essentially invented a job for you in a place where another position could fit seamlessly into the structure already in place. I had to analyze all the jobs from top to bottom, and *this* job is it. I mean, if you want to go work on a construction site, then by all means, we have plenty of jobs. Not sure your back could handle the machinery though."

"Yeah, yeah. My back can't handle much," I agreed.

I knew what Morgan had gone through to get this all to work out. Not to mention, Jensen had helped me with the lawyer, finding an apartment, moving, and most importantly, getting a top-notch physical therapist at the medical center. I was an inconvenience at the moment. I could feel it. No matter how much my family loved me, I was a wreck.

"So, as you can see, this is the best I can offer. I didn't think you'd want to actually work in construction…or even if that was possible for you. And, really, my secretary position is filled." She grinned.

"Ha! I would never work as your secretary. We'd kill one another."

"I'm pretty sure, with the condition you've been in, I'd win."

"We'll see about that."

"So," Morgan continued, "why don't you want this job now that I've gone to all this work to get it for you?"

I shrugged nonchalantly.

I couldn't tell her the truth. That the idea of being Heidi's boss and seeing her day in and day out was absolute torture. I had a hard time keeping my hands to myself when

I was around her, and getting involved with her romantically definitely had to be some kind of HR violation. Fraternizing with your employees wasn't a good idea, and the thought of avoiding her cut deep. It would be easier on us both if none of this had ever happened. Yet here we were.

"Come on, tell me," Morgan said.

"I guess I'm just not qualified," I lied.

Morgan gave me an eat-shit-and-die look. "You have a Stanford business degree. You graduated in the top ten percent of your class. You know how to run a business."

"Well, I don't really have any experience."

"God, stop. You know more about Wright Construction than anyone could because you *are* Wright Construction." She dismissively clicked a few buttons on her computer. "Just do your job, and you'll be fine. Everyone always likes you. They'll see you know what you're doing."

I nodded and stood. "Right. Yeah. Sorry to bring it up."

I felt like an ass for having even asked, but I'd had to. The reality was, I needed this job. I couldn't golf for the next year—at the bare minimum. At least, not professionally. I was in PT indefinitely. Other than that, the only thing I had to deal with was the divorce papers.

My mind, which was used to being cluttered with my game, had gone unnervingly silent. If I went back to golf after a year of this, I'd lose my game. I'd lose everything. I had to be going, going, going. I needed something to occupy the long hours and days and weeks and months before I could become *me* again. And the only other thing I'd ever had in my life was the family business.

When my hand was on the door to her office, Morgan spoke up again, "You'll be back at your game before you know it."

I closed my eyes and breathed out harshly. "What if I'm not?"

"Don't doubt it. I believe in a healthy dose of optimism. You love it too much. And, anyway, Wrights don't give up."

I felt emboldened by Morgan's confidence. She was right. This wasn't the end of everything. I could still make a comeback. The PGA Tour would wait for me at least two years on an exemption because I'd won a tournament in the last year. But, if I didn't meet the requirements for the Tour after that, I might have to qualify again. Something I was not looking forward to.

It was bad enough that I had missed the PGA Championship this last weekend, but now, the Tour were going into the playoff season for the FedEx Cup. A whole month of some of the best golf in the world, and I'd get to watch it from the sidelines. Worse…from a TV screen.

I tried not to think about that. One problem at a time. The one I could deal with presently was Heidi.

It was official. I was her boss. And I would be her boss for the next year—unless, by some miracle, another job opened up in the company. That seemed unlikely, considering my new position.

But I could make Heidi come around.

I needed to talk to her. To make her understand what had happened that day. I couldn't accept that, just because we were in this situation now, we couldn't have something between us again. She'd seemed resolved to walk away, and I was as determined to convince her otherwise.

How much could have changed in the last month?

I exited Morgan's office and took the elevator back down to my floor. My mind was buzzing with all the work that had been dropped at my feet, coupled with the fact that I would have to interact with Heidi on a regular basis. At least I wasn't sitting around, worrying about whether or not I'd ever recover enough to do the one thing I loved.

That was a positive.

Albeit, a strange one.

I rounded the corner that led to my office and couldn't help myself. I turned to search Heidi out. She was resting against her desk, facing my direction. A group of engineering guys was standing around her in deep discussion. One guy was leaning over something on her desk. He said something to her, and she shook her head. Whatever she said next made everyone in the area crack up laughing. Even she tilted her head back and laughed. That mane of blonde hair fell like a waterfall down her back.

God, it was good to see her laugh.

I knew that I should walk away. That I shouldn't stare at her like this.

We'd talked long into the night about how much she loved her job and how proud she was that she had started at the bottom and raised herself up. After everything she had done to get to where she was, she must find me despicable to come in with no experience and become her boss. I'd happened upon this position by sheer luck of birth.

Yet I couldn't stop watching her. She had been this way with me once, and I'd walked away. It was the smart move. But knowing that I was leaving Miranda only made it harder.

Gorgeous, uninhibited, and completely in her element.

This was how she should always be. Not bottled up with anger and frustration. Tense with misunderstandings. From now on, I'd make it my mission to make her laugh.

Her head jerked toward me, as if she had felt my eyes on her like a laser. Her cheeks heated, but she didn't look away. Gone was the fun and playful girl from a minute ago. In her place was that feral creature who kept me on my toes. Never sure if she was going to walk away or devour me whole.

I didn't like the guessing games with her. The best thing about Heidi was, you always knew exactly where you stood. But, right now, I felt as if I were in a fun house with mirrors reflecting back at me, revealing a million different versions of reality.

As I held her gaze, I shattered every mirror but the real one in her eyes.

She seemed to realize that she had given herself away and quickly turned away from me. But I'd seen enough to know the truth.

This wasn't over. This was far from over.

Eleven

Heidi

To say the least, the last five days had been the most uncomfortable of my life. If I'd thought I would be able to avoid Landon, I'd been wrong. Very wrong.

I knew I needed to figure out a way to live with my new reality. But, at present, I wanted to get the fuck out of the office and not have to deal with Landon being there. I didn't do well as a contained creature. Holding on to my emotions was like waiting for a jack-in-the-box to pop open.

That was why I'd agreed to meet Nick for dinner after work. This was the third date, and I couldn't have Landon Wright in my head when I went into this. I could almost convince myself that I was looking forward to it.

My hand strayed to my hair, and I tucked a lock behind my ear. Even though Landon's office was on the way out, I promised myself I wouldn't take a peek and see what he was doing. I didn't need to know if he looked frazzled, as he had for the last couple of days. I wasn't going to see if he'd already taken off his jacket, removed his tie, and rolled up his sleeves. Those things weren't important.

Yet my eyes darted in there anyway.

To my surprise, he had his jacket and tie in place. His hair wasn't mussed, like he had been running his fingers through it in irritation all day. He looked relaxed. And, when he saw me, he smiled.

Oh, fuck.

I'm a goner.

"Hey," Landon said. He stepped out of his office and leaned against the door.

My heart stuttered. "Hey."

We hadn't had a conversation longer than this since he started. He'd given me room to breathe. Even though I couldn't avoid him even if I wanted to.

"You heading out early?" he asked.

I stalled and faced him. "Yeah. It's Friday. Is that a problem?"

He shook his head. "Nope. Not a problem with me."

"Great," I said. "I didn't think I needed permission."

His smile slipped for a second, and then it came back, maxed out. *God, that smile.*

"You don't. Not from me at least."

"Wonderful," I said drily. I wasn't trying to be a sarcastic bitch, but it was a defense mechanism against his charm.

"Heidi, can we not do this?"

"Oh, I'm Heidi now? What happened to Miss Martin?"

Landon leveled me with a you-know-why-I-said-that look. "If we're going to be around each other, then we should maybe try to be civil. Friends even."

"We are friends, Landon," I said with a sad smile. "Just friends."

I pushed past his door and headed for the elevator. I didn't know how much longer I could do this, and it had only been *five* days.

Landon and I were just friends. All we were ever going to be was friends. Him putting on the charm and smiling at me like that was not helping a goddamn thing.

The elevator doors swung open. I stepped inside and hit the button for the lobby. As the doors were sliding shut, Landon's hand shot out to stop them. He held them open with both hands and intently stared at me.

I swallowed hard and felt my body seize up. Here we were. Just the two of us. Alone. Yet…not exactly alone. Anyone could come around the corner and see us together. Wonder why he was holding the doors open like that while watching me like a starved animal.

"What?" I asked when he didn't say anything.

"Don't walk out of here like this."

I arched an eyebrow. "It's only a half hour early."

"You know what I mean."

"I don't—"

"You walked past my office as if we were strangers. We're not. We haven't had a chance to talk. I haven't even had a chance to apologize."

"Well…don't."

"Don't?" he asked, his brows furrowing.

"Don't apologize. What do you have to apologize for?"

"Let me start a list," he said with a half-grin.

"Your wife showed up, and that was that, Landon," I told him with a one-shoulder shrug.

"That is not what happened."

I shook my head and leaned against the back of the elevator. I didn't want to hear this. I didn't want him to do this right now. I prayed that someone would come and interrupt us, but I wasn't that lucky.

"Just don't, okay?"

The elevator started dinging because Landon had been holding the doors open for so long. He did the unthinkable and stepped into the elevator with me. The doors closed noisily behind him, enclosing us together.

"What are you doing?" I whispered, my voice soft and breathy.

"Having that talk."

He walked forward until only mere inches were between us. I was cursing and also silently thanking Wright Construction for having slow elevators. Because, the last time I had been this close to him, we'd made out. And, suddenly, I couldn't get that thought out of my head. I knew I wanted it again. I could tell that he did.

Just because we had a connection didn't mean we should act on it.

"This is not a good idea," I muttered.

I should have said something more along the lines of, *Get the fuck away from me*, but my brain was not listening.

"Everything about you is a good idea, Heidi."

"You are my boss."

"Yeah, I am."

"My job is too important to me. I can't...I don't want to do this."

"Your job isn't in jeopardy."

"It is if you kiss me."

He smiled that brilliant smile. My knees were wobbly. I could tell he liked that I was thinking about kissing him. I mentally kicked myself for bringing it up. But, with him this close, it was getting hard to think properly.

"Next time I kiss you, it will be because you're asking me to, Heidi."

"That's not going to happen," I assured him.

He grinned at me, as if he didn't believe me. Right now...I didn't believe me either.

"Can I see you later?"

"No," I whispered.

"Heidi, come on. Give me a chance."

"I mean, no…I have a date," I said as the elevator reached the bottom floor, and the doors dinged open.

Landon took a shocked step back from me. "A date?"

"Yeah."

"I see."

"Yeah."

Landon followed me out of the elevator. In the lobby, there were too many people with eyes that could be watching us from all directions. I suddenly felt exposed, as if everyone were staring at us. Even though no one else knew what had transpired between Landon and me a month ago…or in the elevator.

"How long has that been going on?" he asked, his voice tight and controlled.

"Dating? My whole life. Some guys take me out for food. Maybe a movie. Pretty sweet deal," I said, trying for levity.

"You know what I mean."

"A few weeks."

"Since I left then?"

"*You* had nothing to do with this," I lied.

"Heidi, you can't—"

"Don't tell me what I can and can't do," I hissed at him. "You made your decision, Landon, and now, I'm making mine." My voice was barely above a whisper, but I still felt exposed from even uttering those words.

His eyes were two open windows, revealing every little thought that fluttered through his head. He was pissed and jealous and frustrated. He wanted to tell me not to go out with anyone. But he knew it was unfair. He knew he didn't have the right to those feelings. He was the one who had fucked this up. Not me. He was the one who deserved to feel this way.

So, why did I feel so horrible when I finally walked away from him?

Emery was at the apartment when I showed up from work early. She would be starting her teaching job on Monday and had been in deep planning mode. She had been going into school early for the past couple of weeks for new teacher orientation. I thought it was smart that she was taking advantage of all this time to get ready for her big-girl job. But she thought I was a dick when I put it like that. I was her best friend, so she was probably right.

"Hey, sexy," I said, wandering into Emery's room.

"Hello, my lover," Emery said with a wink.

"Still in major planning mode?"

"The majorest," she said. "Look what came today." She held up a standard-sized white envelope.

I knew what that letter was. She knew what that letter was. It came in every week. Every single week.

"Great," I said, snatching it out of her hand and stuffing it into my purse, unopened.

"So, how was work?"

I wrinkled my nose. "It was work."

She glanced up at me out of the corner of her eye. "You love your job."

"Yeah, I do, but things have been…you know, rough lately."

"Are you finally going to admit to me that this is about Landon?"

"Absolutely not."

I plopped down onto her bed and watched her as she filed a bunch of paperwork. She was, as usual, dressed in black from head to toe and had her dark hair in a ponytail on the top of her head. No makeup, no fuss, and she was still gorgeous as hell.

"Fine. Then, how is it, having Landon as your boss?"

"Weird as fuck," I admitted. "I mean, I know he's a Wright, but we're the same age. I've been doing this for six years, and he just dropped into the job."

"Well, what do you expect when Jensen pulled strings for him?"

I shrugged. I hadn't expected any different. "He's doing fine, but it's just…weird."

"Weird because you're into him or because of the whole situation?"

"Stop!" I groaned, flopping backward and staring up at the ceiling. "It's because it's Landon. You should get that."

"I get it," she agreed. "But, when you're ready to tell me that you like him, I'll be here to listen." She stood and towered over me, which was a first, considering I was the giant and she was a shrimp.

"Whatever. I have a date tonight."

"Oh, right," Emery said, rolling her eyes. "Sounds fascinating. The wonderful, drool-worthy Nick."

"You're a shitty best friend."

"Yeah, right. I've known you since kindergarten. I know when you're playing along, and I know when you're invested. You're dating this Nick guy because Julia wants to have someone to hang out with her and Trevor."

"But he is nice." I sat up on my elbows.

"Nice? Gross," she said, sticking her tongue out. "Whoever wanted nice? Try passion and fire and need. You can't settle for someone who is nice. You want someone you can't live without."

"Thank you, Queen of Bad Relationships."

Emery swatted at me. "Hey! I might have had some bad relationships in the past, but I give good advice."

"So, you think I should cancel with Nick?"

"No!" she cried. "I think you should definitely go on a date with Nick. Then, you'll realize what you don't want. Because I already know it's not him. You seem oblivious to it."

I wasn't oblivious to it. But he *was* a nice guy. I liked him just fine. There was absolutely nothing wrong with where our relationship was headed. But, as Emery had eloquently said, I could live without him. Very easily.

But that was also a problem with me as a person. I was resilient. After what had happened with my mom and then the shit that went down with my dad, I had to be. I didn't *need* people. I could do everything on my own.

Emery was my real family. I loved her to pieces. She was the only person I'd ever come to say that I really needed. Because, without her, I didn't know if I would have made it through those hard years.

But guys?

They could get in line. I was strong, and I could do without them. And that made me perfectly intimidating. A strong man should hold up a strong woman, not run from her.

I'd thought for a while that Landon Wright might be the kind of guy who did that. The kind of guy I couldn't live without.

But I was wrong. I was carrying on without him.

Or maybe…I'd been wrong all along.

Maybe this was called survival…not living.

Twelve

Landon

A date.
    Heidi had a fucking date.
    God, I'm an idiot.
    Why hadn't I guessed before? Of course, she would move on.
She was the full package. Any guy would be lucky to have her.
I knew that for a fact. But I hadn't thought it would happen
so soon.

While I'd been busy healing and getting my life together,
she'd been running off and trying to find someone else. And
I couldn't even blame her. I wanted to. I wanted to break shit
and demand for her never to see this fucking douche bag again.
I wanted to make things right. To see where this relationship
could go. I wanted her to be mine.

Jealousy burned through me like a fire-breathing dragon.
I couldn't even see straight as she walked right out of the
building and out of my life.

I should have told her about the divorce papers. I should have told her about the injury. I should have told her about why I had moved back and why I needed this job.

But I hadn't wanted to blurt out everything that had happened to me. I didn't want her to think, just because I was leaving Miranda, that automatically meant she should fall into my arms. I didn't want to scare her off. Like I just had.

All I wanted to do was get home and relax. Let my mind do absolutely nothing for a little while. I had physical therapy nearly every day, but on Mondays and Fridays, I went in before work, which meant I could chill tonight.

And obsess over Heidi's date.

About an hour after I entered my new one-bedroom apartment and changed out of my stupid suit, I got a text from Austin.

Drinks?

I sighed and leaned my head back on the couch. A drink sounded nice. Maybe it would be better to go out rather than sit around at home and watch *ESPN*.

Yeah. Where? When?

Patrick and I are going to West Table in a half hour.

Why?

West Table was one of the fanciest restaurants in town. They had a nice bar and coffee shop attached to the building, but it wouldn't have been my first choice.

Patrick is talking to the bartender. She's hot.

Ah, well, that explained it.

Count me in.

I slipped into my standard khakis and a polo and exited the apartment. I'd left my car in Tampa, and I was borrowing Jensen's Mercedes for the time being. I sank into the dark interior and turned on a local radio station before I sped away.

After the day I'd had, I was glad that Austin was offering a distraction. Patrick was always a good time even if he egged on Austin's base qualities. But they had known each other their entire lives and were both still bachelors. I was pretty sure that Austin was because he pushed away any girl who seemed to care about him, and Patrick lost interest in the blink of an eye. A lot of girls flitted in and out of their lives, and no one took any of them seriously.

Though Jensen was certain that Patrick and Morgan had a thing. I couldn't imagine the least serious person I knew ending up with the most serious person I knew.

I ended up at West Table about ten minutes later. I saw Patrick's Lexus SUV already parked on the side of the building, which was good because then Austin wasn't driving. I parked behind them and entered through the side door. The lobby to the building was white marble flooring, a sky-high ceiling, and an enormous staircase. The coffee shop was off to the left, and the restaurant was on the right.

The hostess brightened at my approach. "How many?"

"I'm just meeting some people at the bar," I told her.

"Certainly, sir. Right over there," she said.

I flashed her a smile and then found Austin and Patrick at the bar, each with a glass of whiskey in front of them. A tall, sexy brunette was standing behind the bar, deeply engrossed in whatever Patrick was saying. She was in an all-black outfit with her cleavage gloriously on display. I could see why Patrick was into her. She was right up his alley. Though, with Patrick's track record, I doubted it would go anywhere.

"Hey," I said, sidling up next to Austin.

"Hey. What's up?" Austin said.

"Hey, man," Patrick said. "Good to have you in town. I haven't had a chance to see you around the office yet. Is it weird, working at Wright?"

"Yeah, a little weird," I conceded.

Patrick worked for Wright Construction, too. He crunched numbers and dealt with expenses, and at the beginning of the summer, he had been promoted to a more managerial role. I gathered that he made more money and worked less.

"Well, Austin thinks you'll be playing golf again soon. We're all rooting for you."

"Thanks," I said. I turned to the bartender before I could curse my back again. "Maker's Mark, neat."

"You got it," she said, reaching for the bottle.

"Oh, yeah. Landon, this is Mindi. Mindi, this is Austin's brother Landon."

She winked at me. "Nice to meet you. You're the younger brother, right?"

"I am," I confirmed.

"Cute. I like brothers."

I tilted my head at her, trying to see if I was gathering what she was signaling. Her lips curled into a mischievous grin. Yep, I wasn't wrong. She was definitely interested in a threesome.

She was clearly Patrick's type. Crazy. He loved them crazy.

Austin elbowed Patrick. "Hear that, man? She likes brothers."

Patrick shrugged. "Yeah, whatever. I'm down."

He could say that since he didn't have a brother.

Mindi giggled and topped off his drink. "You boys are silly."

Patrick grinned at her. "That, we are."

"Hey, did you see your girl was here?" Austin asked, clapping me on the back.

"My...girl?" I asked in confusion and also borderline panic. The last time one of my brothers had said something like that, Miranda had flown in from Tampa to corner me.

"Yeah, dude. Check it out," Austin said. He pointed to a table across the room from us.

And there was Heidi. On her date. With some douche bag.

My jealousy, which had subdued in the time that I allowed myself to be distracted, flared up again like an inferno. One second, I had been laughing about Patrick's new crazy girl, and the next, I wanted to walk over there and interrupt Heidi's date.

Who the fuck was he anyway? I'd never seen him before. Not that I'd lived in Lubbock for a while.

"Wait, what am I missing?" Patrick asked. "Who is Landon's girl? God, help us all, not Miranda."

"Nah, dude. Heidi Martin," Austin said, filling him in.

I didn't have it in me to deny it. I wanted Heidi. The month apart after that kiss and all the realizations about Miranda had solidified it. I'd thought I'd come back and we'd pick up where we left off. I hadn't thought she'd already be seeing someone else. "Who is she with?"

Both guys shrugged. Neither of them knew, which meant I was going to need to find out.

"So…you and Heidi?" Patrick asked in surprise. "Didn't you date her best friend?"

"Isn't her best friend dating my brother?" I demanded.

Why did Emery always have to be a sticking point? We hadn't dated in more than ten years. Plus, it wasn't as if she or Jensen had talked to me before they started dating.

"Point," Patrick agreed.

"Seriously, I don't get you two," Austin said. "How can you let her go on a date with someone else? Is this because of you and Miranda?"

"No," I ground out.

"Well, are you going to go stop her? Because I figured that, if you two were fucking, you wouldn't let her date someone else."

"Whoa! Nice, man!" Patrick said, holding his hand up for me to give him a high five. "Moving on from that bitch as fast as possible I see."

"We're not fucking," I corrected them.

"Well, except for that one time," Austin said with raised eyebrows.

"That is not what happened, dude," I told him in frustration.

I'd been so bogged down in dealing with Miranda that I hadn't even told Austin that Heidi and I hadn't been together. And he still clearly thought that we had.

"*Suuurrre*," Austin said, dragging out the word.

"Well, this will be fun," Patrick said.

He had a shit-eating grin on his face, and I was sure that only meant trouble.

"Hey, Mindi."

"Yeah, babe?"

"Can you send a drink to that table?" he asked, pointing out Heidi.

"What are you doing?" I asked.

"You're sending a drink to another girl?" Mindi pouted, sticking out her bottom lip.

"It's from Landon," he told her.

"Do not do that," I groaned. "That would look really bad."

"Ah, have some fun!" Patrick said. "She looks miserable on her date anyway. She'll appreciate it."

"Sure, honey. What should I send?" she asked.

Patrick looked to me.

I shook my head. "No fucking way."

"A nice red wine will do," Patrick said when I refused to answer.

Austin was laughing next to him. "Lighten up, Landon. Heidi is going to appreciate it. Look at how over this date she is."

I'd been trying not to look, to tell the truth. Seeing her on a date with someone else made me want to be violent. But I did what Austin had said. Heidi *did* look uncomfortable. She was leaning away from the guy and had her arms crossed over her chest while he was talking. The beautiful smile that I knew and loved was gone from her face. But she seemed to be trying for a half-assed quirk of her mouth. He was clearly buying it. I didn't want to feel satisfaction from the fact that she wasn't enjoying her date, but a small part of me did.

I watched as the waiter returned to her table with the glass of wine that Patrick had ordered for her. And I meant to look away when she received it in shock, obviously insisting that she hadn't ordered it. Then, the waiter pointed over to the bar, and Heidi's eyes fell on me.

Her frown deepened, and she looked like she was about to get out of her seat and throw the glass of wine in my face. So, I smiled brightly and waved.

Her date turned around and looked at us over his shoulder. I wasn't sure what I read in his expression. Mostly surprise. Then, he was talking to Heidi. She pushed the glass of wine away from her untouched.

Fuck.

"You're such a dick," I said to Patrick

"We're helping you. Aren't we, Austin?" Patrick asked, nudging him.

"Meddling is a fun pastime."

"I'll remind you of that the next time I meddle in your business."

Heidi and her date, it seemed, had come to the end of their meal. I could see the check on their table. They stood and were walking toward the exit. Was she really going to leave without drinking that full glass of wine?

"Hey, Heidi!" Patrick said, waving at her and her date as they passed us.

Heidi stopped in her tracks and sighed. She seemed to be bracing herself for impact.

"Hey, Patrick," she said as she faced us. "Austin. Landon."

"Heidi," Austin said with a knowing look.

I nodded my head at her, but she wouldn't even look in my direction.

"Hey, y'all. I'm Nick," her date said when it was clear that she wasn't about to make an introduction.

"Hey, Nick," Patrick said.

We each shook hands with the guy. I lingered longer than the others and squeezed a little too tight. I couldn't help myself. I instantly disliked this guy. It wouldn't have mattered if he were the nicest person on the planet.

"Austin and Landon," Nick said with a thoughtful expression. "Wright brothers?"

Austin nodded his head. "Yep."

"So, you all work for Wright Construction, too?" Nick asked.

Heidi jumped in right away. "Yep. Landon is my boss." She wielded the word like a weapon.

"Oh," Nick said, his shoulders relaxing.

It was as if that word, *boss*, carried weight and told him I wasn't a threat.

He couldn't have been more wrong.

"You aren't going to drink your wine?" Patrick prompted.

I nearly groaned aloud. *Why had I ever let Austin tell Patrick about what he thought had happened that night with Heidi?*

Heidi gritted her teeth. "We were already finished, and I'm not feeling that well. So, I was going to forgo it. But…thanks."

Her eyes briefly met mine, and they said anything but thank you. The fire in them said, *What the hell are you doing?*, and, *Fuck off.*

"Well, you know what would make you feel better?" Patrick said.

"A Xanax, ice cream, and some sleep?" she muttered under her breath.

I had to fight from smiling at her words.

"Pool," Patrick said.

Nick furrowed his brow. "How would a swimming pool improve her well-being?"

I nearly face-planted into the bar at those words. So, this wasn't a guy she had been dating a while. This wasn't real competition. He didn't even know that she played pool, which showed how very temporary the entire situation was. Not to mention, the faking-sick bit.

Maybe I shouldn't walk away from this. Maybe Patrick had a point. I could play into this and step up my game. I could get rid of good ole Nick in one night. Then, Heidi and I could finally have that talk. I'd be back on track.

"Shooting pool," I corrected him. "If you knew Heidi as well as I do, you'd know it was one of her favorite things to do."

Heidi nearly choked on those words. "That's not exactly accurate. I would say one of my favorite things to do is kicking your ass in pool."

I laughed. "We'll see if you can do that."

"I can't even count the number of times I've done that."

"Wait, I thought you said that this was your boss," Nick said in confusion.

"I…well…he is," Heidi said, backpedaling.

"Landon and Heidi have been friends for years, dude," Patrick said. "He's been her boss for a week. She can give him a pass for the night and play pool. You know where Flips is?"

Nick stammered, "I…yeah, I do."

"What he's trying to say is," Austin cut in, "we're going to head to Flips to play some pool if you'd like to join us."

"Oh, I don't know," Heidi said.

"I mean, these are your friends, right?" Nick asked. "I don't mind going with you if you're feeling up to it."

"I don't—"

"Come on, Heidi," I pressed. "It's only one game. Unless you're afraid I'll beat you."

"The only time you've ever won is when I let you to protect your precious ego."

I shrugged. "You can prove that tonight."

She imploringly looked at Nick, but he seemed not to notice.

"I'm up for it! I didn't even know you liked to play pool. I would love to see how good you are."

"Right," she whispered.

"Great! Then, it's settled," Austin said. "We'll see you there in twenty minutes. We just have to close out."

Heidi glared at me, as if this were all my fault. I was pretty sure she was going to back out and have her new date take her home. Except that I had challenged her to a game, and she was too competitive to let the challenge stand.

I didn't care if I lost horribly to her. I wanted the chance to fight for more than the game.

Thirteen

Heidi

"It was nice to meet some of your friends other than Julia," Nick said with his ever-present smile on his face as we sat outside of Flips. "I really need to meet your roommate now though. Emery sounds nice."

I fought to keep a blank look on my face.

This was a disaster.

A disaster!

"Yeah, we should invite her, too, and then we'd have the whole gang together," I muttered sarcastically.

"If you want to invite her, I don't mind. This has been the best date yet."

I sadly smiled at him. Emery was right. There was no spark here. He hadn't even noticed the tension between me and Landon. Even *after* Landon had sent that drink.

And oh my God! How dare he send me that drink while I was on a date with someone else! What the hell had he been thinking?

"I think Emery is in with her boyfriend tonight," I told him, sinking low in the passenger seat.

"Isn't she dating a Wright?"

"Yes, Jensen. He's the oldest."

"So interesting. I don't know much about their family, just that they're, like, Lubbock royalty. Trevor is more into all that stuff than I am."

"Lubbock royalty." I guffawed. "They're just people who happen to have money. I wouldn't put them on a pedestal."

That was rich, coming from me. I'd been putting them on a pedestal my whole life. But it had been easy to do that when I grew up with nothing. My father's bar wasn't exactly a lucrative business deal. The only money he had ever raked in had been entirely illegal…and we had all paid dearly for it. I was from the wrong side of the tracks, looking up at the mansions, wondering what it was like to live like that. I couldn't help it. Even now that I had money, I had a certain level of fascination with the rich and famous.

Of course, with his golf career, Landon fit that mold better than all of them, and I never really felt that way about him. Probably because I had known him before his career took off.

"You ready to go in?"

I sighed. I was not ready to go in.

I had no idea why I had even agreed to this. Partly because I was competitive by nature and partly because…I wanted to see Landon. After that elevator ride, my mind had been going crazy. I'd thought the date would make me forget about him, but of course, my luck, we'd run into him on the date. Now, I was willingly going to hang out with him and the guy I was dating.

Only one explanation.

I was a masochist.

Nick was getting out of the car before I could even think about changing my mind.

I'm doing this. I'm really doing this.

I let me heels click onto the pavement and straightened out my pink-and-black dress.

Man, I was stalling.

Nick was smiling at me from the front of his car, and I hesitantly walked up to him.

"You all right?"

"Yeah," I lied.

When we entered Flips, it was like coming home.

Having grown up in a bar, I always felt most comfortable inside its four walls. It didn't matter that it frequently smelled of liquor, vomit, and stale cigarettes. It didn't matter that the hardwood floor was stained from years of disuse. It didn't matter that it was dimly lit, making it hard to see all the way to the back of the room, or that it was filled with a wide array of people from all walks of life. This felt right.

And, damn, I needed a drink.

Peter was working. Honestly, I wasn't sure when he wasn't working. He saw me coming and had a tequila shot waiting. He slapped the saltshaker in front of me.

"You look like you need this," he said.

Oh, ye of few words.

"Hey, Peter. Nice to see you. This is my…this is Nick," I said, stumbling over the word *date*.

"Hey, man," Nick said, offering his hand.

Peter kind of stared at it like the guy was out of his mind. "What'll you have?"

"Oh, I'll take a Bud Light." Nick let his hand drop back to his side.

Peter gave me a look that said, *Bud Light? Really?*

So, he didn't have the greatest taste in beer. *Who am I to judge?* Except…I always judged people on what they drank. You could tell a lot about a person based on what kind of drink they ordered at a bar. It was like seeing someone reading a book in the park. You were either instant friends or instant enemies.

I knocked back the shot of tequila even though I needed to keep my wits about me. But one shot would do just fine.

"We're hitting the tables," I told Peter. Then, I nodded for Nick to follow me with his Bud Light.

I had already racked the balls on the table when Landon, Austin, and Patrick breezed into Flips like they owned the place. Not completely out of the realm of possibility for the Wrights. Though probably a bad investment, considering what a mess the whole family was.

Austin procured an entire bottle of whiskey off the shelf and a tray of glasses. It must have cost at least double what it would cost in a store, but Austin didn't seem to care. Austin set the tray down, and Patrick poured whiskey into each of the glasses.

I shook my head. "You're a mess, Austin."

He winked at me. "Come now, Martin. This isn't the worst you've seen me."

"Not the best either."

Patrick grinned. "This is definitely his best."

Landon took a drink when it was offered to him, but otherwise, his eyes were set solely on me. I hadn't even looked at him yet. Still, I could feel his gaze upon me like a caress.

I bit my lip and finally let my eyes drift to his. Suddenly, the room was a furnace. As if the floor was coated in gasoline, and that look had set the place on fire. I hated that he was capable of making me feel that. Of dragging me toward him with one look. Yet I was incapable of pulling away from it.

"You ready to play?" he asked, his voice deep and husky.

"Um," I murmured, "play?"

"Pool." He tossed a pool stick in my direction, and I caught it in one hand. He whispered as he passed me, "Unless you have something else in mind."

I stammered on my words as I felt his hand trail along the small of my back. My eyes hurried to Nick, but he was preoccupied with Austin and Patrick. I felt horrible that this was happening. This was such a bad idea, yet it was Landon. I wanted him to fight for me…even if it was unfair.

"Stop it," I hissed, regaining control of my body.

He arched an eyebrow and quirked a smile at me. "Your break."

I took out my frustration on the pool balls and grabbed everyone's attention. I landed three balls in pockets on the break—two solids and stripe—and smiled. "A hundred bucks says I beat you this game."

Landon pulled out his wallet and laid five twenties on the table without a second thought. "Fine by me."

Patrick scooped up the money and tossed it down on the tray. "Now, we have a game!"

I felt triumphant already. Landon had only beaten me a handful of times, and it was usually when I was belligerently drunk or distracted. Neither of which I was going to be tonight.

"I presume your solids?" Landon asked.

"You know it," I told him as I preceded to I pocketed three more balls before I missed one, leaving the table open for Landon.

"Wow, you are really good!" Nick said, sidling up next to me. "Why didn't you ever tell me that you could play pool like this?"

"Just a fun party trick," I lied.

"Well, I think it's pretty amazing. I'm shit at pool. I've only played once in my life."

"Uh-huh," I said as Landon pocketed a ball. "Sorry kind of concentrating on the game."

"Oh, yeah, sure. Go ahead," Nick said. He stepped back and started chatting with Patrick again.

I strode around to where Landon was standing, assessing the situation. "What do you think? Ten in the upper right corner?" he asked.

I shrugged. "Your call, Landon."

He leaned forward, almost right in my face. "We didn't discuss what would happen if I won."

"I give you a hundred dollars," I said with practiced calm.

Fuck, he was too close.

"That's not what I want."

"That's what you'll get…if you win," I hissed back before stepping away.

He grinned at how flustered I was, and I eased around to the other side of the table. I watched Landon sink the ten he had promised into the upper right pocket.

This was not good. I had a feeling I already knew what Landon wanted if he won. Something that I could not give him, least of all because I was on a date with another guy currently. At present. This very moment!

I nearly screamed when he knocked in two more balls. He was getting cocky though. I could see it in the set of his shoulders and the laughter in his eyes. This was when guys messed up. This was when they thought they could beat a girl because they had started to run the table. I could still win. I *needed* to win.

I stepped forward as he lined up for his next shot. "You sure about that one?"

My hip eased into the side of the pool table, and Landon's eyes traveled down my long, tan legs.

"Trying to intimidate me?"

I laughed lightly. "Of course not. Just helping my opponent."

"You forget that I know you too well for that. You never help your opponent."

"Sometimes, I do. When I want them to win," I added.

His eyes latched on to mine with giant question marks in them. "And do you want me to win?" His voice was laced with temptation.

"No."

He grinned. "And I thought I was a shit liar."

"Come on, you two," Patrick called from where he was seated. "Finish up already."

"I'd go with the twelve," I told him as he aimed for the nine.

"The twelve is impossible."

"Maybe for you."

"Do you want to take this shot, or are you here as a distraction?" His eyes slipped down my dress again. "I don't mind either way."

"Yeah, y'all," Nick said, joining in on Austin's and Patrick's camaraderie. "Don't take all night."

"Where did you find this guy?" Landon muttered under his breath as he lined up his shot again.

"Well, he's not married. So, I think I'll call it a win."

Landon whiffed entirely. The cue ball barely brushed the nine he had been aiming for, and he cursed at his miss. But I knew he was really cursing what I'd just said.

All of that tension from the last week seemed to be hitting its crescendo between us now. If Nick weren't so completely oblivious, he would have noticed how Landon looked at me and the way he talked to me and the feelings that were boiling over in his presence.

"Guess victory will be mine," I told him as I scooted him out of the way.

I landed the two and the six almost without taking a breath. With most of the table cleared, the shots had been easy. Geometry had always been my forte. It was the reason I had gotten into engineering in the first place. I was that weirdo kid who loved math. It paid off in these situations. I just needed to put away the eight to win.

"Come on, Heidi. You've got this," Nick called.

"Yeah, Heidi," Austin agreed. "I love watching you kick my brother's ass."

"You're so thoughtful," Landon muttered.

"What? It's hot when a chick beats you."

"Hey," I said, pointing my pool stick at him. "I'm not just some chick."

"You're right. You're a hot chick," Patrick said.

"Ignore them, and call your shot," Landon said.

I rolled my eyes and lined up for the eight ball. "Eight in the upper right."

In the millisecond after I hit the ball, I had a feeling I was going to miss. I wasn't sure if it was the way I'd hit the ball or the trajectory it went on, but it felt off to me. It rattled back and forth against the corners of the pocket, and we all held our breaths and waited.

"Ugh," I groaned as I watched it with my hand over my eyes. Shockingly, it teetered just far enough backward to land in the pocket. I jumped up in surprise. "Oh my God!"

The other guys all cheered me on.

Austin handed me Landon's hundred bucks. "Never doubted you for a second."

Nick applauded my success. "Great job!"

Patrick put an arm around Nick's shoulders. "Come on! Let's go do shots!"

It was only Landon who looked downtrodden. But he was a good sport. He grinned when I glanced at him.

"Nice game."

"Thanks," I muttered.

I guessed I would never know what I'd have gotten if he'd won.

Fourteen

Heidi

Landon took a step closer to me when Austin, Patrick, and Nick finally walked away. "It really was a great game, Heidi."

"Piece of cake."

"Sure you don't want to find out what would have happened if I'd won."

"Don't think we'll ever know, Landon, because you'll never beat me," I said confidently.

He grinned. "Maybe."

"Seriously, Landon, what the hell are you doing?" I asked before I could stop myself.

"Hanging out with you."

"You've been doing this whole I-know-you-so-well act tonight. And, sure, you might know me, but you can't forget that I know you just as well, which means that I know you are not here just to hang out with me."

"You're right. You *do* know me, Heidi. That's the point. You've been avoiding me and walking away from me and refusing to listen to me all week when I've been standing right in front of you, trying to make things right."

"Maybe I don't want to make things right."

"Why? Because of this guy?" Landon asked, pointing out Nick. "The guy is so oblivious, he can't even see what's right in front of his eyes. I could have made out with you on the pool table, and he would have clapped his hands and applauded at how good you are."

"That is not true," I cried. "Fuck, I don't even want to get into this with you."

I stomped away from him, toward the restroom.

His footsteps alerted me of his presence before he grabbed my elbow. "Heidi, stop."

I should have known he wouldn't let me walk away. And, now, we were alone in a back hallway that led to the restrooms where no one could see us.

I whirled around and smacked his hand where he was touching me. "I don't get what the hell you hope to accomplish here. Following after me and cornering me again? That's not smart. Not only am I here with someone else, but you are also my *boss.*"

"Yeah, I am! Who the fuck cares?"

"I do!"

"Well, Christ, Heidi, I know how important your job is to you. I get it. I'm not trying to get you fired. And I don't think you would get fired even if someone found out."

"You can't possibly know that. That's such an incredibly naive way of thinking. Julia is one of my closest friends. I know that she has fired people or moved people to different branches of the company for less than this."

"Less than what? One kiss *before* I was your boss? Because you keep telling me there's nothing here." He moved forward, caging me in. "Or is it that there *is* something here? And we *are* something more, but you refuse to acknowledge it."

His lips were mere inches from my face, and my body was pulsing in response to his words. His hands trailed down my bare arms. All cognizant thoughts fled my mind. I wanted to give in to this. Just as I had wanted to at the reunion and all those months ago at Christmas. But I couldn't.

"What part of *date* do you not get, Landon?" I asked, shoving him backward.

"The part where you're not with me!" he growled.

"You are *married*!"

"Well, if you'd just fucking talk to me, you would know that I'm divorcing her!"

"Wait…what?" I asked, momentarily dumbfounded.

"Yeah, I'm leaving her!"

I shook my head. "You said that last time, and you still went running back to her like a dog with his tail between his legs."

"Is that what you think happened?" he asked, his voice low and seriously pissed. "Last time, we were separated. I'd told her I was leaving her. And, now, I officially am, Heidi. I didn't know she would be in town that day. I had no clue what kind of shit she was trying to pull. I'm here trying to fix my fucking mistakes."

My jaw fell open at his confession. "You're really leaving her?"

"Yes."

His hands brushed down my arms again. When I didn't say anything in response, he moved in closer. Our anger and frustrations scorched through the space between us. My brain couldn't keep up with my body.

My brain was saying, *Walk away. Don't give in. Keep your defenses up.*

My body was saying, *Touch me, feel me, devour me.*

His fingers grazed my waist, bunching up the material of my dress and forcing us back against the wall. Our gazes met, and my chest was heaving with desire and panic.

I could not give in to him.

I so wanted to give in to him.

He nuzzled my neck with the stubble of his five o'clock shadow. My breaths came out in spurts. And, at the first kiss on my neck, I was a goner. I closed my eyes and leaned my head back. Wanting this, needing this.

"Fuck, Heidi," he groaned.

My hands wrapped around his shoulders, feeling the muscles in his back as I dragged him against me. I forgot where we were or what I was doing. I was just living in the moment. He grasped the back of one of my legs and hoisted it up around his waist. His fingers slipped up my dress and dug into my exposed thigh, leaving indents as he reveled in the taut muscle.

He kissed up my neck and sucked on my earlobe. A desperate, throaty breath escaped my mouth.

"Landon..."

"Come back home with me."

"I can't," I whispered.

His lips grazed mine, and it took everything in me not to give in to that kiss. And, God, I wanted to. I wanted everything he was offering.

"This is what I wanted if I'd won," he said. "Just you."

I whimpered at that. My hands fisted his shirt. My heart beat as fast as if I had run a marathon. His words were so enticing. Exactly what I had wanted to hear all along.

But, if I gave in, I'd hate myself later. I'd hate myself for not waiting until the divorce was finalized...if it was ever finalized. I'd hate that he was my boss, and with one kiss, I could lose the career I'd worked so hard for. And I'd hate that I'd hurt Nick. Though I didn't feel for him what I felt for Landon, it wasn't right to allow this to happen.

Finally, with all the willpower I could muster, I pushed Landon back. "No."

"No?" he asked with a furrowed brow. "No what?"

"This doesn't change anything."

"What the hell, Heidi?"

"You just dropping on me that you're leaving Miranda doesn't change anything," I told him.

"Of course not. I tell you I'm leaving my wife and that I want to be with you, and that means nothing to you? Makes perfect sense."

"But you haven't left her yet! You're still with her!"

"Legally, we're separated. And in another couple of months, we'll be divorced," he groaned. "You want to wait around for her to sign a document that I initiated and already signed. One that says our marriage is irretrievably broken and that we're unable to mend our irreconcilable differences."

"I don't know, Landon. I don't know about any of that. It's all too much at once. I'm on a date with someone else, and you're trying to seduce me. That's fucked up."

Landon took a step back and sighed. He closed his eyes for a second. I could tell that he hated how this had all happened. Maybe not the kissing part, but that it had gotten so out of control.

I was shaking and just wanted to leave. Not that I wanted to see Nick. I obviously had to break it off after what had happened. I'd already been planning to do it, but this thing with Landon made it inevitable. Julia was going to kick my ass for messing up a good thing. If only I'd had the slightest connection with Nick. If only Landon hadn't come back to town.

"You're right," he finally said.

"I am?"

"Yes. This wasn't what I wanted to happen. And I'm sorry for ruining your date."

"You are?" I narrowed my eyes, wondering what the catch was.

"I went about this the wrong way." His eyes were sincere. "I do want this with you, Heidi, but I'm not going to push you if you're not ready. If you want to wait until the divorce is finalized, then I can wait. I'll wait for you."

My heart stuttered at his words. He really meant it, too. He might have pushed me today, but his eyes said he'd wait. Landon and I had turned that corner back in January, when we had been reckless enough to sneak off together. When we had almost crossed that line. Even when he'd told me we couldn't talk anymore, I'd known it was because he cared too much. Not because he didn't care at all.

Yet, no matter how close we had become in the last year, it was hard not to think that I might be some rebound from his wife. Still, I wanted to believe the look he was giving me that said that wasn't the case.

"You'll wait for me?"

"As long as you need. But just don't…settle for that guy in the meantime."

I colored at the accusation. As if I could choose Nick over him.

He nodded when he saw my expression. "I'll rally the troops and head out. I really don't want to hurt you, Heidi."

He leaned forward and brushed his lips against my cheek. I couldn't help myself. I sighed into that touch. With that one touch, my skin hummed, and my body came alive. He might be walking away and doing what I'd asked of him, but my traitorous body told him all he needed to know.

"Landon," I whispered as he turned to go.

"Yeah?"

"Thank you."

He grinned and reached for my hand. He gently squeezed it.

"Hey, guys!" Austin said, turning the corner and finding us standing together, holding hands. "You might want to break up the lovefest because homeboy is going to get suspicious."

I jumped away from Landon, as if Nick himself had just turned the corner. Landon seemed unfazed. He probably didn't care if Nick saw us.

"It's fine," Landon told Austin. "We're heading out."

"We are?" Austin asked.

"Yeah. Let's go."

"But what about Heidi?"

Landon glanced back at me, his eyes sweeping my body one more time, lingering on every inch that he had touched. "She collected her winnings. Maybe I'll come out on top another night."

I watched Landon walk away with Austin, who seemed incredibly confused. I didn't blame him.

How had Landon and I gone from arguing to him pushing me up against a wall to him walking away?

And, worse, how was it that I couldn't even be mad at him?

He was being a gentleman. He was doing exactly what I'd told him to do. Yet…all I really wanted was for him to come back. To break all my rules.

And I realized then that it was *me* I was most mad at.

Fifteen

Heidi

When I made it back into the office on Monday morning, my steps were hesitant and my heart heavy. Emery had thankfully been too preoccupied with the start of work this morning for her to notice that I had been walking on a precipice all weekend.

I'd ended it with Nick as soon as he dropped me off. He'd seemed downtrodden but understanding. He'd even thanked me for the good time that night. I kind of wondered if he liked Austin and Patrick more than me, which would be totally fair, considering how crazy they were.

Now that I wasn't dating anyone anymore, I'd had all weekend to think about what Landon had said…and done. The electricity that had sparked between us obliterated my senses. So much had changed in a year yet still not enough.

I sighed and took the elevator upstairs. The tension was coiled in my stomach like a viper waiting to strike. I didn't know how Landon would react when he saw me. I didn't know how *I* would react.

With the uncertainty eating away at me, I decided to get it over with. I walked right up to his office and knocked twice.

"It's open," Landon called.

I pushed the door all the way open and stared at a frazzled Landon. He was bent over his desk with piles and piles of paperwork scattered before him. He hadn't even looked up.

"Hey," I said.

His eyes shot up at the sound of my voice. "Heidi," he said my name like a prayer.

"Early morning?"

"Christ, what time is it?"

"Nine," I offered.

He rubbed the bridge of his nose. "Yeah, early morning. I didn't even know people were here yet."

"When did you get in?"

"Oh, I was here around six thirty."

"In the morning?"

He laughed. "Yes, in the morning."

"Whatever for? We don't start until nine."

From the looks of it, it seemed that he was mired in work. He'd only been here a week, and already, he was overworked. I wasn't sure if that was because he wasn't used to the work or if it was really piling up. Either way, he looked like he needed some help.

Landon leaned back in his chair and scratched the back of his head. "Well, I have physical therapy Tuesday, Wednesday, and Thursday afternoons and Monday and Friday mornings, so I come when I'm finished."

"Physical therapy?" My voice rose an octave. "For what?"

"Oh, we're asking questions now?" he asked with a smirk.

I opened my mouth and then closed it. He was right. I hadn't wanted to know why he was here. I had refused for him to even tell me.

He waved his hand. "I'm kidding. I injured my back over the summer."

"Again?" I asked.

I knew that he had gone through some issues at the start of his career and that it had bothered him last summer. I didn't know it was still an issue.

"Yes," he said simply.

He looked like he wanted to say more, but he didn't. I wasn't sure if that was my fault because I'd pushed him away or if he legitimately didn't want to talk about it.

"Well, I'm glad you're taking care of it this time," I told him.

"Me, too. It's long overdue."

"So," I muttered, "are you coming to Emery's party today?"

"Already on the schedule to head out early for it."

"Great. This should be fun."

"You do know, she hates birthdays, right?"

"Duh. It'll be more fun this way," I said, cracking a smile.

"She's probably going to kill you."

I shrugged. I was reveling in the ease of our conversation. This was how we had always been before. It was nice to get back to that.

"Yeah, I'm used to her telling me that."

Landon laughed, and my chest eased at how natural that sounded coming from him.

"Well, good luck with that."

"Thanks," I said.

Our eyes met. My smile softened. *Man, I had missed him.*

"Well, I'll leave you to it," I told him, backing away before I got myself in trouble.

"Thanks for stopping in."

The tension I'd seen when I entered his office had evaporated. Perhaps he had been anticipating this conversation as much as I had. And it had gone better than I'd thought.

Neither of us had snapped at the other nor had we torn each other's clothes off. Yet.

I walked out of Landon's office with a bounce in my step that hadn't been there before. Things were looking up. Landon and I were back on speaking terms. I had a surprise birthday party tonight for my best friend. I felt on top of the world.

I almost made it to my desk when Julia scampered out of her office, heading toward me. She was in a sexy black wrap dress that I could never in a million years pull off. She had the most amazing curves. Like to-die-for curves.

"Hey, sexy," I said, whistling at her as she approached.

"Don't use those moves on me, Martin," Julia said. "My office. Now."

I laughed as she shooed me along. "I hope I'm not in trouble."

"You're in a world of trouble."

I shook my head and then plopped down in the seat in front of her desk. She slammed the door shut, as if I were really in trouble, and then smacked me on the arm.

"What the hell happened with Nick? You don't call. You don't write. You can't fill a girl in?"

"Didn't work out."

"What part of it didn't work out? Trevor was the one who told me. I think Nick is really beat up about it."

"He is?" I asked in confusion. "He seemed totally fine when I let him down gently after our date on Friday night."

Julia dropped her head into her hands. "You dumped him *on* your date?"

"Well, we weren't really dating. So, I didn't really dump him."

"It was date three. I thought things were going somewhere."

"I guess they weren't."

"Come on. Give me details. I thought this was a good thing."

I shrugged. I'd known before that Nick wasn't right for me, but after Friday night, I was beyond sure that I couldn't keep seeing him.

"I don't think it was a good thing. I think it was a convenient thing."

Julia sighed. "All right. Back to the drawing board. Maybe Trevor has another friend."

"I don't think so," I said, holding up my hand. "Could you imagine me dating another one of his friends?"

"No," she grumbled. "But I want you to be happy. It's a project of love to find you a man."

I cracked a grin. "What if I just want your body?"

Julia laughed and shook her head. "Don't tell Emery. She'd be way jealous of our love."

"That's a fact," I agreed. "She's a jealous bitch."

"With every right to be. You're an awesome friend and person, which is why I want to find you a guy."

I waved her off. "Don't worry about it."

Apparently, that was the wrong thing to say.

Her eyes narrowed, and she assessed me from top to bottom. "What aren't you telling me?"

"Nothing."

"You've already found someone else!" Julia said, jumping up and down. "Look at how happy you are. Man, I am so excited. Who is he? When do I get to meet him?"

"Julia," I groaned.

"Don't hold out on me. Give me the goods. If there's someone new, I want to hear about it."

"Okay," I said, glancing back out of her door. "But it's not a good idea."

"Your favorite."

I laughed softly. She had no idea. "I kind of have this thing for Landon."

"Landon," Julia repeated. Her face went pale, and she sat down. "Like…Landon Wright?"

"Yeah. We kind of made out at our ten-year high school reunion, and now, he's here, and he's into me. He happened to be at the same bar as Nick and me while we were on our date, and it was night and day. The connection is there with Landon."

Julia's eyes were big and round. "Heidi, he is your boss."

"I know," I whispered.

"He dated your best friend for two years!"

"I know, I know."

"What part of this is a good idea? You cannot have a *connection* with Landon!"

"I know," I said again.

God, I knew all of this already. I knew this a thousandfold. Having feelings for Landon was like waiting for a ticking time bomb to explode. Any moment, it was going to blow up in my face.

"I don't think you know. This is a bad, bad idea!"

"Julia," I groaned. "Seriously, I do know how bad of an idea this is."

"I am head of HR! You can't tell me these kinds of things!"

"Nothing is going on, Julia. Plus, I told you about this as a friend, not as the head of HR."

"Fuck, Heidi," she hissed. She looked flustered and unsure of how to proceed. "You have to stay away from him."

I nodded. "I told him the same thing on Friday night. He's my boss. He's going through a divorce. We can't do this right now."

"Good. Good. That's very mature of you."

"Of course, I told him this after he hiked my leg up around his waist and started kissing up my neck."

Julia put her hands over her ears and started saying, "La-la-la-la," loud enough to get me to stop talking.

I was laughing at her outrageous behavior. Maybe I should have waited until later to fill her in.

"Okay, okay," I told her, raising my hands. "I'll stop talking about it."

"Talking about it? You're going to stop doing more than talking about it. You have to completely stop, or you know I'll have to figure out a way to separate you two. And who do you think they'll move—*you* or a Wright brother?"

I paused at those words. I'd thought about it, of course. It was why I had been so freaked out that he was my boss.

What if I couldn't stay away from him?

I'd have to leave. That was what Julia was saying. Either I'd have to go to another office out of Lubbock or I'd have to take a step down, so he wasn't my boss. They weren't going to move Landon's position. They had just *made* that spot for him. What was one less engineer?

"Tell me you understand how important this is, Heidi," Julia said. Her face contorted with fear. "I'm really worried about you."

"No, I get it. I do."

"Are you sure?"

"Yeah," I whispered.

But I was completely unsure. Despite all the consequences and everything I had told Landon, I didn't know if I could stay away from him forever. It seemed impossible.

"Oh, fuck," Julia sighed when she saw my face. "Just… just don't get caught."

Sixteen

Landon

I glanced down at my phone and swore.

Fucking Miranda.

Why did she have to come and ruin my perfectly good mood?

I'd been thinking about Heidi all weekend. I hadn't been sure if I had made the right move. I'd thought pushing for her and fighting for her would make her see that we should give this a try. But the harder I pushed, the more she gave in, *and* the more she fought me. It was a paradox.

And, when I had seen how upset she was about the entire situation, I'd backed off.

Then, she had come in this morning with some fresh space between us. She'd looked happy. She'd talked to me like we were friends. Like before that kiss a month ago. I knew those feelings were still there, but the fact that she'd asked questions finally seemed to alleviate a little of my pain from walking away on Friday. I'd put the ball in her court. She'd then immediately come back to me. It seemed like a win.

And I had been riding high on it until Miranda sent me a nasty text about the divorce paperwork. I couldn't even turn off my phone to silence her tirade. I had too much work to do, and that was the number people had access to.

So, I spent much of the day ignoring the *beep, beep, beep* from my phone. When it was finally time to leave, I darted out of the office as quickly as I could. I hadn't been home since five this morning, but I wasn't about to head home anytime soon either.

Instead, I went straight to Jensen's house where Emery's surprise party was being held. Heidi was organizing the event, which meant she would already be there. And I wanted to spend as much time with her as I could.

I parked Jensen's Mercedes in the garage and entered through the garage door and into the kitchen.

"Whoa," I said.

Heidi was standing on the island in the middle of the kitchen in nothing but short shorts and a tank top that was riding up her stomach.

Her eyes darted to me. "Oh, Landon! You're early."

She tried to attach a streamer to the spot on the light fixture but missed. The kitchen was already decked out in decorations, but I could see that there were bags with more decor just waiting to go up.

"Need a hand with that?" I asked.

"If you don't mind."

"I'm a bit taller than you."

"Just a bit."

I scrambled onto the island next to her and took the streamer out of her hand. Our bodies were close together, standing there in the middle of Jensen's kitchen. Her blue eyes lit up at my nearness, and then she averted her gaze and took a shaky step back.

"Thanks. I have a ton to do. So, it'd be great if you could help." She hopped off the island.

"That's what I'm here for."

"Great. Great," she muttered.

She seemed nervous around me now. It was as if the easygoing girl who had talked to me in my office this morning disappeared, and I didn't know why.

I brushed off her unease and decided that I wasn't even going to acknowledge it. I really had shown up early to help her if needed and to hang out. I wasn't trying to get crafty and make a move on her.

Once I attached the streamer to the light fixture, I jumped off the island and followed her into the living room. Black balloons were everywhere with a few glitter and hot-pink ones scattered throughout for a bit of color. That was definitely Emery through and through.

"Want me to do that?" I asked Heidi as she sat down to blow up more balloons. "I'm guessing you won't be happy until we cover the room in them."

She grinned up at me and then caught herself and looked away. "Yeah, I want Emery to try to stab me after seeing how over the top it all is."

"This will definitely do," I confirmed, looking around.

Heidi handed me the bag of balloons. "Thanks for your help. I still have a million things to do."

"No problem."

She headed out the door as Jensen appeared at the top of the stairs.

"Landon!" Jensen said with a big smile. "You're early."

"Yeah, I thought I could help out. I knew Heidi had something big planned."

"It's good to see you."

Jensen pulled me in for a hug. He looked happier than I'd ever seen him. It still weirded me out that my ex-girlfriend was the one who brought him that much joy, but I couldn't begrudge him it. I wanted to be that happy, and all I'd been was depressed over the last year.

"Good to see you, too, man."

"How is everything? You've been back for a while, and I feel like you're a stranger."

"I was in church yesterday," I corrected him. I'd made sure to do that, considering how I'd left early so many times before.

Jensen grinned. "Yeah, that's true. Just checking in on you. I'm the oldest. What do you expect from me?"

"Nothing more than this. PT has been great though. I don't know how much progress I've made, but the therapist is a goddess."

"I got the best."

"I can tell. She knows her shit."

"And Miranda?" Jensen asked coolly.

I glanced away. At this point, I hated talking about Miranda. Not that I had ever enjoyed discussing her with my family before, but now, I had to deal with the divorce. It was just messy.

"Still getting texts from her every day, and she says she's refusing to sign the paperwork."

Jensen sighed. "I was afraid of that. She'll come around though."

"We can only hope."

"And the new job?"

I inwardly cringed. I didn't want to bring up the fact that I wanted out of the job. I didn't want to be Heidi's boss, but I also didn't want to be left without a job for a year while I was recovering. My mind couldn't take it. I'd never slowed down a day in my life. I wasn't about to start now. But, after everything Jensen had done for me, I couldn't break it to him.

"An adjustment," I finally said.

Jensen nodded. "I knew it would be, but you'll make it work. You always do. I have to go get Emery now. Everyone should be arriving in the next couple of minutes. I'll see you when I get back with her."

"See you then."

With a sigh, I watched him disappear. I loved my brother, but sometimes, his concern felt like an interrogation. He didn't do it on purpose. He had always been there for us. He had been the one to raise us. He couldn't even help it now.

I went back to blowing up balloons in his absence. A minute later, Heidi peeked her head back into the living room. Pink rose in her cheeks, and she looked slightly sheepish.

"Hey," she said with a nervous little wave.

"What's up?" I arched an eyebrow at her.

"I hate to admit it, but I was kind of eavesdropping."

My mind flittered over everything that I'd said to Jensen, and I came back blank. I didn't think I'd said anything incriminating. Jensen had been checking in on me.

"And?"

"I'm sorry. I shouldn't have."

"What did you hear that has you blushing so furiously?" I set the balloons aside and stepped over to her.

We were alone in the house. We only had a few minutes before people would start showing up.

"I think I'm more embarrassed than anything."

"About what?"

"Well…I didn't know if I should believe what you'd said about Miranda on Friday."

"What part?"

"That you were divorcing her."

I cocked my head to the side and stared down at her beautiful face, those bright blue eyes, the unbelievably luscious lips. "You thought I would lie about something like that?"

"No. Not exactly. I was…cautious."

"Cautiously pessimistic," I accused.

She bit her lip and shrugged. Man, I wanted to kiss those lips. To bite down for her. The way she was looking at me. The blush on her cheeks. The way she gravitated toward me.

"Optimistic," she muttered. "But nervous."

"And now?"

"I believe you. I don't think Jensen would have asked if you'd been lying about it all."

"I'm not going to lie to you, Heidi."

I ran my hand down her arm, and she shivered under my touch. I might have said that I would give her space when she asked for it on Friday. And I'd meant every word when I said it. But, fuck, being alone with her like this, having her look at me like that…it was enough to break any man.

"I'm coming to realize that," she whispered, her voice so soft that it was almost just an exhale.

My hand ran up her shoulder and into her long blonde hair. *This hair. Fuck, this hair.* It was gorgeous and soft, and all I wanted to do was pull it and watch her eyes roll back into her head with delight. A gasp escaped her mouth at my touch, and I took that as answer enough. I tilted her head up to look at me, but her eyes fluttered closed.

I could feel her heart racing away. She wanted this, no matter what she'd said or how she stalled what felt inevitable.

Because Heidi and I *were* inevitable.

There was no denying how I felt or where this was going. I might slow down when she told me to slow down. Pump the brakes when the cracks in her facade began to crumble. But I could never turn around and walk away. There was no amount of distance between us that could make me step back.

"Heidi," I murmured.

"Hmm?"

"Look at me."

Her eyes opened hesitantly, as if she couldn't face her own reality. As if she would give in the minute she saw the depth of affection in my eyes.

"What are you doing?" she asked.

"Falling for you."

There was no accusation in her eyes. It was deep emotional turmoil. One step forward and two steps back. A struggle to reel in how much she wanted this and how terrified she was to let go. Because, if she let go…she could get hurt. She could succumb to something she had sworn she would not do.

Heidi was a fighter. She was resilient. She wasn't going to let me win unless she wanted it, too. Until she was ready.

I could see how torn in two she was. Denying what she wanted and sticking to her guns, all at the same time.

"You can't fall for me, Landon."

"It's too late. It's done."

"Not good enough," she said.

"I'm a goner, Heidi. Can't you see?"

She swallowed hard and nodded. She could see it on my face. She knew that I hadn't been lying to her about Miranda. I was leaving her permanently this time. No separation. Just a good clean break—or as clean as I could make it.

But it didn't eliminate all of our issues. And I was trying hard to meet her halfway about me being her boss. I knew it worried her, but we could get around it. I knew we could.

"I think…I think you need time. I mean, I don't know what I think," she said.

"I don't need time. I've had all the time I needed."

"Well then, I need time," she told me.

I opened my mouth to convince her otherwise. But we'd already been here before. We had been here a few days ago. I would kiss her. She'd give in and then freak out. Then, she'd be pissed at me, and I'd have to start from scratch. Rinse and repeat.

I wanted to stop this endless cycle. But I couldn't. Not here. Not now.

My head nodded of its own accord, and I took a step back. She looked like she was going to say something, but then she stopped. I wanted to say something, but I couldn't. We were both in limbo.

Then, the front door opened, and both our heads darted to the foyer.

"Uncle Landon!" Colton cried, sprinting into the living room and barreling into me.

I laughed because I couldn't help it. I never saw my nephew enough. Jensen and Emery always flew to New York City to go see Colton where he lived with his mom. I hadn't realized Jensen had made an exception for Emery's birthday, but I approved.

I hoisted the seven-year-old up into my arms and groaned. "You are getting so big," I joked.

Truthfully, I probably shouldn't have picked him up with my back the way it was, but eh. I'd deal with the aftermath of that later. Though ignoring the problem was probably how I'd kept reinjuring it the first place.

"I'm turning into a man," Colton confirmed for me.

Heidi and I both laughed.

"Who did you come with? Your nanny?"

"Nanny Jenn flew with me, but Aunt Kimber brought me and Lilyanne over for the party."

And just then Emery's sister, Kimber, walked into the room. She was holding her daughter, Lilyanne's, hand while her husband, Noah, toted their eight-month-old baby, Bethany.

"Hey, Landon. Heidi," Kimber said. She pulled Heidi in for a hug, not noticing how flustered she had been a second before. "Good to see you."

"Hey, Kimber," Heidi said.

"Are you all set for the party?"

"Yeah, pretty much. Just waiting for everyone else to get here."

I set Colton down, and he and Lilyanne immediately started kicking the black balloons all around the living room. I had a feeling they were going to all be popped before Emery even showed up.

"And you, Landon," Kimber said, giving me a hug. "How are you holding up? Emery told me you hurt your back again."

"Nothing some of your famous chocolate cake can't fix."

Kimber owned a bakery downtown called Death by Chocolate. She was an amazing cook and baker and I used to eat her chocolate cake all the time in high school.

She laughed and shook her head. "Well, you haven't changed a bit."

How wrong she was.

My eyes shifted to Heidi's, and at the exact moment, she looked at me. Judging by her expression, she was thinking the same thing. Things had changed a hell of a lot since high school. Right now, I was looking at my ex-girlfriend's best friend like I'd give up the chocolate cake in a heartbeat to eat her for dessert.

Seventeen

Landon

The rest of my family showed up—Austin, Morgan, and Sutton along with her husband, Maverick, and their newborn baby, Jason. Julia showed up last, running into the room as if the house were on fire. She'd taken one look at Austin and parked herself on the opposite side of the room.

I was for sure going to ask him about that later. I had gotten enough shit from him about Heidi that having dirt on him about someone was probably a good way to deflect later.

Emery was stunned when she walked in. She seemed genuinely thrilled to see everyone in a room, celebrating the day of her birth. We all sang "Happy Birthday" with varying levels of skill, and then she blew the candles out.

"So, do we get cake then?" Colton asked. He had nudged Lilyanne out of the way and was leaning on the island in the kitchen, staring at the chocolate cake that Kimber had brought with her from the bakery.

Emery laughed. "Yes, we all get cake!"

She winked at Kimber, who took a cake-cutting knife from the counter and went to work.

Emery hummed under her breath to the Bagel Bites theme song, *"Cupcakes in the morning, cookies in the evening, chocolate at suppertime. When Kimber's in the kitchen, you can eat baked goods anytime."*

"Oh my God," I said as Kimber passed out cake to the kids first. "I have not heard that song in a long time."

"You're lucky," Kimber muttered.

"Does she still sing it to you every time you bake?"

"Often enough."

"Hey," Emery said, "it's a good song! It's catchy."

"It's a commercial jingle for Bagel Bites that you changed the words to."

Emery shrugged. "And? I'm clever."

"Let's not argue with the birthday girl, huh?" Jensen said, butting in between me and Emery.

I took a step back and realized that everyone was looking at us. I hadn't really meant to seamlessly fall into their family dynamic, but I *had* dated Emery for two years. Sometimes, it was easy to be around them. But that didn't mean anything about me and Emery. We were long over, and she was head over heels for my brother…and I was head over heels for her best friend.

Heidi's eyes found me. They were searching, and she looked confused. Julia grabbed her arm and pulled her out of the room without a word. I wondered if Heidi had told Julia. If she had told Emery. Except that now that I'd seen Emery, she looked completely oblivious to it. So, I didn't know. Whatever. Maybe I was overanalyzing everyone's reactions.

I took a piece of cake that Kimber had offered me and followed the rest of the party out of the house and into the backyard. Jensen was planning to grill out for the afternoon, and there were games for the kids and drinks for the adults.

Austin grabbed a beer as soon as we were all outside and offered me one.

I shook my head. "Nah, man, I'm good."

Austin shrugged and was having enough to make up for the rest of the party not drinking. I wanted to keep my wits about me. Morgan and Sutton meandered over to us, and Morgan shot Austin a disdainful look.

"Do you ever do anything other than drink?" she asked.

"Why? You want one?" He offered her the beer he had in his hand.

She rolled her eyes. "No, thanks. I'm just glad we get to have this birthday party in peace without that bitch here. No offense, Landon."

"Offense was intended but not taken," I told her.

Talking about Miranda pushed me to drink.

"And she had to be one of *my* bridesmaids," Sutton grumbled. "You couldn't have divorced her before the wedding?"

"Well, if you hadn't gotten knocked up at twenty-one, then we could have probably fit it into your timetable."

Sutton's eyes moved over to Maverick, who was holding baby Jason. He was holding on to him as if he were precious cargo and not perturbed in the least that Sutton had wandered off without him. Kimber had moved over to sit next to him with Bethany in her lap.

"I have no regrets," she pronounced just like a Wright.

Way to make your mistakes seem purposeful.

"So, are you going to finish school or what?" Morgan asked. This must have been on her mind for a long time.

Sutton shrugged. "Eh, why bother? I want to stay at home with Jason."

Morgan's eyes bulged. "Sometimes, I don't know how we're sisters."

"You run the company, Morgan," Sutton said, affectionately patting her on the shoulder. "I'll do my own thing. I always have."

"That's for damn sure," Austin agreed. "Do you remember that princess superhero outfit?"

"This again?" Sutton groaned.

"It's pretty memorable," I told her.

"What is going on over here?" Patrick asked as he sauntered into the backyard.

"Oh no, trouble is here," Austin said. He shook hands with Patrick and clapped him on the back.

Patrick waggled his eyebrows at my sisters. "Ladies."

"You know you're late, right?" Morgan asked defiantly. Her eyes were trained on Patrick's face. "You missed the surprise."

"Yeah, sorry about that. I had to go pick up Mindi."

Morgan took a step backward. "Who is Mindi?"

Patrick grinned at me and Austin. "The guys will tell you. She's this bartender at West Table. We met when I was there for a business dinner."

"A girlfriend?" Sutton asked when it was clear that Morgan couldn't.

"Uh," Patrick said nervously. "I mean…you know I don't do labels and shit."

"There are children," I reminded him, watching this train wreck crash through the party.

"Right. Sorry, dude. Oh, here she is." Patrick plastered on a smile as the tall brunette from Friday night sauntered into Jensen's backyard in cutoff jean shorts, a white shirt that showed off her stomach, and cowboy boots.

Morgan went pale as a ghost as Mindi approached and waved at us.

"Hey, y'all!" she cried. "Austin. Landon."

We nodded our heads at her and said, "Hey."

Patrick introduced her to the girls, and I zoned out of the conversation.

Having my family all together in one place was the best. We were a close-knit group, and even though we all had skeletons in our closets, it never stopped us from loving each other. This was where it all just felt right.

But that didn't keep me from searching out Heidi. She and Julia had just returned from wherever they had been stashed away. Heidi looked ashen, and her eyes skirted the party. She frowned when she saw our group all piled together.

And, even as Julia hurried over to hug Emery, Heidi stayed in place. She seemed frozen. Heidi wasn't normally an outsider. She was usually a full-loving, center-of-attention kind of girl. She smiled brighter than the sun and laughed with abandon. Her personality was a big joke, and she reveled in being unique and outrageous. I adored all of these things about her.

Yet, right now, right at this very moment, she was not that girl.

Something was wrong. And I didn't think it was me that was causing her this stress. Maybe Julia had said something, but the Heidi I knew would brush off her stresses and put on a brave face. This Heidi couldn't seem to manage it.

Without a backward glance, I walked away from my family and left them to Patrick's antics. My feet carried me across the backyard to where she was standing alone.

"Hey, wallflower," I said. "What are you doing all alone?"

"Oh, hey," she said, glancing away from me before her eyes darted back. "I didn't realize I was making a spectacle of myself."

"I don't think you are. I think I'm the only one who noticed."

She bit her lip and seemed unsure if she liked that I had noted her discomfort. "Well, thanks. I'm fine."

"Heidi Martin is not the kind of girl who is ever just fine."

She raised an eyebrow. "Seriously, I'm fine."

141

"You usually take over the world in a group. Your personality cannot be contained. But you don't seem happy."

"I am happy."

"Liar."

She laughed humorlessly. "Well, I'm happy for Emery. I'm happy that she has her whole family here and her whole humongous new family here. Your family. I'm so happy that there's so much love around her. She deserves that."

"And you don't?" I asked.

"I wasn't talking about me." She tucked her fair hair behind an ear and turned her head away from me.

"Weren't you?"

"It's silly. Forget about it."

"It's not silly if you're upset. Talk to me, Heidi," I encouraged her. "If we have anything at all, it's that we can talk to each other. You know that I'm here. That I'll listen."

She met my gaze and must have seen how sincere I was because her shoulders relaxed. "It's just...I don't have a family. So, sometimes, being around a family like yours is overwhelming. You know?"

I didn't. Not really. I'd always had a big family. I'd always *wanted* a big family. That had been a sticking point with Miranda in the last year. It worried me that Heidi might feel the same.

"Overwhelming how?"

"I don't know. Like...it's hard to be around all these people who know and love each other so much and not feel kind of...jealous. I feel horrible even thinking like that, but the only family I have is Emery. And then I see all of you together and Emery's family, who practically took me in, and I just... *want* that."

Relief flooded me. I couldn't even believe I had thought for a second that she would be anything like Miranda. Heidi felt bad because she was alone, and she wanted more. It was refreshing and a completely understandable emotion.

"You're not alone, you know?" I said.

"Well, the family I do have doesn't count," she said harshly.

"I wasn't talking about your dad, but we can if you'd like."

She shook her head once fiercely. "I don't want to talk about him. He's in prison where he belongs."

I nodded, giving her the room she needed. It wasn't a secret to anyone that Heidi's dad was in prison for money laundering and drug trafficking. When the economy had tanked, he'd almost lost the bar, and he had resorted to illicit means to keep afloat. It had all caught up with him in the worst possible way. It had been a huge scandal, and Hank Martin was a name that everyone in town knew.

"We can talk about your dad when you're ready."

"Don't hold your breath," she muttered.

"In the meantime, you are not alone. Emery might be tried and true, but I'm not going anywhere. You don't have to want a family like that when we're standing right in front of you, accepting you into the fold. It might take some getting used to. I know we're an…interesting bunch. But you never have to search for family again when you have mine right in front of you."

I was offering her my family on a platter. I knew that they all already loved Heidi. Jensen thought she was an incredible employee and a great best friend. Austin thought she was hilarious and a fun person to hang out with. High praise from him. Heidi and Morgan used to cheer together. They were already bonded. And Sutton had always wanted to be like Emery and Heidi when we were in high school.

My family already accepted her more than they had ever accepted Miranda.

And Heidi had no clue.

Heidi breathed out a sigh and seemed to take in what I had told her. "You sure know how to calm a girl down."

"Just you, Heidi."

Heidi laughed. "Knowing your track record, I have to agree with that."

"Now, are you feeling better? Want to come join the cool kids' table?"

"Popularity is so overrated, Landon."

I grinned. That was the exact opposite of the Heidi I'd known in high school. "Come on, cheerleader. Get it moving. Jensen is going to start grilling soon, and you do not want to be over here, standing in his way, when he gets near a grill. Come grab a beer, and hang out with us. We don't bite. Well, I can't guarantee Austin."

Heidi giggled, and her whole face brightened. Whatever demons she had been facing disappeared into the clouds. She was just the confident, bubbly girl I found utterly fascinating.

And, when she seamlessly integrated into my family for the rest of the afternoon, it was like everything in the whole world was going right.

Eighteen

Heidi

Almost two weeks later, on Friday morning, I was called into a meeting before I even made it to the elevator.

"What for?" I asked Max.

He was one of our lead engineers and the least pleasant of the guys in my department.

"Didn't ask. Just said to do it. I'm grabbing people as they get here."

"All right," I said with a raised eyebrow.

I took the elevator up to our floor with a sense of urgency. The last time we'd had a meeting, we'd found out that Landon was the new boss. I sure hoped that this meant that Landon was getting a new job in a different department…or floor. Because walking past him every day on my way to my desk was starting to turn into the best part of my day, and I wasn't sure how I felt about that.

Not that anything had happened. He had been the perfect gentleman. Maybe too much of a perfect gentleman, considering the energy that had been building between us. I thought he was waiting for my move since I'd rebuffed him so many times. And I couldn't see that I would make it.

I sighed and decided not to worry about it. A decision for another day. I rallied a smile for Landon as I passed his office but was surprised to find it empty.

Huh.

He was usually in the office bright and early on Fridays.

Strange.

I shrugged it off and headed into the conference room. Matt greeted me with a wave. He was in a lime-green plaid shirt with a navy-blue bow tie with polka dots and suspenders today. His outfit choices always made me giggle.

"Hey, Matt," I said, taking the seat next to him.

"We meet again, Heidi," he said with a sideways grin.

"Indeed. You know what *this* meeting is about?"

"Nope. They never tell us anything before they want to."

"Yeah, that's the truth." I reached out and snagged a doughnut from the table. "At least they got us some breakfast."

"I'm surprised that you eat that kind of thing."

I stared at him in confusion with half of the glazed doughnut stuffed in my mouth. "Huh?" I managed.

"It's all processed flour and high fructose corn syrup. It's horrible for you."

I swallowed and grinned. "Tastes delicious."

"You should take care of your body. You only have one."

"Noted," I said, giving him a thumbs-up as I reached for a second doughnut.

Just then the engineering manager, Dennis, moseyed into the room. He was a balding man in his mid-fifties with a round belly and an easy smile. I liked Dennis just fine. He was the one who kept giving me merit raises for doing better than the boys.

"Is everyone here?" Dennis asked. He walked to the front of the room, grabbing a box of doughnuts as he went.

I glanced around and noticed that, no, in fact, not everyone was here. "I think we're missing Jim."

"Right, Jim," Dennis said. "Jim is taking a position at the Austin branch. His son just got into Texas, and he and his wife wanted to make the move to be close to him." He shrugged, as if he thought that was a stupid reason to take a position in Austin.

Family was the most important thing though. It was kind of sweet that Jim wanted to move to where his son was. And, as long as it was a lateral move, I didn't see how it was even a bad thing. Austin was a freaking awesome city. I'd gone to visit Emery a couple of times while she had been getting her PhD. It had more to offer than Lubbock; that was for sure.

"So, with Jim clearing out his desk next week in the middle of the new city contract work, we're going to need to get someone prepped and into his job, pronto." Dennis smacked his lips together.

My eyes lit up. They were looking to promote someone. *Oh my God!* A lead engineer spot was open, and they wanted someone to drop right into the city contract work Jim had been doing. Might not be most people's dream, but I wasn't most people.

I wanted that position. No, I *deserved* that position. I'd worked my ass off to get to where I was. I'd spent years in school and training. I had all the certifications. I was up to date on all the proper programs. I even did extra work to prove my worth. This position needed to be mine.

"Company policy says that I have to leave the application up for a minimum of three days. That means you all have until next Wednesday to apply before I close the application entirely. Too much is resting on this project, and we need someone who knows what they're doing right away. So, I'm not going to drag my feet on this. If you don't think you can handle it, then don't waste my time. Understand?"

We all answered in the affirmative.

"Great. Now, get back to work. You're wasting time and money."

I laughed, but most of the other guys grumbled. Dennis was a hard-ass, but he had a good heart.

Matt immediately turned to face me as we stood up. "You seem awfully happy about this," he said.

"Yeah, well, I think it is a great opportunity."

"You're applying?" He sounded genuinely shocked.

"Um, yeah. Why wouldn't I?"

"You just haven't been with the company that long."

I gave him a disbelieving face. "Um…I've been with Wright for six years. Haven't you only been here for four?"

"Oh, yeah. I guess I forgot that I started after you. I did work for another company for four years before this though," he said, as if that somehow made his eight years of experience better than my experience.

"That's cool." *Misogynistic pig.*

He followed me as I exited the room, and we headed back toward our desks.

I'd had enough of Matt after one sitting today. First, he'd criticized doughnuts. *I mean, doughnuts!* And then he'd made it seem like I shouldn't get the promotion because I didn't have enough experience. In this job, that was code for, *You shouldn't get it because you're a woman.*

"Hey, Heidi," Matt said after I turned my back on him and was trying to ignore his presence.

"Hmm?" I asked. I studied the papers on my desk.

"So, I know, the last time we talked, you said that you were dating someone."

My head snapped up at that. *Oh no.* "Yeah?"

"Well, I heard through the grapevine that you're single again."

"There's a grapevine for that?"

He shrugged with a nervous smile. "You know that people gossip around here."

"I see."

"Well, I was just wondering if you wanted to go out sometime. I'm free tonight. We could go to Rain Uptown. I love their pasta."

I smiled in a really nice no-way-in-hell sort of way. Then, I figured I'd let him down easy. "Sorry, Matt, but I don't date in the office."

"Oh," he said softly. "I see."

"It's a personal rule. Better not to mix business with pleasure and all that. You understand, right?"

"Uh, sure. Yeah, it makes perfect sense," he said as I crushed his dreams.

I sank down into my chair at my desk and tried to ignore the pitiful looks I got from Matt, as if the day could get any more awkward. Well, it probably could if Landon showed up and found out that Matt had asked me out. Those Wright boys were a jealous bunch.

But Landon never showed.

His office was mysteriously dark all through the afternoon. I wanted to ask around to find out if anyone knew where he was, but the last thing I wanted was to draw attention to me and Landon. It was bad enough, what we had done so far. It would be worse to make people consider the possibility.

Of course, they already knew we were friends. We'd been friends since high school. I hoped it didn't get misconstrued.

By the time five o'clock rolled around, I was really concerned. I'd gotten used to seeing Landon every day. Three weeks as my boss, and now, it was a thrill to see him and talk to him. Even if nothing was going on.

With him gone all day, I realized how much I missed him. No more stolen glances. No more hidden smiles. No more stupid reasons to go talk to him. No more elevator rides. Today was unbelievably bland without him. And my phone was unbelievably silent.

I checked it once more as I walked over to my car. Nothing.

I plopped down in the front seat and blasted the air conditioner to keep me from sweating from the damn Lubbock dry heat. I wanted to know what was going on with Landon. It seemed strange that he would skip work with no one knowing or talking about it. Maybe he was hurt. Or maybe he'd had something to do.

I knew it was a lame excuse, using his absence to text him...but I did it anyway.

> *Hey! You weren't in the office today. Everything okay?*

It took a good five minutes before I sent it. I laughed shakily at my need to make sure he was all right.

He texted back almost instantly.

> *Yeah. Thanks for checking in. Did I miss anything?*

> *New job opening in engineering. Pretty excited.*

> *That's great. Because of Jim leaving?*

> *You already knew!*

Of course, he'd already known. He was my boss after all. He'd probably had to talk to Jim when he asked for the transfer to Austin.

> *Guilty. But I couldn't say anything.*

> *I get it.*

And I was secretly frustrated that we had this thing between us. This thing that kept us apart. I wanted to talk to

Landon. I wanted to tell him everything going on in my life, like we used to be able to do.

So, why weren't you at work today then?

I waited a solid five minutes between that message and the next. I wasn't sure why it was taking him so long to answer, but when he responded, I knew he had been deciding if he wanted to be bold.

I liked bold.

Why don't you come over to my apartment, and I'll tell you all about it?

Nineteen

Heidi

Going to Landon's apartment fell under the category of Bad Ideas. Yet here I was, driving over to the address he had texted to me and feeling ridiculous that I was doing so. I could try to convince myself that it was simply because I was worried about his well-being.

Actually, let's go with that.

Seemed legit.

Even if it was a lie.

I was going to Landon's because I wanted to see him, and staying away from him fucking sucked. Point-blank.

Just as I pulled into the parking lot of his apartment building, I got a text from Emery. Blood pounded in my ears, and I felt frozen. I still hadn't told Emery that anything was going on with Landon. I mean, nothing was going on with Landon, but she would want to know why I was going over there to see him, and I didn't have a real answer to that. At least not one that I could give her.

Hey! I'm heading over to Jensen's tonight, but I miss you. Can we plan a girls' night this weekend?

I sighed and parked the car. Man, I missed my best friend, too. I should probably head straight home and go hang out with her. That was the sensible thing to do. But there was the door to Landon's apartment, and that was where all my curiosity led.

Feeling like a crappy best friend, I decided not to tell her.

Yes! I miss you, too. How about tomorrow night?

Oh my God, this needs to happen! This damn man always takes all my time.

Yes, because you hate it.

Not in the slightest, but it takes time away from my bestie roomie! So, tomorrow for sure, bitch! You'd better be there.

Definitely tomorrow. I'll be all yours, lover.

Oh, don't tease me!

I laughed at her silly behavior that I adored.

It was officially official though. I had to tell Emery that I was into Landon. I was dreading it. Seriously dreading it. But Emery was my family. One hundred fifty percent. I wasn't going to lie to her. My poor heart couldn't handle dealing with that. I was already tied up in knots over the fact that she didn't know.

It wasn't as if I were cheating. I was just…hanging out with my boss. Who happened to be her ex-boyfriend.

Fuck, I'm screwed.

I tossed my phone in my purse and hurried up to Landon's front door. I knocked twice and tapped my foot on the ground in anticipation. I couldn't believe I was doing this. Sure, I might be able to lie to myself and say that Landon and I had been friends forever, so it wasn't weird to come over here. But it was still a lie.

Landon cracked the door open, and his face brightened. "Hey! You showed."

"I said I would."

"Yeah, you did, but I wasn't sure. With, well…you know."

Yeah, I do know.

He stepped back and gestured for me to enter. With my heart in my throat, I passed him and went into the living room.

The apartment wasn't anything special. I could see everything about the place in one sweep. The small living space had an enormous curved TV that was currently showing some golf tournament, a tiny kitchen with a two-person breakfast nook, and a one bedroom with a too-big bed. This was not the sort of place I would have guessed from someone in the Wright family. Let alone a professional golfer. From what I knew—not that I cared one way or another—the Wrights were all millionaires-plus, and professional golf, even in the midrange, raked in over a million a year. Yet here he was, in a tiny one-bedroom in Lubbock, Texas.

"Nice place," I told him.

He coughed twice as he choked on his own laugh. "Yeah. Sure. Awesome digs."

"It's not what I expected," I said truthfully.

He closed the door behind me and followed me into the living room. "I'm not bitter, I swear, but I went from living in a five-thousand-square-foot house in Clearwater with a pool and Jacuzzi, across from a PGA-regulation golf course, to this. This is…an adjustment."

My jaw hung open at his words. "Well, shit."

"Pretty much my take on it."

"Why did you pick this place? It's not like you can't live somewhere…better."

"That's true. I could move again if I wanted. But, considering all the other changes in my life, I just wanted to go minimalist. I don't need the space. It's just me after all."

"That makes sense actually."

"I think it sounds better in my head than when I said it out loud to Jensen," Landon said. He angled for the kitchen. "You want a drink? Water? Coke? A beer?"

"Coke is fine with me."

He popped open two cans and handed one to me. I made myself comfortable on his couch, which was really low to the ground and clearly very new. The bubbles fizzed at the top of the can and tickled my nose when I went to take a sip. I giggled quietly to myself, and my eyes darted to Landon's mouth. I licked my lips where the bubbles were and tried not to think about what he would taste like without whiskey.

"What did Jensen say when you told him you wanted a one-bedroom hole in the wall?"

Landon put his hand over his chest. "You wound me. It's not actually a hole in the wall."

I laughed. "It's almost comically small."

"Cut me a break. I didn't see it before I signed the lease."

"That wasn't a smart move."

"Nope," he agreed. "Anyway, Jensen thought I was overreacting to the whole divorce and moving away. That I didn't need to live in a tree house to get that far away from my normal lifestyle."

"He's not wrong," I said softly.

"He's not. But I'm not living in a tree house either."

I shook my head and set my Coke down on the coffee table. "So, why weren't you at work today?"

"Ugh! You want to talk about work?" he asked. He scooted closer to me, and my heart raced for a whole other reason. "When I finally have you here?"

"Finally?" I muttered, arching an eyebrow. "I've never been invited to your tree house before."

"I didn't know that all I needed to do was send you an invite to get you over here."

His hand slipped across the space between us and took my hand in his. Our fingers twined together. My stomach knotted at the touch, and I shivered as he ran his thumb up and down my hand. My eyes snagged on his and the intensity in them. I knew I should stop, but I didn't pull away. I hovered on the brink of surrender.

"I'm not sure just any invite would have worked," I murmured.

He drew even closer until his hip was pressed into my side and his shoulder was tight against mine. His lips were only inches from me. The reminder of our one shared kiss hit me over the head with want.

"How about this one?" He eased his other hand up into my hair and brought my face toward him.

Our lips melded together with a heat that suffused the entire room. There was this moment alone. And I could feel this ache that had settled in the pit of my stomach, unrelenting for weeks. This might be wrong, but it felt so right.

I wasn't breathing as I met his kiss, heated and needy. I had wanted this for so long, and now that it was right in front of me, all in front of me, I couldn't get enough. There was no way this could ever be enough.

And, as I dragged him closer to me and opened my mouth to his kisses, I tried to push away that nagging feeling. I tried to ignore that voice in the back of my head, saying that he was my boss and I was going to get fired for this.

I shoved him backward with force I hadn't known I was capable of and stumbled to my feet. "Oh, fuck," I muttered unintelligibly. "Fuck, shit, fuck."

"Heidi, what's wrong?" he asked, jumping to his feet, too.

I stepped back from him and shook my head. I held my hand out. "Stay. Stay right there."

His eyes ignited in frustration. "Why?"

"Because this only ends one way, Landon."

"Hopefully, with you in my fucking bed, Heidi."

"That is not going to happen!"

"And why the fuck not?" he asked.

"If the only reason I'm here right now is because you want to fuck me, then I'm going to leave," I snapped back at him.

I skirted the couch as I headed for the door, but Landon jumped in front of me, blocking my path.

"No fucking way are you leaving right now."

"Watch me!"

Landon slammed his hand out. "You're not leaving."

"You're sadly mistaken if you think that, by inviting me to your tiny tree house, I'll give up all my reasons for staying away from you."

Except that was exactly what I'd been thinking about ever since he texted me and told me to come over. I had known that coming here was a bad idea, and I had done it anyway. I had known this would happen, and I'd wanted it to.

Stupid fucking conscience.

"That's not what I think. I think you came over to talk to me about why I'd missed work. Then, you looked at my mouth and licked your lips, and I couldn't sit next to you and lie to myself about wanting you. I can't do what you're capable of."

"Yes, I want you. But I can't have you. That's it. Full stop."

"I don't accept that," he told me.

"Learn to."

"Are you just blind? Is that what this is? Do you think you can really avoid this *forever*? Because I'm not going anywhere, and what we have isn't just going to go away."

"What do we have, Landon?" I asked in desperation. "Some phone calls, a New Year's mistake, and two whole kisses? That's not much as far as I'm concerned."

"You're joking, right?" His eyes were round and hurt at my accusation. "We've been friends for, like, fifteen years, Heidi. You've helped me more than you could possibly know during the last year. The only reason I stopped talking to you was because I was so into you, and I knew that I had to put distance between us. But let me be clear," he said, stepping dangerously close to me, "there is no distance between us any longer."

"Maybe there should be," I said.

But I'd lost my fire. My back was pressed up against the wall in his apartment, and he was towering over me, even in my high heels. And I felt anything but threatened.

I felt so fucking turned on. Like heart-pounding, legs-shaking, skin-tingly, *wet* turned on. I could hardly control my own body. All it wanted was to grab him and say screw all my misgivings about the situation.

"No, you're wrong. You are fighting this because of work. But I was yours before that, and I'll be yours after it, too."

"That doesn't change the fact that you're my boss though. Fuck, I don't even know *why* you're my boss," I cried.

"Well, you refused to listen to me."

I held my arms wide and tried to tamp down my growing desire. "I'm listening now. I came here to listen to you. For you to tell me why you'd missed work. Not for you to kiss me!"

Landon quirked a smile. He was only a hairbreadth from my mouth. So close that, if I even breathed heavy, I would brush his lips. My eyes were wide with panic, and my fingers were itching to grab on to his shirt. He was teasing me. And it was working.

"Okay, Heidi," he said dreamily. He moved his mouth, so he was grazing it along my cheek and down to my neck. "We'll play it your way. I won't kiss you."

His breath was hot against my skin, and I suddenly felt feverish.

"Then…we're not doing anything wrong." He slid over to my collarbone and to my shoulder. His hands were pressed into the wall on either side of me.

I couldn't keep it together. This was torture. Plain and simple. Perfect, sweet torture.

"This isn't helping," I managed to get out.

"You mean…even when I'm not kissing you," he said, finally planting a kiss on my shoulder and then another one up my collarbone, "even when I'm not touching you…"

He thrust his body against mine, pinning me completely to the wall. I could feel every inch of his rock-hard body under his clothes. His skin was on fire, and every inch of me he touched flamed.

"You still have feelings for me? You still want me? You still want this?"

I stiffened under his scrutiny and those bottomless dark pools.

"Because, if you still want me, then it's not going to go away. It's just going to build. Until it explodes."

And I was an active volcano at his words.

"Tell me you want this as much as I do," he said with earnest. "Tell me this isn't a lost cause. I can see you don't want me to stop. Just tell me you want this. Stop telling me to stop."

His pleading did me in.

I nodded once. "Don't stop."

And then he crushed his lips to mine…and I was lost.

Twenty

Landon

Heidi wasn't fighting me anymore. She slung her arms around my neck and was kissing with the fervor and passion I knew had been lying dormant right under the surface.

I hadn't known that this was going to happen. When I'd invited her over, I'd hoped that we would end up here. But I truly had been planning to talk to her all about the reason I'd missed work today along with everything else going on in my life. I'd wanted it all out in the open so that she would know where we stood.

Then, I just hadn't been able to step back. That one look. The one glance that had said she was thinking about kissing me. It was all I'd needed to completely forget every other reason I'd invited her here.

Yes, I wanted to talk to her. I loved talking to her.

But I wanted to fuck her a whole hell of a lot more at this moment.

Without a second thought, I grasped her by the back of her thighs and hoisted her legs up around my waist. I knew, as soon as I did it, that it was a bad idea. Something small twinged in my back, but I was so set on Heidi that I couldn't even care. I'd deal with it later.

She held on to me tight as I carried her across the tree-house-sized apartment and into my bedroom. I dropped her backward onto the bed, and she met my gaze with lust-filled eyes.

I wasted no time in stripping her out of the pants she had worn to work. There would be time to go slow later, but right now, I couldn't get enough of her.

She sat up and reached for my shorts. Her eyes were alight as she flicked the button open and dragged the zipper down. With an easy push from her hands, my khaki shorts were lying in a puddle at my feet, near her pants. She dragged her own shirt over her head and tossed it on the ground, and mine shortly followed.

"Oh," she murmured softly.

"What?"

Standing, she trailed her fingers over my shoulders and down my biceps. Then, she went back up and over my pecs before dipping over my six-pack and to the V that I'd worked tirelessly on in the gym.

"You should always walk around shirtless," she said.

I laughed as her nails caressed every inch of my body. "Duly noted."

"Might be an issue at the office." She bit down her lip and tilted her head to the side as she enjoyed the view. "I'm willing to take the risk."

"I'll risk everything for you."

My hands gripped her hips and pulled her close to me. Then, I navigated my own path over her thin waist and up to the curve of her bright pink bra. I loved that she was in something so very *her*. She'd been this little Barbie doll in high school, and even though that had chilled out over the years, even though she wore black like she owned the color, she never fully gave up on that girlie girl underneath it all.

She breathed in sharply as my thumbs brushed across her nipples before moving to her back and unsnapping the bra. I reached for the straps and removed them from her arms. Then, she was lying before me in nothing but a blue-striped thong. Her tits were round and perfect, and I ached to claim them.

"Landon," she murmured softly.

There wasn't an ounce of self-consciousness in this woman, and when I looked up at her face, she was practically begging me to continue.

My lips were back on her in an instant, kissing and tasting and devouring her. She grabbed on to me as we crashed back onto the bed together. My body was covering her, and the feel of her underneath was enough to make me explode. She circled her long legs around my waist, pressing my dick against her pussy. Two thin pieces of cotton separated us, and I ground myself against her.

She broke away from my lips to moan my name, which did nothing but make my cock throb. I wanted to feel every inch of her. I wanted her to not just moan my name, but also scream it. I wanted all of Heidi Martin.

I nuzzled her neck, dragging my stubble across it, until she dug her nails into my back. *Fuck, I'm not going to be able to last if she keeps that up.*

"Heidi," I groaned, nibbling on her neck, "I want you."

"Yes."

"I want all of you."

"Please."

"No going back from here," I said. My hand slipped inside her underwear, and I stroked her clit in little circles.

"Oh, fuck!"

She was already wet when I dipped my fingers into her pussy. Her back bucked off the bed, but I had her pinned, allowing her no respite. I worked her into a frenzy that I promised to deliver on. Her breathing was coming out in gasps when I finally slid down and stripped her out of her thong.

"Landon," she groaned, "oh God."

I chuckled softly before slowly licking across her clit. "Was this what you wanted?"

"God, yes."

"Where did all of that anger go, firecracker?"

She snarled at me, and I couldn't help laughing. As much as I adored the way she couldn't contain herself around me, I certainly liked this subdued Heidi, who was about to come at my touch.

"Nothing to be mad at me about now?" I continued teasing her.

"Landon, so help me God," she managed to get out before I bent back over her and started licking her like I was trying to get to the center of a Tootsie Pop.

I pushed two fingers deep inside her and managed two measured thrusts before she came apart completely. And she did scream. And it was amazing.

Without giving her time to pause, I stripped out of my boxers, grabbed a condom out of my nightstand, and then moved back to her panting helplessly on the bed.

"That was...fuck," she muttered with her eyes closed.

"That was just the appetizer."

Her eyes flew open as I eased back on top of her. For a split second, something like fear reflected back at me. I halted.

"Is this okay?" I asked.

All arguing aside, I would never make her go through with this. We both wanted it. That was what made it fucking incredible. And I wanted her to want it right here. Right this minute.

At my question, that flicker of fear dissolved in her eyes, and she nodded. "This is way more than okay."

I grinned devilishly at her. "Good. That was what I thought your screams meant, but I wasn't sure."

"Fucker."

"Excuse me?" I asked with an arched eyebrow.

I pressed my dick against her opening, and she groaned.

"I said, you're a fucker."

I slipped all the way into her tight pussy and grunted with pleasure. "What was that?"

"More," was all she said.

And I happily obliged.

All the sexual tension finally crashed between us in that moment. There was no stopping now. I was inside her. I was taking what was mine. I was fucking marking my territory.

I'd said it all those weeks ago when I kissed her at the back of Flips. Heidi was mine. Mine. All mine.

I didn't care what had happened in my past, in her past. I was only thinking about moving forward. Never moving back again.

My cock thrust deep into her, and I knew I was getting close. Fuck, I had wanted this so fucking bad for so fucking long that I couldn't even keep it together. After watching her orgasm just from my fingers and the sounds she made as she let me pleasure her, I thought I was going to lose it right then and there. This woman did me in like no other. But I needed her to come again. I needed it like my next breath.

I eased up onto my knees and grasped her hips in my hands, lifting her up slightly off the bed. The new angle got me even deeper than I'd been before, and there was no way I was going to be able to hold off. Watching her tits bounce as I bottomed out into her. The flush of red across her body. The glazed look of satisfaction on her face. The round O of her lips as she slipped over the edge again. Then, the cries of ecstasy. My name on her lips, like a prayer.

When she tightened around my cock, I lost it and came with her. I dropped forward over her and panted as my body tried to recover.

"Oh, Heidi," I said, placing featherlight kisses along her cheeks and mouth.

She giggled softly. "I can't feel my legs."

"Am I crushing you?"

"No, I think you killed me."

"In a good way?" I asked with a laugh.

"In the best way."

I claimed her mouth one more time before sliding out of her. She rolled off of the bed, and I couldn't help myself. I smacked her bare ass as she straightened.

"Watch it, fucker," she said with a mischievous grin.

"Yes, I did just fuck her." I winked at her, and she snorted before wandering into the bathroom.

I cleaned up as best I could in the bedroom and then lay back on the bed with my hands behind my head, feeling like a king. I was on top of the fucking world.

Heidi jumped back in bed and snuggled under the covers next to me. She was legit glowing. "I cannot believe I just had sex with my boss."

I humphed and squeezed her into me. "You and your titles. I think you just had sex with *me*. The rest doesn't matter."

"Maybe."

"Are you going to be all right with this?" I asked.

I didn't like where this conversation was going, but she just smiled up at me.

"Are you kidding? All right? We should have done this a long time ago."

I kissed her temple and nodded. "That's what I've been trying to tell you."

"That was a really fun way of avoiding my questions earlier," she said, kissing my chest before resting her head against it.

"Oh, Heidi, that was not to avoid anything. That was for fun, and frankly, it was long overdue."

"Mmm," she said, not arguing.

She trailed her fingers across my chest, and I tried to forget that was how this had all gotten me started. If she kept it up, we might be going for a second round.

"So, why were you out of work today then?"

"Doctor's appointment."

"For your back?"

"Yeah."

"Are you going to tell me the whole story?"

I blew out a breath. "Yeah. So, I went pro right out of college and qualified for the PGA my first year out. It was a pretty big deal. I mean, I know you followed some of it, but they thought, in a few years, I would be a shoo-in for a Masters win and maybe even the whole FedEx Cup."

"I remember some of that. It was right when I started working for Wright."

"Yeah. So, about two years into my career, I fucked up my back. All the doctors said there was no way I could play on it. I needed to drop out and go on medical exemption."

"But you didn't."

"Nope. I played through the pain. Got doped up on pain meds the doctor prescribed and pushed through it."

Her eyes snapped up to mine, wide and concerned. "That stuff is super addicting"

"I'm well aware."

"Did you keep taking them?" she said, her face tightening. "Are you taking them now?"

I knew what that was about. That was about her old man. But I was not like him in that regard.

"No," I told her. "It was a stupid mistake to keep going when I should have taken a break. I was so high on the game. I stopped taking the prescriptions and tried to heal in the off season. And I haven't taken it since."

167

"Never?" she asked.

"Nope. Not worth the risk."

She nodded, relaxing against me again. "Good."

"Anyway, fast forward three years. Something else tweaked in my back, but my doctor gave me the all clear after a couple of weeks. But this summer was the worst. I over rotated. I think I must have put all the pressure into my lower back, and that's when it was all over. The doctor said I needed surgery and a minimum of a year recovery, and even then, I might never golf again, ending my career."

"Oh my God," she whispered, sitting up and staring at me with such shock and pity in her eyes. "So...you're working for Wright because you don't think you'll ever golf again?"

"I have hope that I will be able to golf again, but I'm working for Wright while I'm in physical therapy to try to keep my mind from going crazy. I need something to focus on and something to believe in or else I worry that the mental part of my game will disintegrate if...*when* I return."

"Shit," she muttered. "That's just...awful."

"What's worse is," I said through gritted teeth, "when I got the news, instead of responding as you just did...as most normal human beings would, Miranda told me I couldn't risk ending my career because of a little pain. I think her exact words were, 'Fuck integrity.'"

Heidi winced. "How awful."

"Yeah. Then I caught her telling one of her friends that she didn't want to have kids after we spent the last year in marriage counseling after she miscarried. I'd been planning to divorce her before she got pregnant, but I tried to make it work. Then it was just a slap in the face."

"Wow," Heidi whispered. "Was that right before the reunion?"

I nodded. "That's when I left her. She'd used up her last chance with me, and I was done. Then, there you were." I stroked her hair out of her face. "My little firecracker. And

I realized how stressful my life had become and how much I was hurting emotionally, mentally, and physically. But you and I had always been right. We had always been open and honest with each other. Our connection ran deep. And, suddenly, everything in the world made sense. I wanted you and only you."

Twenty-One

Heidi

My eyes fluttered open to see the early afternoon light streaming in through Landon's window. I was disoriented for a half second before remembering everything that had gone on last night. *Holy hot sex!*

I yawned and stretched out, curling into Landon's side. He was lying on his back with his head turned toward me. His eyes were closed, and he was breathing softly. He looked so peaceful, as if all the worries in the world had fallen off of his shoulders. And, after hearing him talk last night about losing golf, it legitimately felt like the world rested firmly on his shoulders. To be so young, and he'd already had his dreams ripped away from him. It weighed on him in a way that even I couldn't realize.

I'd known about the injuries, but the extent of it all was horrifying. Career ending were not words that any athlete wanted to hear.

Landon's arm wrapped neatly around my waist and pulled me in close. "Morning."

"Good morning," I murmured.

He peeked an eye open. "You look gorgeous in the morning."

I laughed. "Uh, yeah. Sure."

"Most beautiful thing I've ever seen."

"You're ridiculous."

"Mmm," he said noncommittally as he leaned over to give me a kiss. He stopped halfway through the motion and rocked back into the bed. "Shit."

"What?" I asked, concerned.

"Uh…nothing."

"Nothing, huh?"

"I just…think I did something to my back last night."

"You think, or you did?" I worried away at my bottom lip. His eyes said it all. "I did, but it'll be fine. Don't worry."

"Do you need help? Or, like, Tylenol?"

He cringed and then slowly eased into a sitting position. "I guess we were a little too vigorous last night."

I grinned. "You could say that."

"It was probably when I lifted you."

"Oh, shit. Yeah," I muttered. I hadn't known the extent of his injuries then, or I wouldn't have allowed that to happen in the first place. I swatted at his arm. "You need to take better care of yourself. Jesus. Let me get you something. What do you have?"

"There's some Tylenol and a muscle relaxer over the toilet if you want to grab me some along with a glass of water."

I hopped up and hurried to the kitchen to get him some water before entering the bathroom. I felt a little silly, digging around in his medicine cabinet, but he'd told me to after all. My eyes landed on the little row of prescription medicines. I took out a few Tylenol and then found the muscle relaxer as well.

"Find it?" Landon asked.

"Yep. It's right here."

I snapped the cabinet door and walked back into the bedroom.

"Here you go," I said, handing him the pills and water.

"Thanks." He tossed them back and downed the water. "I think I'm dehydrated, too." He arched an eyebrow at me. "Did you have anything to do with that?"

I edged back into bed and grinned. "Nope. Not me."

"Why don't I believe you?" he asked, nuzzling into my neck.

"Because I was totally involved."

Landon pulled me down on top of him and kissed me, slow and steady. Eventually, the medicine did its job, and the pain diminished. I liked to think that the kisses helped too.

By the time we'd eaten lunch and retreated back to the bedroom, I couldn't *believe* the time. It was already well past time that I needed to go see Emery. I'd promised her a girls' night. This thing with Landon was fresh, new, and shiny, and I wanted to succumb to it in every waking minute. Realistically though, that wasn't going to be possible.

"Oh my God, I have to go home," I told him, hopping out of bed and locating all my discarded clothes from last night. "I have a girls' night tonight."

"Don't go," Landon said. He eased back out of bed and wrapped his arms around my waist, drawing me in for another kiss. "Just stay one more night."

"I can't," I barely managed. "I promised Em."

"Have a girls' night tomorrow." His lips grazed my jawline, and he nibbled on my ear in a way that made me want to throw myself back in his bed.

"Can't. As much as I want to stay—"

"Then, stay."

"Oh, you are trouble."

"Yes," he agreed easily.

I removed his hands from my ass with a sigh. "You're making this really difficult."

"I never promised to fight fair."

I laughed. "That's for damn sure."

"When will I see you again?" he asked, following me to the door.

"I don't know. Tomorrow?"

"Good." His eyes lit up at that. "Tomorrow is a promise."

I wrapped my arms around his neck. "I like that."

"Are you going to tell Em?"

"Yeah," I said with a sheepish grin. "Can't hide anything from her. Plus, anyway, she guessed what was going on back in December."

"Of course, she did." Landon tried to pull me back into him again. "You sure you can't tell her tomorrow?"

I smiled and pressed a firm kiss to his lips. "I'll miss you, too."

He finally released me, and I slipped out the door. He stood in the open doorway in nothing but his boxers, and it was damn hard to walk away from that.

That body.

Those abs.

That V!

Fuck, I wanted that body, and everything he was capable of doing with it.

Somehow, I managed to make it out to my car and even start the ignition. He stood there, smirking at me, in the most come-hither display I'd ever witnessed. It took so much self-control to back out of that parking spot and go home.

When I entered the house, Emery was sprawled out on the couch with *Buffy the Vampire Slayer* on for the hundredth time.

"You're back!" Emery said with a big smile. "I thought maybe you'd ditched me."

"Nope. I remembered girls' night. Just going to get into something a little more comfortable."

Emery hopped off the couch and followed me into my room. "Why are you wearing work clothes?"

"That's an excellent question."

"Actually, where were you anyway?"

"Also a good question."

I grabbed some pajamas and clean underwear before retreating into the bathroom without answering Emery's questions. I needed a moment to compose myself before dishing the goods.

When I came back out, she was sitting on my bed with her legs crossed under her like a pretzel. "Avoiding the questions much?"

"No," I said evasively.

"You got another letter today." She held up the same standard white envelope that I had been getting once a week for the last six years. I frowned and plucked it out of her hand.

"Thanks," I mumbled before stuffing it in my closet with all the other unopened letters.

Emery frowned. "Are you going to…"

"No," I told her with more force than necessary. "I'm not."

"K," she said quickly. She knew when not to press. "So, spill where you were and what you were doing. Or else I'll make you talk about the letters."

"Okay, okay," I said, holding up my hands in defense. "I was…with Landon."

"I KNEW IT!" she yelled. Emery jumped off the bed. Her smile was wide and her green eyes bright.

I laughed at her overreaction. "I didn't even say anything else."

"Well, you're finally fucking admitting to me that you're into Landon. I've been waiting for this for months. So, are you like together, together?" Emery asked.

175

"Emery, I do not understand you. Why are you so excited about this? You dated Landon for two years. I was terrified of telling you."

Emery shrugged and flipped her dark hair off her shoulders. "Besides the fact that I'm dating his brother? I think I got over my anger at the Wrights because of Jensen. We were kids, Heidi. Landon left me because he thought he was doing the right thing by his dad. I didn't understand that at the time, but ten years gives you a lot of perspective. I do not begrudge you dating him, like I might have right after high school or something."

"I guess that makes sense. I mean…I still feel weird, telling you about it."

"You haven't told me anything," she groaned, dragging me out of the bedroom and into the kitchen. "Tell me all the details. I think we need ice cream and bubbles to celebrate."

"Oh, champs, yes!" I agreed.

"Champs?" Emery snorted. "You are so *Real Housewives* right now. Oh my God, I hate myself for knowing that. Damn Morgan and her obsession with those kinds of shows and trash magazines."

I laughed. "Does she still watch just to make fun of people?"

"Yes, though I think she's secretly obsessed. Anyway, enough about Morgan. Tell me about Landon. You're together?"

"Yes. Well, no. I mean, not technically since he's in the middle of a divorce."

"Oh, thank fuck about Miranda."

"And there's the whole issue with him being my boss," I reminded her.

"Oh, right. You have that no-dating-coworkers thing."

She plopped vanilla ice cream into bowls for us and drizzled chocolate fudge on top. I took one from her, and we headed back to the living room.

"Julia said that I'd probably get moved if something happened since he's a Wright. But do *not* say anything to Jensen."

"Ugh, seriously?" Emery said, digging into her ice cream.

"I don't want Jensen to know. We'll get in trouble, and I think I'm in line for a promotion. I've worked so hard for this job."

"Okay," Emery said, "I understand that. You got yourself where you are today. But what about Landon?"

"If he wanted to move...he would have asked already," I said a bit defensively.

"So, you're going to wait for him to make the move?"

"I'm not jeopardizing my career."

Emery sighed. "I'm not saying to. I'm saying, if it bothers you this much, then talk to him about it."

"I have. He knows how I feel about him being my boss, but he got this job for a reason. I don't know what to do. I don't want to tell him to get a new job when our relationship is just starting, and he's going through so much."

"Well, if it get serious, then you're going to have to talk about it."

"Yeah," I agreed.

That was a day I was dreading. I knew I needed to talk to Landon about it. As much as he had blown it off, like it didn't matter, I knew that it did. I'd seen Julia's face when I mentioned it. I sighed and decided I'd better bring it up with him. The last thing I wanted was to stress our relationship every day at the office.

"Sorry," Emery said. "I want you to be happy. Landon makes you happy?"

I nodded. "Very."

"Good. Even if it is a little weird."

"I knew it!" I cried. "I knew you were weirded out."

Emery laughed and nudged me. "Nah. I'm joking. Now, the really important question. *Mean Girls* or *Bad Moms*?"

"I'm going to go with both."

"Good choice."

———

All night, I'd obsessed over what to say to Landon about the boss situation. But the minute that I got to his apartment on Sunday afternoon, the words just wouldn't leave my mouth.

I was too happy to talk to him about something that hard. Our relationship had just started. I didn't know where it was going. Only that I wanted it to last. I knew that I should say something, but when he looked at me and touched me and kissed me, my worries disappeared.

Monday morning rolled around, and I still hadn't said anything. My thoughts were swirling around in my head so much that, when we went and got Thai food for lunch, he seemed to read it on my face.

"You're worried about being out together?"

"I mean…yeah," I confirmed. "You're still my boss."

"I know."

My eyes slipped up to his. "Couldn't you just…ask Jensen or Morgan to move you?"

Landon sighed and nodded. "I did already."

"What?" I gasped.

"Yeah. The first day I saw you, I went to ask Morgan for a different job."

"I didn't know that!"

"Well, I didn't want you to think that I was out of line when you were still angry with me."

"What did Morgan say?"

Landon frowned. "She had to restructure the company to get me into this position. There is no other position for me right now. Nothing I'm qualified for at least. The job that I have is it for me until something else opens up."

I rocked back in my chair and frowned. "Wow."

"Yeah, I know."

"Well, I guess that's off the table."

"For now, Heidi, but not forever. We can handle this." He slipped his hand into mine. "I promise."

I numbly nodded my head, watching all my carefully planned suggestions fly out the window.

"Hey," he said, leaning toward me, "we can handle this. I swear. I am with you one hundred percent."

"I know," I told him with a smile.

I'd wanted it to be easier. But, of course, it wasn't easier. Nothing in life was ever easy.

We finished our meal and headed back to the office. My head was up in the clouds on the drive back, and Landon remained silent, giving me the space to come back to the ground.

I knew two things for certain—Landon was my boss, and I wasn't going to give him up for anything.

"Heidi," he said low, drawing me toward his office, as I had instinctively moved to my desk, "let's talk about this."

"What's there to talk about?" I whispered.

"Please," he said more earnestly.

"All right," I said. I didn't know what more we could figure out today, but I was willing to listen.

Then, we walked into his office, and my eyes landed on a woman in a skintight red dress who had seated herself in the middle of Landon's desk with her legs crossed seductively.

"Hello, darling," Miranda said.

Twenty-Two

Landon

S hit.
　　Oh, shit.

My eyes were wide with alarm. What in the ever-loving fuck was Miranda doing here? I'd been ignoring her calls, texts, and pathetic messages to try to get me to reconsider the divorce. I'd only responded to tell her to sign the paperwork or talk to her lawyer. I'd made my decision, and I wasn't going back to where we had been the last miserable year.

"Oh," Heidi said. Her cheeks were bright red. "I'm just… going to go back to my desk then. Good talk, boss."

"Heidi," I said softly.

"We'll chat about that…thing later."

And then she all but dashed out of the room, leaving me alone with the most conniving woman I knew.

"What are you doing here, Miranda?" I demanded.

"I came to see my husband, of course."

I nearly rolled my eyes. Why was I even surprised that she was playing that card? Nothing surprised me about her anymore.

This was the worst fucking time for her to show up. All I wanted to do was run out of this room and go talk to Heidi. I didn't know what she must be feeling right now and I didn't want her to think that anything was happening with me and Miranda.

I wished that I could go tell her not to worry and that there was nothing between Miranda and I anymore.

Instead, I had to deal with Miranda.

"Are you going to sign the papers?" I demanded.

She stuck her cherry-red lip out and flipped her blonde bangs out of her eyes. She'd gotten her hair cut since I last saw her, and it was angled around her chin. I tried not to look lower than that. She'd picked her outfit with purpose, and I didn't want to give her the satisfaction of assessing it.

"Do we have to talk about that silly document you sent me?"

My anger flared. "I'm at work. Either you're here to sign the paperwork or you're going to leave."

She hopped off the desk. The Louboutins I'd bought her for her birthday last year clicked as she hit the ground. "I flew all the way here, and you're kicking me out?"

"Yes," I said bluntly.

"I thought we could talk."

"Please, just stop this, Miranda. Just sign the divorce forms and get this over with."

She strode toward me with a feline's prowl, and it took everything in me not to shudder and back away from her. She trailed her French-manicured nail down my tie and smirked, as if she thought she would get a reaction, as if she had some sort of control over me. But she didn't.

At one point, I'd loved this woman. And seeing her here like this made me wonder how that had ever been possible.

"But I don't want to get this over with. I want you, Landon."

She leaned forward against me, and I took a step back.

"What part of *divorce* are you not comprehending?"

"The part where we got married and said our wedding vows. I took those seriously, Landon. I guess you didn't."

I sighed. This was a conversation I did not want to have. "I took them seriously," I told her. "You know I meant those words when I said them, but things have changed. We've changed. I think it will be better for both of us if we move on with our lives."

"I can't just stop loving you," she said, her voice soft and hesitant.

An act. I saw it for what it was. There was nothing soft or hesitant about Miranda. There never had been. She was commanding and fiery and filled a room. It was what had endeared her to me once upon a time. But our fairy tale wasn't ending in a happily ever after.

"We're not having this conversation."

"Yes, we are," she snapped back.

"I'm afraid not. I have work to do. And you should go home."

"How can I go home to an empty house?" Miranda demanded. Her hands were on her hips, and she'd gone from pouty to angry in the blink of an eye.

"Why should I care?"

"Because I'm your wife!"

"And, soon, you'll be my ex-wife."

"How can you be so uncaring?" she asked. "How can you just throw me aside like this? Is there someone else?"

My face pinched at just the wrong moment, projecting that I was seeing someone else…Heidi. And Miranda knew me too well not to judge my facial expressions, my annoyance with her question, as anything else but the truth.

She gasped. "Who is it? Are you cheating on me?"

I sighed and rubbed my forehead. "I have never cheated on you. And I can't currently be cheating on you because we're separated. And, if you'd just sign the paperwork, we'd be divorced."

"So, you are seeing someone then?"

"This conversation has no purpose. If you're here to annoy me, then congratulations. You've succeeded." I held my hands up in frustration.

There was no way in hell I was going to tell her about Heidi. No way that I would ever mention dating someone else until the divorce was completely final. Nothing would make Miranda drag her feet more than knowing I had already moved on. No matter that I had checked out of my headspace with Miranda a year ago. I did not want this to last any longer than it had to.

"Is that what you think? That I'm here to annoy you?" She sank into her hip, and her nostrils flared. "I think this entire thing is fucking insane, Landon. I'm your fucking wife. There has to be a reason for this motherfucking madness. Either you've found someone else or you've gone clinically insane."

I huffed. "Really sweet. Now, I'm clinically insane?"

"No," she grumbled. "I think you're with someone else."

"What is it going to take for you to sign the papers?" I demanded to change the subject.

She bit her cherry-red lip and looked at me as if this were the first time she had thought of the question. I knew by her eyes that it was not. "Nothing."

"I don't believe you. You're already getting half of everything that's not covered in the prenup. What more could you want from me?"

"Everything."

"Well, you can't have everything."

"Then, just you."

"No. You know what? I'm not having this conversation with you any longer. I'll have my lawyer contact you, and if we can't settle this in a reasonable way, then we'll go to mediation, or we'll go to court. Your choice, Miranda."

Her eyes were wide with alarm, as if she had *finally* realized that I was serious.

"Take me to dinner tonight. Have one more night with me."

"No," I said at once. I didn't want to spend any more time with her than I had to.

"And I'll sign."

I paused. Was she serious? One dinner, and she'd end all of this? It seemed too good to be true. And you know what they said about things that were too good to be true.

"I don't believe you."

"I swear it."

Just then the door crashed inward, and Morgan's face appeared in the door.

Oh, man, how I loved my sister for her impeccable timing.

"*Heyyyy!*"

"Oh, Morgan," Miranda said deprecatingly. She raised her chin a notch and flashed her a fierce smile that could only be seen as a threat. "How good to see you. As always."

"Same, Miranda. What are you doing here? Just took a wrong turn and ended up in Lubbock, huh?" she asked in the slow voice usually reserved for misbehaving toddlers.

"I'm here to see my husband. You don't have to be so patronizing."

"Oh, big words. So adorable," Morgan said.

I tried not to laugh. "Morgan."

"Are you going to let her talk to me like this?" Miranda asked, whirling on me.

"You think I have any control over her?" I asked.

"He doesn't," Morgan confirmed.

"How did you even know she was here?"

Morgan shrugged. "Gossip travels quick." She whirled back on Miranda. "Ready to go home now? Buh-bye!"

"You can't make me leave."

Morgan touched her hand to her chin and contemplatively gazed up in the air. "Hmm…last I checked…I was the vice president of this company. That kind of makes me…in charge around here. I know that must be hard for you to comprehend since you don't have a job. Your idea of work is being a stay-at-home wife, which means spending all of my brother's money and generally being a bimbo."

"Fuck you, Morgan."

"So, as you can see, I can make you leave."

I laughed. I couldn't help it. Morgan had been waiting for this moment for too long. She was enjoying herself way too much.

"It's okay. She's going to go. Aren't you, Miranda?" I asked.

"What about dinner?" she asked.

I knew she had asked on purpose, right in front of Morgan. Not her smartest move though because there was no way that Morgan would think that was a good idea. I was still on the fence and leaning toward holding on strong and not giving in. Seemed the smartest option. But, still…if there were a chance.

"I'll think about it."

"Don't think about anything," Miranda said. She eyed Morgan disdainfully. "Just text me."

"It's time for you to go!" Morgan interrupted. "You're trespassing on private property, and if you don't get out of here, I'll call security."

Miranda shot her a vicious glare. "You're such a bitch, Morgan."

"Fine by me!" Morgan shot back. "Now, out!"

Miranda gave Morgan one more angry glare before sending me a simpering look and stomping out of my office. I was glad to have her gone, but I knew we had made a spectacle of the whole ordeal. That meant, Heidi had probably heard some of it, which was probably not that great. I needed to talk to her and clear the air.

"You are not *seriously* considering going to dinner with her?" Morgan said, rounding on me. "What the hell did she say before I showed up that would make you consider that?"

I shrugged. This was a conversation I didn't want to have with Morgan either.

"Oh my God, you're not getting back together." She reached out and grabbed my arm. "Please, for the love of all things holy, tell me you are *not* getting back together with her!"

"We're not getting back together. Calm down," I said with a laugh.

"Oh, thank God. I thought I was going to have to stage an intervention. I would get the entire family together. We'd meet at Jensen's place. It would probably involve a PowerPoint presentation and lots of whiskey."

I held my hand up to stop her from continuing, but I was grinning. "I get it. No one in the family likes her."

"Understatement."

"And you're all thrilled that my marriage is dissolving, and we're divorcing."

"Very."

"And you don't care how it happens as long as it's done."

"Well, more or less. I mean, I want you to be happy. And I'm certain you'll come out of this happier than you were before. I don't know how you lived with her this long."

"You know, she wasn't always like that with me."

"Or you were just banging and didn't care." Morgan put her hands over her eyes. "Horrible mental image."

I laughed. "You're a riot, Morgan. Now, really, what are you doing here?"

"Hello? I saved your ass. I heard—and I quote—'Landon's hot wife is here.' So, I ran as soon as I could to take care of it. You're a softy. Like this dinner thing…"

"Look, she promised she'd sign the divorce papers if I went to one more dinner with her."

Morgan scoffed. "She'll sign anyway."

"She hasn't yet."

"We're not in dire straits here. She's going to sign. She has to."

"I'd like her to do it today."

"And do you think going to dinner with her will somehow miraculously make her do that?"

"I don't know, but if it will, isn't it worth pursuing? I will do anything to make her do this faster," I told her.

Morgan grimaced. "Don't say *anything*. You don't know what she'll come up with."

"I'll think about it. I don't know what I'll do."

"Please do not do anything stupid. There's still time to stage that intervention."

I laughed and patted her on the back. "You've done enough for me, Morgan. The divorce will be finalized soon, and then we can all move on from this train wreck."

"I won't hold my breath," she muttered.

"Always a ray of sunshine."

"I run a business. I don't need to be a fucking ray of sunshine. I just need to get shit done."

I held up my hands in defense. "If only we were all as amazing as you, Morgan."

"Don't do anything stupid, okay?"

I flashed her a grin. "Do I ever?"

"All the time. You and Austin. You're going to give me gray hair." She shook out her long brown hair before moving toward the door. "If you're going to do something stupid, then don't blame me when it backfires in your face, okay? I'm warning you now."

"Warning noted."

I wasn't an idiot. I knew that Miranda had something up her sleeve. But I wasn't sure if it was enough to let this all go or to give in to her demand. Either way, I knew that I needed to talk to Heidi and make this right. Because Miranda was right.

I *was* seeing someone else.

And the reason I wanted this divorce finalized as quickly as possible was all for her.

Twenty-Three

Landon

Morgan left my office and headed back upstairs. I peeked my head out of the office and found a wall of eyes staring at me.

Apparently, none of that had been subtle. Morgan and Miranda weren't exactly inconspicuous. I guessed that everyone at least had known that I had marital problems if they hadn't heard our discussion of a divorce. Thankfully, much of it had been muffled before Morgan catapulted into the room.

But the one set of eyes *not* on me was the one I was looking for. Heidi had her head buried in her work. She was purposefully not looking up. I wondered if she was even reading or if she was just staring.

Well, fuck working the rest of the day. I straightened my tie and strode toward her. I knew she didn't want anyone to know about us while I was her boss, but I wasn't about to wait around all day until I could see her after work. I didn't want to stress her like that.

Before I reached her, however, one of the other engineers stood up and blocked my path.

"Hey, Landon!"

I tried to reach for his name in my mind. I'd been trying to memorize all my employees' names, but I hadn't been here that long. This guy did not ring a bell.

"Hey, man," I said with a Wright smile. "What's going on?"

"It's Matt," he said in a rush.

"Right. Matt. What can I do for you?"

"I wanted to give you a high five, man," Matt said, holding his hand up.

I gave him a blank look but high-fived him anyway. *Why was this guy treating me like we were best friends when I was clearly his boss and didn't know him at all?*

"What for?"

"You have a really hot wife!" Matt said.

Heidi's head snapped up at that. Her gaze settled on Matt, as if she could burn through his skull with laser beams from her eyes.

"I mean, they don't make them like that around here, if you know what I mean." He chuckled twice.

I was barely able to control the disgusted feeling that washed over me. Heidi was not.

I straightened up and stood a head taller than him. "You should remember who you're speaking with. I won't condone people degrading women in such a manner in my office."

Matt stammered, "Uh, yeah, totally. Sorry. I didn't mean anything by it. I thought it was a compliment."

"That's what concerns me."

Matt opened his mouth and then closed it. "I, uh…"

"Don't worry about it. Just try to be more respectful in the future."

With that, I eased past Matt and straight to Heidi.

She glanced up from her work. "Can I help you?"

"Yes. As a matter of fact, I need to see you in my office."

"Did I do something wrong?" she asked, tilting her head at me.

"On the contrary, I wanted to discuss Jim's old job. I'll be talking with everyone throughout the week, regarding the new position."

"I see." She stood slowly to her feet and stared up at me with part confusion and part fear in her eyes.

"After you." I gestured for her to go ahead.

She took a deep breath and then walked right into my office. She didn't look around once. She strode past all her male colleagues, ignoring their questioning stares. I snapped the door shut as soon as she was inside.

"That was…interesting," Heidi muttered.

"More like outrageous."

"Which part? Morgan or Miranda?"

"Yes," I told her, striding to the desk.

She plopped down into the chair in front of my desk and warily looked at me. "I'm guessing I'm not here to discuss the new job."

"Not exactly," I admitted.

"I figured. So…Miranda is back. What does that mean? Are you back together?"

"Did you not hear the shouting match?"

"I heard Morgan bossing Miranda around. I don't know where *you* stand on her."

"Same place I've stood with her since the reunion. I'm leaving her. It's over."

"But she doesn't want that?" Heidi guessed. She picked at her nails and tried not to look up at me.

I sighed heavily and walked around to where she was sitting. I reached out and took her hand in mine. I was surprised that she let me. "Hey, this still doesn't change anything between us. That's why I wanted to talk to you."

"So, you're *not* going to dinner with her then?" She watched me, as if nervous that I would lie.

"I don't know. I wanted to talk to you about that."

"What's there to talk about?" She slid her hand out of mine. "You clearly want to go."

"Hold up. I clearly do not want to go, but she said, if I went, she'd sign the divorce papers. That seems like a good thing for me and you."

"Just dinner?" she asked suspiciously. "That's what she said."

"Yep."

"And do you believe her?"

"I don't know," I told her honestly. "What do you think? Is it worth a shot?"

"Honestly, it sounds like a horrible idea," Heidi said.

"Then, I won't go. Easy enough."

"But," she said softly. She cringed, as if she hated even having this thought. "I do want it to be over, Landon. I hate hiding. I hate all of this." She dramatically splayed her hands out. "It sucks."

I reached for her and pulled her close to me. I hated seeing her hurt. I hated knowing that I didn't know how to fix all of this.

"Me, too, Heidi. You know I hate this as well. I don't even want to hide you."

My lips softly brushed against hers. She dissolved into me for a heartbeat before breaking away.

"Landon," she hissed. "We're at work!"

"I know. I'm sorry. I can't help it around you."

"You are my boss. I am your employee. There is a line we're not supposed to cross, and you keep hurdling it."

"With pleasure."

She shook her head. "I hate the idea of you spending any time with Miranda. She's unpredictable, which makes her a liability. However, if you think you can make headway, then go."

"Heidi—"

"I'll be fine. I'll just…go hang out with Em. She'll understand."

I winced. Yeah, I'd hurt Emery. I'd been a total dick. I regretted how I'd acted, and I still carried a great deal of guilt over how that had all gone down. But to have Heidi insinuate that Emery would understand because Heidi was feeling the same way Emery had all those years ago? That felt like a punch to the gut.

"I'm not going. Not if you're hurting half as much as Emery was."

Heidi sighed. "No, I didn't mean that with you. I meant, Vanessa," she said, mentioning Jensen's ex-wife. "Em goes to see Colton every month and has to deal with her. She can commiserate. Seriously…just go, but don't enjoy it."

A small smile quirked on her lips, and all I wanted to do was take them for my own. To take her right here on this very desk.

"I could never enjoy a single moment spent with her… when I could be spending it with you."

She leaned forward and offered me a short peck. "Good. Now, make the bitch sign the damn paperwork."

I laughed. "Deal."

I was on my way out of the office, contemplating how to address Miranda about dinner, when Austin and Patrick came up on either side of me.

"Hey, bro," Austin said, nudging me.

"Hey, hey," Patrick said.

I could smell the whiskey coming off of Austin. *Jesus Christ.*

"Have you been drinking on the job?" I asked Austin.

He shrugged unapologetically. "Maybe?"

"One day, they are going to fire you."

"Doubtful."

"And not why we're here," Patrick said with a grin. "We heard that wifey showed up at the office today."

"God, have you been talking to Morgan?" I asked.

"She said that you were going to dinner with Miranda," Austin said. He raised his eyebrows in question.

"Yeah. I'm going to get her to sign the paperwork."

"Not a good idea," Austin said.

"What would you know about good decisions regarding relationships?" I asked with a laugh. "Either of you actually. Have you ever had a serious girlfriend?"

"Oh, there was that one time," Patrick said.

"No, there wasn't," Austin said.

"I mean…you were serious with that HR chick for, like, a hot minute."

"Julia?" I asked. "I didn't know y'all dated."

"We didn't," Austin said with annoyance. "This isn't about us. This is about Miranda. I mean, I know you're banging Heidi…"

"Could you keep your voice down?" I ground out, looking around the parking lot wildly. Luckily, there was no one nearby. *But, Jesus!*

"And Miranda has a way of fucking you over, dude. I mean, you had to marry her before you realized she was a massive bitch."

I stopped walking once we reached Jensen's Mercedes that I was still borrowing. I stared at both of them. I knew they meant well, but they couldn't possibly understand where I was coming from.

"Appreciate the concern, guys, but she's signing the paperwork. That's it," I told them.

"Should I take care of your girl while you're away?" Patrick asked with a laugh.

Before I knew what I was doing, I had slammed Patrick backward. He was pressed up against the SUV next to my car, and my hands were fisted in the front of his suit coat him. His eyes widened in alarm.

"Dude, I was joking!" Patrick cried.

"Do not ever make a joke like that about Heidi again," I growled. "Ever."

"You know I'm just fucking around," Patrick said.

"Landon, bro," Austin said, placing his hand on my sleeve.

"Ever," I repeated.

"Got it," Patrick said. "Clear as day. No jokes about Heidi."

I released him with a shove and clicked the key fob to open the car. "I'm going to this fucking dinner with my soon-to-be ex-wife, and it's the last goddamn thing that I want to do. I want this marriage to be over. I want to move on with my life. So, while I appreciate y'all trying to steer me in the right direction," I said, looking them in the eyes, one at a time, "back the fuck off."

Patrick straightened out his suit and gave me a two-fingered salute.

Austin just nodded. "Text if you need an out. We'll be happy to make a scene."

"Thanks," I said with a genuine smile.

Miranda had put me on edge. I hated that I'd gotten into an argument with my brother and his best friend. I'd just lost my shit. The idea of someone else getting near Heidi while I was trying to eliminate my baggage had made me see red. I wouldn't let that happen.

With a heavy sigh, I sank into the driver's seat of the Mercedes and sent Miranda a text.

K.A. LINDE

I'll do dinner if you agree to sign the paperwork.

*See you at seven at West Table, darling.
Wear my favorite suit.*

Twenty-Four

Landon

I showed up right on time. Not a second before or after seven. I wanted to keep my time with her to a minimum. I was already dreading this whole fucking thing. Not to mention, the last time I had been at West Table, I'd been hitting on Heidi while she was with someone else. Now, here I was, with Miranda.

And, of course, she showed up a full ten minutes late. I cringed at the fact that I had walked right into her setup. She had the upper hand already because she had kept me waiting. And I'd stayed.

Like a fucking idiot.

"Sorry I'm late," she said, not rushing in the slightest as she catwalked up to the table I'd reserved for us.

She'd changed out of her red dress for a black number that I'd never seen before and hoped to God never to see again. It was…slinky. Clearly meant to be seductive. And covered very little.

"I was about to leave," I said as way of a greeting.

She shot me a smooth smile. "No, you weren't."

I ground my teeth together. She sank down into her seat, which was a blessing since I could now only see her top half. The other problem was, now, I could see her top half.

"You wore the suit," she said with a big grin.

I looked down at the charcoal suit I had picked out with disdain. I'd probably never wear it again.

"Did you bring the paperwork? Are you going to sign now?"

"Didn't you get a good look at me? Where would I hide divorce papers? Feel free to try to find them though." She winked at me.

"I'll pass."

"Shame." Miranda flipped her blonde bob and reached for the wine menu. "I'll sign when I get home. No rush."

"So, none of this is necessary?" I glared at her and started to stand up.

"Sit down, Landon. Have some wine with me. Relax. I'll sign your precious papers. Just…" Her soulful eyes looked up into mine. "Just…let it be like old times for one night."

I didn't relax. I just stared back at her blankly. She ignored my expression and ordered a vintage bottle of her favorite French wine. She was through a glass of wine by the time we ordered our food. I had a glass in front of me, but I'd only had a sip. What I really wanted was some of Austin's whiskey. I should have stolen his flask to get through this evening.

"So," Miranda said once the waiter disappeared with our orders. She twirled the stem of her wine glass around in her hand and smiled at me.

"So?"

"I'm ready to get pregnant now."

My mouth dropped open in shock. Of all the things I had thought she would say, that hadn't been one of them. "You what?"

"Pregnant, silly. I think we should try again."

I shook my head and blinked rapidly. "Um…no."

"Well, that's why you're divorcing me, right? Because I lost the first one and then jokingly said that I didn't want any kids."

"That's not—"

"God, I get it, Landon," she said. "I mean, I understand where you're coming from. You want a big family. You come from a big family. I didn't think it was that serious. I didn't think you'd want to walk away just because I was scared."

"That is not what I'm doing."

Her eyes were bright. "Then, let's figure this out. I know I've been moody the last year. I know I haven't been my best me with you, but that doesn't mean we give up. We can try harder. We can try for another baby. Just…don't leave me."

"Miranda, you cannot do this right now."

"Do what?" she asked. "Try to save our marriage?"

"Our marriage is in the process of being dissolved. I'm here so that you'll make it official," I told her as calmly as I could. "The last thing I want is have a baby with you."

"That isn't what you said a couple months ago! You were yelling at me because of some throw away statement I made."

"Throw away…" I closed my eyes and breathed calmly through my nose. "It's more than one statement. This is bigger than that. But I am not changing my mind."

"Is it Emery?"

"How many times do I have to tell you that Emery is with Jensen, and I have no feelings for her?"

"Another time I guess because I don't believe it. It's something else."

"I can't believe I even have to say this because you already *know* why I'm divorcing you. But do I need to tell you again?"

Miranda downed the rest of her glass of wine. Clearly, this wasn't going as she'd planned. "Fine. Tell me again. Because I think you're making a huge mistake."

"I'm divorcing you because what we have is broken," I told her, clasping my hands together in front of me. "We are two different people, and it has taken me years to realize that."

"This is insane, Landon. I've given you everything. I moved to Tampa for you where I knew absolutely no one. I quit my job for you so that I could support you while you golfed. I gave up holidays with my family in Augusta to be here in this desert wasteland with your family who *hates* me. I've dealt with golf fans and cling-ons and all of that bullshit. You think I ruined your life, Landon? Look a little closer."

I almost laughed, except she really believed what she said. She was utterly delusional, and there was nothing I could say that would change her mind. She would never see that she had done all those things of her own free will to get access to my money. That *she* had been one of those golf fans and cling-ons, and I hadn't realized it at the time. That her quitting her job was because she hadn't wanted to work while I was on Tour…so she could go to all the lavish parties and act like a celebrity.

No matter what I said at this point, it wouldn't make a difference. It only proved my point.

"The answer is no," I told her as our food appeared.

"No to what?" she spat, shoving her salad away from her.

"Everything. We're here for you to sign the paperwork. That's it."

"You're not even going to consider?"

"I don't have to. This is over, Miranda."

"Then, I change my terms," she said at once.

Oh, Plan B. This should be good.

"You can't change the terms. You said dinner. That's it."

"Well, if you really think that we're never getting back together, then this won't even matter."

I cocked my head to the side. I really didn't even want to know. "No."

"One more thing, and then I'm out of your life forever… just like you want."

"What? What thing?"

She smiled and leaned forward, exposing more of her cleavage. "Make love to me one more time."

I gaped at her and then burst into laughter. I couldn't help myself. It was so…outrageous. Of course she wanted to fuck again. Probably somewhere in her sick, demented head, she thought that, by having sex once more, I would magically change my mind. That I'd realize she was still the perfect woman for me, and we'd end up together.

Or worse, she'd try to get pregnant and get me on the hook forever.

I shook my head in disgust and pulled out my wallet. I threw a hundred dollars down for the meal and tossed another hundred at her. "For the good time I'll be missing."

She gaped at me. "Landon!"

"The answer is no," I said as I stood. "Actually, the answer is fuck no. I'd rather see you in court than sit here another minute."

"Landon, wait!"

As I exited the restaurant, I chuckled at myself for how stupid I'd been for coming. Everyone was right. She wasn't going to sign the papers just because I had gone to dinner with her. It had been worth a try but worth nothing more than that.

I tried Heidi's number when I got back to the car, but she didn't answer. I revved the Mercedes and peeled out of the parking lot, on my way to her apartment. I didn't care if Emery was there. I needed to see Heidi. I needed to get the slime of that dinner off my body. It was a mistake to go, and while I had known that deep down, I had wanted it all to be over so fucking bad.

And fuck Miranda and her fucking stipulations. She didn't get to put stipulations on this divorce. She'd had plenty of time to fix our marriage. It had been falling apart for a year.

I'd defended her to everyone, and then I'd just realized they were all right.

I was almost to Heidi's apartment when I got a text from her.

Flips.

I cursed and pulled a U-turn, on my way to the bar she adored. Considering her history with her father, you'd think she wouldn't love bars as much as she did. But I knew they still held happy memories for her. Maybe that was what she always clung to when she came to Flips to hustle pool from unsuspecting victims. It probably helped her forget her dad as much as it brought positive memories. For someone who'd had a pretty rough life, she was unbelievably buoyant. I admired her for that. For pushing through all the bullshit and coming out ahead. And, one day…I'd get her to talk about it all.

I parked out front of the bar and killed the engine. The place was surprisingly busy for a Monday night, but it always had its regulars.

My regular was standing in low-slung jean shorts and a black tank top that said *Hank's* in distressed white letters. She had a pool stick behind her neck, and she was holding on to it with both hands. The guy standing next to her was looking at her as if she were his next meal, but she just urged him to take his shot. When he missed, her laugh rang through the bar, and she stumbled forward, dropping the pool stick to her side.

She was drunk.

My face fell as I approached her.

I could see it in her languid body movements and the tilt of her shoulders as she stepped up to the table. She bent over to aim for her shot, and half of her ass cheeks hung out the back of her shorts. It was hot as fuck. But it wasn't on display for me. It was on display for every fucking dick in this place.

And, suddenly, I was furious.

Not with Heidi. With myself.

I had been out at some shit dinner with my horrible soon-to-be ex-wife. I had made Heidi come here where she needed to play pool and get sloppy drunk to forget. I had done this.

And, now, everyone in the room was getting a full view of her ass because of my goddamn mistake.

No fucking way.

My appearance was noticed before I made it all the way up to her.

"Hey, man," the guy she was playing said to me. "What's up?"

I ignored him as Heidi's eyes locked on to mine.

"Landon!"

"Time to go."

"No way! I have, like…a whole beer here, and I'm totally slaying Tommy over here."

I arched an eyebrow at her.

She rolled her eyes back at me. "You were *busy*."

"I'm not busy anymore," I said, my voice low and uncompromising.

"I'll just finish this game."

"No."

"Hey, pal, why don't you let the lady do what she wants?" Tommy said.

"Why don't you find another half-naked drunk girl to hit on?" I spat back at him. "I'm going to be here, taking care of this one."

Heidi walked up to me and poked me in the chest. "I don't *need* to be taken care of."

I stepped up to meet her. "You're right. You don't need to be taken care of, but I am going to take care of you anyway. You can't convince me otherwise. And, right now, I would like to put some clothes on you and get you away from every guy in this place who wants to whip his dick out right now."

"Oh, you want to put clothes *on* me?" she said with another eye roll. "That's new."

I shrugged out of my suit coat and slung it around her shoulders.

She protested, "I'm fine!"

"We should get you home."

"Ugh, why?"

"You have work in the morning. You're drunk. You need to talk to me, and this isn't helping as much as you want to believe."

Her eyes glazed over, and she quickly glanced away from me. She was hurt. I knew that. I could see that.

"I'm staying here," she said halfheartedly.

"Don't make me throw you over my shoulder and carry you out of this bar."

"You wouldn't," she spat. "Your back."

I arched an eyebrow. "Watch me."

She bit her lip, as if she had more concern for my injury than she had for trying to talk to me. I appreciated the sentiment because throwing her over my shoulder would probably be a really dumb move. But I'd do it anyway.

"Fine," she said, throwing her pool stick onto the table and storming out before me.

I sighed heavily and followed after her. "Heidi," I called when we made it outside. "Hey, are you okay?"

She whirled around on me. "You know, I made out with that guy Tommy on New Year's."

I clenched my jaw. "No, I didn't know that."

"Yeah. He's, like, a totally normal guy. We hit it off real fine. And when you left me there all alone, I went and found someone else. I made out with him because you weren't there. You were married. You couldn't be with me. And I wanted to forget you."

"You can't forget me, Heidi. No matter how far you try to push me away or come up with reasons that we can't be together, we will always end up right here." I pointed at the pavement between us. "Because I am yours, and you are mine. And we are not just a finite point on a line; we are limitless."

Twenty-Five

Heidi

"Jesus, Landon," I whispered, crumbling at his words.

I had been so busy being drunk and frustrated and freaking jealous that I wasn't able to see past my own ego. I didn't know what had happened at that dinner with Miranda. I only had worst-case scenarios running through my head even though I'd told him to go. Or maybe because I'd told him to go.

When I wanted to tell him to stay.

Stay.

Just stay with me.

Don't give in to her.

Don't listen to her.

Please, God, don't fuck this up.

Landon bridged the short distance between us and placed a soft kiss on my lips. The fire extinguished out of me in a rush. I melted into him, throwing my arms around his neck.

"I'm so glad you're here," I whispered.

"Me, too, firecracker. Me, too."

I laughed. That goddamn nickname.

"Can we get you home now?" he asked, pointing toward the Mercedes.

"What about my car?"

"We'll get it in the morning."

I nodded with a sigh. "Yeah. Okay."

We piled into the car, and he drove me back to my apartment in silence. I had a million questions buzzing around my head, but I wasn't sure if I wanted to ask them. My brain was fuzzy, and I knew that I'd had too much to drink. Like, if I could tell that I was pretty drunk, that was a bad sign. I was one of those people who would constantly claim, *I'm not drunk*, when I clearly was.

But Peter knew what week it was. So, I wasn't surprised that he never cut me off tonight.

Landon helped me stumble up to my apartment, and I was happy to see that Emery wasn't there. She slept over at Jensen's all the time anyway. And I did not want to have that awkward moment with her and Landon. It would have to happen one day. Preferably not while I was wasted.

"Which way?" Landon asked as he shut the door behind us.

I was suddenly self-conscious of the fact that Landon was here, in my apartment. I'd been to his, but he'd never been here.

"Uh...that room." I pointed out my bedroom.

He put his hand on the small of my back as we walked across the elaborately decorated living room and into my bedroom. It was pretty big for the size of the apartment. I liked that I could have a massive king-size bed, and it didn't fill up the entire room. That had been the selling point...along with the walk-in closet and stand-up shower.

"Fuck," I said as I nearly ran into my four-poster bed. My head was spinning. "How much did I drink tonight?"

"I'm going to go with a lot. You were this drunk that night we played pool with Em last Christmas."

"No way," I slurred. "Em was way drunker than me that night."

"Yes. But you were wasted, too."

"And you wouldn't even help me inside."

"Yes, well," he said, glancing away from me.

"What?"

I leaned against a post of my bed and stared at him. His eyes met mine, full of desire, and suddenly, I was so fucking turned on. One look, and I was a goner.

"I didn't trust myself to come inside," he admitted.

"Oh? Why not?" I asked with a grin.

"Because I wanted more than I was allowed to have that night, and you would have given me what I wanted."

"I would have," I agreed softly.

I'd wanted him so bad. He'd driven me home from Flips that night because I was drunk, and all I'd wanted to do was kiss him. I was sure that I had been blatantly telegraphing that. He'd read it all over my expression. And, instead of coming inside where he surely would have cheated on his wife, he'd left.

Part of me had been frustrated because of the connection that was clearly there, but part of me, the sober part of me, appreciated that he'd left. He could have been the dick who cheated to get out of his marriage, but he wasn't that guy. He hadn't been that guy on New Year's either. He'd stopped talking to me. Even though I'd hated it. And then he'd waited until it was the right time for us.

Like now.

"But you can have it tonight," I told him.

He grinned. "I think you're a bit drunk tonight."

"So? You wouldn't be taking advantage of me."

"Oh, I most certainly would be."

I shrugged off the suit jacket he had thrown on my shoulders earlier, leaving me in nothing but my jean shorts and tank top. I moved over to where he was standing, half-in and half-out of my bedroom. My hands fell to his belt buckle.

"You don't look like you want to be in this suit anymore."

"I'd be happy to burn the suit."

"Did she touch your suit?" I asked, my voice gritty and sharp.

"She looked at it. That was enough for me."

"Me, too. Definitely burning it." I unbuckled the belt and then fumbled with the button before sliding down the zipper. My eyes were still glued on his. "We'll probably have to take it off first."

He chuckled hoarsely. "You're going to be the death of me."

I grinned. My fingers slipped the knot of his tie free and let it loose. Then, I worked up the buttons of his crisp white shirt. I fumbled a few times as I tried in my haste to get the shirt off, but he grinned and eased out the last few buttons. I pressed my hands against his rock-hard abdomen and then up his smooth, cut chest. My nails dug into his shoulders as I pushed his shirt off his smoking-hot body.

God, he was sexy as hell. I wanted him naked like I hadn't wanted anything else. The alcohol might be fueling me, but it didn't change anything about how much I wanted him.

"Fuck, Heidi," he said.

He leaned into me and captured my lips. His kiss was urgent and needy. He wanted this as much as I did. Our bodies crashed together, and soon, I was pressed back against a post on my bed. His hands reached for my jean shorts and popped the button.

"Every guy in the fucking bar wanted in these shorts." He grabbed my ass with one hand as he shoved his other down the front of my shorts. "It killed me that I wasn't with you, that I couldn't claim you right then and there."

He swirled his finger around my clit, and I gasped against him. Everything felt heightened. My skin tingled. My heart jackhammered in my chest. My fingers dug into his biceps. My body gave in to the sensations that only Landon Wright elicited. He was a match that struck a fire within me.

"Oh, yeah? Is that why you were willing to throw me over your shoulder?"

"I was willing to do a lot more than that. I would have been perfectly happy with bending this hot ass over the pool table."

"And here I thought, I was the jealous one," I told him.

He gently lifted my chin until I looked up into his dark eyes. "You do not have a single thing to be jealous about. You are my one and only."

I leaned into his embrace and tenderly kissed him.

He was too good to be true. He was proving to be everything I'd ever wanted. It was hard for me not to think that something might happen to change that. Especially with Miranda in town. But here we were, in my bedroom, and he only had eyes for me.

He stripped me out of my shorts, and soon, my tank top followed. Every place that he touched me, my body was scorching. A trail of heat spread straight between my legs. I whimpered at his touch as he leaned me backward onto the bed.

His cock jutted out of his boxer briefs, and he easily freed himself, dropping his underwear to the floor. I reached out and wrapped my hand around him. I stroked him up and down until his eyes glazed over, and he practically ripped my underwear off.

"You don't want me to finish?" I asked, licking my lips.

"God, yes, but I want inside your pussy more."

He gripped my hips and pressed the tip of his dick against my opening. I moaned and arched backward. He pushed a little further and then eased out. I thought I was going to explode if he didn't continue. We'd talked over the weekend about the fact that I was on the pill, but I could still feel him hesitate.

"Landon, please," I whimpered.

"You're sure?" he asked.

I wrapped my legs around his waist and pulled him closer to show him how sure I was. "God, please, fuck me."

He didn't need to be told twice.

Landon thrust forward then all the way. Our bodies collided together, roughly and fully. He grabbed my hands and pushed them over my head. Holding them in place, he gripped my hips and started driving into me. All the frustration and tension and jealousy that had bottled up between us seemed to explode in that moment.

Here, we were together.

Here, the rest of the world didn't exist.

Here, he wasn't my boss.

We were just two people taking what we could get—to hell with the consequences.

"Oh, fuck, Heidi," he said, leaning over me to steal a kiss. "You feel so fucking good."

"Oh God, yes," I panted.

He picked up his tempo. Our bodies rocked together. And, soon, the bruising pace sent me straight over the edge. I cried out his name into the night as he came with me.

Our bodies were slick with sweat, our lips swollen. And I had never felt better.

"I think I need a shower."

I giggled unavoidably. "Yes. We both do."

"Come on, firecracker. Let's get you cleaned up."

Landon eased out of me, and then we both headed into the shower. Exhaustion settled over my whole body as soon as the hot spray hit my skin. I could have slept for days after that. Landon must have noticed the fight go out of my limbs because he did most of the work. He took his time in lathering up my body with the eucalyptus bath soap I adored. His hands were deft and slippery. He ran his fingers through my long hair and massaged my scalp. It was heavenly, and it made me forget for a little bit longer what was to come later this week. The real reason I was irritated and weary.

Once we were both clean, Landon wrapped a towel around my shoulders and kissed my lips. "You look tired. Why don't you crawl into bed, and I'll find you some clothes?"

I nodded absentmindedly and walked to the bed. I toweled off most of the water and then knotted the towel in my hair before climbing into bed. My body succumbed to the soft comforter and down pillows on contact. I vaguely heard Landon slip back into his boxer briefs and rummage through my drawers.

"T-shirts are in the closet," I mumbled.

"You hang up all your T-shirts?"

"Yes. I'm a bit obsessive."

He laughed and then entered the walk-in closet, flicking on the overhead light. He returned a minute later with a high school cheerleading shirt in hand and a pair of underwear.

"No shorts?" I asked, pushing the covers back and sitting up to slide into the clothes.

"I'd love to keep you naked all night, but I think you need to sleep. And I want to be able to grab your ass."

I laughed as I tugged on the T-shirt. "You're ridiculous."

"Probably," he said with a shrug. "Hey, what are all those letters in there?"

I froze in place, my hand halfway to pulling my hair out of the towel. "What?" I squeaked.

"You realize you have a huge collection of letters in a box in your closet, right?" he said with an easy laugh as he walked around to the other side of the bed.

"You went through my letters?" I asked, panicked.

"No." He turned to look at me, as if just realizing that I was freaking out. "I just saw them. They're sitting out in the open."

"They're nothing. Forget about them," I said a little too hastily.

"Heidi—"

"I said, forget about them." I raised my voice and stormed into the bathroom to hang up my towel. My hands were shaking as I put it on a hook on the back of the door, and my stomach was in knots. I hadn't even thought about him seeing the letters. I hadn't considered he would ask.

Landon knocked twice on the bathroom door and sighed. "Heidi, come out here, please."

I took a deep breath and opened the door. "Hey."

"I'm sorry. I didn't realize that would upset you. I was legitimately curious."

I nodded twice and then stepped into his open arms. "It's…it's okay. I just…I wasn't prepared."

"It's okay. Let's go to bed, all right?"

I nodded.

We crawled into bed, and Landon turned off the last light, casting us into darkness. He pulled me tight against his chest and kissed my shoulder. I lay there, completely content with just listening to the rise and fall of his chest and his gentle breathing. I waited until I was sure he was almost asleep before getting up the guts to say anything.

"They're from my dad," I whispered.

It was the first time I had ever said that aloud. I was pretty sure Emery knew, but we didn't talk about it.

"I thought they might be," Landon said into my shoulder.

"I don't answer them."

"Ever?"

"Not once in six years."

Landon sighed softly. "Is that when he went to prison?"

I nodded. My voice was hoarse when I said, "Six years on Saturday."

"That's a long time not to talk to him."

"Not long enough," I countered.

Landon pressed another kiss into my shoulder. I thought he knew not to press me on it and that it was a big step that I had even told him this much. As often as we had talked before and as much as everyone in the town knew about Hank Martin's illegal affairs, no one ever dared to talk about it with me.

"And, on Saturday…are you going to be okay?"

"I usually spend the day alone," I admitted.

"I don't want you to be alone this year," he told me. "Not anymore. Not when you have me. Okay?"

I nodded because words were failing me. "Okay."

Twenty-Six

Heidi

I woke up to the sound of the door slamming, and Emery yelling my name, "Heidi?"

"Oh, fuck," I murmured.

Landon groaned next to me and tugged me closer to him. Either he was the deepest sleeper ever or he simply didn't care that my best friend, his freaking ex-girlfriend, was about to walk in on us while we were half-naked.

"Landon," I said, shoving him. "Get up. Get up. Get up. You need to…like, hide in the closet."

His brown eyes slowly opened and stared up at me. He had a sexy grin on his face and said, "Morning."

"Landon, come on."

"Did you say, hide in the closet?" he asked, as if just processing what I'd said.

"Yeah, Emery is—"

Just then Emery burst into the room, dressed in a pair of tiny black shorts and an oversize black T-shirt. It could have been Jensen's.

"Oh, shit," Emery said.

"Home," I finished.

Landon languidly rolled over and stretched his arms over his head. "Morning, Em."

"Oh my God," she said, holding her hands up over her eyes. "That was not...I mean—fuck. I'm just going to—yep, all right then." She stumbled backward out of the doorway.

I groaned. "Ugh!"

Landon laughed, reaching for me. "Why are you so embarrassed?"

I pushed him back into the pillow. "You are *such* a dude."

"Hey, hey," he said, holding up his hands. "She's the one dating my brother."

I threw my pillow at him as I jumped out of bed. "And do you want to see her in bed with him?"

He scrunched up his nose.

"Yeah, I didn't think so."

I knotted my hair up on the top of my head as I left my bedroom to go find my best friend. "Hey, Em?"

"In here," Emery called from her bedroom.

"Hey."

She waved her hand as she dug through her closet for clothes to wear to work.

"Sorry about that."

"It's no big," she said. "I just...was a hundred percent unprepared for that."

"Yeah, I guess it's probably pretty weird."

Emery shot me a no-shit look. "That's a word for it."

"I know you said that you were cool with it, but I really don't want you to feel uncomfortable in your own apartment. We don't have to be here if you don't—"

Emery held up her hand. "Bring it down a level, hooker. I don't care that you're together, and I don't want you to have to go somewhere else."

"But?" I prompted.

"But…I don't know how long I can keep this from Jensen."

Landon stuck his head in the bedroom. Thankfully, he'd shrugged back into his button-up and slacks. "Sorry, just happened to overhear."

Emery rolled her eyes at him. "Yeah, because we're so quiet."

"Telling Jensen would be a really bad idea for Heidi at this point."

Emery threw down the pair of shoes she'd been holding. "I'm going crazy over here. Secrets are a big thing between me and Jensen, and if he thinks I'm holding something back, then he's going to get pissed. And, trust me, no one likes when that happens. Least of all, me."

"Yeah, but if we tell Jensen, I could lose my job," I said.

"Or we could figure something out!" Emery cried.

"I love my brother, but we all know he solves problems with a blunt instrument," Landon said.

"What if we talked to Morgan?" Emery asked.

"Already did."

"Fuck," Emery groaned. "Okay, okay. I can figure this out, but if he shows up and y'all are together, I never knew!"

"Got it," Landon agreed.

I nodded. "Thanks, Em."

"You owe me," Emery told me. "And you…you should be lucky it's my best friend."

Landon held his arms up. "We both appreciate it, Emery. Even if we don't both deserve it."

She nodded her head as Landon eased out of the bedroom.

"I have to get ready for work," Emery said with a sigh. "Will you please be careful? I could have easily had Jensen with me, and we'd be having a much different conversation."

"I'd like to avoid that conversation if at all possible."

"Me, too," she muttered. Emery's eyes cut to mine again. "This is so weird. You're sleeping with Landon Wright. Like... Landon Wright."

"Yeah," I said with a one-shoulder shrug. "Guess so."

"And it's the week of...and you seem okay."

I swallowed hard. "I'm holding up. I told him last night... about everything."

"Holy shit, Heidi. That's huge. Y'all are really serious, aren't you?"

I bit my lip and did a brisk nod. "I feel like it all happened so fast, yet...I've been waiting for this moment for so long. Just finding a guy who really gets me, you know?"

Emery looked down and grinned. "That, I do. And I'm also queen of realizing that it's not always the guy you expected you'd fall for."

"What is it with these Wright brothers?" I asked.

"If only I knew."

"Seriously."

"Falling for them only pads their egos," Emery said.

I snort-laughed. "As if their egos need padding."

"Yet we love them."

"We do," I agreed softly.

Emery laughed. "Okay, seriously, work. Go put some clothes on, you slob. You're super naked."

I tugged on the T-shirt I had on, suddenly remembering I'd never put on shorts. "Whatever. You like it, ho."

"Oh, yeah, baby. Take it all off."

I tugged at the bottom of my shirt, giving her a peek of my stomach. "Come and get it, lover."

Emery winked at me before I disappeared around the corner.

I breathed a sigh of relief. I was the luckiest fucking person in the world to have a friend like her. It was no joke when I said that she was the only family I had left. I worried more about what she thought than about losing my job at this point. I knew that she was putting on an act, too. She wasn't a hundred percent comfortable with me and Landon, but she loved me and wanted me to be happy. I hoped that we could all figure out how to handle this over time.

"She okay?" Landon asked when I stepped back into my bedroom.

"I think she's adjusting."

"Yeah, welcome to the club."

"You know what? Don't use that tone with me about Emery. You were the one who ditched her on graduation day and left her in tattered pieces that I had to put back together for years, Landon."

He held his hands up in defense. "Whoa. Okay. I didn't mean to upset you like that. I meant that I had to adjust to her and Jensen. At least you told her about us before she walked in on us."

"I know," I said with a shake of my head. "I get defensive about Emery. You really hurt her, you know."

He scratched the back of his head. "Yeah. Trust me, I carry around the guilt from it. I was mad about what had happened with my dad, that the last thing I'd ever said to him was that I chose Emery over him and that I would every time. When he died, I blamed myself, and I stupidly blamed Emery. I couldn't even look at her or think about her or talk to her without that pain. So, yeah, I get that you want to protect her. I was a dick to push her away when I was grieving, but it was high school. I have apologized for how I acted. And what happened with me and Emery has absolutely nothing to do with what's happening with me and you, Heidi."

"That was what you said to your dad?" I asked softly.

"Uh…yeah," he said, glancing off. "Did I never tell you that?"

"I…no. I knew you got into an argument about college."

"Yeah, well, what I wouldn't give to redo those days. But then I don't know if I'd be standing right here, and I know this is where I'm supposed to be."

I stepped into his arms, rested my head on his shoulder, and closed my eyes. This was where I was meant to be, too.

"We should probably get my car," I whispered, tightening my grip on him.

"And get to work," he agreed.

"But there's a bed."

His hands slipped down to my ass as he toed the door closed. "And this ass. Fuck."

Needless to say, we were both late to work.

———

I beat him to the office because he still had to go home and change after dropping me off at my car. But I made a mad dash as soon as I hit the building. My heels were not cooperating with me either, and for the first time in a while, I wished that I'd chosen flats. Even though the heels made me feel empowered.

I was feeling pretty empowered regardless of my shoe choice today.

Julia was waiting at my desk when I arrived. She was impatiently tapping her black flats as Matt tried to engage her in conversation. Julia had a total don't-fuck-with-me vibe that Matt had to either be too stupid or too self-absorbed to realize. I was starting to suspect both.

"There you are!" Julia cried, jumping up from my seat.

"Yeah, sorry about that. Car trouble."

"Landon must have had the same kind of car trouble," Matt muttered under his breath.

"What?" I asked, hoping I sounded confused. Even though my heart was thwacking away inside my chest like a bird in a cage.

"Landon isn't in yet," Julia informed me.

"Really? Weird. Did he really have car trouble?" I asked.

Matt eyed me suspiciously, as if not buying what I was saying. "We don't know. He's just not here."

I shrugged. "Doesn't he have physical therapy or something?"

"For what?" Matt asked.

"Golf injury."

"How do you know so much about Landon anyway?"

"Well…we've been friends since high school. He dated my best friend."

"Huh," Matt said. His eyebrows scrunched together, as if he were contemplating something really hard.

I hoped he was thinking that the line I'd fed him was the truth.

Sure, Landon and I were *friends*. Yep.

"I didn't realize that," Matt said finally.

"Anyway," Julia said, "we're not here to talk about Landon. I'm here to schedule your interview."

"My interview for the lead engineer spot?" I gasped, bouncing on the balls of my feet.

"Yes. That's right."

"Congrats, Heidi," Matt said. "I scheduled mine yesterday."

I nearly turned and glared at Matt. *Way to steal my thunder, dude.*

"Oh my God, yes. Let's do this."

Julia nodded toward her office, and I followed her inside.

She shut the door and whirled on me. "Please tell me that you and Landon are not both late because you were together."

"We're not both late because we were together," I told her.

225

"It looks bad, Heidi."

"I know," I admitted.

"That creep Matt is picking up on things, and I don't want him to put the pieces together about you two. I thought you were going to be smart about this. Showing up late, missing work at the same time, hanging out in his office, going to lunch together? Heidi, come on."

I bit my lip. I knew she was right. I knew that we were being reckless. We definitely needed to be more careful if even dummy Matt was starting to see through things.

"I got it. I got it," I said.

Julia leaned forward, her hair swishing in front of her face. "You are a serious contender for this promotion, Heidi. I shouldn't even freaking tell you this, but you are."

I beamed at her, but I understood the underlying sentiment. I wouldn't get the job if someone found out about me and Landon. I'd get fired. "I got it, Julia."

"Good. Now that that's over, let's pen you in for Thursday morning at nine o'clock with Dennis."

"Sounds good."

"Now, what are you doing on Saturday? Because I could desperately use some shopping for the Wright Charity Benefit."

I opened my mouth and then closed it.

Julia had only been working for Wright Construction for about a year. We had become friends almost immediately, but she knew very little about my past. She definitely didn't know that Saturday was the anniversary of the day my dad had been thrown into prison.

"Uh…Saturday isn't good. How about Sunday?"

She wrinkled her nose. "Trevor is dragging me to church with him and his entire family."

"Oh, you're meeting the family?"

"Yeah. Should be interesting. Unfortunately, they go to the same church as the Wrights."

"That means…Austin will be there?" I guessed.

"Yeah. Dick."

I laughed. "Okay. Not Sunday. We'll figure it out. Still plenty of time before the Benefit."

"True. Just let me know if you change your mind about Saturday. I could use some time with my girls!"

I nodded even though I had no intention of doing so, and I waved bye to Julia.

Landon was entering the premises when I left Julia's office. He looked hot as fuck in crisp khaki pants and a blue blazer. It was the most *him* I'd seen him dress since he started working here. His khakis and polo—i.e., typical golf attire—suited him better than a suit.

He grinned at me. "Good morning."

"You're late, Mr. Wright."

"Had a busy morning."

"Me, too. Found out I have an interview for Jim's job," I said, falling into step beside him.

"Congratulations," he said with an even smile.

"And that Matt suspects something is going on," I quietly told him.

Landon quickly masked his surprise. "Huh. Is that right?"

"Yep. We should be more careful."

"Duly noted, Miss Martin. Good luck on your interview."

He nodded at me and then headed for his desk, as if he didn't care one way or another if I wanted to talk to him. He acted like my boss. And I could feel Matt's gaze on mine as I walked away from Landon without a backward glance. I despised what we were doing, but I couldn't stop now. And, frankly, I didn't want to.

"So, why was he late?" Matt asked me when I sat down.

"Don't know. He said he had a busy morning," I said with a shrug.

"Could you imagine if I used that as my excuse?" he huffed.

"Well, he's the boss."

Matt nodded his head and turned his attention back to his computer. "Fucking Wrights," he muttered under his breath. "They could get away with murder."

He wasn't wrong.

Twenty-Seven

Heidi

S aturday morning started like any other day.
The world turned. The sun rose. Life went on.

Except it didn't.

Today was the only day of the year that my life *didn't* go on. Today was the day that my dad had been charged and sentenced to prison. In my world, that meant, he'd died. And I mourned his death only on this day.

I woke up with the sun—alone and strangely buoyant. Normally, I pushed away the thought of my dad…the death of my mom. I didn't think about it. I didn't let it hurt me. I stayed strong and powerful, despite my circumstances, but today, I'd let myself feel it all.

Landon had wanted to stay the night. After staying as far away from each other as possible at the office, we'd be glued together at night—hot, sweaty, and desperate to be close to each other. But I'd needed last night alone, and he'd promised to come over in the morning.

I changed into jean shorts and a pink T-shirt with tennis shoes. Nothing fancy for my old man. I'd been a daddy's girl my whole life. His little pink princess. With a sigh, I laced up my shoes and headed out into the living room.

Emery was seated at the counter with a stack of papers in front of her to grade for school. She pushed a cup of coffee toward me.

"Thanks," I said, adding cream and sugar.

"How are you doing?" Her eyes were wide and wary.

She knew what today was. She knew I was normally messed up all week, anticipating it.

"Ready to face the day."

Emery placed her hand on mine and squeezed. "You're an incredible person, you have a brilliant mind, and you are my best friend. You know that, right?"

I smiled. "Thanks."

"Come here."

I stepped into my best friend's arms, and we held each other tight.

"I love you, Heidi."

"Love you, too, Em."

"Call me if you need me."

I nodded and then pulled away. I was used to doing this routine alone, so I'd told Landon that I would pick him up. It helped me to be in control of the situation, to have my hands on the wheel and know exactly where I was going.

I drove across town to his apartment, and he was waiting for me in khaki shorts and a blue polo with tennis shoes, Ray-Bans, and a hat. He looked comfortable and laid-back, which was what I'd suggested. It was nice to see him out of his stuffy suit...and in something other than his birthday suit. Though that one was my favorite.

He popped open the passenger door and sank into the seat. "Morning, gorgeous."

"Hey," I said with a sad smile. "You ready?"

"As long as you are."

I bit my lip and then put the car in drive.

We didn't speak as we drove. He seemed comfortable with the silence. I needed it. There were too many thoughts—ideas, stories, memories—running through my head and cluttering my mind. Everything I never let myself think about, which overloaded me on this day. I was the queen of compartmentalization, but when I stepped back and looked at the file drawers of memories categorized in my mind, everything just tumbled out. Rows and rows of cards and videos and letters that just took over. I let myself feel it, breathe it in. It ached like nothing else. But I needed to feel it to stay sane.

We pulled into the cemetery a few minutes later, and Landon inhaled sharply. It was the biggest cemetery in Lubbock with enormous headstones and even a crypt or two. And everyone knew someone who lived here.

I maneuvered into a huge parking lot and killed the engine. I'd deposited flowers in the backseat before coming to get Landon and grabbed them as we got out of the car. He wrapped a strong arm around my shoulders as we silently threaded through the tombstones.

My mother was waiting in the center of the stones.

MARY ELIZABETH MARTIN

JUNE 21, 1969—OCTOBER 17, 2000

A GOOD MOTHER, WIFE, AND FRIEND

I placed the flowers in front of her gravestone. Orchids—her favorite.

The worst part was, I never knew what to say. It was why I didn't visit as often as I probably should have. Because, when

I talked to my mom, it was hard not to mention my dad. She'd asked about him. And the answers hurt too much.

He's not the guy you knew.

He's not a good dad anymore.

He gave up on you. On me. On himself.

You'd be ashamed of him now.

Landon gently rubbed my back. I was glad he was here. Even if it was hard for him since both of his parents were buried here, too.

"Hey, Mom," I whispered. "I, uh…just wanted to stop by and introduce you to Landon. He's, uh…a, uh, Wright. You probably knew his dad." I glanced over at Landon, and he just smiled. "He's kind of my boyfriend, and I thought you should meet."

"Nice to meet you, Mrs. Martin. You have a real great girl here," Landon said. Then, he turned to face me. "So, I'm kind of your boyfriend, huh?"

"That's right."

"I'm looking forward to the day we can get rid of that *kind of* part."

"Me, too," I whispered. "You know, few years I'll be as old as my mom when she died. It's scary to think that I'll live longer than she did."

"I know how that feels. I was only seven when my mom died. I was older than her almost two years ago. It was disorienting."

"Do you want to see her while we're here?"

He kissed my forehead. "How about we do it when I can introduce you to both of them as my girlfriend…not just *kind of?*"

I grinned, despite myself. "I'd like that."

"What else do you do on this day?" he asked.

"I usually do all the things that I would have done with my parents before my mom died. It's like I get to mourn them both on the same day. It's kind of like…I give myself permission to be a kid again. It's dumb. I know. I never tell anyone about it."

He placed a finger on my lips. "The way you grieve is never dumb. It is unique to every person. Allowing yourself the time to do it is what's important."

I threw my arms around his middle and held him tight. I didn't know how I had gotten so lucky to have someone like Landon Wright. But I was thanking all things holy for sending me a person who understood me so completely.

We left the cemetery with an improved mood and headed out to The Orchard, which was an apple orchard about twenty minutes outside of town. They always held the Apple Butter Festival, an apple-picking event, this time of year.

Landon carried the basket while we walked around the orchard and filled it with apples. And, the whole time we meandered through the craft vendors, listened to music from local artists, and even tried to hit an apple with a slingshot, I told him stories.

The stories I always replayed in my head as I did this alone every year.

"Dad used to put me on his shoulders when I was kid so that I could reach the high branches in the trees. It was my favorite part, getting to throw apples down to my mom," I told him.

He smiled at the fond memory.

"Sometimes, I would swing back and forth between their arms. We came every year, you know. My mom adored fresh apples. Later, when we got home, she would make me a homemade apple pie. She'd always remind me to blow on it to cool it down. As a kid, I always wanted to eat the ice cream, but now, I would kill for a slice of her pie."

"Let's make one when we get back," he suggested.

I shook my head. "No, I don't have her recipe. It's different. I tried."

"All right, love," he said, kissing me on the cheek.

"Ready for our next stop?" I asked.

He arched an eyebrow. "There's more?"

I nodded. "Yeah."

"Lead the way."

We left the festival, only to stop halfway to our next destination to get ice cream from Dairy Queen. I ordered both a large M&M Blizzard and a Peanut Butter Cup Blizzard and set them both in front of me. Landon got a chocolate-dipped cone.

He curiously eyed the extra Blizzard.

"For my dad," I whispered.

"You used to come here a lot?"

"Over the summer, he would bring home extra super-large DQ Blizzards that would last me the whole summer. My mom hated it, but she'd sneak some of his ice cream when he wasn't looking."

"And, normally, you'd come and eat one of these alone?"

"Yeah, well, it was a reminder of happier times, you know? Before the…drugs and…and everything." I hiccuped over the last word and glanced away.

"I get it," he said, covering my hand. "I like knowing this side of you."

"Thanks for being here with me."

"I wouldn't have missed it. If you need me, I'm here."

I nodded my head and then returned to my Blizzard. Truly, there was no way I was going to finish it, but I couldn't bring it back to the apartment with all the memories it held. So, when Landon finished his cone, I dumped the rest of the Blizzards, and we headed out.

"I hope you know how to roller skate," I told him as we pulled into the parking lot.

He laughed. "Uh, I haven't skated in years."

"Just don't break your back."

"Too late for that."

We each rented a set of crappy skates and laced them up on a black, neon-green, and neon-pink carpeted bench that glowed in the black lights. A couple of regulars, middle schoolers, who could skate circles around everyone in the place, were already showing off to the shitty techno music blaring through the speakers. But the stale smell of burned popcorn, overloads of sugar, and cheap pizza, coupled with the feel of wheels under my feet, brought me to a different place. A different place.

It was as if I had been transported.

"I'm really not good at skating," Landon admitted as he eased onto his feet.

"Color me surprised. A Wright actually isn't good at something."

"We're bad at a lot of stuff."

"Well, I'll hold your hand, pretty boy. Come here."

He took my hands, and I skated backward like a pro, guiding him and getting him back into a rhythm. After we did a lap or two, he stopped thinking so hard about what his feet were doing and started enjoying himself. That meant I could show off, and it was fun. God, it was so fun.

"Where did you learn to skate like that?" Landon asked in awe.

I grinned as I weaved my feet back and forth. "My dad."

"Hank Martin roller-skated?" he asked practically uncomprehendingly.

"He was amazing. Grew up in an age where roller-skating was cheap, and all the cool kids did it. Showing off was my dad's pastime."

"Don't know anyone else like that," he said sarcastically.

I laughed, comfortable with the statement today. Most other days, I wouldn't appreciate the comparison to my father. "I do have a flair for the dramatic."

"I like that about you."

"What don't you like, Wright?"

He cocked his head to the side. "Nothing."

"Give me time."

"I've known you for a long time, Heidi. Not going to change how I feel now."

He took my hand and tugged me back around so that we could skate like a brand-new middle school couple showing off to our friends. It was strangely romantic in a completely unassuming way.

By the time the later afternoon birthday crowds started showing up, Landon and I decided to call it quits. Roller-skating wasn't the best thing for his back anyway. I could tell he was in some pain but didn't want to ruin my day with it.

I ordered him to return our shoes as I snagged us some pizza and a Coke. We ate like it was fine dining, laughing over how the cheese seemed to slide off the entire slice and the bottom had the consistency of cardboard. But it was delicious. And being with him like this was equally delicious.

"Where are we going next?" he asked as the sun was finally setting on the horizon. "Flips? For pool?"

"No," I said with a sigh. "Hank's."

Landon glanced over at me in confusion. "But Hank's was demolished."

"I know." I swiped at the tear in my eye at the mention that my father's beloved bar had been torn down by Wright Construction to put up high-end condominiums. And that I'd then gone and worked for the people who had done it.

I stopped the car in front of the condos, and Landon and I both slid out. I nodded my head at the small park across the street. It was deserted at this hour, and we easily found a park bench that faced the condos. As I faced the building that used to be my home away from home, where I'd spent more hours than my own home, tears poured out of my eyes. And I let them. I let myself feel all the pain.

"I miss him," I finally admitted. "I miss him so much."

Landon wrapped an arm around my shoulder. "I know."

"I miss the man he used to be. When he used to be a good father. When he didn't do drugs, then sell drugs, then fucking bankroll the bar with his drug money to try to keep it afloat. I wished he hadn't been the kind of dad who brought strange women over all the time. Married women. The kind who I never really knew their names, and they switched too often for me to care. I wished I hadn't had to clean up his fucking messes all the time. Help him in his drunken stupor and cry myself to sleep when he was in a drunken rage so bad that only passing out would get him to stop.

"But he loved me. You know…despite all of that…he loved me. He tried to provide for me and let me do anything I wanted. But it…wasn't parenting. After Mom left, he was surviving. And letting me do anything I wanted wasn't charity. I'm lucky I had Emery and that her mom helped me out as much as she did."

"Maybe he's changed. Why don't you reach out and talk to him? You don't know; he might surprise you."

"No, I can't." I swiped at my eyes.

"But why?"

I shook my head. "Because."

"Heidi—"

"Because he spent all of my college funds on drugs!" I shouted, standing up and throwing my arms out. I let out the last ounce of depressing news. The part I'd held back from everyone. "He spent all the money that my mom had left me for college. He pawned off all her jewelry and every last thing that had ever belonged to her. And he left me with nothing. Now, even though I'm working my ass off, I'm broke as hell, Landon. I need this job more than life itself. And it's all his fault."

"Fuck," Landon whispered.

"Yeah. So, he gets one day. I give myself one day to miss him. That's all he deserves."

Twenty-Eight

Landon

Spending that day with Heidi, when she was at her most vulnerable, had changed everything. I had fallen for her. Completely, utterly, unequivocally.

And I was a fucking asshole.

I knew why she needed this job. I now knew without question why this was so important to her. Yet I was gambling with it. I was gambling with her. I could feel the delicate tightrope we were walking on, and I feared our feet would slip if I wasn't careful.

I didn't know how to be more careful.

Sunday morning, Heidi was wrapped in my arms when I got a text from Jensen.

You still coming to church?

"Fuck," I spat.

"Hmm?" Heidi asked, peering up at me with sleep-deprived eyes.

.A. LINDE

"I forgot it's Sunday. I'm supposed to meet Jensen for church. Want to go with me?"

"Won't that look bad?" she mumbled.

I gritted my teeth and nodded. "Yeah, probably. Fuck, I'm sorry. You can stay here and keep sleeping. I'll be back in about an hour, okay?"

"All right," she said with a big yawn. "Come back to me soon, okay?"

"God, I wish you could go with me."

"One day," she said, leaning into me for a kiss.

"One day soon," I promised.

I hastily changed into a suit and darted over to the church we'd been going to since I was little. My mom had been an avid churchgoer, even before she found out about the cancer. Of course, we hadn't known how bad it was until she was on her deathbed. But it made sense now why she had been so religious about the church service. She must have been scared with five children and a life-threatening illness.

I arrived just in time to make the service. Jensen, Emery, Austin, Morgan, Sutton, Maverick, and little baby Jason were all seated in the front row, like a defending army. Even though my family was super fucked up and carried more baggage than an airplane in a year, we were always here.

Lubbock was one of those towns where church service was mandatory, but we Wrights took it to an extreme. It was new for me though. I'd been gone for a long time. I'd only gone to church when I was home for the holidays. I definitely hadn't gone when I was in Tampa. So, remembering that this was a thing we always did tripped me up on Sundays.

"Sorry," I muttered as I sank into the seat Jensen had left for me at the end of the aisle.

"Where were you?" he asked.

"My alarm didn't go off."

Jensen shot me a look that said he didn't believe me. And he was right. Not that I'd let him know that.

Emery leaned forward and waved. "Hey, Landon."

"Em."

Her eyes said enough to me without words. She asked, *How's Heidi?*

Doing okay.

Good. I worry.

I know. I'm watching out for her.

She nodded her head at Jensen. *You going to talk to him?*

I sighed and nodded. *Yeah.*

Thank God. She breathed out in relief and sat back.

Jensen shot me a questioning look, but the service started before he could say anything. My mind was filled with the conversation that I knew I needed to have with Jensen, and I couldn't seem to concentrate on what was being said. I also felt pretty shitty about leaving Heidi in my bed even if she was going to just sleep away the rest of the morning.

Luckily, the service was over soon enough, and the congregation stood and began to mingle. Emery jumped up and hurried over to her sister, Kimber, who was holding her youngest daughter, Bethany, and trying to corral Lilyanne. Austin fingered his pocket for what I guessed was a flask and tried to leave, but Morgan was smacking his arm and silently arguing with him. I knew it wouldn't do much good. Also, I should probably help, but I didn't.

Sutton was the one who came over. "Here, hold your nephew, you heathen," she said, thrusting Jason into my arms.

I laughed and softly cradled the baby. He was completely passed out and hadn't made a peep all service. And holding him in my arms like this made my chest ache. A family was something I had wanted ever since my father died.

"He's too cute and little," I told her.

"He's adorable, and thank God. With how little sleep I'm getting, he'd better be."

I laughed, and she grinned.

Sutton was the baby, only twenty-one years old, and, she'd somehow had her own baby before everyone, except Jensen. It was almost unfair. But I couldn't begrudge her the happiness. She was still glowing with joy. We had all thought that Sutton's shotgun wedding was because of this little guy in my arms. Yet she seemed to genuinely love her husband, Maverick. Against all odds, Sutton was the happiest of us all and the one with the least amount of baggage. Maybe because she had only been one when our mom died and eleven when our dad died, she didn't have as acute memories of the pain. Either way, I envied her.

"What are you doing for your birthday?" I asked. "It's coming up. Big twenty-two."

"Ugh," she groaned. "Jensen planned the freaking Charity Benefit for the same weekend. So, probably getting a babysitter and going to the dumb event."

"I didn't schedule the date for the Benefit," Jensen said. "I wouldn't have put it on your birthday, but Emery and I would be happy to babysit the night before if you would like a night out."

Her eyes lit up. "You're serious?"

"I know a thing or two about babies. We can manage."

"You're the best!" she said.

Maverick appeared at the sound of her squeal, and she filled him in.

"Thanks, man," he said, holding his hand out to Jensen.

Jensen shook it and gave him a curious look. I was sure Jensen still believed that Maverick only wanted Sutton for her money, but it sure didn't look like it.

Maverick took Jason from me, and I turned to face Jensen.

He raised an eyebrow. "You want to talk?"

I nodded. "Yeah. Outside?"

"Sure."

We left the chapel together and wandered out into the brisk morning air. Lubbock had that strange sense of being desertlike. No matter how hot it got during the day, mornings and nights were always significantly cooler. Texas weather was strangely erratic.

Being around Jensen always made me realize how much I missed him when I didn't see him. No matter that we lived in the same town again and he worked only a couple of floors above me, I never saw him. He was a loner by choice, which had only intensified post-Vanessa. I was glad that he had someone even if that someone had to be Emery. But I couldn't talk; I was dating her best friend.

"I assume this is about Miranda," Jensen said as we headed out to his truck.

"No actually," I said. I hadn't even thought about Miranda since she left.

"Oh?"

"I've started seeing someone," I told him.

"Oh," Jensen said with a sigh. "Already? You couldn't wait until the divorce was finalized?"

"Yeah. It kind of happened unexpectedly."

"And you're telling me this…because it concerns me somehow?"

"I'm telling you this as my brother, all right? Not as the CEO of Wright Construction," I carefully told him.

"Oh, boy, here it comes. Wright family drama. Lay it on me."

"I'm seeing one of my employees."

Jensen sighed and looked up at the clear sky above us. "Seriously? What did I do to deserve this?"

"You're an ass," I told him with a laugh.

"Fuck, Landon. Did you come to me because you wanted me to tell you how bad of an idea this is? And, God…don't tell me who it is. Otherwise, I'll be complicit."

"I came to you for advice, I guess," I told him. I really wasn't sure what I'd come to him for. "And maybe a new job?"

Jensen laughed at that. "Advice and a new job? Jobs just appear out of thin air now? Grow on trees?"

"You're the CEO. You can move me."

"Well, you're talking to your brother, not the CEO, and your brother thinks you're an idiot for not being able to keep it in your pants."

"Thanks, dick. It's not like that."

"I'm sure."

"It's not about the sex."

"Don't you know that rule number one is, *Don't fuck your employees?*"

"Can you move me or not?"

"I really don't want to know who this is, do I?" Jensen asked me.

I hesitated for a second and then shook my head. "No."

"I'll talk to Morgan," he said with a shake of his head, "but I can't promise you anything. If I were you, I'd straighten your shit out first. We don't need to pay a fortune for the best therapist in the state of Texas because you lost your game while your head was wrapped around some girl you'd known for a couple of weeks."

I opened my mouth to protest. I'd known Heidi a hell of a lot longer. But he was right; I didn't need to tell him any details about who I was seeing. There was only one person on my floor who I'd known before getting the job, and deduction skills weren't that difficult.

"Just stay away from her until we can figure this out, okay?"

"How long will that be?" I asked.

He shrugged. "I don't know, Landon. Maybe, in a few weeks, you'll find someone who doesn't work on your floor, and we won't have to move you at all."

I gritted my teeth. "I don't think that's happening."

"You fall for someone faster than any of us," Jensen said, as if it were a crime. "You fell for Miranda this fast and married her six months later. Imagine if you had slowed down and gotten to know her. Maybe we wouldn't be dealing with this shit at all."

"I don't even want to hear it. You risked everything for Emery after only knowing her a few weeks, and now, you're lecturing me?" I asked in disbelief. "I came to you for help as my brother. Don't fucking judge me, man."

Jensen held up his hands. "You're right. I just worry. I thought you had enough on your plate without adding something else to the mix. It took four weeks to make this position for you. So, I'll look into it, but stay away from her until then."

I swallowed hard. "Fine."

Even though I knew that I wouldn't.

When I got home, I didn't share my conversation with Heidi. I wanted to tell her that I was working on fixing the problem that kept us apart, but Jensen had made no promises. I didn't want to get her hopes up, only for them to be dashed if he couldn't come up with a solution.

The next morning, I went into physical therapy bright and early. Anjee greeted me with a friendly smile and started me on my warm-ups and stretches. Moving home to start physical therapy and getting a job with the company was supposed to help me de-stress, yet I was more stressed than ever. That meant my mental state was totally fucked up right now, destroying my whole reason for moving here in the first place. But Anjee always calmed me down, reminded me to keep my head in the game, and to heal right the first time so I could get back on my feet.

I knew she was right. In more than one way. I needed time, and it was the only thing I couldn't actually rush.

I finished therapy at exactly the right time, feeling worn out and achy all over. Monday mornings were the worst because I had taken the weekends off. But I was glad that I'd gotten it out of the way. Then, I could play catch-up at work before everyone got there.

I slumped over in my chair when I finally made it to my office. My back was throbbing. I had really worked hard today. Harder than I had before. Something Anjee had said made me really want to do everything I could every minute I was with her to get my back to start improving. And, now, I was hating myself for it.

I popped a few Tylenol and then went through my emails. When I found the one that most interested me, I stopped and stared at the subject line.

Lead Engineer Job Offer

This was the job Heidi had applied for. I would know before she did whether or not she'd gotten it. My mouse hovered over the email. I wanted to read it. I wanted to find out if she had gotten the spot. I wanted to be the one to tell her and congratulate her and hold her.

But I couldn't do it.

If she'd gotten the job, then she needed to hear it from someone else. Even if no one else knew that we were seeing each other, I knew, and it would feel like favoritism.

I forwarded the email over to Julia and Dennis, the head of engineering, and asked them to inform whoever had gotten the job. They probably thought I was being a dick by delegating out one of my tasks, but I didn't care. Everyone thought that the Wright family were all dicks anyway. I didn't mind feeding into our reputation a little bit if it saved my integrity.

Twenty-Nine

Landon

Heidi appeared in the office an hour later. We tried not to talk to each other or look at each other when she was here. But I caught myself doing it anyway. No matter how troublesome it was, it was impossible to look away from her. Especially when all I could think about was getting her back to my place and stripping her out of all those sexy work clothes she strutted around here in. Though today, of course, I was excited to find out about the promotion.

And I was glad that I didn't know. If she had gotten it, I couldn't spoil it, and if she hadn't, I couldn't ruin her day.

Julia rushed over to Heidi's desk as soon as she showed up, and they chattered away. I caught a glimpse of them together as I headed for the restroom. My stomach was actually cramping. I was so nervous for her. I knew what this meant to her. I knew all too well.

When I stepped back out of the restroom though, I was shocked to find Heidi waiting for me.

"I got it!" she cried, biting her lip and looking like all she wanted to do was throw her arms around me and make out with me.

"You got it?" I said, playing dumb.

"The job! You're looking at your new lead engineer!"

Her eyes darted back and forth, as if waiting for someone else to come around the corner and find us talking to each other.

"Congratulations!" I said. I wanted nothing more than to grab her around the middle and swing her around.

"Did you know?" she asked, beaming. "Did you already know? Had you known all weekend?"

I shook my head. "No, I didn't know. I wouldn't have been able to keep it a secret all weekend."

"Oh my God, Landon, I just…you know how much this means to me."

"I do," I said, taking a small step forward. "I really want to kiss you right now."

"You can't."

But her eyes were bright, and her fingers curled into fists at her sides. I imagined them curling into my suit jacket, and I took another step forward.

"Just one."

God, I knew I was supposed to stay away. I knew that I should step back and not take advantage of this situation, but I wanted to. I wanted to run my hands through her long hair and knot it in my fist as I fucked her from behind. I wanted to kiss her perfect pink lips—both sets—until they were swollen. I wanted to taste every inch of her body and then let her taste herself on my lips.

I wanted everything in that moment. And I could have nothing.

She could see the desire written plainly on my face, and she released a breathy gasp that only made me want to re-create it.

"Landon," she whispered.

I tilted my head toward the empty restroom. She shook her head, eyes wide. I grinned as I dragged her inside and locked the door.

"What are you doing?" she panted as I pressed her back into the wall.

"Celebrating you."

My lips crashed down onto hers, and she returned the kiss with fervor. As if we hadn't just been together last night. As if we hadn't been together all weekend. Yet I couldn't get enough.

Patience flew out the window. Jensen's warnings flittered out of my mind. All my thoughts about integrity disappeared entirely.

"Landon, we can't," she said as she grabbed on to my suit and tugged me closer.

"I know."

My hand slid up her bare thigh and shoved her pencil skirt up to her waist. I thrust her thong aside, and she whimpered at my touch. My fingers delved in between her folds and felt her slick need.

She was already wet for me. *Fuck.*

"Oh God, I want you right now," I told her.

She closed her eyes and tried to control her breathing as my dick hardened uncomfortably in my suit pants. I moved my wet fingers to circle her clit. She tensed all around me as she tried not to whimper, and I knew it must be difficult because she was very vocal. But I kept circling her sensitive center until she was biting down on her own hand to keep from crying out. Then, I shoved two fingers up inside her.

"Congratulations," I growled into her ear as she came on my fingers.

I desperately wanted to take out my cock and have her against the wall. But we were out of time.

I removed my hand from her underwear, and she sagged against the wall. Her breathing was erratic, but she hastily straightened out her skirt.

"How do I look?"

"Hot as hell."

"Landon," she said, smacking my arm.

"Fine. You're fine."

"What the hell were you thinking?" She was glaring at me now.

She looked pissed as all hell even though I'd just given her a hot fucking orgasm.

"I wasn't," I admitted.

"Don't fucking do that again. Maybe wait until after work next time."

I grinned. "Sounds good. I'll see you after work."

She shook her head and sent one more look pointed my way—half-desire and half-anger. Then, she peeked out of the restroom and disappeared. I took a minute to steady myself against the sink. I'd been so close to fucking her right then and there on the restroom sink. And I hadn't given two fucks.

Discretion was causing me physical pain. *Fuck, Jensen and his stay away from her.*

With a sigh, I ran a hand back through my hair and eased back to my desk.

I was finally getting through the rest of my emails for the morning when there was a knock at the door. I glanced up and saw Matt standing at the door. "Come on in."

"Hey, Landon," he said, entering the room.

"How can I help you, Matt?"

Matt's face darkened, and he glanced away. Then, he firmly shut the door and took the seat in front of me. "I wanted to talk about the lead engineer position with you."

"What about it?"

"I know you had some role in choosing who got the promotion. I thought our conversation regarding the position went really well."

I leaned back in my seat and assessed him. "It did."

"I thought so. I'm a very experienced engineer. I have all the certifications. I work on all the biggest projects. I've been here day in and day out, putting in the hours, making sure everything is right, and generally holding this department together."

"Okay." I had a feeling I knew where this was going, and I wasn't going to like it.

This Matt guy sure thought highly of himself. In my experience, the people with the best credentials didn't have to flaunt them.

"Then, why exactly did Heidi get the promotion over me?" He crossed his arms and waited.

"Matt, while I understand that you might be upset because you did not receive the promotion, I cannot disclose the contents of Heidi's interview or credentials. She was the most qualified person for the job, and that was why she was chosen."

"Sorry to say so, *sir*, but that seems ridiculous."

I stood from my desk and buttoned the top button of my suit jacket. "We're very sorry that we were unable to offer you the job, but there will be more opportunities in the future."

Matt looked disgusted with me and then turned and walked out.

My day didn't get any better. No less than three other men in the department came to talk to me about picking Heidi over them. From what I gathered, they didn't believe that a woman could accurately do a man's job. When the last guy flat-out told me that, it took all my energy not to punch him in the teeth.

"That'll do," I said, my voice short and irritated. "Heidi is perfectly capable of being a lead engineer and more. You should get used to the idea. Now, get out of my office."

I spent the rest of the day in silence and solitude. I knew that I had been short with everyone because they were talking about Heidi. But I also felt the general attitude was reprehensible. Morgan could handle all of Wright Construction just as well, if not better, than Jensen. There was no reason to say otherwise about Heidi.

Before I realized it, the time had flown by, and suddenly, I was well past the end of the day. I rubbed my tired eyes and stood from my desk. Today had been exhausting. As I was about to shut my computer down, one last email came through.

Ryan Copeland.

I laughed. I hadn't heard that name in a while. I opened the email from probably my best golfing friend and read the contents.

You know you want to.

I scrolled down and saw what he meant. I frowned and then contemplated. *Hmm…maybe he's right.*

I pulled out my phone and shot Heidi a text message.

Go away with me this weekend.

A ding sounded from down the hallway, and I found Heidi herself walking toward me. She looked just as worn down from the day as I did.

"I didn't know you were still here," I said.

"I didn't know you were still here either." She held up her phone as she wandered into my office. "What's this about?"

The floor was eerily empty when I closed the door behind her. "Do you want to go?"

She leaned backward against my desk. Her pencil skirt slid up her thighs, and I couldn't help my gaze from shifting there.

"Landon, we should talk about this. You know it's a bad idea for us to be seen together. What you did earlier…"

"Yes?" I asked, stepping up to her. I was close enough to touch her, but I didn't.

"It was not smart."

"Is anyone else here tonight?"

"No," she told me. "Everyone left an hour ago. I was still filling out paperwork and figuring out everything I needed for the new job."

"Good," I told her. Then, I brought my lips down on top of hers.

"Landon, I said, after work," she groaned into my mouth. But she didn't stop me.

"This *is* after work."

"I meant—fuck," she said as she felt my dick press up against her.

"Go away with me this weekend." My hands trailed down to her ass, and I greedily grabbed it. I loved her ass.

"Landon…"

"I want to celebrate your promotion."

"Oh, Landon."

"Say yes."

I slowly eased her skirt up her legs once more, and she gasped slightly.

"What am I saying yes to again?"

"Everything," I told her.

I took her thong in my hand and tugged it down her legs. She stepped out of it, and I stuffed them in my pocket as I winked at her.

"Landon, this is complicated," she said, her voice barely above a whisper.

"I know I should wait. I should be patient. But, Heidi, as you can see," I said, pushing my hand between her legs, "I'm not patient. I don't want to be patient. Not with you."

"Oh God." Her head dropped back as my fingers caressed her most sensitive spot.

"Is that a yes?"

"Yes, Landon. Always. God, yes."

I flipped her around so that she was facing my desk and then bent her over at the waist. I unbuckled my pants and let them fall to my ass as I pulled my cock out of my boxer briefs. Heidi whimpered softly. I caressed her pert ass and then kicked her feet a little further apart.

I wanted to take my time with her here, on my desk, like I'd been fantasizing about since I took this job. But, even though everyone was gone for the day, that didn't mean we were completely alone. I knew we had precious few minutes.

The anticipation made me rock hard, and I slid my dick deep into her pussy. She was already soaking wet for me. I had no trouble whatsoever.

"Fuck," I grunted as I pulled out and slammed back into her. "I fucking love this view."

"You get so"—I rocked hard into her—"deep."

My hand smacked her ass, and she yelped softly at the touch. The noise went straight to my dick, and I knew that I wasn't going to hold out for long. Not with her making those noises, not with her ass in my hands, not with my dick buried deep inside her while she was bent over this way.

I picked up my pace, and soon, we were coming together. I gritted my teeth as I finished and then pulled back. I hastily cleaned up after myself and tossed the tissue into the trash can. Heidi tugged her skirt back down and then collapsed into one of the chairs.

"You know this was not what I meant by after work."

I grinned. "I know. But are you complaining?"

She shook her head. "You're going to get me in so much trouble."

"Go away with me," I said, bending down and capturing her lips once more.

"Where would we go?" she asked, already giving in.

"You showed me a part of your life this weekend. Let me show you mine."

Thirty

Heidi

It was hard to stay mad at Landon for being so reckless at work. I knew that I should have tried harder, especially since I'd gotten the promotion. But being with him was like living on a perpetual high. No matter the withdrawals I might have to suffer later, I wanted the next fix.

So, I'd agreed to go away with him.

It hadn't actually even been a question. Mostly because, when he'd told me where we were going, I'd squealed with excitement.

His world was golf—more specifically, the PGA Tour Championship in Atlanta that weekend. It was the finals for the golf world where the best of the best came to compete for the FedEx Cup and the coveted first place ten-million-dollar prize money. The Masters was still the be-all and end-all of golf as far as I was concerned, not that I knew *that* much about the sport, but the Tour Championship was an amazing opportunity.

Landon's friend Ryan Copeland had sent over tickets for some big event that weekend. Landon could get in pretty much anywhere off of his name, but I was pretty sure Ryan's thoughtfulness had won him over.

We arrived late Friday night after work. We couldn't risk being seen leaving work early together again. It was bad enough that Julia had suspected I was up to something when I told her again that I couldn't go shopping. Luckily, Emery was with Jensen in New York City this weekend to see Colton. So, it was pretty easy to get out of shopping.

I'd packed more than my fair share of clothes for this trip. Even though we were only going to be there for two days, I wanted to be sure that I was prepared.

When Landon got a look at my outfit on Saturday morning, he grinned and pulled me back into the bedroom. "Forget the tournament. Let's stay in."

I laughed throatily. "I am in a khaki skirt, polo, and tennis shoes!"

"Sexiest I've ever seen you."

"Oh my God, you get turned on by golf attire! I've heard of everything now."

He kissed my lips. "I get turned on by *you* in golf attire. You look sexy as hell in everything you wear, but you wore this for me. So, how can I not like it?"

"Are you trying to stall so that we don't have to go out there?"

He gave me a searching look. "Why would you think that?"

"Because…you're not playing," I said softly. "I thought that would be hard on you."

"It is."

"Yeah, I could tell."

"How do you read me so perfectly?" He tugged me closer.

"Because I know you."

"I approve of this."

"You'd better."

He laughed. "Oh God, I'm so glad that I brought you with me."

A knock on the door startled us apart, and Landon waved away my anxiety. I wasn't completely comfortable with being here with him. Even though I knew no one and clearly no one here would know me, I couldn't relax. This was Landon's element, not mine.

Landon opened the door and shook the hand of the guy at the door. "Hey, man!"

"Landon fucking Wright," the guy said, strutting into the hotel suite as if he owned the place. He was an exceptionally tall and handsome African American man with the most amazing smile. "Finally got your ass back to a golf tournament." His dark eyes shot to me, and his eyebrows rose. "Well, hello there."

"Hello," I said with a raised brow.

He reached out and placed a kiss on my hand with a boyish grin. "I'm sure Landon has told you all about his charming single friend."

Landon rolled his eyes. "Heidi, this is Ryan Copeland. He's on the Tour."

"Um…hi. You're the one who got us the tickets for tonight." I deftly pulled my hand out of his.

"Us?" Ryan said, glancing between me and Landon. "You left Miranda and already found the hottest replacement on the course? The man with no game always gets the hottest fucking girls. How do you do it?"

"Heidi isn't a replacement," Landon said with a shake of his head. "Heidi is…her own person. She's not a real PGA."

"A real PGA?" I asked in confusion.

"It's awful," Ryan said with a grin, as if he didn't find it that awful. "Party Groupie Association. Basically, the putt sluts who chase down our balls, if you know what I mean."

257

I opened and then closed my mouth. I hadn't really thought that much about what the girls who followed them around on Tour were like. Sure, everyone knew that Tiger Woods had fucked more people than the average porn star, but it just hadn't registered with me.

"I suppose I do," I finally said.

"Try to avoid the locker-room talk," Landon said. "Y'all are disgusting enough without bringing it to my girlfriend."

"Girlfriend? Girlfriend." Ryan sighed. "I thought you were bringing me a treat. I'm so disappointed in you."

"No luck. You'll just have to settle for someone else."

"Alas," Ryan said. He winked at me. "Well, come on. I tee off in a couple of hours, and we should head to the clubhouse before I have to warm up."

We followed Ryan out of the hotel and met his caddy, Gerald, waiting in the front seat. I slid into the backseat with Landon.

"Who is your caddy?"

"Jake Gibson," Landon told me. "We've been together from the start, but I had to let him go when I got injured."

"Jake is your main man, Wright," Ryan said from the front seat. "He will be back when you are."

Landon didn't comment. I knew that he was thinking that he might never be back. Though he seemed fine when he was sitting behind a desk and pushing papers, I knew that he was not ready to swing a club...not even to walk a full course.

The clubhouse was Southern and gorgeous. I couldn't get over the number of trees and hills and the overall humid nature of the late September tournament. Atlanta was about as different from Lubbock as anything could be. I wasn't sure that I liked that my hands were sweating just from walking outside, but it was undeniably stunning.

People were everywhere. Thousands of people were already lined up on the course, being held back by a flimsy rope and held to silence for the players. Camera crews hovered around like early spring bees. As far as the eye could see, everyone was dressed in golf clothes.

Ryan ushered us into the clubhouse, and we were brought to a huge room with a balcony overlooking one of the greens. Landon gently put his hand on the small of my back to get me to follow Ryan to the bar.

"There are so many people here," I told him in surprise.

He laughed. "Yes, golf is a spectator sport. Most people in here are professionals waiting for their tee time or those who didn't make it to this round."

"There are a lot of women in here."

"Yeah, well, wives show up to this tournament a lot. It technically closes out the season until January. And, really, anyone can get in here as long as they know someone."

We were stopped four times on the way to the bar—all golfers who were excited to see Landon at the tournament and asking about when he'd be back. He chatted merrily with all of them. Clearly, a lot of the golfers were close even though Landon had told me it was a pretty solitary life. The amount of time they got to see other golfers was pretty limited, and unless you were already out of the tournament, most guys liked to stay in the right frame of mind to play.

I suspected that Landon had been that kind of player. He had that sort of intensity about him. Plus, he had taken a job so that he could keep his mind active. He took this seriously. I could see it in the respect everyone gave him.

Being here, in this world, with him was a new and crazy experience.

To me, Landon was still a Lubbock-area Wright brother with the Texas charm and easygoing personality. But here… he was so much more.

"You're a celebrity," I whispered in his ear when we caught up with Ryan again.

Landon's eyes glittered with humor. "I'm a professional golfer, love."

"I know. I just…you're a celebrity, Landon. I still remember you from high school when you were…wait, you were the star quarterback. I suppose you were a celebrity then, too."

"Different scale."

"Did you say you've known him since high school?" Ryan asked with a big smile on his face. "Oh God, is this your high school sweetheart who you told me about that one time?"

"No," Landon said at once, his voice clipped.

I frowned at that. *He had told other people about Emery?* I wasn't jealous about that or anything, just surprised. I'd figured he never talked about what had happened at all. That was what Emery and I had always assumed with the way he'd moved on.

"We never dated in high school. I've just known him for a long time."

"Interesting." Ryan passed Landon and me beers even though it was only eight o'clock in the morning and got a coffee for himself. "Need the caffeine to get through this day now that I've fucking kicked smoking."

We moved over to the balcony and took a table from someone who had gotten up and left the clubhouse to go play. Our view was pretty stellar, and the guys talked shop in a way that was undecipherable to me. I knew as much about golf as Landon did about engineering.

By the time Ryan had to go warm up, I was pleasantly buzzed from the beer and in need of a water. I was about to get up when a camera crew buzzed over to us.

"Landon Wright, so good to see you back at a tournament today. Mind if we do a short interview about your injury and recovery?" the man asked.

I hopped out of my chair. "Go ahead. I'm going to get a water, and I'll be back."

"Okay. Be quick."

I could see Landon didn't really want to give the interview, but if he was half the celebrity he seemed to be, it wasn't going to be the only one he'd give today when people realized he was here.

The cameras started rolling as soon as I hopped up from my seat.

"We're here today with a PGA favorite, Landon Wright. This is his first appearance since he dropped out of the US Open in June. Good to see you here today, Landon."

I watched as Landon layered on the charming charism. This was the guy I'd fallen head over heels for. The one who I'd held hands with while roller-skating and eating ice cream and snuggling in his bed. The one who I called my boss and fucker. I was his firecracker. And, somehow, that reality merged with this one.

I disappeared then, letting him have his moment for the camera, and stepped up to the bar. "Two waters, please."

"Sure thing," the bartender said.

"Come on, Ben," a familiar voice squeaked from the end of the bar.

My eyes rounded in horror as I turned my head and found none other than Miranda.

"Fuck, fuck, fuck," I breathed.

She was seated on a barstool with a man who was one of the golfers that had stopped to talk to Landon earlier today. She was leaning into him and giving him a come-hither look. The term *putt slut* took on an all-new meaning.

"Miranda, I can't do this. Not when I'm buddies with Landon."

She trailed a finger down his front and grinned devilishly. "You've wanted me for years, and we've stayed away from each other. Time's up."

He put his hand on hers, as if to push her away, but he didn't. She sidled up closer to him when he did nothing.

And I'd seen enough.

I felt sick to my stomach. I snatched up the water bottles as soon as the bartender handed them to me, and I hurried away. I needed to get Landon out of here. As if it wasn't bad enough that Miranda had been refusing to sign the divorce paperwork, now, she was trying to find a replacement for Landon, so she could go from one golfer to another.

I shuddered and moved to Landon's side. The interview had just concluded. He gave me a confused look when I appeared frantic.

But then I said the magic words to get him to move, "Miranda is here."

Thirty-One

Landon

"What the fuck is she doing here?" I asked as I herded Heidi out of the clubhouse.

I probably shouldn't be walking the course. Okay, I definitely shouldn't be. But I couldn't stay in the clubhouse and run into Miranda. That would be suicide.

"Do you really want to know?" she asked.

"Yes."

We took the stairs and were outside when Heidi finally sighed and told me, "She's looking for a new you."

"A new...me?"

"Yeah. She was talking to that guy Ben that you know. Telling him that they've wanted each other forever and that he could now have her."

I gave her a disgusted face. "God, she gives the term *nineteenth hole* a whole new meaning."

Heidi snorted. "Nineteenth hole? God, you golfers are really gross!"

"You don't even want to know. *Double bogey* and *water holes* have double meanings, too. You can probably guess."

"Oh…wow. I probably can."

I laughed at her adorable face as I had her thinking about anal play and blow jobs. "You know, if you're interested…"

"Concentrate, you," she said, playfully smacking my arm.

"Right. Escaping my crazy ex is the number one priority. Dirty bedroom play can be considered at a later time."

"Oh, you are only going to be thinking about that now, aren't you?"

I arched an eyebrow in her direction and wrapped an arm around her waist. Then, I dropped it lower and grabbed her ass. "Can you blame me?"

She leaned over and kissed me in a way that brooked no argument. She did *not* blame me.

"Maybe later," she whispered into my ear.

Hell yes.

Now that I was out of the clubhouse, away from Miranda, and out on the course, I felt more like myself. There were plenty of people mingling around who could recognize me, but with my hat pulled low over my eyes and without a club in my hands, most people just walked by. It was only the occasional wide-eyed PGA girl or devoted middle-aged man. Both were harmless in small quantities.

Heidi took it all in stride. I was so used to this environment that I hadn't even thought to prepare her for what was to come. Of course, I was just the guy she'd known in high school when we were in Lubbock. I was a different person out here, but I was enjoying her perception of it. Everything was a new adventure, and she wanted answers to all of her questions—how many tournaments I played, how much you could win, the dynamics of the game, who everyone was, what the importance of different clubs were, and on and on.

I enjoyed telling her all about my first love—golf.

The more time I spent with Heidi, the more I realized she was my second.

———

By the time we returned to our hotel room later that day, we were both exhausted and starving, and Heidi was a little sunburned.

"Fucking sun! I put on sunscreen," she groaned.

"You are kind of pale."

"Kind of pale?" she asked, sticking her arm out for me to investigate. "I was a ghost, and now, I'm a lobster."

"You're just a little pink. We'll get you a hat for tomorrow and some better sunscreen."

She sighed. "I am going to look ridiculous in my dress tonight. Nothing like tan lines in a strapless dress."

"Why don't we skip it?" I suggested.

"What? That was the whole reason we came—because you got the tickets from Ryan."

"That gave me the push to bring you, but really, I just wanted to spend some time with you and show you a golf tournament. One day, I want to get back to this. I hope I can get back to this. And, when I do, I wanted you to see what it was like."

"Golf groupies always throwing themselves at you?" she asked.

"That is an unfortunate part of the job, but most of the golfers on the Tour are deeply devoted to their girlfriends or wives and would never deal with that nonsense. And that's all it is—nonsense."

"Is that how you met Miranda?"

I sighed and nodded. "Well, she wasn't exactly a groupie. She was a nurse for the Tour. So, I saw her all the time since we traveled to a lot of the same events."

265

"She was a *nurse*? Didn't see that coming."

"Yeah. She quit after we got married."

"Huh. And you didn't think that weird. Like she planned it all along?"

"There are a lot of things that I regret about being with Miranda," I told her. "And, though I see her for the person she is now, I didn't at the time. None of it matters now. All that matters is that I have you." I kissed her forehead and then her nose and then her lips. "You never hide yourself from me, and I don't have to be someone different for you. That is why I think we should skip the dinner."

She laughed lightly. "That's why?"

"I'd rather do anything other than run into my ex. How about you?"

"All right," she said with a nod. "What do you have in mind?"

"Anything. Let's go find a restaurant and have our own dinner."

"That sounds nice," she said. All the tension left her shoulders. It was as if she had been afraid of seeing Miranda, too. "But I'm going to need a shower first."

I tugged Heidi into the bathroom. The best part of the suite we had was the enormous stand-up shower with waterfall jets. We eased each other out of the clothes we had worn all day on the course and stepped into the steamy spray. My hands slid up and down her wet body and then up into her long hair. She released a soft moan when I ran my fingers across her scalp.

"Mmm, Landon. We're never leaving this shower," she whispered.

"You're damn right about that."

My fingers slipped between her legs and tenderly worked on her clit.

"A whole new definition of water hole," she said with a laugh.

Then, she dropped to her knees before me.

"Fuck," I groaned.

I'd been thinking about all the fun we could have today, but fuck, I hadn't expected her to just drop like that. Then, my dick was in her mouth—hot and wet and fucking amazing. I lost all conscious thought at that point. Her tongue was lapping at my cock. Her hand worked it up and down. She even made this low humming sound that sent vibrations straight through my body. I shuddered as she bobbed up and down, fucking me with her mouth.

"Heidi," I groaned, sinking my hand into her hair.

"Mmm…"

"Let me fuck you."

"Mmm," was her response.

I felt my dick twitch in her mouth. Fuck, she was goddamn good at that. I was barely holding on. If she kept at it, I was going to come in her mouth, and I really, *really* wanted to get inside her.

"Heidi," I said, "bend over right the fuck now."

Her eyes popped up to mine, and she slowly released my dick. "Right now?"

"Ass in the air, love."

She could barely fight a grin as she turned around, put her hands on the bench in the shower, and showed me her ass. God, I loved everything about her, but she had an awesome ass.

I moved my hands to her cheeks and spread them wide for me. Then, I palmed my cock and eased into her pussy. She moaned and pushed back against me, getting me just that much deeper.

I wanted all of her. Every last inch. And so much more.

There was not a part of me that she hadn't touched. And, whether she knew it or not, I was a goner. No matter the barriers between us, Heidi Martin had managed to eradicate them all from my mind. There was only her and here and now. And, when we were together, nothing else mattered.

Just the feel of her and the taste of her. That smile. That touch. That moan.

Everything about her.

And she had no idea what she was doing to me. How completely and utterly she had stolen my heart.

Our bodies rocked together in perfect sync. The hours at the course slipped away. She tightened around me. I slipped one finger between her cheeks and moved it against her pucker. When she clenched even harder, greedily pushing back against me, I eased a digit inside her. She cried out in pleasure at the feel of being filled, and my dick lengthened almost painfully as her body shook.

We came together in the heat of the moment with the water beating down on us and the steam clouding the room. Heidi dropped to her knees, panting, as her orgasm took her over. And I stood, staring down at her in awe. She might have fallen to her knees, but I felt as if I had just given her a piece of me that I'd never given away.

I knelt beside her and brought her lips to mine. "I love you," I whispered into the embrace.

She stilled and pulled back to look at me. Her eyes were wide with excitement and terror. As if she had wanted to say it all along but had been holding back. "I love you, too."

Thirty-Two

Heidi

We kissed passionately under the water and then cleaned ourselves up. Once out of the shower, we changed and found a local seafood place that had fish overnighted from the coast each day. It was incredible, and Landon assured me it was way more relaxing than a big PGA dinner could ever be.

I wanted to go to one eventually, but it wasn't worth it to go to this one. Not when Miranda could show up and ruin everything. I didn't want Landon to have to deal with that, and I couldn't handle the headache.

It was enough for me this time that he really wanted me at the tournament to show me the life he led outside of Lubbock. And what a life it was.

We spent the next day wandering the golf course and meeting his friends. Ryan fell pretty quickly out of the top of the tournament rankings, but Landon told me he would still be assured a substantial prize for getting this far.

And the rest of the weekend was just…amazing. Hanging out with Ryan, enjoying the game, and finding my place in both of Landon's realities.

After the winner was announced, we had to hurry and catch our flight home. I was sad to go. This had been a pretty wonderful weekend. Just the two of us actually having the opportunity to live our lives. It was refreshing. And it'd made me all the more nervous to get home.

Because we couldn't have that life at home.

When we returned, he would be my boss again, and I would be a lead engineer in the company I'd been working for since college…the company his family owned. Everything was stacked against us back in reality. And I didn't want to have to deal with it. Not after the weekend we'd had.

"You're awfully quiet," he said as we boarded the plane home.

"The weekend was so perfect."

"So, you're sad about that?"

"Only that…we're not *together* at home. That's not our reality. And I got used to you being my boyfriend here."

"Heidi," he said with a sigh. "We'll figure it out."

"When?" I asked.

"I might have…already talked to Jensen."

"You did what?" I screeched. A few people turned to look at us, and I dipped my head to my chest. "I mean…what were you thinking?"

"I didn't tell him it was you. Only that I was dating someone on my floor, and I wanted him to find me a new spot."

My breathing got shallow. "He's going to figure it out."

"No, he's not. There are a lot of girls on the floor. They're just not in engineering. And, anyway, he said to wait it out, and he would figure a way to make it work."

"When did you talk to him? Why didn't you tell me?" I asked frantically.

"Um…at church, a week ago. I didn't tell you because I didn't want to get your hopes up. I don't know how long it could take. He doesn't know it's you. He thinks that my new girl is someone I just met and that I'll get over it."

"How charming."

"Jensen is just looking out for me."

"I know, I know. He's a great guy. He'd have to be to be with my best friend. Still, I wish you had told me."

"I'm sorry. I wasn't trying to keep it a secret or anything. I wanted to wait to figure out what Jensen could do." Landon took my hand as we settled into our first-class seats. "Trust me, okay? We'll make this work out."

I nodded. He was right. If Jensen didn't know, then it could theoretically be anyone. There were a ton of other women that Landon could be with, and if Emery kept her mouth shut, then Jensen would never have a reason to suspect me. In fact, he'd probably think that I was the last person Landon would pick, considering his history with Emery.

Landon planted a kiss on my cheek, and the rest of the flight was smooth sailing. My bad mood about having to hide our relationship again vanished. Maybe I was overreacting anyway.

Did I want our relationship to be known to everyone? Of course.

Could I wait until Jensen moved Landon to a new spot? Probably.

I didn't want to wait, but it wasn't the end of the world. Landon was worth waiting for as far as I was concerned.

Our descent into Lubbock was a little rocky. They'd had some storms unexpectedly blow through, and it was keeping a lot of flights in Dallas. Luckily, we'd gotten out just in time. But my stomach was queasy by the time we made it to Landon's car. I sipped on a bottle of water as we drove through the flooded streets back to my apartment.

That was such an issue in Lubbock. Because it rained so infrequently, anytime there was rain, all the streets would overflow. The ground couldn't soak it up. There weren't enough drains. And, basically, the rain always hit like a flash flood. I swore, it was bad planning from some poor government civil engineer. A better sewer system would have handled that, but I didn't work for the government. So, it probably wouldn't get fixed anytime soon.

Landon lugged my suitcase inside while I checked the mail. I tucked the mail under my arm as I dashed inside to try to get out of the rain.

"Oh my God, it's like a monsoon out there," I said, throwing the mail onto the counter and shaking out my soaking wet hair.

"Yeah. No joke. You would never guess that we were normally a desert climate."

I laughed. "No way. I'm going to change out of these wet clothes."

"Can I watch?" he asked with a grin.

"Why do I have a feeling that's not all you're going to do?"

"No idea." He tried and failed to give me a look of innocence.

"I'll just be a minute."

I traipsed into my bedroom and stripped out of my travel gear. I changed into pajama bottoms and a T-shirt before towel-drying my hair. I looked like a wet dog but whatever.

When I walked back out to the living room, Landon was sitting on the couch, holding a plain white letter in his hand. He was gently tapping it against the coffee table. His eyes found mine across the room.

"What are you doing with that?" I asked, my voice small.

"Just saw it in the pile of mail. You still haven't read any of them, have you?"

"No. Because I'm not going to ever read them. I don't want to talk to him."

Landon stood to face me. The letter between us felt like a barrier. "You shouldn't compartmentalize this the way that you do, Heidi. I know that you miss him. I know that you only allow yourself one day a year to think about him. But it's here every single week as a reminder. Aren't you the least bit curious?"

"No," I said fervently. "I'm not curious. I don't want to hear from the man who did everything he could to ruin my life."

"You and I both know that's not true."

"Yes, it is!" I cried.

"You didn't think that way about him in high school, and he was using then. He might have fucked up. He might have done horrible things. But he loves you. He put you through cheerleading. He came to all of the football games. He threw you that graduation party."

"Ancient history! I can't forget about all the times that I had to take care of his drunk ass when I was the kid. I was the one who needed to be taken care of. Throwing money at a problem doesn't make it go away."

"No, it doesn't," Landon said with a sigh. He walked forward to me and handed me the letter. "But the last thing I said to my dad before he died was something horrible, and I would give anything to have one more day with him. One more moment to make things right. But I will *never* have that. You have that, and you're throwing it away."

I felt like I had been burned with a cigarette. I recoiled back from the statement as tears sprang to my eyes. Never in the six years that my dad was gone had I once thought about actually reading his letters, actually talking to him. But I'd never thought about it like Landon had. If I could, wouldn't I do everything to have one more day with my mom? My dad might be horrible. He might have ruined my life and his own, but maybe I was in the wrong for not giving him a second chance.

273

Landon's arms were around me as all these emotions hit me at once. "Hey, it's okay. You don't have to decide today. I just don't want you to ignore him forever and live to regret never having a relationship with him again."

"I don't know if I can." I sniffled.

"You'll know when it's time."

I pulled back and peered down at the letter. My heart constricted. I didn't know if I had the strength today. I needed more time to contemplate it.

"Not yet," I whispered. "Will you…will you be here when I'm ready?"

"Always," he told me. "I will always be here when you need me."

I leaned back into his embrace, my mind trapped on the box of letters hidden away in my closet. The thought of going them, of ripping open years of wounds, left me drained, and I hadn't even touched them yet. I was scared of what I would find—that, as right as I thought I was about my father, I might also be wrong. What if I had wasted six years for nothing? And worse…what if everything I had done to shield my heart from him was for no good reason?

Landon left later that night when I got a text from Emery, saying that she was on her way home. He needed to get his stuff home and change out of his own travel clothes. Plus, he didn't want to run into Jensen just yet. I knew that conversation was probably going to have to come up again, but neither of us wanted it to be like this.

Emery showed up with Jensen, as expected. It made me happy for my friend and jealous that she didn't have to hide anything. But, when she saw me sitting in the living room, watching *Moana*, she shooed him out of the apartment, and we spent the rest of the night catching up while she finished some last-minute grading.

"So, you're actually going to read the letters?" Emery asked in shock.

"I don't know. I think…I'll know when it's the right time. Right?"

"Lover girl, you've been waiting this long. Are you sure you'll know? Maybe you should do it now and get it over with."

"No, Landon said he'd be here with me. I think I'll need all the emotional support I can get."

"Well, I'm here, too."

"I know," I said as I leaned over and kissed her cheek.

"Oh, Heidi, so forward."

"You like it."

She giggled. "Totally. I would so be bi for you."

"Same."

We looked at each other and then burst into laughter. It was a fun night. A chill night. One that I hadn't realized how much I needed. I had the best, best friend in the world. And I knew I was lucky to have known her my entire life.

Our night ended too soon, and then it was back to the grind. I knew that Landon would be in early on Monday morning as usual, and I made sure to avoid his desk at all costs. I didn't trust not to give myself away when I looked at him.

I plopped down next to Matt.

"Hey, Heidi!" he said with buoyancy I hadn't seen from him…ever.

"Hey, Matt."

"How was your weekend?"

I froze momentarily, surprised by the question. "Uh… good. I didn't do much. How about you?"

"I met someone," he gushed. "She's gorgeous, and it just clicked."

I breathed a sigh of relief. He hadn't asked about my weekend because he actually cared. As per usual Matt. He had asked because he had news, and he wanted to share.

"Oh, yeah? A new girl? That's exciting. Where did you meet her?"

"I was at a bar with some friends, and I met her there. Her name is Wendy, and she's perfect for me. I just know it."

"That's amazing, Matt," I said with a genuine smile.

If he had a girlfriend, that would mean he might stop asking me out.

"Yeah. I can't wait for you to meet her. I know she'll love you."

I found that doubtful but told him how excited I was to meet her as well. I returned my gaze to my computer as Julia showed up at my desk.

"Heidi, can we talk?" she asked, nodding her head toward her office.

"Hey, babe. Yeah, totally."

I followed her into her office and sank into the seat.

Julia slowly closed the door behind her. She stayed facing the door and sighed. "I want to know why you lied to me."

"What?" I asked in confusion.

"Why did you lie to me, Heidi?"

"I don't know what—"

"You said that you didn't want to go shopping with me this weekend because Emery was out of town." She turned to face me. "But you were with Landon this weekend."

I opened my mouth and then closed it. How did she know that?

"Right?"

I nodded. "Yeah."

"In Atlanta at a golf tournament."

"Yeah. How do you know that, Julia?"

She didn't answer my question. She slowly walked to her desk and pivoted the computer screen to face me. On the screen was a video of me and Landon out on the course in Atlanta. He had his hand on the small of my back, and you could clearly see me leaning in to kiss him.

My hand flew to my mouth. "What...what is this?"

"It's one of many videos forwarded to Dennis this morning. Then, they ended up in my inbox."

Her hands were shaking when her eyes finally met mine.

"I'm sorry, Heidi. You're fired."

Thirty-Three

Heidi

Shock hit me with the force of a tidal wave.

I was knocked back, hurtling into oblivion, drowning in my own disbelief. I couldn't process the words that Julia had said. They didn't make sense. They weren't logical. They weren't something anyone had ever said to me.

A couple of days ago, I had been promoted, and now... this.

I opened my mouth to ask the most obvious questions. *What? Why? How?* But they didn't come out. Nothing came out.

Tears hit me in the backs of my eyes, and I fought with everything not to let them fall. I swallowed them, refusing to submit to such humiliation. I wouldn't ask. I wouldn't beg. I wouldn't grovel. I certainly wouldn't fucking cry.

Not here.

Julia was one of my closest friends. I knew this was killing her to have to be the one to tell me. But, as head of HR, this was part of her job. She'd complained about firing other people before. It was her least favorite part of human resources. She thought it should be handled in each department, but everyone was always foisting responsibility off on someone else.

And now...she was...she was...

I stood abruptly. "Okay," I managed to get out.

It sounded hollow and brittle. More a gasp than a word.

"Heidi," Julia said. There was anguish in her voice. Her eyes told me she wanted to reach out to me. Her body said that she wanted to comfort me. Her hands told me to stay... to figure out what was going on...to let her answer all the questions I had bubbling under the surface.

But I bit my lip and took a frantic step backward. "Okay," I repeated.

"Are you sure you don't—"

"Yep," I interrupted her.

If I didn't leave now, I wouldn't be able to hold my head up high as I walked out of that office. And I needed that. I wanted to hold on to my pride until I was gone.

I wrenched the door to her office open and stormed out of there like a thundercloud. As soon as I was out of her office, I went from near to tears to anger to pissed to wanting to fucking murder someone in about three seconds flat. My hands were clenched into fists at my sides. My heart was galloping at breakneck speed. My ears were ringing. I was seeing a tinge of red to everything.

My head snapped into Landon's office. I was ready to blow a gasket, but I was unprepared for him not to be there. The office was dark, and the door was closed. I never looked in there anymore for fear of this. Exact. Fucking. Thing. And then, the day that I did, the day after we'd gotten back from the PGA Tour Championship, he was missing.

"Fuck." I slapped onto his closed office door and then marched over to my desk.

"What was that about?" Matt asked.

He could clearly tell something was wrong. He looked confused and concerned. I just wanted to tell him to fuck off, but I held my tongue.

"I'm going home," I told him instead of the truth. I scrambled to collect a bunch of my personal effects. I'd worked here for six years. I couldn't get everything in one trip, but I wanted to make sure I had the things I really needed.

"Why?"

I slammed my hand down on the paperwork I was organizing. "Do I *look* like I want to talk right now?"

He shrank back. I was usually a sarcastic bitch, but I didn't raise my voice.

"No."

"No, I don't."

I tossed everything I had managed to get together into my oversize boho bag, wiped any personal files and passwords I had off of the computer, and left everything else. I for sure thought Matt was going to try to say something else to me, but he didn't. He just let me pass. He probably thought it was PMS or something equally sexist. That was the MO in the office.

I left the office in a daze. I somehow made it out of the Wright Construction building, past the sign out front with the company motto, *What's Wright Is Right*, and to my car without being accosted by anyone. Tossing the contents of my purse into the passenger seat, I threw myself into the driver's side and just fucking sat there.

My gaze drifted up the side of the building I'd worked at for so long, and everything hit me at once.

I had been fired.

I would never work here again.

I had no source of income.

Everything I had worked for was for nothing.

My life as I had known it was over.

The tears that I had been holding back with shock and anger released like a torrent from my body. Suddenly, I was sobbing into my steering wheel, my hands on either side of it, as I uncontrollably heaved up and down. A choking sound came from my mouth, and I tried to suck in oxygen that couldn't seem to get to my brain.

There was no oxygen. There was no air. There was nothing.

I couldn't breathe.

My body shook as the tears continued to stream down my face, and I turned into a blubbering mess. I started to cough loud and desperately. My chest ached, my fingers and toes felt numb, and my head felt fuzzy. I hiccuped over the tears, fighting my body's response to the horrible news.

I was hyperventilating.

I was having a panic attack.

I needed to calm down.

"Fuck," I gasped out through the tears. "Calm down. Calm down. Calm down."

No matter how many times I told myself to stop what I was doing, it didn't matter. Panic attacks weren't rational. There was nothing that anyone could do to be logical about the situation. *Calm* was not a word that you even understood when it hit you. There was only that moment when your brain stopped functioning, you stopped breathing, and the tears refused to stop falling.

It had been so long since I had an attack. Years, in fact. The last one had been the day when my dad was sent to prison. I hadn't cried in front of him. I hadn't said a damn word. He'd pleaded with me. Begged for one more minute with me. A chance. I'd coldly stared into his pale eyes that were so like mine and then turned and walked away. When I'd gotten back to my car, I hadn't been able to leave the courtroom for nearly an hour.

I couldn't do that today.

I couldn't be here another minute.

Despite the dangers, I revved the engine and peeled out of the parking lot. My breathing was erratic, and my tears refused to stop. My face was hot, and my eyes burned. Still, I didn't stop. I didn't pull over.

I made it home without remembering a single thing I'd done to get there. As soon as I was inside, I went straight to the shower, turned the water on as hot as it would go, stripped out of my work clothes, and stepped under the spray.

The tears eventually subsided to a low keening and chest-rattling breaths. I moved into the living room and turned on some mindless TV, staring at it, unseeing.

That was how Emery found me when she got home after school. "Hey! You're home early!"

I slowly turned to look at her and then back at the TV. "Yeah."

"What's going on?" she asked after seeing my splotchy red face and the clothes she had dubbed my Tinder breakup pajamas. Emery hurried to the couch and sat down. "Did you and Landon break up? What did he do to you? I'll kill him."

"I…I…" I coughed over the words, trying to get them out. "I got fired."

Emery whipped back, shocked. "You got fired?"

"Yep."

She gaped at me. "You're the best employee they have. On what grounds could they possibly fire you?"

"Probably fucking my boss."

"It's just rumor and speculation," Emery insisted. "I mean, what do they know? They're grasping at straws. You can deny it. Landon will stick up for you. We'll tell Jensen and Morgan. We'll get this straightened out. They can't do that. It's unlawful."

"They have proof."

"What proof?" Emery squeaked.

The tears came again when I thought about it. "Landon and I went to a golf tournament together this weekend, and someone took videos of us together. I watched one of us kissing."

"Oh." Emery tucked her legs up underneath herself and chewed on her finger. "Well...fuck."

"Yeah."

I bent forward, putting my head in my hands. Emery rubbed my back and held me as I cried.

"Who sent in the videos?" she asked after a couple of minutes.

I sniffled. "I don't know. I had to get out of Julia's office..."

"Julia?" Emery gasped. "She fired you?"

"She didn't want to, but...yeah."

"God. Okay, I'm going to text her and see if she'll come over. Maybe we can figure out who sent it in."

I went back to watching the TV and contemplating how horrible my life was at the present moment when Julia showed up in my apartment.

"Hey," she said tentatively.

"Come on in," Emery said.

"Is she..."

"A wreck but not mad at you."

Julia deflated. "Thank God. That was the hardest thing I've ever done at work before."

I dismissively waved my hand and then turned back to the TV. She was just doing her job. I couldn't blame her. I was busy blaming myself and Landon for this catastrophe.

"Did it say who that email was from?" Emery prodded.

"No, it was anonymous." Julia frowned. "I thought it was weird, but there were enough different images that we couldn't think that they had been doctored. Then, Heidi agreed that they'd gone away together."

"I didn't know you were going to fire me if I said yes," I muttered.

"I know. I'm sorry. I feel like the worst friend ever."

"How is Landon taking all of this?" Emery asked.

I frowned and glanced away. I hadn't asked about Landon. I hadn't even checked my phone to see if he had texted or called. My fury was building again, and I didn't know if I could handle seeing him when I was like this.

"I have no idea," Julia said. "He was in some meeting for the higher-ups all day. I never saw him."

"Does he even know?" Emery asked. "I mean…he has to know, right? You ran this by him first?"

"I…I don't know. I thought that everyone had done what they were supposed to do in this situation. It wasn't my job to follow up with Landon. I mean…I thought he had already been questioned."

"Heidi, you should probably text him."

I shook my head. "No."

"He might not even know."

"I said no," I spat.

Both girls stilled. They could feel my anger from where they were standing next to the couch. I couldn't seem to get it under control.

If Landon and I had just waited, if we had listened to everyone else, if we had done the smart thing and stayed away from each other, I never would have been in this situation.

Emery and Julia shared a meaningful look, but they didn't say anything further about it. They just put on *Mean Girls* and brought me ice cream. We were only twenty minutes into the movie when my front door sounded like it was going to be broken down.

My eyes shot to Emery's. "What did you do?"

She gave me an innocent look. "Who me?"

"I hate you."

"I know. I love you, too, buttercup." Emery nudged Julia, and they both headed to her room.

Slow and creaky, I eased my body off the couch and wandered to the front door. I felt like I'd aged a lifetime in the few hours since I left work. I turned the doorknob and found an irritated Landon standing at the entrance.

"Is it true?" he asked.

"Like you don't know."

He narrowed his eyes. "Can I come in?"

"I guess you can. Doesn't matter anymore," I said as I walked away from the front door, leaving him room to follow me in. I heard the door click shut behind him.

"Emery said that you were fired," he said.

I winced, as if he had slapped me. *Fired*. That fucking word. Poisonous and toxic. One word able to do so much damage.

"Happened this morning."

"Why didn't you call or text me?"

His arm landed on my sleeve, and I jumped away from him. A look of horror flitted across his face and then disappeared.

"What would I have said?"

"I could have been here. We could have worked this out together."

"I think we already did. And it happened *just* like I'd said it would, Landon. That time I told you what would happen and you didn't listen. You just had to move forward. You had to have me. You couldn't listen to me when I told you that this couldn't work, that my job meant something to me, that I needed it. I even told you *why* I needed it, and that didn't seem to be enough. You had to push. You had to demand. Well, congratulations! You got exactly what you wanted."

"You think I wanted this?" he asked in disbelief. "You think I wanted you to lose your job?"

"I think you didn't care one way or another as long as you got what *you* wanted," I said with venom in my voice. My hands were trembling at my sides.

"That is not true, and you know it."

"No, I don't!" I shouted at him. "Because here I am, without my job, and you get to keep yours because you're a fucking Wright brother."

"I didn't even know that this was happening. I never would have let them do this to you."

"Well, it seems we've found something you're not good at. I thought what we had between us felt so right." I shook my head and looked away. "I was wrong."

"Heidi," he moaned. He ran a hand back through his hair. "Please, love, let me fix this. I can make this right. I know I can."

"No, you can't. And you don't really want to. You all have millions of dollars. You're a fucking celebrity. How could you possibly understand someone like me?" I threw at him.

"I didn't think any of that ever mattered to you," he said stiffly.

"And here I thought that I mattered to you. Guess we were both wrong."

Landon recoiled at my words. I was hurting him on purpose. I knew I was. But I was so angry with me and him and the world. He was just an easy target. Because we could have stopped. He could have not pushed me the way he had, but he didn't stop or back down. And, now, I was the one paying the price. Not him.

"You should leave," I told him.

"Please, don't do this."

"I said, leave."

"Heidi, I won't just leave you."

I turned my back on him. "Just *go*, Landon. Now."

Tears welled in my eyes again. I heard him breathing deeply behind me. I knew that he didn't want to go. And part of me wanted to turn around and beg him to stay.

But I didn't.

And he left.

Thirty-Four

Landon

I tried to put my hand through the brick wall outside of Heidi's apartment when I left. It didn't go so well.

"Fuck!" I cried as I stomped over to the Mercedes.

I shook my bleeding hand out before getting into the front seat, but it didn't do much good. The knuckles were broken, and it hurt like a motherfucker. At least the pain kept me from thinking about the train wreck I had just walked into.

When Emery had texted me and told me to come over, I'd expected it to be bad. But I certainly hadn't thought it would be as bad as it was. I couldn't fucking believe that Heidi had been fired without anyone even *talking* to me. It was so unbelievably fucked up that I was beyond livid. I had known Heidi would be a pissed, but I hadn't prepared for her to take it out on me. I hadn't been prepared for it to be my fault.

And I should have been. Because it was my fault.

I'd pushed and advocated for this. I wanted to be with her, and I didn't care about anything else. Of course, I never wanted her to lose her job. Never in a million years. But we hadn't been careful. Hell, we'd never been careful. It was fucking amazing that no one had caught us before now, considering all the shit we had done together.

But I wasn't going to let Heidi walk away from us.

We were meant for each other.

Nothing was going to stand in my way.

I drove over to Jensen's with a blind determination. I broke at least three traffic laws on the way, but I could really give zero fucks about it all.

After pulling into the garage, I wandered into Jensen's house and called out for him, "Jensen!"

"Up here," he called back.

I found him sitting in his second-story office, staring at his computer screen. My hand was still on fire, but I slapped it down onto his desk.

"What the hell did you do?" I demanded.

He glanced at my hand. "You're bleeding on my desk."

"Let me repeat myself. What the fuck did you do?"

"Landon, I didn't do anything. But I know what you're going to say."

"No, you don't!"

"Yes, I think I do. Now, have a seat and talk to me about this."

"I quit!"

Jensen sighed and rubbed the bridge of his nose. "Sit," he repeated, pointing at the chair.

"I'm not going to sit down and be a good boy, Jensen! This is outrageous. I told you I was seeing someone, and then Heidi got fired before I was even told about what was happening. Don't you think that's fucking ridiculous? I would never have let that happen to her, and now, you have lost one of your best employees," I snapped at him. "So, yeah, I quit. I need the job, but I don't need it this much. Give Heidi her job back, and let me fucking figure out my own thing."

Jensen leaned back in his seat. "Are you done?"

"Am I fucking done? That's all you have to say?"

"Well, are you going to clean up your hand, was second, but I thought I'd lead with the more important question."

"Did you hear a word I said?"

"Of course I did, Landon. But you're not quitting the company. I didn't know that Heidi had been fired until it had already happened, and I'm working on discovering who is behind the videos that surfaced."

"Who cares where the videos came from? What matters is that Heidi needs this job, and you stole it from her because of me."

"I understand that you're upset," Jensen said calmly. He slowly got to his feet and put his hand on my shoulder. "But you can't think clearly when you're like this."

I smacked his hand away and ignored the pain from that movement. "Heidi broke up with me because of this shit. I don't need to think clearly. I need to fix this."

"What happened to Heidi was…unfortunate," Jensen said, carefully choosing his words. "It was handled poorly. I understand that the employees in her department believed they were doing the right thing to contain the situation and avoid a scandal. However, as you were not notified, no investigation was put into it other than to assume that the evidence hadn't been doctored. We both know that this isn't good for the company. And, obviously, it's not good for your relationship with Heidi. And, by the way…Heidi? No wonder you didn't want to tell me."

"Yeah, well, I did want to tell you, but I didn't want her to get fucking fired."

Jensen sighed and crossed his arms over his chest. "Look, speaking as the CEO of this company and your boss, the evidence was pretty damning, and everyone reacted quickly to minimize the damage. Have you seen the videos?"

I shook my head. "I didn't even know what they had."

Jensen moved back to his computer and pulled up the email that he had received with the evidence of Heidi and me together. It was a series of videos and a couple of pictures of Heidi and me on the golf course, in the clubhouse, and even at dinner at the seafood restaurant that we had picked at random. Whoever had taken these shots had clearly been following us because no one else had known where we were.

"Well, fuck," I groaned, finally sinking into the seat.

"I agree. After watching these, do you see why she was fired?"

I hated myself, but I nodded. "I know why they did it, but I still want to fix it."

"The way to fix this is to figure out who sent these. It was anonymous. I already have someone looking into it. The way these images were sent to us feels like a threat. It was pointed. Not sent to me or Morgan, but directly to Heidi's immediate supervisor. Does Heidi have any enemies? Anyone who would want to see her fired?"

I shook my head. "I don't know. I don't think so. Wait, maybe this Matt guy who works in her department. He wanted the promotion that she got."

Jensen drummed his fingers on the desk. "He has motive, but would he have had access to these videos?"

"Fuck, I don't know."

"And do you?"

"Do I what?"

Jensen averted his gaze, and that was when I realized he had already come to a conclusion. He looked back at me then. "Do *you* know anyone who would benefit from Heidi getting fired?"

I opened my mouth as the conclusion Jensen had come to dawned on me. "Miranda."

"Yeah. That's where I landed, too."

"She was at the tournament," I told him. "Heidi saw her briefly. She was trying to pick up a golf buddy of mine to replace me, but we didn't see her the rest of the weekend. We skipped a dinner and everything to avoid her."

"Didn't seem to work," Jensen said, touching his screen.

"Fuck. What a conniving bitch!"

"I wouldn't put it past her."

"Oh, I'm going to call her and give her a piece of my mind."

"I'm certain that's what she wants from you—a reaction. It's best for us to dig a little deeper and see if we can nail her on something like this. Let's make sure it's really her and not this…Matt guy. Then, we'll decide where to go from there. A judge will not look kindly on threats if she's trying to get more money."

"I could wring her neck."

"I would also advise against that," Jensen said with amusement. "Though I know the feeling well."

I leaned my head back and stared at the white ceiling. "What the fuck do I do, man? Heidi freaked out on me and forced me out of her apartment. I'm head over heels for that girl, and she won't even talk to me."

"As your brother, I'd tell you to fight for her. If you're willing to throw everything away for her, she must be worth it."

"She is. She is worth it."

"You know, Emery suspected something was going on with y'all back in December, but I thought she was crazy."

"Yeah. She was right. I tried to deny that anything was happening back then and tried to say we were just talking a lot. But that's a lie. I'd fallen for her, and I stopped talking to her when I realized I had feelings for her." I shrugged. "Didn't want to be a cheating douche bag."

"I think that was smart. All things considered."

"Yeah, but now, when I finally get her, it all blows up in my face."

"You'll work through it," Jensen confidently told me. "You should just try and talk to her."

"No, she won't listen to me. She unloaded when I stepped into her apartment. The last thing she wants to do is talk to me. She's blaming me for this."

Jensen ran a hand back through his hair. "What if I tried to talk to her?"

I narrowed my eyes. "You'd do that?"

"She was my employee after all. Until we get this all cleared up, I can't do anything about her job, but I can try to fix how this was handled and let her know that you were not at fault."

"I…yeah," I said with a nod.

I'd texted her half a dozen times after Emery messaged me, but she hadn't responded. She actually hadn't responded to my texts all day. I'd been messaging her through my meetings.

"That'd be great."

"Okay. I'll do that now. You go clean up your hand."

I nodded and disappeared into the guest bedroom. I ran my hand under cold water, hissing the whole time. It hurt something horrible. Dumb fucking idea. Yet it had seemed perfectly logical at the time.

My stomach was in knots over everything that had happened. And the helplessness that had settled over me. Quitting had felt like the only logical thing to do. If I weren't her boss, then she could have her job back. Yet it wasn't that simple. There were more things to consider than our relationship. Too bad I couldn't concentrate on any of them but the way that Heidi had looked at me when she told me to get out of her place.

Once my hand was bandaged—another freaking injury for me to deal with—I moseyed back into Jensen's office. He was staring down at his phone, and he looked bleak.

"What?" I asked. My stomach dropped, and I waited for the bad news that I knew was coming.

"She didn't answer."

I waited. "And?"

"Nothing."

"And, Jensen?"

He frowned. "She texted back."

"What did she say?"

He shook his head. I snatched the phone from him and stared at the text from Heidi.

> *I know you're only calling me because of Landon. So, just…don't. I don't want to talk to him. I don't want to talk about him. I want nothing to do with him or any of his family. Leave me alone.*

My hands shook as the words filtered in and out of my vision. If it had been my phone, I probably would have thrown it against the wall and shattered it into a million fucking pieces. As it was, I tossed it to Jensen without care and left his office.

He followed. "Hey, man, where are you going?"

"To find Austin."

"What? Why?"

"Because I know he'll have a spare bottle handy."

"I have alcohol here."

"Fuck off, Jensen. I want to get wasted and not think about how my girlfriend broke up with me or how I lost the best thing that had ever happened to me."

"Shit," Jensen muttered. "I'm coming with you."

"Fine," I spat.

I didn't care one way or another who was there. Austin and Patrick were good for a distraction. And I needed one. Desperately. Because, otherwise, I was going to end up doing something really stupid.

Tonight, I would be pissed.

Tomorrow, I would put my life back together.

Thirty-Five

Heidi

Two days later, I still hadn't moved from the couch. I was in the same clothes, and my hair was in the same topknot.

Emery took one look at me when she got home from work and started to force me into the shower. "You cannot do this. You can't wallow."

"Yes, I can. What else do I have to do?"

"Heidi Anne Martin! You are a strong, independent, unbelievably incredible woman. You will pick yourself up from this and keep going. This is not the end of your life. You are a brilliant engineer, and anyone would be lucky to have you. Just because you are no longer gainfully employed by Wright Construction does not change a damn thing about your awesomeness."

"You're a great friend, Em."

"Damn straight!" She shoved me toward the shower. "Now, go."

I complied. By the time that I was clean, had blown out my hair, and had chosen a new set of pajamas to lounge around in, Julia was here with her hand on her hip, looking fierce as fuck.

"What is this? An intervention?" I asked.

Emery and Julia were both dressed in cute black-on-black outfits. And they looked ready to take me down if I resisted whatever plot they had come up with.

"Hell yes, it is," Julia said. "Now, turn your cute ass around, and put on something presentable. We're going out."

"I'm not going out."

"Don't make us come in there," Emery threatened. "We're trying to get you back on your feet. You haven't left the house in three days. It's time."

I gritted my teeth. "Where are we going?"

"Shopping."

"God, y'all are the worst," I muttered.

They were playing to my weakness. They knew I loved shopping. Even if I didn't need anything. Though maybe some retail therapy would help.

"Whatever," Julia said. "Just hurry up!"

I matched their morose attire and slipped into black skinnies, a black tank, and some old beat-up Converse. I skipped all my makeup, except mascara. Emery handed me her wallet, and I stuffed it in my purse. The weirdo still didn't like to carry a purse.

We took Julia's SUV to Malouf's, a local clothing store that was essentially the Nordstrom of Lubbock. It had all the fancy designers and did custom-tailored suits. Even though I shouldn't spend money here, I loved to do it.

A sigh escaped me as we entered because I realized there was no way I could afford anything in here now. With my job gone, I would have to use my savings to cover rent and my student loans.

Normally, I was the one grabbing dresses off the racks and throwing them in my friends' unwilling arms, but today, I trailed behind. I might be able to suffer through window shopping, but I didn't have to enjoy it. The thought of spending money at the moment made me panic.

I knew I needed to be looking for another job. I just couldn't get myself to do much of anything. I was mourning the career I'd always thought I would have.

"This one," Emery said, tossing the dress to me.

I reached out and caught it before the silky material could fall to the ground. I looked at the dusty-rose satin slip dress that Emery had handed to me. It was stunning. My color and long enough for my build, too.

"Where the hell would I wear this?" I held it up for both girls to examine.

They wore matching grins.

"Oh no. Is there a bigger plot happening here?"

"Just try it on," Emery encouraged.

"You'll look so hot in that!" Julia said. "I'm going to go with something black, of course. But pink? Man, no one can pull off pink like you. With that long blonde hair and those bright blue eyes."

"Whoa," Emery said, putting her hand out. "Stop moving in on my woman."

I couldn't help it. I laughed. It was the first time since I'd left work that I'd done anything other than frown or cry. It felt…nice.

"Success!" Julia said.

"I knew shopping would work," Emery agreed.

Then, they gathered me up and hurried me to the dressing room. Their arms were full of almost exclusively black apparel…and I had one dress. I wasn't sure if they thought I'd bolt if we took too long to look or what. They seemed anxious to get me healthy. To see my smile and hope that I would turn back into the bubbly friend they were used to. I just…wasn't sure I would be able to do that. Not yet at least.

Still, I humored them. I slid the sleek material over my head and down my narrow hips. It cut low in the front and had a relatively high slit up the right side. When I stepped out of the dressing room, I was shocked to see the transformation. The girls were right. This was my color.

"Oh my God," Emery muttered. "It's not even fair. Your genetics are unreal. Why were you given all the good genes? You're as bad as Kimber."

I laughed. Emery's sister, Kimber, had been prom queen in high school, and they were night and day in appearance. I looked more like Kimber than Emery ever had. In fact, in high school, it had felt more like the three of us were siblings, and I wasn't an only child.

"You have to get it," Julia said as soon as she stepped out of the room.

"I have nowhere to wear it, and I'm sure I can't afford it."

"Look," Emery said with a sigh, leaning against the three-way mirror. "We're all really worried about you. I know how much this job meant to you."

"I really don't think that you do."

"Heidi, I've known you my whole life. I know that you have wanted to succeed in this forever."

I shook my head. "You don't know everything, Em."

"What? What don't I know?"

"My dad," I choked out. "My dad used my college funds."

"He used your…" Her mouth hung open. "Oh. Oh God."

"What?" Julia asked. "What am I missing?"

"He used my college funds on drugs and shackled me with student loan debt and then some," I spat angrily. "So, I needed the job more than anyone even knew. And, now, I don't know what I'm going to do."

"Heidi, I'm sorry," Emery said. "Why didn't you tell me?"

"Because I was handling it," I said with a sigh. "And now…now, I'm not."

"Well, I think you should talk to Jensen. We talked, and I know he's worried about you and Landon. He's been going out and drinking every night with Austin and Patrick. We all know that's not a smart decision."

"I don't want to hear it," I said, holding up my hands.

"Well, I'm sorry. You need to. Jensen has been trying to get ahold of you. I know that he wants to apologize to you about how this was all handled and that they're looking into the circumstances behind it."

"Em, just stop."

"Come on, please. Talk to him."

"I already texted him back."

"I know," Emery said with a frown. "But—"

"There is no *but* to this conversation, Em. I know what you're trying to do. But I do not want to talk about Jensen Wright or Landon Wright or *any* of the Wrights."

"But it isn't their fault," Emery said.

"It isn't? I wasn't just *fired* from the company that they own and operate?"

"You were, but—"

"Are you really going to try to stand there and defend them to me?" I gasped. "*You*, of all people?"

I turned around and walked back into the dressing room. I didn't want to have to deal with this shit. My body was shaking from the effort to not explode. I loved Emery to pieces, and I knew that she meant well. I hadn't wanted to yell at her. But she had been talking nonsense to me, and she fucking knew it.

"I'm not defending how it all went down. It was shitty," Emery said through the dressing room wall. I could hear the desperation seeping into her voice. "But I know none of them knew that it was happening. They weren't even aware that you were fired or that you were dating Landon until after it all happened. You need to talk to someone. If not Landon, at least talk to Jensen."

With my clothes back on, I hung the dress back on the hanger and stepped out. "No."

"Heidi—"

"It's over, Emery. I got fired because of Landon. No matter how you try to twist it around, that is what happened. It's on him. Don't you remember that Landon who shattered your heart, lied to you, and ignored you for months? This shouldn't be that hard for you to grasp."

"That was ten years ago, Heidi! And he's different with you."

I snorted. "Yeah, right."

"Um, can I cut in?" Julia asked. "I didn't know Landon ten years ago. I don't really know him now. But I do know that he has been awful at work since you left. I have never seen a grown man mope like that."

"Jesus," I said. I leaned my head back and sighed. "I don't know. Okay? I don't know anything. I don't really even want to be discussing this. I lost my job and boyfriend all in one day. I am broken and beaten and depressed. My heart is an empty wasteland where Landon Wright used to occupy. And I want things to go back to the way they were. But how can I be with someone who was so careless with the thing I held most dear? It's not something that is going to be fixed overnight."

"Okay," Emery said slowly. "We didn't mean to push. I think you should talk to Jensen when you're ready. Even if that's not today."

"It's a good idea," Julia agreed. "Keeping this all bottled up does not help. Trust me, I know. I've been in therapy for years, trying to get over my crazy ex. I wish I'd had friends like you and Emery back then. Running away doesn't always solve the problem. That's all I'm saying."

"Yeah, maybe. I know your situation is so crazier than this, Julia," I said with a sigh. "I don't know. I'll think about it, okay?"

Emery and Julia nodded. They couldn't ask for more than that. I wasn't prepared to give more than that.

I held up the dress still in my hand. "What were you trying to get me to buy this for anyway?"

"Charity Benefit," Julia said.

I groaned. "You thought I'd go to the Wright event after this week? Are you out of your minds?"

They glanced at each other and shrugged.

"Maybe a little," Emery said.

"We could make it a girls' trip," Julia said. "Free champagne?"

"No."

"Humph," Emery muttered. "Just think about it."

"No."

"I'm buying the dress," Julia said, ignoring my protests. "Just as a backup. In case you change your mind and go with us."

That wasn't happening.

But, in the end, I couldn't change their minds. And the dress came home with me.

Still, my mind wandered back to Landon. Even though I didn't want it, too. I wondered what he was doing. If he had been getting drunk with Austin every night, like Emery had said. If he had been moping around, like Julia had said. If he was hurting as much as I was. My heart ached with the loss of him. I'd only just gotten him…only just fallen in love…and then it had all been tragically ripped away.

I couldn't turn back the clock.

We'd known it was wrong, but it'd felt so damn right.

Now, it was all up in flames.

Thirty-Six

Landon

Day four of no response from Heidi.

Not even a text telling me to fuck off and leave her alone.

I was going totally insane. The only thing keeping me from banging her door down was the reassurance from Emery and my family that Heidi needed time.

Time.

That sick fucker.

It was turning into my least favorite word in existence. Something I had no control over. Something that constantly hounded me. Something that was impossible to run from or escape.

An endless snake eternally eating its tail.

Laughing at me.

And how finite my life was.

I brushed aside the thoughts that continued to plague me and sent Austin's third call to voice mail. I knew he wanted to go out and drink. We'd done it every night since Heidi was unceremoniously fired and then dumped me. It had been a welcome reprieve from the ache that was so brutal, it was a fissure in my chest. But I needed a night away from it all. To be alone and decide my next move.

Without even knowing exactly where I was going, I pulled into the cemetery parking lot and cut the engine. It was a clear night, and the moon hung heavy in the sky as I stepped out of the car, threw on a North Face jacket from the backseat, and wandered out among the gravestones.

When my mom had died, I'd only been seven, and cemeteries had creeped me out for a long time after that. But, when my dad had died, I'd just stopped coming. I'd told Heidi that I wanted to introduce her to my parents when we were official, but the truth was…I hadn't been out here more than a handful of times since they passed. And never alone.

But I felt drawn here tonight.

No more alcohol.

No more wasted nights.

No more forgetting.

I found my parents buried next to each other in the middle of the cemetery. They had ostentatious headstones that couldn't be missed. The word *Wright* was in big letters on each of them. I sank into the grass between my mom and dad and just stared, unseeing. It was enough to be out there tonight and let my parents take the brunt of my pain.

Headlights pulled me from my seat, and I hopped up to see a flashlight coming toward me. But the person never made it. They stopped a few rows short of me, and I was shocked when I realized I knew exactly who it was.

Without a second thought, I walked right over and cleared my throat. "Heidi."

She whipped around and held the flashlight like a weapon. Her breathing was shaky, her eyes wide in terror.

"Landon?" she asked softly.

"Yeah."

"What are you doing here?"

"Same as you."

She shook her head and turned away from me. "You scared the shit out of me."

"Sorry about that. I wasn't expecting anyone else to be here."

"Me either."

"Heidi, I—"

"Landon, don't," she muttered. "Please don't."

"No," I told her. "I can't just shut down. Not around you."

She blew out a heavy breath. "I thought you'd be at a bar with Austin."

"Why?"

"I don't know. Emery said you'd been going out."

"Yeah, well, it's hard not to want to drink when your girlfriend breaks up with you."

She grimaced. "I bet."

"Man, I didn't come over here to guilt-trip you. I…I wanted to see you. I've missed you like fucking crazy."

"I know."

"Emery tell you that, too?" I arched an eyebrow.

She shook her head. "No. Personal experience."

I managed a quick smile at that. She'd missed me. Fuck, just seeing her was eating me from the inside out. I wanted her back in my arms, in my bed, in my life.

Sometimes, love cracked your heart open to show you what really mattered.

Her. Only her.

I held my hand out. "Come with me."

"Landon…"

"Just…trust me."

With a sigh, she placed her hand in mine and let me walk her over to my parents' gravestones. She dropped my hand when we got there and stared down at their names on the stones.

"Your parents," she whispered.

"Yeah. Um…I've never done this before," I said, feeling totally out of my depth. "But, Mom…Dad…this is Heidi. She's, uh…well, a friend. Actually, she broke my heart, but I love her so much that I wanted to introduce her to you anyway."

"Landon…"

"Stop saying my name like that," I said, turning to face her. "You sound so dejected when you say it like that. I want to remember the way you said it when you were moaning it on top of me."

She jerked her head to the side and took a deep breath. "I should go."

"Heidi, I understand why you blame me for this."

"You don't seem like you get it," she said. Her hands were clenched at her sides.

"I do. I get it because it's my fault." I sighed. "Jensen is looking into who sent the videos to the company, and my guess is, it was Miranda. And, if I'm right, then you're right. It is my fault that all of this happened. Because my bitch ex is trying to get back at me."

"You think Miranda took those videos?"

"I think it's a real possibility that she would want you to get fired after finding out we were together."

"But wouldn't she have sent them to Jensen?"

I laughed humorlessly. "No. She hates my family. All of them. She would know that Jensen would side with me and keep this quiet. And, you know, I should have seen this about her all along. You asked me once, 'Why her?' Why did I marry her?" I shook my head and glanced at my father's gravestone. "I've been saying for a long time that it was because she wasn't this person when we met and I thought she loved me. I don't think I was willing to see what I'd actually done."

"What do you mean? That you married a psycho?" She crossed her arms.

"Yes. I thought I was making the right choice. My dad wanted me to be with someone worthy of the Wright name. That's why he didn't want me with Emery. He didn't think she was good enough. So, when I met Miranda out of college, she came from old money, worked as a nurse on the Tour, seemed to know the ins and outs of golf, and fit right into my life. I thought…I thought it was what my dad would have wanted. Even after I found out her parents were bankrupt and I helped them get out of debt, I was still blinded."

"You paid off her parent's debts?" Heidi gasped.

"Yeah. No one knows. I thought it was the right thing to do at the time. I had married their daughter after all. But, if I'd just realized then how crazy she was and how much she was using me, we wouldn't be here right now."

"Maybe. Maybe not," Heidi said.

"I don't want to talk about Miranda or think about the person I was when I was with her. I only want to be exactly who I am when I'm with you."

She closed her eyes and turned her head to the stars. She was shaking slightly from the chill. Lubbock was so windy all the time that it would make nights cold. I slipped off the North Face I'd put on earlier and slung it around her shoulders. She looked like she wanted to protest but was too cold to do so.

"Thanks." Her eyes dropped to the ground and then back up to mine. "I'm sorry for yelling at you the other day."

My jaw nearly hit the ground. "You are?"

"I was angry and frustrated and so, so pissed off. I took all of that out on you. Whether or not you think it's your fault, you didn't deserve how I treated you."

"Heidi, my firecracker," I said with a chuckle, "I could never love you less for yelling at me."

I took a step toward her, and she took one back.

"But I can't do this."

"What?" I asked, my voice coming out harsher than I'd intended. "What do you mean?"

"What I'm feeling is crippling," she told me. "Completely physically debilitating. It is turning my entire world upside down, and I'm trying to find where I still fit in. I lost my job and my identity all in one fell swoop."

"Don't you think that I, of all people, understand what that's like?" I asked. "When I injured my back, golf was gone. Something I had been doing my entire life. The only job I had ever known. And not just that, but I was physically limited from that point on. I was half the man that I had been all because of one bad swing. I think I can understand what it feels like to have an identity crisis."

"Fuck, I know. I do know that you have been here before. And I'm sorry that I yelled at you, but it doesn't really change how I feel. It doesn't change the fact that what happened...I associate with you and your family. So, it makes *this* hard." She gestured between us.

"Being with me?"

"Being *near* you," she corrected. "Seeing you and knowing that I love you and that I can't let this go. That I can't forgive and forget. That, right now, I hate the Wrights and everything they fucking stand for. Because I lost myself, got caught up in you, and did exactly what I'd sworn I wouldn't do. Now, I'm fucked."

"I see," I said, suddenly miserable again.

She loved me, but she didn't want to even be near me. Miranda had hated my family for no reason, and now, Heidi hated them with good reason. I couldn't fucking win.

"So, I just...I need time, Landon."

Hello, time, my old friend.

"Of course," I found myself saying. "It's the last thing that I want to give you, but I will if you think it will help."

She took a stutter step forward, as if she wanted to throw herself into my arms. Then, she seemed to catch herself and stopped. She shrugged out of my jacket and offered it back to me.

"Keep it."

"I can't."

"Please, Heidi. Let me take care of you even if you don't want to be taken care of."

I bridged the distance that she had been hesitant to cross before and tugged the jacket closer around her. Her eyes were round with concern at my nearness. But she didn't pull away.

"You might hate me right now, but I'll be right here. If you need me, if you think you can move past what happened. I'll be here, trying to fix what I broke between us." I leaned forward and pressed my lips to her forehead. "I should have waited for you. I should have probably waited until Jensen or Morgan moved me. There are a ton of things I could have done, but I can't regret our time together. I never will. You stole my heart completely with that first kiss in the back of Flips, and I don't even want it back."

A tear slipped down her cheek, and I gently swiped it off her face.

"No more tears, love."

"I'm sorry, Landon," she said in a choked gasp.

Then, she turned away from me and fled through the cemetery, leaving me with nothing but the dead to console my broken heart.

Thirty-Seven

Heidi

"I cannot believe that I let you talk me into this," I said with a heavy sigh as Julia parked her SUV in the parking lot of the Overton.

"It'll be fine," Emery insisted from the passenger seat.

I was seated in the back in the dusty-rose slip dress that Julia had gotten for me. I had no idea why in the hell I was wearing it or why I was about to attend the Wright Charity Benefit.

"I have it on good authority that Landon isn't even going to be here, and you know most of the company doesn't even show up. It's mostly for hoity-toity types with a lot of money to dish out," Julia reminded me again. "Engineering would never show up for this."

Well, that was true at least. No one in the department I had worked for had any interest in dressing up and going to some high-class function. But I didn't understand why Landon wouldn't be here. It was a Wright event. He was a Wright.

"And why isn't Landon coming again?" I asked.

Julia and Emery passed a look between them.

"Jensen said he was busy," Emery said at the same time Julia said, "I think he's busy."

They both laughed nervously, and I sat straight up. "He's going to be here, isn't he?"

"No!" they both said at once.

"Oh, Jesus, y'all lied to me?" I groaned. "Take me home! I am not dealing with this tonight."

"How else were we going to get you here?" Emery asked, swiveling to face me. "So…Landon *might* be here. I don't actually know. But we can still have a good time either way. I really didn't want to go without you. Think about how much fun we had at Sutton's wedding because you dragged me there."

"You're both shitty friends."

"Free champagne. Free dinner. And a reason to wear a fancy dress. Fuck all the Wrights tonight, and let's just have a good time. What do you think, Heidi?" Julia asked with a smile. Her red hair was flipped to one side, revealing the shaved undercut.

"Okay, but steer me clear of them tonight, or I can't promise that I won't flip my shit." I popped the door open and stepped out with my nude strappy heels.

"Excellent," Emery said. She hopped out next to me in her floor-length black dress and flats.

Julia had gone with mile-high black heels. She was rocking it with a short black one-shoulder dress that showed off her tattoos. I wouldn't fuck with her.

"Shall we?" Julia asked with a wicked grin.

I nodded reluctantly and was ushered inside between my two best friends. I knew that they were only trying to be good friends, but I was not looking forward to this.

Wright Construction had fired me, and I had broken up with a member of the Wright family. Now, I was showing up at one of their events. It was pretty ballsy.

The ballroom was decorated to match the casino theme with enormous signs that said, *Wright Charity Benefit Casino Night: Double Down for Charity*. Roulette tables were set up in the center of the room. Blackjack and poker tables were already crowded with players. The noisiest area of the room was already the craps table. Women blew on the dice before men threw and hoped to win. It was outrageous and genius. All the money spent would be donated to the local Lubbock Children's Hospital. From the looks of it, it would be a very generous donation indeed.

We angled toward the least crowded bar, and Emery passed out pink champagne.

She held her glass aloft. "To free champagne, best friends, and a girls' night out."

"Let's get fucked up," Julia added.

I just laughed. "I might have to get fucked up to live through this night."

"Y'all are ruining the toast!" Emery spat.

"To Emery being shitty at toasts," Julia said, lifting her glass again.

"I'll toast to that," I said.

Emery sighed, and we all clinked our glasses together.

She muttered, "Bitches," under her breath as we tipped our drinks back.

Julia's eyes lit up as we approached the craps table. I had only a vague idea of how to play. I had never been a big gambler, but I could see that Julia really knew what she was doing as she placed her bet.

"Done this before?" I asked.

She grinned. "Not for a long time. I prefer blackjack or poker, but craps is pure entertainment. Less thinking."

I stared at the board with my head spinning. *Yeah, less thinking. Sure.* But then again, this was probably what people thought about pool, and it all fit for me like a puzzle.

Julia had a crazy stack of money in front of her after only a half hour of playtime. She shrugged her shoulders, as if it didn't mean anything, and then pocketed her earnings.

"You do know that this is for charity," Emery said with a laugh. "You're supposed to lose."

"Oh, I don't lose," Julia said. Then, she frowned and looked uncomfortable. "Um, maybe I shouldn't play?"

"I was kidding," Emery said. "Of course you should play."

We moved over to the blackjack tables where Julia's eyes were lasered in on the cards popping up. If I didn't know better, I would think she was actually counting the cards. *Could she do that?*

"Didn't expect to see you here," someone said next to me.

I whipped my head over and found Austin and Patrick standing and grinning at me. Patrick's date, Mindi, was drinking a dirty martini and staring blankly at the blackjack table in a silver micro-mini dress.

"I didn't expect to show up," I admitted.

Patrick smiled back. "Don't blame you."

But Austin's attention was on Julia. "Hey," he said.

She glanced over at him with indifference. "What do you want?"

"Need a drink?"

"No," she said. "I don't have to have a drink to have fun."

"But what does it hurt?" He tilted his head at the bar and grinned like the cocky bastard he was. "Come walk with me. We should catch up."

"No. Not with you," she told him. Her hands were on her hips, and she looked fierce.

I certainly wouldn't want to mess with her. Emery pinched my arm, and I saw that she looked worried that Austin and Julia were making a scene.

"Maybe just leave her alone," I said.

"I was simply asking her if I could get her a drink."

"I don't want a drink from you," Julia said.

"Then how about a walk?"

"I don't want to go anywhere with you either."

"That's not what you said last time."

Julia's nostrils flared. "You used me and then ignored me, Austin. You're disgusting, and I'd rather go anywhere than be around you. You're a user. That's what you do."

"Takes one to know one," he said, his jaw clenched.

Julia slapped the shit out of Austin. His head whipped to the side, and the table we were near silenced. Everyone was staring in our direction now. But Julia didn't seem to notice. She was shaking with anger.

"Fuck you," she hissed.

Austin rubbed his jaw, looked back at Julia, and laughed. "However you like it, babe."

Julia fumed and looked ready to do more than just slap him when Emery intervened and guided Julia away from Austin. But I was staring at him. He was hurt. I was shocked to see anything but the look of a drunk idiot on his face. His tone had been reactionary. He'd been offended, so he'd gone for the jugular, and when that hadn't worked, he'd made it a joke. It was a defense mechanism.

I stepped forward and got in his face. "If you ever hurt my friend again, I will rip your balls off and put them in a blender. Are we clear?"

"Crystal," he spat.

I stormed after Julia, but she was holed up in the restroom and wouldn't let Emery or me near her. I knew that feeling. She probably just needed to compose herself before she could go out there again.

God, why did guys have to act like such dicks?

I was standing against the wall, sipping on another glass of champagne that a waiter had brought by, when I saw

Landon break away from Austin and Patrick and aim straight toward me. It was like he had a radar to find me standing like a wallflower against the back of the room. Part of me wanted to turn tail and hide in the women's restroom, but I didn't. I kept my dignity.

"Hey, you showed," he said with some surprise in his voice.

"Yeah. I, uh…was told you wouldn't be here."

He deflated for a second before a quick recovery. "Of course you were. That sounds right."

He stared at me for a second too long, like he was drinking me in. I had completely forgotten about my sexy dress and high heels.

"You look incredible," he told me.

"Thanks." I bit my lip as I assessed him for the first time.

Because…holy shit! He was in a tuxedo. A tailored tux that fit his body like a glove, and I wanted to slowly take it off. He was clean-shaven where he normally had a bit of scruff, and he must have gotten his hair cut. I really wished that he wasn't so hot. It would make all of this easier.

"You look nice, too."

He grinned. "Sorry about Austin. Patrick filled me in."

"Yeah. Your brother is a grade-A jerk."

"Unfortunately, that's how you can tell that he likes her."

"Well, we're not on the playground anymore, and mean boys weren't cute even then."

Landon held his hands up. "I wasn't defending his actions. I think what he said was wrong. But this is Austin. He's a total shit when he likes someone."

What I wanted to say was, if he wasn't such a raging alcoholic, then maybe he wouldn't always find himself in this situation. But I didn't really know Austin. Definitely not like Landon did. So, I just let it go.

"Do you want to…" Landon trailed off and gestured to the room behind him.

It was full of happy partygoers frivolously spending their money for charity.

"Do you really think that's smart?"

"I find that I don't care in the slightest."

It was nearly impossible to stay aloof to Landon when he was staring down at me so earnestly, begging for a little time with me. Of course, this was what had gotten us into the mess to begin with.

"Yeah. I guess everyone already knows that I was fired because of you," I said with a sigh.

"Actually, they don't. Besides your supervisor, Julia, and me, no one on your floor is aware of the reason for your absence."

"Absence?"

"Yes."

"Everyone thinks that I'm taking some time off?" I asked in disbelief. "What kind of bullshit is that? Saving your own asses?"

"They were trying to avoid a scandal, Heidi. This could have been damaging to the Wright Construction brand. Far beyond the scope we'd thought about. I, obviously, have been primarily focused on your needs, but I do understand what Jensen and Morgan are dealing with."

"Right. Fire the expendable girl, cover it up so that you don't look bad, and then talk about how it could have hurt *you* and not her," I spat.

"That's not what I'm saying at all. I'm trying to get you back!" he said. "I already tried to quit, hoping to get you your job back."

My eyes rounded. "You did?"

"Yeah. I went straight to Jensen after you broke up with me. I told him I'd figure out my own shit."

"I didn't know that," I said, my voice small.

"Yeah. But he refused. He said that, even if I quit, it wouldn't guarantee you your job. At least not until they find out who sent the videos and if they were going to issue any more threats. Or at the very least until he could find me another position."

"Wait, threats? You think the videos were a threat?"

"Don't you?" he asked. "And it worked, too."

"You think Miranda was threatening the company?"

"Any threat against a member of the Wright family is a threat against the company. And those videos being leaked strategically show me with an employee. Yeah, that's a threat."

I hadn't thought that far ahead. I had been in my own bubble all week. Dejected and depressed over the loss of my job. I hadn't once thought about this like a pool game. Lining up the balls for three moves from now. Seeing where your opponent would move to get you in the right position. It was strategic. And, if Miranda was playing this game, then it absolutely was more than just getting me out of the way.

"Fuck, she is trying for a bigger game, isn't she?" I whispered. "She wants something more than me out of the way."

Landon nodded. "Yeah, we're waiting for her to show her hand, and Jensen is trying to anticipate it. I'm so sorry that you got caught in her crosshairs."

I glanced over his shoulder and froze. "I think we're about to find out."

"Why do you…" Landon started.

Then, he followed my gaze and found Miranda striding straight toward us.

Thirty-Eight

Landon

Miranda's painted-on cherry-red dress drew eyes from all directions. And it was exactly what she wanted. So, I purposefully looked away from her and searched out Jensen and Morgan in the crowd. They weren't hard to find, standing at the front of the room with a handful of big donors. As if she could sense me watching her, Morgan nudged Jensen, and he frowned in my direction when he realized Miranda was here.

Showtime.

"Don't engage her," I told Heidi. I moved in front of her, so I was shielding her from Miranda.

"Landon, I am not going to sit back and let her assault you. If she's the bitch who made me lose my job, then I'm going to give her a piece of my mind."

Oh, Heidi. God, I love you.

"You'll be giving her what she wants. It'd be better if you let me handle this. She wants to fuck with me anyway. You're just…in her way."

"Fuck that," she muttered.

"I second that, love," I whispered before Miranda came face-to-face with me.

Miranda stopped only a foot from me and smiled, as if she were truly excited to see me. As if the last time we had come face-to-face, I hadn't thrown money at her like a common whore.

"Hello, darling," Miranda said with a seductive smile. "I've missed you."

"Can't say the same," I said.

Her eyes darted behind me to find Heidi standing there. I was sure she was glaring.

Miranda huffed. "I guess Wright has really lowered their standards this year on who they let in to their biggest charity event of the season."

I gave her a pointed look. "It seems so."

"Oh, you're so adorable when you're upset."

"Did you do it, Miranda?"

"Do what, pet? I've done a lot of things," she said with a wink.

"Did you take the videos and send them to the company?"

She batted her eyelashes at me. "What videos?"

"You know damn well what videos."

"I asked you point-blank if you were seeing someone else, Landon. You told me no." She cocked her head to the side. "I wanted proof for myself."

"What did you hope to accomplish by this?" I asked. I had to clench my hands into fists to keep them from shaking in anger.

"I thought you would see the error of your ways and come back to me," Miranda told me.

Heidi snorted behind me and then dissolved into laughter. That did nothing for Miranda. She went from Southern sweet to bitch mode in about two seconds. She sneered at Heidi, and I had to hold myself together.

"That's not ever going to happen, Miranda," I told her. "You should turn around and leave here now. Just sign the fucking paperwork and get out of my life with all your fucking manipulative ways and scheming. The fact that you could take those videos and send them to the company to try to get ahead disgusts me."

"You were the one going behind my back and cheating," she snapped. "Of course I hired a private investigator to look into my interests!"

"I never cheated on you," I said as calmly as I could. "But I would never in a million years choose you over Heidi."

There. I'd laid it all out.

Everyone in the building could hear what I had to say. It didn't matter to me any longer. Miranda's threats weren't valid. Whatever she wanted from me, she was never going to get. And I was tired of hiding my feelings for Heidi. She was the one for me, and I didn't care who knew it.

"You're not serious," Miranda cried. "You're so desperate to be with someone that you hooked up with your ex-girlfriend's best friend? Were you disappointed that Jensen had claimed Emery, so you went for second best? I mean, God, it's fucking repulsive."

"Shut your mouth."

"Just face it, Landon. You can't be alone. You're addicted to being in love, to being in a relationship."

"Maybe I don't like to be alone, but I'd rather alone than be with you any day. And, fuck, Miranda, you have no room to talk. You were already trying to replace me with another golfer in Atlanta."

Miranda rolled her eyes. "I had no interest in Ben. I was trying to check up on you. And it turned out, you had been lying to me, so I had good reason to do so. And, God, look at what you are trying to replace me with."

She sneered at Heidi, and I felt her shift, as if to defend herself, but I shook my head. It wasn't worth it.

"Miranda," I warned.

"I mean…you went *slumming*," Miranda said with a coquettish laugh. "So cute that you think Texas trailer trash with a drug-dealer daddy could ever replace someone like me."

Heidi lunged out from behind me. Really, after that comment, I didn't blame her.

"Go to hell!" Heidi cried. "Why do you have to try to ruin everyone else's lives just because you're miserable?"

"Oh, honey, I'm not miserable. I had the best years of Landon Wright. Are you enjoying my sloppy seconds?"

Heidi's back straightened, and I saw more fire in her in that moment than I'd seen all week. It was like my firecracker was back…and she was about to explode.

"You're not even worth his time. You're certainly not worth mine. The fact that you flew all the way out here because you were so desperate and thought you could get him back if you got me out of the way is really pathetic." Heidi tilted her head and furrowed her brow. "I actually pity you."

Miranda laughed. "I don't need anyone's pity."

"You're a sad little putt slut who snagged herself a pro golfer and now will do anything to keep him. He's finally seen you for who you really are," Heidi said. "And you can insult me all you like, but you're never going to get him back. Not with your winning personality."

"Fucking bitch," Miranda croaked. "You don't know what you're saying."

"She does," I said. I placed my arm around Heidi's shoulders and squared off against Miranda.

Miranda opened her mouth to respond, but my family stepped up on either side of me and Heidi. We were all facing her—Jensen, Austin, Morgan, Sutton, and even Patrick,

Emery, and Julia. Us against her. I knew who I would place my bet on.

"You should go," I said firmly. "You're not wanted here."

"Fuck all of you fucking Wrights. I'll take the scandal to the press!"

Jensen shook his head. "I bought out your PI. I don't think that will be happening."

"Yeah, it wasn't even that hard to track down when I knew what I was looking for," Morgan said. She changed her tone of voice and grinned at Miranda. I knew she was enjoying herself. "So, you can go bye-bye now."

Miranda's eyes roamed between my family before landing back on me. "God, I am so glad that I got that abortion."

My stomach dropped out of my body. My head felt dizzy, and I couldn't seem to process what she had said. "You… what?"

"Yeah. You fucking thought I miscarried? No, I just didn't want to have your fucking kid and have it grow up and be a Wright. So, I got rid of it," Miranda spat at me.

The last year sped before my eyes. All the times I had defended her and catered to her and moved mountains for her comfort because of the miscarriage that I believed we were both mourning. Even when I'd wanted out, I'd been there for her through everything. Then she had done this without even telling me and lied about it for a year.

"Get the fuck out," I said, pointing at the door. "Right now."

Miranda opened her mouth to respond, but Jensen, Austin, and Patrick took over, acting as my own personal guards to escort her out of the building. I hoped this was the last time that I would ever see her. I'd wanted out for a long time, but I'd never fathomed the depths of her deceit.

Heidi put her hand on my back. She knew what that meant to me. She knew how much I had wanted a family and what I had sacrificed to try for one.

"Hey, that's not your fault," she said softly.

"She killed our unborn child."

"I know," she whispered. "And nothing could ever make that right."

"She actually did it."

"I know," she repeated. Her hand ran circles around my back, trying to ease my pain. "But...but I'm here, Landon. If you need me."

I saw the sincerity in her eyes. That she was still upset with me but couldn't walk away from me when I'd found out something like this. I loved her even more for it.

"I can't believe it."

"I think it explains a lot about her behavior. The way she's always acted so jealous and angry. When you first told me she had the miscarriage, I thought her actions were from guilt that she might not be able to have a child," Heidi explained. "Now, I see it's guilt because she got rid of the one you wanted and lied about it. The fact that she wielded the news like a weapon just showed how desperate she was. She wants to hurt you."

"It worked," I admitted.

"How could it not?" Heidi asked. "What she did was despicable. Going behind your back and lying and then making you cater to her for so long about something that wasn't even true. She's just crazy. Aren't you a little glad a child isn't involved?"

My eyes moved to Jensen, who was striding back toward us. He was proof enough that a divorce was bad when a child was involved. I nodded. I was glad. I didn't want children with Miranda or to be shackled to her forever.

But I would never forgive her for terminating the one we could have had. The possibility. It felt like losing the baby all over again.

"God, what a bitch!" Morgan said. "I mean...phew! You picked a real winner, Landon."

"Thanks, Morgan," I said with an eye roll.

"She sure knows how to put on a show though. And, seriously, I wouldn't take anything she said to heart." She gave me a pointed look. "At this point, she would do anything to hurt you—lie, cheat, steal, hire a private investigator to get your girlfriend fired. You know, totally normal psychotic behavior."

I couldn't help it. I laughed. "Well, there's one good thing that came out of all of this."

"Yeah?" Heidi asked.

"You're talking to me again."

"Um…yes, that's great," Morgan said, "however, I have to say that the best part is that when Jensen escorted her out, he threatened her within an inch of her life. I'm pretty sure we'll have the signed divorce paperwork by tomorrow."

I took that first breath of relief at the thought. Even though Miranda had wrecked my life and slaughtered my heart with that last comment, it was going to be over soon. I could move on, and hopefully, I could do that with Heidi on my arm.

Morgan winked at Heidi and then disappeared toward the small stage at the front of the room. I turned to face Heidi, who was still staring at me with round blue eyes full of concern.

"You know that I am totally in love with you, right?" I asked.

She nodded. "Yeah, I think I noticed that."

"I don't want us to be apart. I don't want what happened here or with our jobs to pull us apart. I'll really quit this time, Heidi. I'll get you your job back, and we'll make this work. It's not worth not having you."

She waved me off. "Look, I didn't want to break up with you. I want us to be together. That's what I've wanted for so long. I just blamed you for everything. And, sure, it was Miranda's fault, and we both could have been more careful, but we should have worked through this together. I'm sure that's why Emery and Julia insisted I come here."

"I would love to make this work as a team. I don't want to go through life, wondering about what-ifs. I want you."

I cupped her face in my hands and then gently pressed a kiss to her lips. She leaned into me, and I tasted sweet victory in that little movement. Heidi was mine.

"Ladies and gentlemen, if I could have your attention," Jensen said from the stage. "I'm Jensen Wright, the CEO of Wright Construction, and I wanted to thank everyone for coming out tonight for our annual Charity Benefit. I hope you're losing all of your money at the tables, so we can donate an enormous check to the Lubbock Children's Hospital!"

The crowd laughed and cheered at his comment, raising glasses to toast the night.

"While I have your attention, I have a special announcement. Wright Construction has recently opened a new division of the company where a percentage of all proceeds will go to our partnership with Lubbock Children's Hospital. We'll be opening Wright Golf Club, a PGA-style golf course focused on teaching the beginner to bringing the professionals in town."

My heart stopped beating. My jaw dropped open. Time itself stopped.

"And here to run this new division, I give you my brother Landon Wright."

Thirty-Nine

Heidi

Landon's shock oozed out of every pore.

His family was grinning at him. They had all been in on it. Even Sutton, who was the only Wright not working for the company. And my heart went out to them all. They had seen his depression and the toll that losing golf had pressed on him. And then they had done something about it. I didn't know how long this had been in the works, but I couldn't be happier for him.

Landon went up onto the stage and shook hands with Jensen and Morgan. After they said a few words to each other, Landon turned on the charm as he thanked the crowd for this incredible opportunity and then said he hoped to see them all out there on the course.

Emery nudged me. "How about that?"

"Did you know?" I asked her.

"I had an idea about it, but I think it was a glimmer of an idea. I wasn't sure, and I didn't want to say anything if you didn't know. Especially if Landon didn't know."

"I'm so happy for him. This is where his heart is. I think he eventually would have died from working in an office every day."

"You're probably right," Emery agreed. "So...aren't you glad you came?"

"Is this why you lied to me?"

"Jensen told me I had to get you here, no matter what. So, I did. And I'm so glad that I did, too." Emery nodded her head behind me. "Speaking of."

I turned around and came face-to-face with Jensen Wright.

"Heidi," he said with a dimpled smile.

"Hey," I said. "Um...sorry about that text the other day."

"Forgiven. I probably deserved it."

"That was a really nice thing you did for Landon."

"He's my brother. I love him, and I want to see him happy. I knew he'd never really be happy at Wright. He might have the business degree, but he belongs on the course. And I wanted to give him something that would actually keep him occupied until he could get back out."

"That's really amazing."

"That is why I wish you had answered your phone," he continued.

"Yeah. I...this wasn't a good week."

He nodded. "I imagine not. Had you answered your phone though, I would have told you about what I had in the works for Landon. I wanted it to be a surprise for him. When he told me he was dating someone, I never guessed it was you, so I ignored the problem. I deeply apologize for that error and how it resulted in you losing your job."

"Oh, yeah...getting fired. Pretty much one of the worst days of my life."

"I know that I can't make up for the emotional strain that the company has caused you, but with Landon in a different position in the company, I would be happy to offer you your job back."

I froze in place. My mouth popped open. My eyes were wide.

He laughed. "Is that a yes?"

"I…I don't know. I mean, yes, I want to come back," I admitted quickly, "but I don't want to return to an environment where people believe that the only reason I got my promotion is because I slept with my boss. There's enough sexism in the engineering department without that bullshit, too."

"I understand," he said with a nod. "We've had your boss and Julia sign an NDA where they would be liable if they disclosed the information they had found in that email. That means that the only people left who know about the videos are you and my family. I would never want to place you in a position where you would be uncomfortable."

"And I would…keep my promotion?" I whispered, thinking this all sounded too good to be true.

"I don't see why not."

"What's the catch?" I asked with a laugh.

"No catch. What happened was a mistake. Losing you would be a huge loss to the company. We really want you back, Heidi."

My heart stuttered, and I felt faint. "Okay."

"Okay?"

"Yeah," I said with a nod. "I'll take a ten percent pay raise for my emotional discomfort, and I'd like a real office."

Jensen laughed boisterously. "Oh, man. I see why Landon loves you."

I shrugged. "Didn't hurt to try."

He nodded and extended his hand. I put mine in his, and we shook.

"Done."

"Oh my God," I whispered. Then, I saw Landon striding toward us, and I couldn't help it. I dashed toward him, throwing myself into his arms. "Oh my God!"

"What?" he asked, his voice half between concern and excitement.

"Jensen just gave me my job back."

"Heidi, that's amazing."

"With a raise and an office!"

Landon laughed. "You outmaneuvered Jensen Wright. Bask in the glory of that feeling, love. Happens only once in a lifetime."

"God, Landon," I said. I pulled back and sighed heavily. "I am really so sorry for this week."

He held up his hand. "You don't have to apologize to me. I can understand exactly how you felt. I'm sure I was not nice to anyone the week after I injured my back."

"Yeah, I know. It's a reason but not an excuse. I should have believed in you and trusted you. Blowing up like that was just...reactionary. I hurt, so I was blind. It didn't matter how much I loved you or any other thought. Just the pain. I don't ever want to feel that again. I don't want to lose you over something like that."

He pulled me closer and planted a kiss on my lips. "The truth is, you never lost me. I've been right here all along, and I always will be."

I knew that now.

The fog that I had been walking through all week cleared, and I could finally see what was in front of me. Landon Wright was the best damn thing that had happened to me. We might have had our ups and downs, but there were no longer any barriers between us.

"Do you want to get out of here?" I asked.

He grinned. "I'd like nothing more."

He held out his arm, and I placed my hand in the crook of his sleeve. Without a backward glance, we left behind our friends and family and the entire party. With the week we'd had, I wanted to get away from the crowd and fall back in love with him.

He had valeted the Mercedes, and we waited until the valet returned it to us. Then, he drove me across town. He didn't even ask, *Your place or mine?* He just drove to my apartment and helped me inside.

I didn't know how he knew that I wanted him to come to my place instead of his little tree house. But I wanted to erase the negative memories I had here with him.

My hands slipped under his tuxedo jacket before I even got the door closed. He laughed at my eager behavior, but when I kissed him with everything I had in me, his humor evaporated. I wanted him and needed him like nothing else. I'd felt warranted in my anger over the last week, but I wanted to forget that it had ever happened.

"Heidi," he murmured against my mouth.

"Mmm," I groaned, tossing his jacket to the floor.

His hands were clutching my slip dress. And it was the thinnest material possible, so he was actually digging into my skin. And, fuck me, I wanted him.

"I want to savor you."

"I want you to fuck me."

He slipped his tongue across my bottom lip. "I want to taste every inch of your body."

"I want it rough and fast."

"I want to make you come so many times, you see stars." His fingers met the slit of my dress and eased up to my hips where I was without panties for the night.

"Harder," I practically breathed against his lips. "Much harder."

"And only remember my name." He moved his hand between my legs and stroked my pussy before exploring my clit.

I purred at the touch, my body heightened with arousal. "Take me," I pleaded. "Own me."

"You're not the kind of woman who can be owned," he told me as he did a damn good job of owning my body.

"Prove me wrong," I groaned.

"Fuck, I missed you."

"I know. It was awful."

"I wish I could fucking throw you over my shoulder and carry you into the bedroom. This injury is…" He shook his head.

I leaned forward and tenderly kissed him. "Your injury is of no consequence to me. You are not less of a man because you can't act like a caveman. Trust me, I have firsthand experience."

He grinned. "Would you like more firsthand experience?"

"Yes, please."

He removed his hand and directed me to the bedroom. As I walked past him, he smacked my ass. Once I was in the bedroom, he took his time in pulling my dress over my head and discarding the expensive piece of material onto the floor. I couldn't seem to care.

His hands traced their way down my body. Then, he leaned me backward on the bed and used his lips to follow where his hands had been. It was sweet, blissful torture. I wanted him inside me, and he wanted to devour me. He was winning.

His tongue set siege to my clit, and his fingers ravaged the inside of me, bringing me to orgasm twice before he was satisfied. I was incoherent.

There was no separation between me and Landon. There was no space or distance or emotion that we couldn't bridge. No feeling he hadn't captured. No touch he hadn't embraced. Living without him had been agony, and I refused to endure it again.

I flipped Landon so that he was lying on his back and then moved on top of him. He gripped my hips and eased me down onto his dick. I tipped my head back with pleasure at the feel of him filling me. Then, I started to bounce up and down on top of him. My tits were moving with me, and I knew he was enjoying the view.

"Fuck, Heidi," he moaned. "You're going to make me come."

"Come with me," I pleaded. I could already feel my orgasm building again, and I was eager for him to finish me off.

He wrapped his arms around my waist and held me tight against his chest. Then, he thrust up into me over and over again. His eyes were dark pools of lust, and I was a mirror for his desire.

"Don't close your eyes," he told me.

And, when I came, I was looking directly into his orbs and screaming his name as I fell apart. He came with me, and we both lay, panting from exhaustion and satisfaction.

He placed a light kiss on my shoulder. "I think you wore me out."

"You'll be ready for round two soon enough," I told him with a wink before sashaying into the bathroom.

When I came back out, he had his boxers back on and was lounging back on the bed, looking mighty pleased with himself.

"Something you want to say?" I asked, slipping into a pair of panties and an oversize cheer T-shirt.

"Just thinking about you coming three times."

"Want to try for more?"

"Fuck yes, I do."

I laughed and snuggled up next to him in the bed. I pressed my face into his chest and breathed him in.

This was real. All of this was real. Landon would be divorced in twenty-four hours. I had my job back. He was going to be working in golf again. The hardships had been insufferable…but they were worth it if I got all of this in the end.

He ran his fingers through my long hair, and I felt myself being lulled to sleep.

"Thank you," he whispered into the stillness.

"For what?"

"Not completely giving up on us."

"This is what I want. It always was."

I felt so fortunate. Landon and I had fucked up. We'd almost been destroyed. But we'd come out ahead. It made me feel like I could do anything. And there were more things that I had left to do.

Forty

Heidi

"Do you…do you want to read those letters with me?" I whispered.

Landon froze. "Right now?"

"Yeah. I just…I thought now might be a good time."

He leaned over and switched on the side table light. "Let's do it."

"You're sure? You still want to?"

"I think you need to."

I took a deep breath and then padded into the closet. I carried out the box of letters. It was pretty heavy. The last time I'd counted, there were over three hundred unopened, unanswered letters in there. I was sure it was closer to three hundred fifty now. It was a daunting task but one that I felt I should finally dig into.

My dad had made mistakes, like me and Landon, and I hoped that, by reading through the letters, I might actually discover the truth in all of what my father had done.

Landon took the tub from me and placed it on the bed. We sorted through the letters that were mostly in order by when they had been sent, and I pulled out the very first one.

"Are you ready?" he asked.

I nodded, feeding off his strength, and I tore the envelope open. I was surprised to find that it only had a few lines on it.

My dearest Heidi,

You deserve better than me for your old man. I hope, one day, you'll forgive me and come visit. I don't know that I'll survive this place without you.

Love you, princess.

Dad

My heart stopped over every line. It was so little. So simple. Just an apology. Just his need for me to be with him, and I hadn't even been able to open it.

We tore through letter after letter. The first fifty were all apologies, pleading with me to answer, to come see him, to understand. Asking for more than I had been able to give during that time of my life. I'd been too upset with him... unable to forgive...never able to forget.

Then, suddenly, the letters changed. The first one that was different started out with one last plea.

Heidi,

*My desperation must not be clear enough to you,
or you are refusing to respond to my letters. I can
understand why you're upset, but I can't say that I'm
happy that you won't even talk to me. Even just to
tell me to stop writing. I won't ask again for you to
come see me. When you want to come see me, I'll be
here. Same place. Waiting.*

And then, of all things, he started talking about my mom.
The first time he had seen her. The first time he had gotten up
the nerve to talk to her. Their first date. Their first kiss. Their
wedding day. The day I was born.

The last six years of letters was a collection of every
happy memory my father had ever had of me and my mom…
and I'd missed it.

All of these memories that I didn't have and events that
I couldn't recall. Everything I'd ever wanted to know about
my mom and my dad, and they had been sitting in my closet,
neglected for the past six years.

There were enough letters of our history to fill a book.
And Landon and I stayed up until the wee hours of the
morning, reading every last one. I cried through a few of them.
We smiled through most of my childhood. And my heart
swelled to bursting with each new entry, like I was getting to
see directly into my dad's head in a way he had never done for
me when I was a kid…and certainly never after that when he
was using.

This was a different man. This was the man I remembered
every year with ice cream and a good cry.

He'd been here all along. Sitting in prison, not more than
five miles out of town.

339

We finally reached the last one, and I slowly opened it, unsure of what story I would get to hear next. My eyes were drooping, yet I was still wide awake and anxious.

My Heidi,

I thought of another one that you probably don't remember. You were only three or four at the time. Tall for your age, of course. You're still tall. Just like your mama. Just like me. We thought you'd be a volleyball player or even a basketball player. We had high hopes that you'd want to be a professional athlete and get a scholarship to put you through school later. Of course, we couldn't afford much, so we were always hoping you'd get to live your dream if you wanted.

But you had different ideas. You wanted to be in gymnastics. It was the summer of the 1992 Olympics, and after watching the girls fly through the air, you decided that you wanted to do that, too. Your mama insisted that you go into lessons. I was working three jobs just to get by. I hadn't opened the bar yet, and we barely had enough to cover rent and keep food on the table. So, I told her no.

Well, your mom had taken some gymnastics lessons when she was young. So, while I was working, she was teaching you how to do crazy backbends and other things I don't have names for. I came home one day to find both of you hanging upside down, and you had already figured out how to do some kind of walkover thing.

It had only been a week, and your mom, she looked me right in the eye and said, "Hank, you get this girl into gymnastics lessons and let me worry about the expense."

I never asked how she got the money to cover it. I suspect she begged her parents. Something we both hated. But you got your lessons, and it was worth it in the end. Because that's how you got into cheerleading, and I have never seen you happier than when you are cheering. I didn't understand it much. Didn't even realize it was an actual sport until you were in it, but I was proud of you.

I wanted you to have the world, and even when I couldn't always give it to you, I hope you know that I tried.

I always tried.

I love you so much.

Dad

I felt Landon's hot gaze on mine as I stared down at the last letter. Heat expanded in my chest, and then I burst out laughing.

"Heidi?" Landon asked.

I couldn't stop it. I couldn't stop laughing. It came out of me completely unbidden and uncontrollable.

"Hey. Hey, what's wrong? What's going on? Why are you laughing?"

I clutched my sides and leaned back on the bed as I let the emotions of the night wash over me. "Nothing," I managed to get out.

"Nothing?"

"I mean…no—God, it's just…funny."

"What is?"

"I have had so much stress over these letters. They've been sitting in there, in my closet, tormenting me for years. Years, Landon," I told him, biting back another laugh. "And this is all it is. Memories from my childhood. Memories of my mom."

"I think it's pretty amazing. I wish I had something like this from my parents," he admitted.

I leaned forward and kissed him. "Oh, I love you. You are right. This was so worth it. I should have opened these a long time ago. Though, maybe if I had, I wouldn't have been as forgiving. Maybe I needed someone to show me that it's okay to make mistakes. That we can forgive and we can move on from what happened."

He brought his lips to mine again. "I'm glad that I could be of service."

"Oh, you have been of great service," I said, moving my eyebrows up and down.

He laughed. "Are you saying you're ready for round two?"

"Um…yes, but also sleep?"

"In that order?"

"You've convinced me."

Landon carefully put all the letters back in the box and set it on the floor. "What are you going to do about all of that?" he asked as he climbed back on top of me.

I fell backward on the bed and enjoyed the feel of his body pressing into me. "I think I know exactly what I need to do."

His eyes swept over my face, and he smiled. "Good."

Then, his mouth covered mine, and all talking ceased.

The next morning, Landon and I presented our identification to the security guard at the gate outside of the prison where my father was housed. I was dressed in a simple blue sundress and a distressed jean jacket, and I was shaking like a leaf. I'd been so confident when I planned this trip the day before, but now that I was here, I couldn't believe it was actually happening.

After clearing our IDs, we were told where to go for visiting hours.

Landon put his arm around my shoulders and steered me into the building. "It's okay," he told me. "You can do this."

"I know I can. But I'm…what if he doesn't want to see me?"

"The man has been writing you letters for six years. He wants to see you."

I knew he was right, but still, I couldn't shake the fear from my veins. This could be a disaster.

I took a deep breath and walked inside.

Landon and I found a table at the back of the room, but I couldn't sit. I was too jittery. Nerves were fighting their way through my body, and I clenched and unclenched my hands. Landon stood by me and was my rock through the whole thing. Other visitors came in and waited, sitting casually at tables. This clearly wasn't their first time.

A buzzer by the door announced that inmates were being let into the room, and I snapped to attention. My eyes were fixed on the door, as I waited for that moment.

Anxiety crept through my body, and I shook my head. "Maybe we should go," I whispered.

"We can if you're not ready." He took my hand in his. "But I think you're ready."

I squeezed his hand. He was right. I was ready. I could do this.

Then, my dad walked into the room. He looked as if he had aged significantly in the six years that he had been here. His hair had thinned and grayed. His skin was pale. His eyes were deep set. He carried himself as if he had a weight on his shoulders. And that weight was about to bury him.

I gasped slightly at the sight of him. I might have noticed all of that at once, but what I saw next was just...Dad. My dad. The man I had sworn I would never see again. The man I'd sworn I would never forgive. The man...who I was giving a second chance.

His eyes scanned the room in confusion. I wondered if he had ever had a visitor in the six years he had been here.

Then, he saw me.

And the world stopped.

His mouth opened, and tears welled in his eyes. A hand went to his chest. I thought he was going to collapse.

I hurried forward with Landon on my heels. My dad stared in awe. His lips quivered, and then real tears fell down his cheeks.

"Heidi?" he whispered. "It's really you?"

"Yeah, Dad. It's really me."

He moved slowly and touched the sleeve of my jacket. When he discovered that I was real, he tugged me against him and held me. I wrapped my arms around him as he sobbed.

"I thought you would never come. I'd given up hope."

"I know," I whispered. "But we read your letters, and...I decided that it was time."

"I'm so glad," he said.

He hesitantly released me and then seemed to realize that I had someone with me.

"Dad, this is my boyfriend, Landon Wright."

My dad furrowed his brows, as if he were trying to reconcile Landon Wright being with his daughter. Then, he stuck his hand out, and Landon shook it.

"Good to see you again, son."

"Pleasure to meet you again, sir."

"You taking care of my girl?"

"Dad," I whispered. It had only been a few minutes, and already, he was interrogating my boyfriend.

"She's the most important thing in my life. I'll take care of her until the end of time."

My dad nodded, and they seemed to have an understanding. "As it should be."

Landon wrapped his arm back around my shoulders and kissed my forehead as my dad moved us to a table.

"Thank you," I whispered.

"Meant every word. You are and always will be the most important thing in my life. Don't ever forget that."

As we turned to go and sit with my dad for the first time in six years, I knew that I wouldn't forget that. Not ever.

Because, when you found a love that was inescapable, you held on and never let go.

Epilogue

Landon
Two Years Later

I stared down the green in shock. I had just hit the last ball in my very first tournament back in the world I'd thought I lost forever. And, even better, it was on the Wright Golf Club course. The course I had helped design and run for the last two years. It was one of the most rewarding experiences of my life, and getting it added to the PGA docket for the upcoming year was an even sweeter victory.

Not that I had come back with a bang or anything. I'd ended this tournament in the middle of the pack. My recovery had been long and arduous, but it had happened. And my physical therapist, Anjee, continually reminded me that it would have been quicker if I hadn't been such a shit about pushing myself.

My old friend and caddy, Jake Gibson, had come in for the tournament to play with me again.

He picked up the ball I'd hit and passed it to me. "Congrats, man. It's good to have you back."

"Yeah, it's good to be back."

"And probably not to have Ryan hounding you."

I laughed. "True. That part was annoying."

"Start full-time training next week for the PGA Qualifiers?"

"You bet," I agreed.

Then, I walked off the course and found my beautiful fiancée waiting for me. Heidi's face split as I approached, and she bounced up and down on the balls of her feet.

"You did so well!" she cried, throwing her arms around me.

I kissed the top of her head and tugged her in close. "I kind of sucked, love."

"Well, whatever. You're golfing again!"

"Dreams do come true."

"Do you have any other obligations today?"

I looped my arm around her waist as we walked back up to the clubhouse.

"Nothing else today. Why?"

"I might or might not have planned a surprise party."

"No. No way," I said. "And, anyway, it's not a surprise if I know."

"Oh, you'll be surprised."

"Do we have to go now?"

She nodded her head in excitement and bounced around some more. "I'm really, really excited."

"I can tell that," I said, grabbing her for another kiss. "Let me just clean up and change. Then, we can head out."

"Great!"

"You can always surprise me with a blow job if you want."

"Landon Wright!" she snapped.

I just laughed. "Later then?"

Then, she gave me a mysterious look. "Probably…yeah."

I grinned devilishly, and she smacked my arm as I passed. I loved her to pieces, and our sex life was unimaginable. I never thought that I could be this happy.

After six months together, I'd popped the question and asked her to move in and marry me, all in one fell swoop.

She'd turned me down.

I should have seen it coming. Heidi was her own incredible woman, and she did things her own way.

After a week, she'd conceded that she had only said no on principle and that she wanted to be with me forever anyway. But, from there, we'd been taking things slow, and we still hadn't set a date for the wedding. I was waiting for her to tell me when she was ready. If she was in no rush and she was in my arms and my bed every day, then I could wait for her. I thought a part of her was waiting to see if her dad would get out on parole to be there for the wedding. So, I didn't push her.

We'd gotten rid of my tree house and her apartment, and we'd bought a house by the golf course. Emery had moved in with Jensen the same weekend.

Best friends and brothers. Who would have guessed?

Once I was changed, I found Heidi leaning back against the Jeep I'd gotten after taking over my new position at Wright Golf Club. It'd felt more permanent once I had my own car here. No more borrowing Jensen's Mercedes. She was in cutoff jean shorts and a cropped tank top with sandals, and I wanted to eat her right up. Damn surprise.

"Where are we heading, firecracker?" I asked, swinging the keys around on my finger.

She held her hand out. "Hand them over."

"You're not driving my car."

"Watch me," she countered.

I laughed, knowing which buttons to push, and tossed her the keys. We piled into the Jeep, and she drove me to the north side of town. I couldn't figure out where we were headed until she actually pulled into the parking lot.

"You're kidding," I said with a look of disbelief.

"It'll be fun!"

I stared up at the sign for miniature golf and burst out laughing. "You are so ridiculous."

"Yeah, you love it."

"True."

When we walked into the outdoor putt-putt course, I acted as surprised as I'd promised I would be. My entire family was there, waiting for us. Jensen and Emery were bent over, talking to Colton. Austin and Patrick were trying to figure out how to juggle the golf balls. Morgan was shaking her head at the pair of them and talking animatedly to Julia. Sutton was chasing after a two-year-old Jason, who was toddling along ahead of her.

Heidi cleared her throat, and they all turned to look at us. "We made it!"

Everyone cheered and congratulated me on my first tournament back, and it was truly amazing to have my wacky, damaged, incredible family all in one place. Then, as the excitement wore off, everyone moved to pick up their equipment.

"I'm blue!" Morgan called.

"I call hot pink!" Patrick said in a pretty good imitation of Morgan's voice.

She slapped him on the arm. Hard.

"This putter is way too short," Jensen said, holding up a crappy putter. He shrugged, taking it with him anyway.

"I'm going first!" Colton yelled.

Heidi and I moved up to the putt-putt station last. I claimed a mustard-yellow ball that no one else had wanted, and she grabbed a magenta-colored one.

"You do realize, I'm going to win, right?" I asked with a cocky grin.

Heidi rolled her eyes. "No way. I am kick-ass at mini golf."

"This is my job, firecracker."

"Well, listen here. I'm very competitive."

I laughed and kissed her. "We'll see."

"No, you'll see!"

When I lined up my first shot, Heidi leaned in behind me and kept trying to sneak in kisses.

"Distraction is not working."

"Oh, yeah?" she asked.

Her head darted back and forth, and as I was about to putt, she lifted her shirt and flashed me. I whiffed, knocking the ball down the green without a single ounce of precision.

"Told you."

I smacked her ass with my putter as I passed to try to finish the horrible job I'd done. "You'll pay for that later."

"Promise?"

"Yeah," I said as I sank my second putt. "You can put me down for a birdie, love."

She wrote down my score and then wrapped her arms around my waist. "Love?" she whispered.

"Hmm?"

"I think I'm ready."

"I hope so. It's your turn."

"For a baby," she whispered.

I froze and stared down into her face. She was suddenly serious, even with her cute, scared smile. But I couldn't stop my giant smile.

This was what I'd wanted for so long. A life and a family with the girl of my dreams, and here she was, offering it on a platter.

"Think we should get married first, or do you want to start here?"

"Not *right* here." She laughed. "I was thinking we'd get married the weekend after the Championship."

"That's six weeks away," I reminded her.

"Guess we have some planning to do then, huh?"

"I guess we do. And you're sure about this?"

She stood on her tiptoes and gently kissed me. "I've never been surer of anything in my life."

"What about your dad?"

She shook her head. "I love him, but I won't put my life on hold for him. He understands. I talked to him about it. I want to be with you. I want to be your wife and have your children. I'm ready."

I picked her up and swung her around in a circle. Our game forgotten. Everything else falling away. Just me and the woman I loved with the entire world ahead of us, ready for the taking.

The End

The
Wright
Mistake

I always wanted a nice normal boyfriend. The kind you could bring home to your parents. Instead, I fell for Austin Wright. We tried this once and failed. Hard. I swore, the bad boy Wright who set my body on fire would never get a second chance because our love is heroin-laced gasoline— addicting and destined to go up in flames.

One

Julia

"I'm really…so sorry," I said with a sad smile. "I don't think this is going to work out."

Trevor stared back at me his face a mask of hurt and shock. We'd been together almost a year. A year in two days actually. Which made it all that much worse.

"You're…you're breaking up with me?" Trevor asked. "But Julia…"

"I know. I know."

"It's been a year. I had this whole," he breathed in deeply and looked away from me, "this whole thing planned for you for our anniversary."

I winced. Of course, he did. Because Trevor was this perfect, normal, nice guy. He was the guy who came over to your place to do your laundry while you were with your friends and filled up your gas tank when he noticed you were running low and called your mom to chat every Thursday. Or he would have done that last one…if he'd thought my parents were alive.

"I'm sorry," I repeated.

"Why?"

"Why what?"

He gave me a disbelieving look. "Why would you do this? There has to be a reason."

"Oh. I…don't think we're compatible."

"We've been together for a year. Don't you think you would have noticed that before now?"

I had. I couldn't say that. Not to him. But I'd definitely known it. Trevor was…safe. He made me complacent.

And he was trying to get too close.

Much too close for his own good.

"Yeah."

"You can't handle commitment, can you?" he asked. "You can't let anyone in. You won't let anyone know the real you."

I didn't say anything in my defense. That all was truer than he would ever know. I had let someone in, and it had fucking backfired like nothing else. It wasn't that I was commitment phobic; it was just when I got to the point of admitting everything that had happened in my life, I always realized it was too fucked up to continue. So, I ended it. Perfect normal Trevor couldn't handle the real Julia Banner.

"You should go," I told him, crossing my arms over my chest.

He looked like he was going to plead with me, fall to his knees and beg. But he shook his head, turned, and walked out of my one bedroom apartment.

I sank into the couch and put my head in my hands. Why did I keep doing this to myself? Was this anyway to live?

My phone buzzed on the table and Heidi's name flashed on the screen. Heidi and I had met day one when I'd started working at Wright Construction as the head of HR almost two years ago. I loved her to pieces.

I picked up the phone. "Hey."

"Did you do it?" she asked.

I sighed. "Yeah. He hates me."

"Psh. Trevor from accounting couldn't hate a fly. He's hurt. He'll get over it."

"Yeah. I guess."

"Want to get fucked up to feel better about it?"

"I want to get fucked to feel better about it."

Heidi laughed. "That's my girl."

"Flips?"

It was the local bar that we always went to. By anyone else's standards, it was kind of a dump. But Heidi adored the place.

"Actually…we're all heading to Ransom Canyon for Memorial Day weekend. Lake, boats, barbeque—the trifecta. You in?"

"And how exactly am I going to get laid out of this plan?"

"Well, there will be a lot of alcohol," Heidi hedged.

"And?"

"And…a lot of hot eligible men."

I rolled my eyes. "Like who?"

"The Wrights all invited a bunch of people to come hang out. I know your…issues with Austin, so I didn't mention it before. But I don't think that should stop you now."

I groaned. "Austin Wright is the biggest alcoholic jackass on this side of the planet! You know how he treated me when we were together."

"True," she added. "But…that was a year and a half ago. And since you slapped the shit out of him last fall, he's kind of avoided you like the plague. Which means you should be fine."

"Heidi!"

"Get your ass over here and bring a bathing suit. I want to see those tattoos you're sporting. I won't take no for an answer."

And then she unceremoniously hung up on me. I glanced down at it with a sigh. Maybe Heidi was right, and I needed some girl time to get over this break up.

I stripped out of my work attire and into a pair of cut off jean shorts and a black Queen tank top. I piled my dark red hair up into a messy bun on the top of my head and admired the recently shaved undercut. I filled up my travel tote with enough clothes for a week away from home. Now, I just needed my favorite olive green bomber jacket. Not that May in Lubbock, Texas was cold by any stretch of the imagination, but the dusty, windy, and flat place I had called home for almost two years now, got cool on summer nights. But the jacket was nowhere to be found. I tore my apartment apart looking for it. I swore I'd left it hanging in my closet, but nope. No luck. Must have left it at work or in the car or something.

I finally added a black Beatles sweatshirt I'd picked up at a thrift store and headed over to Heidi's place, where she lived with Landon Wright, the middle sibling in the Wright family dynasty. They'd gotten together last year and were totally crazy in love. They'd gotten engaged practically right away and now lived together in a brand new house that they'd had built on a golf course. Country clubbers, man.

When I pulled up in my oversized black Tahoe, Landon was packing up his Jeep. He waved as I parked.

"Hey Julia. I'm glad to see that Heidi convinced you to come with us."

I hopped out of the car and moved my bag into the trunk. "Yeah. She's persuasive all right. Told me to get my ass over here and hung up on me."

Landon laughed congenially. He had the goddamn Wright good looks—dark hair, dark penetrating eyes, perfect smile, and so tall you could climb the fuckers.

"This sounds like my fiancée."

"I swear you say it just because you like the sound of it."

He grinned not at all sheepish. "Can't blame me."

"Not in the least."

Heidi appeared then in tiny white cut offs and a pink bathing suit top. She had a huge floppy hat on her head, her long blonde hair falling to her waist, and sunglasses to cover her entire face. "I'm so fucking ready!"

She clobbered me on sight, planting a kiss on my cheek.

"You're insane," I told her.

"And you are wearing too many clothes."

"Don't say that around Emery," I said about her best friend. "She might get jealous."

"Can I watch?" Landon asked from where he was standing with his arms crossed, eyeing us appraisingly.

"You can join in," Heidi said with a wink. Then she smacked my ass and hopped into the front seat. I climbed into the back, and once Landon was in the driver's seat, we were off and away.

It was only a twenty-minute drive to Ransom Canyon, and Heidi kept me from brooding too much about my recent break up. Not that I was actually upset about leaving Trevor. I was more upset that he had been right. I liked uncomplicated fun. Preferably with a lot of mind-blowing sex.

"So, who all did you say would be here?" I asked again.

"Um…" Heidi trailed off.

Landon shot her a look of frustration. "My family mostly."

"Mostly?"

"Heidi and Emery and her sister Kimber and her husband Noah and their two kids will also be there."

"And?" I added.

"And Patrick," Landon said as an afterthought.

"What happened to all the hot eligible bachelors, Heidi?"

She chewed on her bottom lip and her big blue eyes searched my face. "About that…"

"Oh, you're such a bitch."

Great. I was going to be the only single girl here who wasn't related to the Wright family. And the two single guys here—Austin and Patrick—were totally off limits. Just perfect.

Heidi laughed and shrugged. Clearly this had been all part of her evil plan. The little witch.

Landon parked his Jeep next to a giant truck, which I vaguely recalled belonged to his oldest brother, Jensen, and then we all hopped out. Landon waved us off when we tried to help. "Go on and check out the lake. I've got this."

Heidi kissed his cheek, grabbed my hand, and dashed down the hill to the dock below. Ransom Canyon was a town of only about a thousand people, but the lake filled up all summer. It was craziest on Memorial Day and Fourth of July. As in…today. There were boats everywhere on the lake, and I could see parties happening all up and down the lake. Maybe I wouldn't be at such a loss after all.

We skipped to a stop when we got to the end of the dock and Heidi laughed before peeling her shorts off.

"What are you doing?" I asked.

"Taking a swim. Come with me, lover."

"Uh, no. I do not have a swimsuit on."

"That's no fun." She handed me her floppy hat, tied up her blonde hair, and then cannonballed into the water as if she didn't have a care in the world.

I laughed as she splashed water on me and took a step back. "You're crazy!"

"Oh my God, get in! The water is divine!"

"No chance in hell. I need to change first."

Heidi pouted as she treaded water. "You're missing out. Emery would do it."

"Don't care. You can't goad me into this."

"I want you to have some fun. Since you finally ditched Mr. Boring."

"He was not boring."

Heidi rolled her eyes and ducked under water. "He was so boring," she said, when she came up for air. "My girl is fire and passion and tattoos and top-shelf whiskey."

"You must be thinking of someone else," I teased.

"Come on. Show me those tattoos!"

"Later! When I have a freaking swimsuit on. Unless you are just dying to see my thong."

Heidi raised an eyebrow. "I bet everyone here would die to see your thong."

"You're incorrigible."

"Would you rather talk about Trevor?"

I shook my head. "Let's go back to my thong."

"Did someone say thong?" a voice called from behind me on the deck.

I took a deep breath, closed my eyes, and then exhaled slowly. Exactly what I didn't want to deal with. I turned and came face-to-face with Austin fucking Wright.

He looked…fucking gorgeous. His almost black hair was sharp on the sides but longer in the front. He had dark haunted eyes and a smile like a razor blade. His cheekbones were hollowed and jawline chiseled out of marble. And he was fucking shirtless.

His swim trunks rode low on his hips revealing the carefully maintained six pack beneath and the sexy V. I didn't know how he managed it with the amount of alcohol in his system, but he was cut as fuck. Bulging biceps and ripped pecs with a half sleeve bleeding into his chest. Ink that I had touched every inch of.

I shook myself out of my reverie. Fuck.

"Shocking that you showed up right when we were talking about my underwear."

"Good to see you too, babe," Austin said with a grin.

"Wish I could say the same."

His best friend Patrick trailed behind him with a dopey smile on his face. They both looked loaded. But Austin always held his alcohol better than everyone else. Probably because his tolerance was through the roof considering he drank all the time.

"What's up, Julia?" Patrick said.

I nodded my head at Patrick.

"Y'all coming in?" Heidi called from the water.

"Hell yes!" Patrick ran and jumped into the water next to Heidi. She giggled and splashed him back when he surfaced. "Austin, man, we need something to float our beer!"

"Oh, you're drunk already and still drinking," I snarled. "How shocking!"

Austin set his dark eyes on me and he smiled wickedly. "Heard you broke up with that tool you were seeing."

"Not that it's any of your fucking business."

"Just trying to figure out why you're still acting like this."

"Like what?" I demanded even though I knew it was a bad idea.

"Like you've got a stick up your ass."

I narrowed my eyes and clenched my hands into fists.

"And not even the way that you like it either, babe." He winked, and I flushed scarlet.

"Why are you such a dick?"

He held his arms wide. "Just your average Prince Charming."

I snorted. "There's nothing about you that's charming."

"Nothing about me that's average either."

Then he looked at me in a way that made my clothes melt off. That seductive, eye-fucking, take-me-right-now, all-consuming look of desire that had set me on fire and pushed me into his bed the first time. The same smile that said he was bad, bad news, and I was happy to be on the front page.

"Fuck off, Austin."

I turned to leave, smoke pouring out of my ears. But Austin latched onto my wrist as I tried to break away. "Come with me."

"What part of *fuck off* did you not understand?"

"Swimming."

"What?" I asked, realizing a half second too late what was about to happen.

He tugged me toward the edge of the dock. I stumbled into him, losing my footing completely. Then vertigo hit. I was weightless suspended in mid-air for a split second with Austin's chest pressed against mine. His smile was magnetic. His lips so fucking inviting. He looked…younger, happier, freer than I'd ever seen him.

Then we crashed into the water. I came up soaking wet in my fucking street clothes, sputtering for breath. Austin popped to the surface right after me. His hands slid down my sides and twirled me back around to face him. He yanked me tight against his body and all cognitive thought fled my mind as I felt the press of every inch of him up against me.

My body went into hyper drive, imagining all the ways he could touch and lick and caress and pleasure my body. All the ways that mouth could make me come. All the ways his dick could lay claim to my body. And I didn't pull away.

I leaned in letting my body take over for once and ignoring my mind entirely. His lips were so close.

So inviting.

So easy to forget.

"Fuck, I love getting you wet, Jules," he breathed seductively.

And then reality crashed back into place.

363

The
Wright
Mistake

COMING AUGUST 8TH!

PREORDER EVERYWHERE NOW:

WWW.KALINDE.COM/BOOK/
THE-WRIGHT-MISTAKE

Acknowledgments

First, I'd like to thank the readers and bloggers who support me! It's because of all of you that I keep getting to do this, and I couldn't be more appreciative. Everyone review, blog post, share, link, comment, Tweet, mention to your friend and on and on help authors so much, and I know you all do it out of the goodness of your heart!

As always, this book is a labor of love. So many people put their hands on it and shaped the story. Thank you to all of you for helping me—Anjee Sapp, Rebecca Kimmerling, Katie Miller, Rebecca Gibson, Polly Matthews, Rachel Brookes. Danielle Sanchez for keeping me sane and running my life, Sarah Hansen for a swoonworthy cover, Jovana Shirley for your amazing editing and formatting, Kimberly Brower for her agenting miracles, Alyssa Garcia for your stunning unbelievable graphics that save my life, Michelle New for images that blow me away, and Nita Banks and Becca Manuel for amazing trailers! You have a gift!, and Wander Aguiar for the cover image that I was in desperate need of.

Also to my #squad girls, the amazing group of people in the K.A. Linde Books group, my Shop Talkers, and all the amazing authors who share my release and I have the privilege of calling my friend—Diana Peterfreund, Corinne Michaels, Staci Hart, Kandi Steiner, J. Sterling, Jillian Dodd, CD Reiss, Laurelin Paige, Meghan March, Melanie Harlow, Jessica Hawkins, A.L. Jackson, Ilsa Madden-Mills, Amy Daws, Sierra Simone, Kendall Ryan, and more!

And, of course, my husband Joel for endless hours binge-watching *Once Upon A Time*, long walks to figure out plot holes, and all the care and understanding that I could ever need. Plus Riker and Lucy, who keep life interesting!

About the Author

K.A. Linde is the *USA Today* bestselling author of the Avoiding Series and more than twenty other novels. She grew up as a military brat and attended the University of Georgia where she obtained a Master's in political science. She works full-time as an author and loves Disney movies, binge-watching *Supernatural*, and *Star Wars*.

K.A. LINDE

She currently lives in Lubbock, Texas, with her husband and two super-adorable puppies.

Visit her online at www.kalinde.com and on Facebook, Twitter, and Instagram @authorkalinde.

Join her newsletter at www.kalinde.com/subscribe for exclusive content, free books, and giveaways every month.